Nathan Jeffries' father had been a naval hero, but his Quaker mother Amy wanted a peaceful career for her golden boy. All that changed after the disastrous Embargo of 1807 and by 1812 Nathan had lost his freedom, his fiancée Barbara Steward, his best friend Peter and perhaps soon his life. The world was suddenly at war, and Nathan lived in torment and fear. The Jeffries' enemy, Richard Auster, engaged to the bewitching Catherine Charles, wanted Nathan to suffer final reprisal at sea, ruled by the British lion. But the enterprising Nathan finds a way to wage a war of his own.

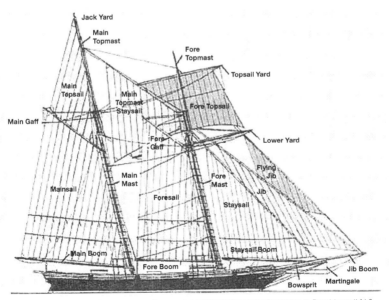

BALTIMORE TOPSAIL SCHOONER - COURTESY OF THE WHITING PROJECT @ PROMARE/NAS

For Gloria, Henry, Lynn and Scott
Siamo tutti nella stessa barca

1812:
Rights *of* Passage

BERT J. HUBINGER

CAPSTAN
COMMUNICATIONS
ANNAPOLIS

Published by Capstan Communications, Annapolis MD

ISBN-13: 978-0615530239
ISBN-10: 0615530230

Printed in the United States

Background cover image "Attack of Fort Oswego, on Lake Ontario, North America, May 6th 1814." Drawn by Captain Steele. Engraved by R. Havell & Son. Collection of Paul Lear.

Acknowledgments

To Carol Callahan, Jack Saunders, Mitzi Mabe and my wife Shelley, who have shared (or suffered) my love of war at sea.

One

Baltimore - *July 4, 1807*

A liveried black servant opened the massive oak door of the Steward mansion, and the newly arrived guests, wearing honest homespun, squinted in the bright light of enormous beeswax candles that showered the foyer with gold. And here was the host himself.

"Welcome, Captain Jeffries and young Mr. Nathan!" said the host Abraham Steward, approaching a bit too enthusiastically, resplendent and corpulent in black and white silk, his blue and red waistcoat bulging.

"Good evening, sir. War at last!" said Captain William Jeffries, too loudly. "Huzzah!"

Abraham Steward grasped the Captain's hand and then Nathan's in embarrassing false cheer, the fleshy palm grip of an overripe Polonius.

"Please come in, gentlemen!"

Nearly three sheets to the wind already, Nathan's father, Captain Jeffries, squeezed their host's narrow shoulders as they entered the mansion, and leaned over to his right ear.

"You know, Mr. Steward," said Captain Jeffries, "I must talk to your friend the General about those Fort McHenry defenses. Captain Barney and I agree that sooner or later—"

"Oh, yes, of course, Captain," Abraham laughed, nervously pulling away and looking over into the west wing ballroom.

"You know, if we leave the harbor defenses up to Auster's man, the mayor, we will—"

"Pardon me, please—"

And Abraham Steward, their distracted host, was gone.

His father also left in Steward's wake, thundering across the oak floor toward the nearest supply of brandy, leaving Nathan alone. Then Nathan heard a familiar voice behind him.

"War at last?"

Nathan spun around.

"Peter!" he yelled. "My old friend, it has been too long!"

To the amusement or shock of those near the foyer, he strode over to the dark-skinned man and grasped his shoulders, ignoring the gasps of the servants on the other end of the room. Peter's clothes, a threadbare waistcoat, aged broadcloth dress coat and loose-fitting cotton trousers, contrasted with his smooth and robust physique. His handsome, ruddy face gave him away as a half-breed.

"Well," asked Peter, fighting a smile, "do you think it is war at last, Nathan?"

"Quakers believe—"

"Your mother, Amy," said Peter, "is a Quaker, but you—"

"Peter, killing another human being is wrong, and I have promised—"

"Even your father's sworn enemy, Jacob Auster?"

"Let's not talk about *that*, Peter."

"Nathan, ever since your accident aboard *Bucephalus*—"

With a fierce scowl, Nathan suddenly grabbed the smaller man's right arm to pull him off balance. Peter whirled around with blinding speed, kicked and hooked Nathan's left leg, and Nathan fell to the floor, his shoes banging loudly on the polished oak. The two men laughed, calmly ignoring the ladies watching this strange tableau.

"You have improved," Nathan said, holding up his left hand.

"Maybe," Peter said, "and maybe you are slipping." He grasped Nathan's hand and pulled him back up. "How is your father really, Nathan?"

"My father is . . . about the same. My mother keeps us going, somehow."

"I am sorry, Nathan, I had hoped—"

"And how is your beautiful mother, Peter?"

"I am trying to find her."

"What do you mean?"

"She is not at the cabin here or in Boston."

"What? What does Mr. Steward say?"

"Nothing. He waves off my concern, and insists she must be with her . . . patron, shall we say, perhaps out of the country." Peter could not hide his bitterness.

"Meanwhile Mr. Steward complains about this war fever, insisting that we have no reason to fight England over *Leopard* attacking *Chesapeake* or impressment or anything else—that challenging their navy is absurd. All this echoed by Captain Jacob Auster and his minions."

"Ah, God. Then tell him to shut his mouth, or shut it for him," Nathan said. "Or better yet, heave him outside, head first. I have to agree that war is wrong; violence is—"

"Precisely." Peter smiled. "But this is strange coming from a Jeffries."

"I honor my father's patriotism and courage," Nathan said, "even though I am still opposed to violence. But—"

"But the drum beats of war call to us again to fight for freedom of the seas, I know."

"My father rants about the Austers and their cabal and talks about nothing else except getting a command. He wrote to President Jefferson, tried to find some 12-pounders for *Bucephalus*, went on and on about privateers until my mother told him to stop it. Sometimes I think he is mad, Peter! Or both of them are. Those two are tearing me apart."

"I understand, my friend." Peter's ruddy skin and intelligent brown eyes glowed in the light.

"When my mother is not present, all my father talks about is launching a swarm of sea raiders like *Enterprise*, *Hornet*, *Argus* and *Wasp* against the British merchant fleet. He says our fast little public ships and privateers can play hell with them—make them give up impressment soon enough, he says. I fear we are losing him, Peter. 'Amy,' he says, 'You will turn our son into a coward.' But I cannot break my promise to my mother to stay ashore."

"Nathan—"

"Peter, have you seen Barbara? What are you looking at?"

"Brandy or Madeira, gentlemen?"

That lovely, coy voice behind him.

Nathan whirled around to see the green-eyed beauty herself at the door to the west wing; long blond hair elaborately coiffured, with lips shaped like a gentle bow wave that generously broadened into a musical laugh. Europe had not completely forged Barbara Steward into a lady— or perhaps it had. Her emerald gown matched her eyes, the bow matched her hair, and her voluptuous figure enhanced perfectly. Peter and Nathan had difficulty breathing, mesmerized by this golden apparition in the ripe, living flesh.

"Your faces!" she said delightedly, pulling both Peter and Nathan aside. "Do I look that frightful?"

"You look—my God, Barbara. I . . . could hardly recognize you," Nathan stammered.

"And I hope the change is not displeasing?" She spun gaily in the hall, her golden hair, bare white shoulders, regal carriage and full shapely figure revealed by the subtly yielding Empire gown.

"I *am* in love with you," Nathan blurted.

Delighted, she laughed again and turned to Peter, and as she held his hand, reveling in his admiration, Peter realized that she was once again flirting with him, the renegade half-breed, not Nathan. Nathan was a large, innocent lamb. Peter was a plaything for the whites, cleaned up nice for the wealthy, white gentlefolk. The gentle white ladies.

Peter suddenly stopped walking and broke away, saying nothing, but Barbara's smile wilted briefly when she saw Peter intending to leave.

"Do not say that," she said coyly to Nathan, letting go of his arm and restraining Peter, then leading both men across into the east hall of the house. That view of the harbor was spiked with the spires of two churches and the courthouse not unlike Bullfinch's golden capital dome in Boston. She pulled Peter near and breathed in his left ear.

"So good to see you clean, young brother. We need to get you out of the barn more often."

She kissed his cheek and quickly tongued his ear as they passed into the east foyer where bedlam reigned after the music ended—blue and red uniforms, silk broadcloth, linen that shone in the glistening candlelight.

Peter wondered if Barbara would once again try to lure him upstairs, irresistible as always, and play with him like an exotic toy. He felt helpless to resist, though he knew she thought of him as little better than a slave, a low ranking servant, really useful only in private.

Now she escorted both men with a twinkle in her eye, as stunning as the color and movement of the ball itself—the classic motif, with its false white columns and molding, Greek and Roman scenes in subtle, pleasing, black-and-gold wallpaper, the warmth and glitter of the candles in their escutcheons. They were surrounded by the brilliant uniforms, long suits and gowns of the guests, military and naval men, loyal Republicans, a few disloyal Federalists, even a few British friends of the Stewards.

Outside, carriages, wagons and drays flooded down the hill on the Baltimore-Annapolis pike, crowding the miserable red dirt ruts that passed as roads, even here in the outskirts of Fells Point. Baltimore's forest of ship masts and busy wharf now vied with Boston, New York, Philadelphia, Charlestown and Savannah. But as rough-hewn as Baltimore and Fells Point were, in Nathan's eyes their crude denizens were esquires compared to the nasty political creatures in that dismal swamp, the new capitol called Washington City, huddled along the pestilential Potomac. In that respect he would have to agree with his father's enemies, the Austers, who stayed in the new capital often, but mocked its pretensions of grandeur and civility.

Abraham Steward had adopted Peter with the help of a mysterious benefactor. This handsome half-breed—this sometimes uppity Shawnee whose dark ruddy face was a dead give away, unlike his beautiful Shawnee mother known as Elizabeth Hughes—constantly probed for more information, especially about his father, whom he had never seen. Nathan and his parents were the only ones who treated Peter as an equal—in fact they knew he was far superior to most white men and highly intelligent. Both Peter and Nathan were targets of seductive looks from women, usually hanging off their men's arms: Nathan, tall, wide-shouldered, fair-haired and muscular, a seemingly gentle young man, hesitant and slow, unassuming; and Peter, wiry, smaller, dark and usually quiet but proud, constantly chaffing at the condescending and superbly hypocritical Stewards,

Austers and Charles contingent in Philadelphia.

At the prestigious Baltimore Academy, Peter had made no close friends and found himself under attack by a number of students. One large white bully lost a finger and vomited for hours, but no charges were filed. Peter's prowess in the classroom irked his professors—so brilliant that a relentless pack of professors hunted down every compelling phrase in a futile attempt to discredit, for instance, Peter's essay "War with Great Britain." His varied inventions and investigations, his work with Robert Fulton, the great naturalist Linnaeus and others, led many to call him a "damned pagan prodigy." But no one really liked or trusted him, except the Jeffries and his Shawnee cousin, Tecumseh.

Nathan had always dreamed of marrying Barbara Steward. What man did not? Barbara was one of the most eligible young ladies in Maryland, and a few people spoke of his "engagement" to Barbara. But everyone knew that the Stewards' finances were tied to the Austers, who owned slavers out of Delaware, Maryland and Virginia, even up north; Tories, so powerful no one dare question their operations. Abraham Steward's Bank of Baltimore was in bed with Lloyd's of London and Liverpool slavers.

So many enormous beeswax candles and spermaceti lanterns gleamed that it looked like the entire mansion was on fire. From the ballroom in the west wing, Nathan could hear the Mozart vying with the raucous entertainment outside, up and down Bond Street. The small, lithe Peter in his brown train suit—in the flickering lights of the celebrations and lamps, as if through a mist; these were the two people he loved more than any other, excepting his parents, of course. Nathan, a tall, broad man in his best dark, homespun broadcloth coat, hopeless shoes, but a pleasant and honest smile that everyone loved; at least nearly everyone. Especially, he thought, the love of his life, Barbara, and his dearest friend, Peter Hughes, the "Redskin Experiment." And then there was a mysterious benefactor who helped the Stewards, Elizabeth and Peter Hughes, anonymously, remotely, secretly. Nathan knew that Peter felt nearly ready to kill over the mystery, and Nathan dreamed of helping him, in medieval fashion. They could laugh together over the absurdity of their lives.

Nathan made fun of Peter's burnished looks and academic prowess, and Peter ridiculed Nathan's lack of sophistication and book learning. Nathan's pale, unassuming face, pleasant enough when properly groomed, still seemed boyish, and his body, full grown now, more than six feet, seemed clumsy, even docile, but was dangerously powerful if aroused. On the rare occasion when this happened, there was only one punch, except when he and Richard Auster had fought in the water beside *Bucephalus*. Nathan and his father had once saved Peter's life when he was ambushed by a pack of wharf rats they could never prove were paid off by the Austers. That had been two years ago. The Jeffries were the only white people in Baltimore who seemed not to care about Peter's being a half-breed.

But then Peter had been sent north to Dartmouth College in New Hampshire and Barbara had been sent to London.

Under the bright lanterns that glistened off the vast colonnaded portico, escutcheons shook their fists at Nathan in the flickering light, the music swelling inside and the crowd noise about as he lost sight of Peter and Barbara. He saw a horde of guests constantly milling around the two Hepplewhite sofas and two vast Chippendale tables at the other end the main ballroom, all long walnut and mahogany, with cheeses and early summer fruit and vegetables from the south, venison and pheasant, fresh baked corn bread, pies and cakes. The candelabra near the fireplace picked out great war scenes in the oval Persian rug before the sofa. Barbara acting strangely. The joy of seeing Peter. Those glorious candles. Nathan knew he had already drunk too much, and felt lost, alone.

At the other end of the hall, Peter noticed Abraham Steward staring at him with a strained look. Peter felt a nudge from Barbara.

"My dear brother," she whispered, grasping his arm. "See? We have already lost poor Nathan. Let us not go in right now—we must not upset the other guests—but may I show you a new book by Lord Byron, and our project by that Dutch painter? Please," she insisted, and kissing him on the neck, pulled him away.

The night slid into utter chaos, ship shattered on the rocks, Madeira and brandy flowing on. Nathan barely avoided capture by Barbara's father and one elderly bejeweled woman seeking him for some reason. He looked everywhere for Peter. Who could have expected the way the evening ended?

Nathan spoke briefly with affable Captain Isaac Hull, commanding the frigate *Constitution*, who knew his father from the Quasi-War in '01. He met a young lieutenant, Oliver Hazard Perry, but mostly he forced himself not to search for Barbara, who always seemed just out of reach, or to stare at the dark-haired woman who always seemed to be facing him from halfway down the large ballroom, near the west hall. She was standing with Abraham Steward and Captain Jacob Auster, with his son, Richard and another young lieutenant whom Nathan could not immediately place. Long-tailed broadcloth coats with high stocks and wide lapels, pants and high boots—cut in the latest British country gentleman fashion. But who is she? That proud, slender figure in a pale blue evening gown, her long hair unfashionably straight but slightly braided and gathered on top, off the bare shoulders.

Her nose was prominent with a slight curve, but otherwise straight and narrow, her cheekbones high, brows gracefully arched, lip curled suggestively when she smiled; lips thin but demanding, an exciting mouth. She was a bit taller than Barbara, and lacked her voluptuousness. Nathan felt a tidal pull of desire for her, even as he remembered his promise to steer clear of the enemy. Those intelligent eyes, willing to engage; dark and flecked with gold. They seemed to beckon him; innocent and seductive, haughty and honest. Her skin was darker than most white women. Nathan, glancing lingeringly and then away, feared the openness of that perfect, oval, aristocratic face, exquisite but unusual, somewhat like his mother's. Suddenly when he turned, that utterly entrancing woman was standing calmly before him, not even waiting for a formal introduction.

"Mr. Jeffries?"

Nathan, stunned, closed his mouth and grasped for words.

"Yes ma'am. Nathan Jeffries, at your service. May I—"

She laughed, musically, delightfully. "I am Catherine Charles, sir; please call me Catherine. You know my fiancé Richard Auster."

"Uh, yes, Catherine—"

"Nathan? If I may—"

"Oh, certainly—"

"I know the Austers and Jeffries are not fond of each other, but—"

"There you are!"

Barbara, hanging on Peter's arm, entered from the east hall. Nathan knew instantly from their faces and slight dishevelment that they had just risen from the same bed. His best friend! With Barbara! Watching his world fall apart, Nathan noticed others staring at this dark-skinned creature with the hostess, few guessing the whole truth.

"If you will excuse me," said Barbara. "Father would like me to discredit Mozart in front of our esteemed guests. Catherine, have you met Peter Hughes, my adopted brother?"

"It is a pleasure to meet you, Mr. Hughes," said Catherine. She held out her hand.

"For me also, Miss . . . Charles," he took her hand, bowing slightly. He would not look Nathan in the eyes.

Barbara glanced at Nathan and walked over to the harpsichord by the far wall. A few guests nearby clapped politely as she began to play a minuet. A quartet beginning to set up their instruments quieted down, and a crowd began to gather for the dance.

"Are you also a man of the sea, Nathan?" asked Catherine in a soft voice.

"Hardly," said Richard Auster, whose father, Jacob, nearly as rotund as Abraham Steward, was also making his way over.

Nathan stared at his enemy. "I help my father in the countinghouse, but I hope to soon begin my studies at Harvard," he said, "and enter a career in law. Following my mother's beliefs, I am a man of peace."

"At which you will no doubt command the same success your father has. Shall we dance, my dear?"

And they were gone. Nathan glared at the couple until Catherine turned back to look at him again, and Nathan caught himself staring at her dark beauty. Soon a dazzling circle of pink and blues and yellows, ruffled petticoats and empire gowns and courtly gestures formed as the minuet ended. Then Abraham Steward conducted the reel, followed by a newfangled waltz. In the excitement and beauty of the ballroom, Barbara's pretty, full and sensuously curved lips quivered slightly as she played with the quartet.

"Nathan." Peter's voice. Nathan started to leave.

"Nathan, please let me—"

Lieutenant Perry was approaching, and then they heard a loud voice from behind them.

"Well, well! This is a truly democratic gathering!"

Jacob Auster, more drunk and walking with a slight stagger, wearing dark blue with "bullion buttons" and a sneer on his face, approached Nathan and his father. Nathan's heart chilled. Richard's short, fleshy faced father, weaving, nodding at Nathan, laughed as Richard came over, a chip off the old block, but sober.

"You are drunk, father," he said.

Captain Jacob Auster nodded. "Yes . . . but my face is not as red as . . . that one!" he said, pointing at Peter. Someone cut short a laugh. A few people giggled, but were hushed up. Everyone in the room was quiet now, and guests were crowding around. Nathan, embarrassed, frightened and angry, knew what he had to do. Then his father burst out with a quarterdeck roar.

"I thought we had settled this years ago when we agreed it requires more than the right parentage to make a gentleman!"

Young Richard Auster suddenly laughed in the most blatantly derisive manner, but nodded toward Nathan, as if mocking his own father.

"Come, sir," said Richard to his father Jacob. "I must—"

"Sir!"

There was a scuffle behind them.

"Jeffries!" Jacob said to Nathan. "I understand that your father is having some difficulties in business."

More dreadful silence. No one looked at Nathan or his father.

Fighting to keep his temper, Nathan held his father's arm to quiet him. "My father's company is sound, thank you . . . whatever you have heard."

"Yes, quite. In any case, your father is an old fool, what? But at least no coward."

Nathan could not believe what was happening. Peter shook his head. Richard Auster returned Nathan's gaze with a calm that was chilling. But it was too late. He could not stop it.

Again. What had happened tonight was . . . Peter, damn him, would have known the right words.

Captain William Jeffries walked back to Captain Auster.

"Please explain that, sir."

"Your son obviously decided not to follow in your wake, because it would have required some small amount of courage. We know what this so-called 'Quakeree' is all about—a convenient excuse for cowardice."

William and Nathan stared at their tormenter in stunned silence. Then Captain Jeffries tossed the rest of his drink in the man's large, round face.

Abraham Steward dropped his head and arms in defeat. Richard seemed amused. The looks on the faces of Barbara and Catherine sickened Nathan.

Wiping red drops from his face with a handkerchief, Jacob Auster stared at William in amazement, then grinned. "Since even you are not likely to apologize, I shall of course require, as they say, *mano a mano*?" He rubbed his hands in anticipation. "Delightful." He forced down a chuckle. "Shall we say, then—"

"Please, Captain Auster, Richard," said his host Abraham, turning to Nathan for help. "This is not—"

"Be quiet, Abraham," said Auster. "We will come to agreeable terms with your friends, say, tomorrow afternoon, if that is convenient? And to whom shall I send a representative?"

Peter strode forward and grabbed Nathan's arm, but the latter shook it off and ignored him.

Suddenly more sober, Captain Jeffries turned to Lt. Perry, whom he had known for several years. "Will you act as my second?" he demanded of the young man, ignoring his own son, too young in any case.

"Yes, sir," said Perry, sadly, while a furious Abraham Steward shook his head.

"Lieutenant Perry has kindly made himself available," Nathan's father said to Jacob Auster.

"Yes. Quite." Auster grinned, weaving slightly. "My dear?" He offered Catherine his arm but she ignored him, accepted her fiancé Richard's arm, and strode gracefully out without a word, with no more lingering glances at Nathan or anything else.

Captain Jacob Auster, now alone, unflappable, bowed to the crowd, shrugged and faced his opponent. "This has been a pleasure, Captain Jeffries, Abraham, Barbara, my friends. Adieu."

Duel at Bladensburg Grounds - *August 18, 1807*

In a few hours Nathan's father's approaching demise, which had begun its countdown at that catastrophic July 4th ball, would be complete. He felt he never would see his father again, or Peter, after that bitter betrayal. Of all people, Peter and Barbara, the finest woman, he had thought; two people who rose above others in his exacting estimation. His father Captain William Jeffries would at least not have long to suffer, as dawn approached. Sleep of course had been impossible. He knew he sometimes lacked judgment, and he certainly lacked Peter's intellectual powers, but he needed to witness the duel. His father had no idea he was there; Nathan, hiding near the dueling ground, spying on his father, knew that his mother Amy would never forgive him for not telling her. William Jeffries, with his son's help, had finally succeeded in destroying her life—she would shortly find out that her husband broke his promise. As for Nathan, his future, like his father's impending death, would be "the undiscovered country" as Peter had quoted from Shakespeare, and nothing to look forward to. But surely there was no choice, no choice, and so the nightmare dragged on until—and they had managed to keep the secret—he would lose his father today. Nathan's mind raged; may God forgive me for my sins, I surrender myself to your care. Perhaps he would challenge Richard, and then his mother would be left alone. Nathan fought the urge to vomit. Now he could hear the men by the carriage.

"Is there anything else I can do?" Perry asked Nathan's father. It was half past five, before dawn and still dark outside. Nathan gulped, seeing the men appear and disappear in the flickering light of the oil lanterns.

"No, thank you, my friend," said William Jeffries calmly. "Just accept my thanks for all of your . . . for your assistance. I am—please make sure that letter gets to my wife Amy, and . . . tell my son that . . . I have always loved him."

"I will return shortly."

Captain Jeffries nodded, as someone leaned out the carriage window; they heard the screech of a mockingbird, the mourning doves, the hoot of an owl. Fog reflected the light from the lanterns, and the shadowy limbs of the sweetgum, chestnut, poplar and white oak snaked into the gray overhead; in pre-dawn mist, thin patches of dew lay scattered in the lower shadows. William Jeffries wore his old uniform, complete with dark blue half-moon fore-and-aft cocked hat. In the flat glen surrounded by oaks, Nathan saw a carriage silhouetted in more lamps. All had agreed that no one else must be told. A message would be sent to the appropriate people, merely to advise them that a man, for all his love of family, cherished his honor and pride above all other considerations. The madness of the challenge and sudden execution.

The true sun was now moments away. The opponents met at the northwest corner beyond the cow pasture. A personal brace of Belgian dueling pistols had been provided by an associate, Michael Fredericks; weapons that had "never failed to fire."

A deathly thin figure in a beaver hat approached them, holding another lantern that revealed all.

"Ah! Lt. Perry and Mister Jeffries, is it? Upon my word, this is a pleasure!" The man bowed politely, his large smiling face stretched ancient pock marks on skin taut and ruddy, a face undoubtedly reflecting a life at sea. Neatly dressed in silk and flannel, his raspy yet resonant voice seemed compassionate and confiding. He reminded Nathan of an enormous spider.

"Archibald Coxe, master of *Scourge*, at your service and speaking for Captain Auster—I only wish we had met—"

"Yes, we know," said Perry curtly. "Wait here, sir, please," he said to William.

A smiling Coxe and Perry slowly walked toward the other carriage, the hostility almost palpable, so that the final arrangements could be quietly confirmed.

Nathan could make out phrases. " . . . in the event of a misfire . . . no cases yet prosecuted . . . but I would caution against discharging weapons a second time, sir . . . it would alert . . . after shots are exchanged . . . not admit publicly . . . not an acceptable retraction . . . apology . . ."

A voice inside Nathan screamed that he must stop this, throwing his life away if necessary, that this was mad and senseless suicide. But that was the voice of fear. The men on both sides stood by and watched the proceedings; shivering, Nathan feared his hands and voice were starting to shake. Before the sun fully rose, his father would be dead.

The agonized look on Perry's face made it difficult . . . and his mother and his ex-friend Peter Hughes, the woman of his dreams Barbara Steward . . . Barbara's wet full lips pressed against Peter's, her body pressed to his; Nathan almost froze, and backed away involuntarily.

"Sir?"

"Are you ready, Captain?" Here was Lt. Perry.

Did his father silently nod? Was he actually—

The beautiful ebony and mother of pearl inlaid case contained a matched pair of pistols, charged with powder, wad, and ball. "Impressive," said Jacob Auster. His eyes flickered past his opponent.

"Your choice of weapons, sir," someone said to Captain Auster. Where was his son, Richard? After Jacob selected a pistol from the case, William Jeffries took the other. Nathan watched, fighting his terror; he could imagine the dark hardwood,smooth, almost slick; the barrel cool, alien. William handed it back to Perry to load and prime. Nathan felt numb and feared that his father, the hero of the 1799-1801 Quasi-War, stood no chance.

A few moments later, Lt. Perry handed him the weapon again. "Loaded, charged and primed, Captain Jeffries."

"Please position yourselves back to back, gentlemen," said a stranger, tall and imposing.

"Cock your locks!" They clicked back the hammers, muzzles held high.

This was it! Nathan could feel a dozen of pairs of eyes fixed on the two men. At least I know my father will not flinch, he said to himself insanely. Was he shaking? Auster was silent, seemed at ease. Nathan thought he heard the hoot of an owl.

"You will each advance fifteen paces, at my count, turn and fire at will," the somber man entoned. "Ready, gentlemen?"

"Ready," they said.

"One! Two! Three! Four ... Five ..."

Nathan fought the urge to run.

"... Fourteen ... Fifteen."

He felt like his heart would burst, as he watched his father slowly turn. Auster was equally measured; both pistols were raised to the level almost simultaneously. Nathan could imagine looking over the hammer and barrel of his pistol, seeing the black hole of Auster's pointed at his father's face, then in a moment it seemed to lower, down to the level of his ribs and then his belly. In that moment, would his father decide to lower his weapon and fire it into the ground? But Nathan saw the flash in the pan, heard two deafening cracks, almost in unison, as pistols jerked and both weapons exploded loudly in acrid fire, but did one discharge prematurely? Impossible—both had waited properly for the count. A misfire?

For what seemed like eternity, Nathan stared through the smoke to see his father's adversary standing, pistol at his side, a wide-eyed look of astonishment replacing his habitual disdain. The smelly, powdery cloud dissipated. The two men gazed at each other. Apparently, both shots had missed. But then Jacob Auster rolled a furious, hateful eye at his opponent and dropped his weapon, twisting slowly like a feeble tree branch in the wind, weaving backwards and forwards before falling to his knees, and then on to his hands and elbows. Finally he rolled over on his side, curled in pain. Nathan saw briefly a look of shock on Jacob Auster's face, staring, mouth agape in astonishment. No one moved as he groaned; the doctor walked over and knelt by him with his bag. He shook his head. Coxe followed and stood watching as Captain Jacob Auster heaved convulsively, then thrashing briefly, head back, gasping, arching like a fish out of water. Then he was still.

Suddenly Nathan saw Richard Auster charge out of the underbrush behind his father, and looked at Nathan's father with pure hate.

"You fired early, you bastard!" he said loudly.

Two

Baltimore

Now aged twenty in late November 1811, a godsend and a curse to man, Catherine Charles had known London, Rome, Florence, Venice, Paris, Barcelona, Prague by way of Brussels, then ran hard aground and stranded with the Charles clan in Philadelphia. But Philadelphia, after seeing Boston, New York and especially Baltimore, loomed in Catherine's mind as by far the most sophisticated, educated and urbane, cynical New World center of some cultural efforts—that is to say the inhabitants were the least "American," in this original capital of the Continental Congress. There were more Tory Loyalists in Philadelphia than in Canada, who openly regretted and complained bitterly about their separation from England, and about this awkward relocation of the capital to those rude infested swamps of the Potomac and Anacostia basin. Everyone respected and admired the genius of nearby Baltimore's burgeoning shipping and industry. But the thought of being stranded in Maryland on the Chesapeake, the far side of civilization, among those tobacco-chewing primitive tribes from Ireland, Scotland and God knows where, not to mention the native-born, more violent rustics—as bad as the lower elements of Boston—chilled the heart of any truly civilized soul.

Catherine, especially since puberty, had lured most men for all the usual reasons. She had been attacked by royal princes, wealthy shipping men, not to mention denizens of the wharf in harbors from Portsmouth to Baltimore. Men who bully and men who ambush supposedly weaker prey—one of whom lost an eye in the battle before Richard Auster came to her aid. Richard feared nothing and no one. By the time she was 15, Catherine drew every man to her, and they drowned in the relentlessly dark sea of her large, hypnotic eyes. Richard trusted her, and only her. And in truth she cared as little about any of that as did the sea itself. Besides, she was to marry Richard Auster, the envy of every woman. Catherine could remember how Richard had laughingly pronounced his undying love for her when it had been arranged for them as children—one adopted, already wonderfully cynical, in fact, when she was 12—both were familiar with loneliness, isolation and privilege. Richard was a worthy match for Catherine's keen intellect and extensive education.

But everything had changed in 1807. When she met William and Nathan Jeffries, and saw how vicious Richard became after his father died, Catherine could no longer dismiss the insufferable arrogance of the Austers and their British cronies. Her loyalties were Federalist—or at least had been, and the Federalists hated the Virginia "Monarchy." Instead of declaring war or at least attacking the British at sea, Jefferson and his Democratic-Republican Congress passed the catastrophic Embargo. In spite of his generosity and charm, she began to see Richard Auster as a monster. He was neither Federalist nor Jeffersonian, but a genius at manipulating both sides, young John Quincy Adams as well as James Madison, into unwitting betrayals of United States interests and values—not to mention secretly aiding young congressmen from the west, like Henry Clay.

That evening in 1807, when she first set eyes on Nathan and listened to Captain Jeffries weigh in on the evils of slavery and impressments, she lived among the very wealthy in the civilized island of Philadelphia and was constantly turning down invitations. But there was no one, least of all Barbara and Abraham Steward, in whom she could confide her true feelings about those same evils.

Those few European friends who shared her hatred for slavery could not help her now, and she trusted no one in her native land. That July of 1807, she felt the patriotic surge that she and Richard had often laughed at. She would not admit it, but she had felt instantly drawn to Nathan— she would spend the rest of her life denying it, but when she saw these two men, father and son, treat Peter Hughes just like any man … she was intrigued. Most Americans cared little for the fate of the Indians or the Negroes; that did not make it right, but only reinforced the work that must be done.

Even after the Embargo was lifted in 1809, Captain Jeffries, his reputation now sullied, drank his way toward ruin; Catherine's fiancé Richard Auster laughed with satisfaction. Catherine hid her true feelings behind a mask of sophistication and cynicism. She decided to play a dangerous game, and attempt a secret correspondence with the one person who she thought might be receptive to her inteference—Amy Jeffries. And she knew that thousands of Negroes died thanks to Richard, and thousands of American seamen were impressed, flogged, lives lost in blood and horror from Chesapeake Bay to the Indian Ocean, while the Austers grew more powerful and wealthy.

To the Austers, Catherine behaved as if she had dismissed the Jeffries and faintly disliked those who cared about the misery of the thousands of Indians, Negroes and impressed seamen treated so brutally. She despised dueling, but seeing how the Austers behaved at that unforgettable ball at the Stewards, her heart went out to William and Nathan, and the duel that followed so quickly felt as if it had happened yesterday. Catherine also knew that her life as she had known it was over. Since 1807, with all the shipping businesses sunk by Jefferson's and Madison's disastrous Embargo and the later bills to restrict sea trade or take all American ships from the seas, brilliant opportunist Richard Auster had blossomed into a dark and menacing man, worse than his father—who frightened other men and attracted too many women.

Captain Jeffries, his friend Captain Joshua Barney and a few allies insisted that the United States urgently needed a vast fleet of small warships, sea raiders, public and private, dedicated to destroying British merchant ships, especially in home waters and the Mediterranean. At least a few ships must venture around the Capes and attack British whaling ships and others in the Pacific and the Indian Ocean. Richard laughed when she mentioned this, but admitted in theory British trade could be crippled by dedicated commerce raiders—the *guerre de course*. But soon the omnipresent British warships would smoke out and bottle up every little American wasp and hornet and enterprise, a mere handful of small vessels suited for attacking British merchantmen. That the puny American squadron of frigates also would be quickly run to ground went without saying. Less than two dozen active war ships in the U.S. Navy, not one larger than fourth or fifth class! The American frigate *President's* attack on the innocent and far smaller HMS sloop *Little Belt* had irked many British—none more than Richard Dacres, captain of HMS frigate *Guerriere*. By the time he commanded her, the great Dutch and French fleets had been virtually destroyed or captured by the British Navy.

The befuddled landsmen in Washington City, against the stern warnings of the first president, had ignored the obvious dilemma now facing the United States—how to enforce their rights without any deterrent. The French and British laughed at American threats now. Catherine knew that American ships were easy pickings, mostly for the British; the same Royal Navy allowed certain American merchantmen to pass, to supply grain and other essentials to Wellington's army in Spain. During these years, she had known long and bitter spells, just as many seafarers had suffered impressment and other insults against the United States, the flag with 15 stars.

Since the formal engagement of these two beautiful young people, Catherine had watched Richard become a ruthless and hard slave owner, through his South American task masters, a slave runner, accused on sea and land but seldom to his face, a deadly shot. He often politely ignored her efforts to discuss the failed economic policies and moral issues. A man accustomed to winning by any means necessary, he became increasingly impatient with her postponement of their union, which she dreaded, now planned for June 29, 1812, as the country, once again, seemed to be stumbling towards war, both within and without.

Catherine looked on her upcoming marriage as a duty, impressment almost, rather than a glorious new life. She felt that her life in any meaningful, intellectual sense would be over. She could read some of the more thoughtful women writers, mostly in England, or even the local fare such as Charlotte or that naturalist Barlow. But Catherine had no illusions about marriage—the magic and then misery of that life, like frail, quiet, docile and nearly invisible Mary Auster, who lost two children before Richard, and Barbara Steward's mother who had died giving birth. She would love and care for her children. Other than that, Richard would dominate her more than ever, and they would grow even more distant.

Catherine knew all of the clinical details of love and its physical delights, but she had not experienced any of them. The Charles family was not warm. Not even to their own. And they refused to tell Catherine about her real parents—on either side. Catherine remembered how Mr. Charles had lured her and other girls to his lap with sweets, and they kissed him, even though it was distasteful and wrong. Stories about Charles and children were rampant and vicious.

In Boston of all places, one brave soul who dared to print the truth about the Charles cadre died in a mysterious fire with his printing press. Not even one small voice escaped punishment, "like the wrath of Cod," Richard often laughed. Everyone knew that some merchants were hit much harder than others. Much harder.

Catherine feared Richard, his associates, his plans for the Jeffries, his plans for her. He was dangerous . . . her horrible thoughts of some accident—but she must not favor those thoughts. Her feelings were shredded and boxing the compass, like a ship drifting aimlessly, in circles, in all directions. Richard had recovered the pistol ball removed from his father, and he did not laugh about that. His honor was not satisfied, but eventually it would be. She knew he was determined to ruin Nathan and his family—spreading stories about Jeffries' cowardice in shooting early, a matter often discussed in private meetings to which his fiancée was pointedly not invited. She found herself longing to see Nathan again, that annoyingly uneducated, persistent, oddly endearing flat face, a tall blonde young man one step up from the trades—struggling to save his father's business and obey his Quaker mother. Catherine knew that Nathan was overmatched by the harassment from Richard's men, which the latter laughingly denied—just as he laughed charmingly when she or anyone spoke of newspaper reports of press gangs and British ships abducting Americans, seamen and landsmen, ignoring any proof of U.S. citizenship.

Now, in the carriage on their way to Hammond Hall in Annapolis, she could feel Richard's eyes on her, caressing and probing her, basking and hungering for that glow that seemed to surround her, in spite of, or perhaps because of, those fathomless dark eyes, silky black hair, unfashionably dark skin and outspoken haughtiness, proud, sharp face of classical beauty, nose a bit arched, upper lip a bit long, not smiling now. Now her thin lips were demanding. "Did you hear what I asked you, Richard?"

Who could know what course would lead to disaster? But Nathan knew his nightmare would never be over. Even now, he wanted to honor their families' agreement. Even now, after her betrayal with his once best friend, he wanted her desperately.

"It's only for a three or four months, my love," said Nathan. "You'll see. This will be better for both of us. A spring or summer . . . wedding . . . will be better," he added desperately, risking this trial balloon, again, although he did not know why.

"Perhaps, as you said, we will see," Barbara said. Her pretty face was stony and severe. "Go if you must. I cannot stop you."

He reached out to her and hugged her to him, but her arms remained stiffly at her sides, and when he made to kiss her, again, she turned away. He kissed her cheek, feeling awkward, and it seemed as if she were already thousands of miles away. He held her loosely by the shoulders, but she would not look at him.

"Please, Barbara, I don't want to leave like this."

She gazed up at him now, her green eyes cold and distant. "How did you want to leave, Nathan?"

"I—oh, hell, you know that I love you. Why do you torment me?"

"I . . . torment you? Foolish man!" She jerked away. "You have a curious way of showing your love for me."

"And you . . . I . . . I only leave because I must! You should understand, you . . . you will understand . . . I . . . I—"

"Please leave now, Nathan, if you must go," she said dismissively. "Speak no more."

He could not talk to anyone effectively; maybe he could redeem the

Jeffries name through brilliant action—maybe. As he walked away from the Steward mansion, Nathan thought bitterly how the lives of the Jeffries had deteriorated in the years since William's fight with Auster, and his bitter departure from Peter and the Stewards. Amy could not forgive William's temper and she became furious when Nathan chaffed at his countinghouse duties. William's drinking worsened as rumors persisted that he had fired early and killed Jacob Auster in a dishonorable duel.

When President Jefferson ordered the Embargo instead of war in 1807, that had been the final excuse for William to spend most of his time at Saucy Sal's and other favorite taverns near the wharf. His shipping business foundered, as did most shippers, relegated to coastal runs and occasional illegal voyages to the West Indies with grain, tobacco, beans, butter and hams. Some captains even sailed to Portugal and Spain to sell flour to Wellington's army fighting Bonaparte. Nathan resented visits from Catherine Charles, that haughty do-gooder, and felt keenly Peter's betrayal, the loss of his only true friend, God rot his soul.

Enoch Earliegh, William Jeffries' most trusted man and last loyal partner, an older man with a family to support, skirted the law more often than William. He was a skilled seaman, well-versed in Bowditch and the new sextant. And there were still enough crew to hand, reef and steer with the best of them, and cut a sharp bargain at either end—the men did not mention smuggling to Amy. By 1809, Earliegh had become *de facto* master and supercargo aboard the large, fast brig *Bucephalus*, the last of William's array of vessels. Meanwhile, the U.S. Navy and a few revenue cutters interdicted not the British or French, but their own countrymen.

Nathan and William tried to convince Amy that Nathan must return to sea if their business should be saved. Amy finally fell silent and would only look coldly at the men who had reneged on their promises to her. Her chilly demeanor reminded Nathan of the slick and treacherous snow and ice that survived from earlier rains, snows and sleet. He felt sickened by his broken promise, but he must go! Earliegh agreed to Nathan's passage only as a favor to William.

As *Bucephalus* stood out from Baltimore harbor for this short cruise to Boston, Nathan, nominally and only superficially master of his father's ship, was cast as a journeyman, a mere tyro, working safely east-north-east beyond the Virginia Capes on the safest possible route to Boston; Delaware Bay, still dark, now just a league to the west. That's when the lookout shouted that a topsail schooner had appeared near the rising sun.

Nathan had to admit the schooner was a beautiful sight—to his practiced eye, in the growing light of dawn, she bore all the signs of a fast Baltimore boat. Earliegh concurred, after shouting at one of the crew for fouling the spanker. The sharply raked schooner swooped alongside from windward, seemingly out of nowhere, topsails now furled, and politely invited *Bucephalus* to heave to. Since the schooner was heavily manned and her ten carronades were cleared for action, there was little choice and Nathan watched Earliegh roar out the commands;

"Two points larboard . . . back the mains'l! You there, snap to on starboard braces!"

"Remember," Nathan said quietly, trying to keep his voice steady, "I am in command, you are the mate again—at least, for now."

"Nathan, I really think—"

"No debate, Mr. Earliegh!"

The schooner's long boat was already being hoisted out and fifteen minutes later in the calm swell, a pale, gaunt British lieutenant climbed aboard the brig backed by four armed crew, knuckled out of habit and asked to see the captain.

Before Earliegh could utter a sound, Nathan stepped forward and said, "I am master of the vessel. Why have you interrupted our voyage?"

The lieutenant smiled. "Sir, my name is Wickes and my orders are to search for British deserters who we know are aboard your vessel—"

Nathan saw the nightmare developing before him like an angry purple squall. "Sir, we are all Americans and can prove it, and—"

"Name?"

Nathan stared at the man.

"Your name, dammit ye rascal rebel Yank—"

There was a stunned silence. Then Nathan smiled.

"Nathan Jeffries at your service—and your captain or second is—"

"Shut yer damned . . . Sergeant, yew . . . bring your men—Mister Jeffries, summon your crew—anyone aboard if you please, and now!"

Nathan looked at Earleigh, who stared back along with the rest of the men. Nathan knew he could easily take on two of the likes of this precious dove in a fair fight. But arguing with 12-pounder carronades, muskets, pistols, cutlasses, pikes and vastly outnumbered? "Roust the lot," Nathan said quietly to his mate.

Earliegh nodded, clearly shaken, but blew his whistle, the code for "Abandon ship." The ten crewmen, none of whom trusted Nathan particularly, were quickly gathered around the main mast, some fearful, some bravely smiling, all fully aware of the situation. The lieutenant, not used to even this modicum of independent command, insisted on studying every "bloody face." Sunrise broke on those young wizened faces, records of the life at sea that his father had always wanted for Nathan.

"Jeffries! Jeffries—do you understand me, sir, you must surrender the deserters aboard!"

Nathan almost felt sorry for this fuzzy-faced twit. He said the only thing he could say. "Again, sir, there are no deserters aboard my ship."

"So? What about yer mate? Your name?"

The officer looked at Earleigh, who had last seen Scotland as a child. The master had a family onshore and looked distraught.

"He grew up in Baltimore, same as me," said Nathan. "I can vouch—"

"This man's not American, you rascal!" cried the lieutenant, his voice rising, "and yew ain't no sea lawyer—"

"You listen to me, you Cockney—"

"Shut yer mouth!" Wickes shouted, actually reaching for his short sword, touching the leather scabbard, then staring at Nathan again.

"Where're yer citizenship papers?" he asked quietly.

"Let me show you in my cabin—"

"No! We have no time for that. You two and that man over there are obviously British subjects—"

"No!" Nathan shouted.

"Take them!"

Two British sailors grabbed a terrified Earleigh and one of the American seamen, Tom Howard, then reached for Nathan.

"No! Lieutenant!"

Nathan grabbed at young Wicke's thin wrist as he wrestled with the clumsy sword, then a fist to his chin, his automatic punch—blood spurted from that arrogant nose—but suddenly a resounding collision against the back of his head, the fist of a large and powerful British crewman, ended Nathan's day.

Nathan woke up in pitch dark on a heaving, slimy deck, timbers and hemp groaning through his soul, the terrifying crashing and pounding of heavy seas. A few feet away, stale and sour smells of rotten fish and moldy cheese and excrement permeated the air and sharply penetrated his nostrils. He vomited a blood-speckled torrent and tried to roll away. An oaken cask behind him shifted with a menacing hiss. He had seen this done to lost souls, the damned slaves and doomed prisoners, gagged and trussed up lying on his side, his back bent, arms tied and pulled behind toward his bent, hogtied legs. He lay helpless, knowing he was in the orlop, near the sloshing bilge, surrounded by loose barrels, deep in the cargo hold in a violent storm. The throbbing, whipping waves of pain in his shoulders and ribs were almost as bad as the blinding flashes in the back of his head. His throat burned. There was a metallic smell of blood, perhaps from his own scalp or lungs. His body felt cold and numb; out of breath with bile rising again, he fought against his bindings and a choking panic. Nathan suddenly realized he was choking himself, then passed out again.

Later, cold and groaning from the hemp bindings and beating, he woke up to a more urgent nightmare—he was aboard a strange ship, pressed into an unimaginable life of pain and danger, a slave to the lash. Stripped of everything but shirt and trousers. No shoes. No cover. Suddenly a light from above blinded him as the grating lifted, boots and bare feet thundered down the companionway ladder two yards from his head.

"Up, laddie!" shouted a harsh and pitiless voice as he was untied and lifted. Nathan heard unfriendly laughter as his muscles screamed in agony and he thumped to the deck again.

"Time to meet the Cap'n."

Three

Tippecanoe

Peter Hughes and Tecumseh had argued with the Prophet so often; the three men had smoked many times during these past four years, 1807 to 1811. But this time the Prophet, Tenskwatawa, was alone trailing a dozen sycophants and bodyguards. Tecumseh was recruiting far to the south, and for a full moon Peter had found himself arguing against the Prophet alone. It was now before dawn, November 7, 1811, the battle, the target and now suitably the dying moon appeared before him in what might be the last few moments of Peter's life—as he felt his spirit slide towards the gray mist. The residents of Prophetstown had watched through the night as another ocean of stars, so many campfires of white soldiers that it seemed to reflect the numberless great jewels of the night stretching into the distance—no doubt a stirring sight, for a white man.

"Please, with all respect, Prophet, you must wait for Tecumseh—"

"It is not your decision, Wapalaneathy!"

After a moment's silence the two men faced each other, and the Prophet grabbed Peter's shoulder, standing on a ridge now looking to the south, overlooking the Wabash Valley.

"Let's go inside again," said Tenskwatawa. "I want you to meet my beautiful niece Connumoch. None will marry her, Walpalaneathy."

A young Winnebago brave ran up to them, sneered at the half Shawnee and shouted at the Prophet, pointing to the west.

"*Saymacanekee!* Much more of Harrison army here!"

"*Keathway?* How many?"

"*Metcheay!*"

"All of them," said Walpalaneathy, the half-breed Peter Hughes, shaking his head, shivering in his blanket on that wooded knoll near the west bank of the west branch of Tippecanoe River where it joins the eastern branch and then the great Wabash River a few miles to the south. It was still dark; in the faint moonlight, Peter could see the bare branches of nearby trees snaking into the mist. Prophetstown, the great village on the Tippecanoe River near the Wabash, stretched out to the south, and he could see figures moving among the *wickiups*. Even though dawn was still hours away, he knew his arguments had failed once again, and he still did not know who he was. Through the oak and birch, not half a mile to the west, he could barely make out dozens of campfires marking the position of the white man's army, at least 1,000 strong.

Peter had tried to encourage negotiations and begged the Prophet to wait until his brother Tecumseh returned before taking any action. But the Prophet, urged on by sycophants and urging on over 600 men of the combined tribes, insisted that the Indians could laugh at white man's bullets; he had swayed those who were still dubious about the wisdom of an attack against Harrison's camp.

It was a chilly fall morning, and Tenskwatawa was wearing a long robe of soft deer skin and fox fur. He had one feather and the necklace of bear teeth that was one of the trappings of his rank as spiritual leader of the tribe. A slim, attractive young squaw bowed her head and left shortly after Peter entered the tent. A pot was boiling on the fire, and Tenskwatawa, seated, gestured to a place near him on the hide covered floor.

"Sit, little brother. Smoke. *Wessee? Lekaw?* Some dog? Goose?" The two men ate and smoked for a few minutes in silence, studying each other. Though not a handsome, prepossessing figure like his brother, the Prophet had a commanding visage with skin the color of dark cedar and a large, broad, hooked nose, even more pronounced than Tecumseh's. His one dark eye was usually a penetrating slit, and widened only when he was relaxed and approving. Lean and sickly as a very young man, he was now more robust and vigorous. He pointed his chin at Peter.

"Remember, our best braves will penetrate the enemy headquarters, attack and kill Harrison himself—the Long Knives will then scatter like the young quails, back into the prairie."

The Prophet knew perfectly well they were heavily outnumbered and outflanked, but he had convinced himself and his followers that he had "seen" Harrison coming out of the west through the bare trees, that a "noontide sun" would show the way for the night attack against him. The dozens of campfires supposedly proved Tenskwatawa right; they would light the way to victory, showing where the soldiers were.

"And it would be more dangerous, and more costly in the long run, Little Brother, to let them march into our village, making further ridiculous demands. It is here we must put an end to their arrogance."

"Surely you do not see victory, Prophet! You are outmanned and outgunned—"

"Of course I see victory!" the Prophet interrupted loudly and nervously. Then he took Peter aside. "You must not remain here and speak thus . . . if you are not with us in spirit, then you must not be with us at all!"

"I fight for my brothers, you know that!" said Peter. "But this is a mistake, it is not yet time—"

"Leave us! Go join the white devils, return to your eastern cities. Take what you wish to survive; but you no longer belong here."

Peter was forced to agree but said, "I shall do none of those things. I shall remain a . . . neutral observer." The Prophet snorted and turned away. Peter strode out from the tent and left the village, selecting a hidden viewpoint. Why did he stay—merely to spy on "his" people, rather than simply depart? He would be able to hear and see the lead and arrows ripping through the trees and thudding into bodies. Some Indians would leave their good cover to attack over open ground, thinking themselves safe from the white man's bullets, as ordained by the Prophet. They would be cut down by troops using cartridges loaded with buckshot. More shooting, war whoops, bayonet and buckshot, soldiers falling back, then regrouping and pressing closer again.

And then he heard a nearby shot, and another; a soldier silhouetted near a fire screamed and doubled over. Arrows flew; he could hear them. It had begun. The scene he had dreaded was being enacted before his eyes, just this moment. The Shawnee, Kickapoos, Winnebagos and others were attacking Harrison's camp from just south of his position. To the east, he could no longer hear the river or the creatures of the night. It began as the Prophet had promised Peter. Suddenly the yelling and screaming erupted with renewed power from the south, very near him. The soldiers were charging, circling to counterattack around the Prophet's left flank. A man spun and fell not fifty yards away, holding his hands to his face. Peter could hear sharpshooters reloading, shouting and saw Indians retreating. One dropped as a red stain appeared in his back. Balls ricocheted off rocks and broke branches. Arrows buzzed and whined. Now men were fighting all around him, but he lay still unseen. The smoke and smell of powder and blood was nauseating. The Indians were being driven back, and everything was lost.

Most of the action was over now and Peter cautiously raised his head above the level of the bushes. What lay before him bought tears to his eyes. He realized the several hundred dead were mostly white men, but they had won the battle. He was alone, listening to the occasional shot as sporadic fighting continued. He saw a wild hog sniffing at a bloody, mangled body, smelled urine, bile and metal wafting in the acrid, smoke-filled air and almost vomited. I can still smell those sweet birch fires from my bitter, earliest years, he thought. Now scattered on the ground, new flintlock rifles, paper cartridges bitten by desperate men, powder horns and lead balls used by marksmen as long range trade muskets, Springfields, bayonets, "Brown Bess".75 caliber, even a brace of pistols with a new kind of ignition called a percussion cap, still in their fancy box.

The acrid powder smoke rising with campfires throughout Prophetstown was oddly soothing to Peter's nostrils, even with bitter memories. At dawn, most of the Indians melted into the marsh, and the town was burned by Harrison's troops. Peter could see several white officers in blue and gold uniforms on horseback, and knew that the braves had failed to get Harrison.

As the sky lightened near dawn, he saw the dreadful pools of blood, men flopped on the ground, scattered body parts, bloody, scalped heads. Dozens of corpses lay scattered in the woods. Peter wondered whether it was hours or minutes that passed as he remained almost motionless, watching the horror. It was near sunrise. Almost prone on the ground, he would be hard to detect in his dark buckskin and was safe enough for now; he carried only a knife, and could no longer believe in weapons.

As he rose and turned to head south to work his way around and swing back southeast to where the remains of the town would be across the river, he saw a soldier a hundred yards away, who saw him at the same time and began aiming his long rifle. Peter started to run as he heard, "There's one heading towards the fork! Cut him off at the river!" But Peter was confident he could outrun any pursuit and hide successfully until nightfall, even if there were an outside perimeter of soldiers. Why had he remained? Bare twigs snapped and slapped at soldiers crashed through the brambles. He entered a clearing with few trees, a gentle sloping rise, and though exposed, he made even better time. Then he saw another soldier straight ahead of him step out from behind a tree at the top of the clearing and raise his rifle. The muzzle pointed at him, flashed and roared as he plunged toward the ground. The air was alive; he felt a blinding pain as the ball entered his leg. He saw distant fires and maybe humans—impossible to tell—approaching? Or growing? No doubt here his body would feed hungry foxes and pumas, or . . . as he drifted in and out of consciousness, he couldn't help thinking of Nathan, Barbara, the Austers, leaving his mother's house in flames—that ignoble summer of 1807, when he lost his old life and his few friends among the white folks. In his last moments of lucidity, he looked again at the stubborn flickers of Prophetstown.

Aboard *Scourge*

The memory was surely just a nightmare, Nathan prayed, but this Hell told him otherwise. A long thin knife had sliced the back line of his bindings and blood rushed back to his straightening legs. Nathan whined in pain, lying curled on his side. He heard several cold laughs. Where was he? He could not remember—wait, he did remember, a line from that Englishman—Byron, Shelley? No . . . Wordsworth—from a book of poems his mother had recently given him. How strange that he could hear the lines in his head: "The child is father of the man." He could remember his father's commanding bellow—how many hours or days or weeks ago? And his mother. With heart pounding . . . Peter, Barbara, the bewitchingly and irritatingly superior Catherine on Auster's arm . . . Peter's mother and his fight with his best friend seemed more real than . . . how everything had changed after 1807, pleasing his madman of a father, violating his promise to his mother. On his cruise as supercargo; then he remembered—pressed off his own ship, his father's beloved *Bucephalus*.

The suffocating fear, drowning in waves of pain, returned full force. A wiry grip pulled his shoulder. "My, my, look what we got here," said the grating voice and the thin, cruel face came down to his; angry, pale and bony, an almost bare skull, heartless black eyes and downward-curving mouth, black stubbly beard, ears sharply dropping lobeless, against that skull, like a raptor or snake.

"How dare you impress me?" gasped Nathan, half angry, half fearful. "You and your . . . made a bad mistake, beat me down like a . . . you forced me off my own ship—I am a free American, you bastard, whoever the hell. . . you cannot press— "

A boot kicked him in the back, and he cried out as the sharp pain shot through him.

"And you'll take a civil tone with me. I'yam Mister Eller Clough, oy'please, His Majesty's master at arms and master's mate o' t' *Scourge*."

Eller and his men laughed. "And you got it all wrong, boy. You up and signed on, of your own free will, you did—or you will! The Captain will see you now—as we stow summore o' your cargo."

More laughter.

"What! . . . not this side of Hell . . . you damned—"

Nathan gasped as a boot probed and buried itself in his groin.

"Get 'im cleaned up a little," rasped Clough, "then bring 'em back to Cap'n's cabin. Might as well see it once before we throw 'im to the sharks . . . or sell 'im to the Musselmen!" There was another brief explosion of mirthless laughter.

The men roughly lifted Nathan and untied him completely. He groaned as circulation returned to his limp limbs. They forced him to stand, his bones cracking and his sore muscles burning with sharp spasms. Through his agony, they laughingly poured the Atlantic on him by the buckets full, since "they's workin' on the pumps. Get on those slops!"

The crew half-dragged the new volunteer toward the stern and up ahead, Eller Clough knocked on the Captain's door. Nathan could see bare-chested men in the dim light of the berth deck staring and snickering as they passed.

"Enter!"

"Ah! Mister Nathaniel Jeffries, is it? Son of war hero Captain William Jeffries! I am so glad to see you again—Captain Archibald Coxe, at your service—how long has it been?"

He stood nearly as tall as Nathan, thin, very civil, clean and polished, with a large, smoothly pleasant face, neatly dressed in the same formal black, beige and white silk and flannel he had worn for the duel. His large, expressive face studied Nathan pleasantly, smiling, as if shopping for a good horse.

Nathan finally placed the face, and nearly lost his balance again, "You're Auster's man—"

"Well, I feel relieved you finally figured it out, Natty. Now first I need you to sign—or make your mark, like most of these nigger-lovers you see, mostly a matter of signing."

Nathan stepped back, managed to hock up enough saliva to spray those smooth cheeks with red spit. The ruddy mucous dripped in the silence.

The man suddenly erupted in laughter. "By Gad, sir, you are no coward, not what I was led to expect—not yet, anyway."

Eller Clough whispered in his master's right ear.

"Yes," said Coxe. "That man fought a duel over some foolishness. Then he dove into the bottle and got drunk forever—" Clough laughed.

"And that beautiful girl, Amy—now your mother—what is to become of her now? And her man? Maybe both father and son will be tarred and feathered together AND keel-hauled AND maybe flogged a couple hundred times for good measure."

Eller Clough suddenly punched Nathan in the lower back with his "knuckler." Nathan screamed and bent like a snapping string on a fiddle. The other men laughed.

"You kin look forward to that treatment, Natty, my boy," said Clough.

Coxe seated himself at the small writing desk, the late sun just starting to slant in the after cabin windows on either side of the ship. Out the stern gallery windows, Nathan could see only occasional small whitecaps and five-foot swells loping under the stern, seas that made him nervous but seemed friendly enough; no ships to attack or flee, no sanctuary.

Calmly ignoring the blood streaks on his shirt, the Captain looked again at the younger man and his pale, penetrating blue eyes missed nothing. Coxe was tall in upper torso with gangly arms, but moved like a cat. His attire was clean and orderly, as was the cabin, everything in its place, tidy and efficient. His cravat was still carefully tied, his shirt and satin vest well fitted, black belt and shoes rather elegant for a pirate, a Caribbean sailor, Nathan thought. But there was nothing elegant about the man himself as he stood under the skylight, the one place he could stand in the little cabin.

"Captain Archie A. Coxe, boy, master of His Majesty's privateer *Scourge*, not pirate, and I only acted for the Austers as a friend in the unfortunate matter of your father's distasteful, dastardly, premature firing—"

"HE did nothing of the kind, you bastard—"

"Not now, Nathan—disgraceful and cowardly, we would say, going off half-cocked, as it were."

Clough guffawed.

Archibald Coxe showed Nathan a crew list on foolscap. "You write your name right there," he said, pointing to a blank line. "Or make your mark! No—you are some kind of scribe, am I right? Keeping Daddy's books, maybe a few free guineas for yourself? You'll be ordinary volunteer—clerk's mate—a handy waister, except probably no skills at all, not able-bodied, not really a seaman, just big, strong, we hope, good for the heavy work at least, muscles for scrubbing the deck, hauling on lines. Can you hand, reef or steer, as they say, or anything? Sign here, I said."

"My name will not appear. I will sign nothing," said Nathan defiantly.

"You will if you ever want your folks and friends to hear from you again!" Cap'n Coxe snickered as Eller Clough snorted while he cracked Nathan's back.

"My family and friends—" gasped Nathan, fighting back tears of pain.

The pleasant laugh erupted again from the Captain.

"They will miss you, dear boy. Remember, they have no idea what has become of you—"

"Why are you doing this to me? Do you get paid by Richard Auster to do his dirty business? I—"

"Shut your mouth, boy, and listen. If you don't sign, no one will know what happened to you, either."

"But they will suspect—"

"Now, if you want to live, if you ever want to see your folks again, you will want to write to them to let them know you shipped out of your own free will . . . understand? I am master of *Scourge*, and we earn profit for the owners."

Nathan smelled blood on the fresh breeze wafting in the stern windows, and felt like sobbing, hopelessly trapped into making an ugly choice—the horror and bitterness of his present predicament already seemed like an ongoing nightmare.

Cap'n Archibald Coxe now spoke sharply, impatiently. "Well, what's it gonna be, boy? Will ye volunteer to join this British privateer? Remember we only attack the French."

Nathan almost laughed, knowing his days were numbered in any case, then tried to conceal the trembling of his hand as he took the pen and signed his name. Clough half-dragged him from the cabin and the Captain's laughter rang shrilly in Nathan's ears as he was thrown forward, nearly falling over the leeward side with cold Atlantic spray and rain pelting his back.

"Go find Davis, cap'n's clark; he'll have to do with this, for the time bein'—no, there's the bosun, Logan! He's the one to sort you out!"

As Nathan stumbled down the deck to the bosun, he collided with a burly sailor heaving on the leeward topsail brace line as *Scourge* fought east by north. Nathan, much the slighter in build, was knocked on his backside. A few men stopped to look, but no one spoke.

He looked at the burly sailor and forced a smile but the other scowled and looked like he wanted to fight.

"Pardon me," Nathan said coldly.

"Pardon me?" echoed the man. "It's a school boy we have here, mates, another sprat for the frying pan!"

A few men laughed, but whereas they seemed sympathetic, all Nathan could see in the cold blue eyes of his accuser was implacable hostility. He stood up and glared at the man.

"You might try being more civil, sir," Nathan said, attempting to embarrass the man with courtesy.

"I'll civil you, you young whelp." With that, the seaman, about Nathan's height but perhaps forty pounds heavier, closed on him with murder in his eyes. Nathan froze on the deck; his feet wouldn't move.

"Morgan! Get back to work! You, boy, come over here!" How much had the bosun seen? Morgan grunted, then produced an evil smile before turning and walking away.

"We'll finish this later, *boy*."

With his heart pounding, Nathan said nothing but walked forward to where the bosun waited.

"Jeffries, do you know what this is?" the bos'n, Mr. Jack Logan, roared, holding up a holystone.

"Yes . . . sir," Nathan stuttered quietly, wondering if Logan believed that.

"The clerk'll not object if you do your work, and no harm comes to you."

"Yes, sir." Nathan narrowly avoided another collision as two men rushed by him carrying a new jib to bend on the forestay. Logan and Nathan were now standing between the bow and foremast. Another group of men were working around the capstan; just abaft that was the mainmast. Some unmade rigging and loose line still cluttered the deck. Two men were shaking out the topgallant sail on the small yard high above.

"Steer clear of Morgan," Logan told him. "He doesn't like newcomers, and he hates anyone who is younger'n him. But once you get to know him, you'll like him even less! Well, he's a good topman—if you can trust him on a yard, that's about it."

Four

Philadelphia

Catherine sat in the white, rococo game room of the Charles Mansion on Beacham Street, drinking tea with Mrs. Charles. Catherine's penetrating brown eyes were fixed on her hostess as she made another determined effort to politely cross examine the older woman. Hung all around the spacious room were heavy gilt-framed paintings of the Charles dynasty, beginning with Sir Frederick Charles, Chief Magistrate of the Commonwealth of Pennsylvania in the early 1700s. There were gaming tables against the walls. But mostly tea tables and the greatest variety of enticing chairs and sofas Catherine had ever seen, colors and shapes pleasing to the eye. It was her guardian and hostess' private room. The 100-year-old paintings of Philadelphia nobility with enormous lace ruff and heavily brocaded silk finery echoed the elaborately high-frilled dress that Mrs. Beatrice Charles wore. The woman herself seemed almost a part of the lofty paintings and heavily upholstered English and French furniture.

Catherine had to force herself not to study the enormous jowls above which floated a perfect, round chin and small, almost dainty face; red lips perpetually pursed and pouting in an implacably amiable manner, her face folded to the side, and above her small forehead, a pile of light, skimpy hair, mostly her own and graying now. Beatrice talked out of the side of her mouth, eyes close-set but open. She was short and stout with stubby, capable fingers and powerful arms. Her fully boned polonaise dress showed a large expanse of white breasts and seemed designed to make her form even bulkier, though its ornate frills and bows of pink and lavender satin were impressively excessive.

Oddly contrasted to this, Catherine wore a long green Empire gown that clung loosely but lovingly to her slim form. It was somewhat more conservative attire than she had chosen when visiting Barbara, though similar, in the latest Continental style.

"But why won't you tell me?" she said again to Mrs. Charles.

"But why do you want to know?" The older woman's confident hazel eyes crinkled, smiling into Catherine's. The young woman realized with a slight chill that she was not really a match for the woman she never considered more than a cool and distant "aunt." Beatrice was tough, shrewd and intelligent—perhaps more than Catherine herself.

Her hostess and guardian had no intention of revealing the truth about Catherine's beginnings—not now, not ever. That smile, though filled with generations of decorum, concealed a ruthless, indomitable will. Knowing what she now knew about Mr. Jonathan Charles, Catherine suspected that Beatrice "commanded the ship." Her smile broadened, and she decided to play out the losing hand anyway.

"Why do I want to know my origins? Why, indeed! Who would not wish to understand her origins—the cause of who she is—and show the love and respect due the memory of her progenitors?"

Beatrice, with all the arrogance of her Philadelphia tribe, put Catherine in her place with a regal wave of the hand and laughed.

"Ah, my dear, how delightfully naive you are! Has it not occurred to you that your ignorance of these matters is a blessing? That there might be excellent reasons for keeping this particular information from you? It has been judged—quite rightly—that you are better for not knowing. I myself have in fact always agreed with the reasoning, and who knows? Perhaps you would too."

"So there is some truth which is ugly or unpleasant?" Catherine pursued her interlocutor doggedly.

"Catherine! Your wit and stubbornness would do you great credit if they were displayed under more appropriate circumstances! Perhaps someday the occasion may arise!"

So that was it. She had been warned. She looked out the window at the extensive south gardens. At least, she thought, Nathan Jeffries might be alive. Odd that, thinking of him now instead of thinking of her own dilemma; in any case she would play the game to the end.

"At least, ma'am, I know enough not to commit the ultimate impropriety against my hospitable family here in Philadelphia! Worse than ingratitude for all the kindness you've shown me, would be boorishness and redundancy. I shall certainly drop this inquiry—for now."

Beatrice laughed again. "Well said! You are a beautiful, quick child. I envy you, my dear! Your talent, your sophistication, your experiences in the world. I mean Europe, of course—not to mention your happy decision to favor us with a visit!"

As if I had a choice, Catherine thought. As she turned to the window, she wondered if she should ever return. There had been no talk of a trial against Jeffries perhaps, but that did not mean the Austers had no other ugly plans for any who crossed them.

"Yes, Beatrice—who is that man over there?"

"Where?" Mrs. Charles' eyes quickly darted toward the garden, and then returned to Catherine's face. She didn't budge.

"Over there, talking to Jonathan, with his back to us. There, he's leaving now."

The two men were partially hidden by a small maple tree, and now the taller one, in a sky blue silk suit and cocked beaver hat, was walking away from the house, toward the stretch of Commerce Street that ran along the other end of the garden.

"I . . . imagine he is a business acquaintance of Jonathan's."

"But why are they meeting out there?"

Beatrice's chuckle seemed somewhat forced. "You certainly are a curious soul! So many questions! Why don't you ask Jonathan yourself?"

"Ask me what?" Jonathan Charles, wearing a brown broadcloth coat with matching cravat and lighter pants, strode into the room from the west entrance. Of medium build and pleasingly plain features, he seemed permanently sanguine. His calm manner just escaped being deferential. *Smooth* was the way Catherine thought of him. Perhaps filled with secrets, as

Richard was, but smaller and less threatening. Too smooth to be as real, as substantial as Beatrice. But he might be attractive to the kind of woman who wanted a tractable, malleable, cooperative man. And again, there was the money both of them had brought to the marriage.

In spite of his seeming congeniality, Catherine wondered if Jonathan had sought excitement elsewhere as his wife became perhaps too much for him. The ideal shape of the new century woman was definitely slimmer than that of the preceding era. A woman like Catherine would have been too thin a decade earlier, but was more than acceptable now. Beatrice, the flesh of her arms beginning to sag and jiggle heavily when she moved, would have been regarded as too weighty even a hundred years earlier. Catherine assumed that these two seemingly generous souls still had the desire; they were in their fifties, but vigorous enough.

"Catherine was wondering who you were with in the garden," said Beatrice.

Jonathan nodded to both women. "Just a business associate who did not have the time to come in." He walked over to Catherine to kiss her outstretched hand with perfect British aplomb.

"How delightful to see you, my dear. I had been at the office, earlier, of course. When did you arrive?" Jonathan sat in the large wing chair near the fireplace.

"I guess it was about 11 o'clock, wasn't it, Beatrice?"

"Yes. We have had a pleasant time of it, a bit of dinner and catching up on things."

"I remember when I used to hug you and sit you on my knee, Catherine," said Jonathan. "That was—well, not too many years ago, it seems!"

"I remember, Jonathan," said Catherine with a smile. "I guess I'm too big and too old for that now."

"Certainly you have grown up!" said Beatrice. Only she laughed.

But Catherine again refused to retreat. "I was told that the authorities and Austers did not want their good name soiled by the travesty of . . . but I worry, as Richard's fiancée, that I should know more—I worry that . . . certain people . . . will never speak to me again, perhaps understandably. But is there perhaps more to this bitter fight among the ship owner cabals, information of which I should be made aware?"

"You are worried? Perhaps about the Jeffries? There's nothing to worry your pretty head about, my dear," said Jonathan.

"Don't patronize her, Jonathan," said Beatrice. "What else have you heard, Catherine, or what do you suspect? You probably know as much about the political situation as we do—perhaps more."

"Yes, yes, the fight between the Austers and the Jeffries, and his son Nathan's apparently been taken aboard a British ship from *Bucephalus*, and are we even certain the other ship—"

"Of course it is British ... Madam ... a small warship can slip in unnoticed and seem to be just another schooner, or small cutter—"

"What if it actually is American, a United States vessel of some notoriety? I do worry about that boy Nathan, insofar as it might tarnish our reputation. Long before that, I heard the way the captains, mostly the Austers and their people, talk about Jeffries and the 'old Revolution gang.' It almost sounds like war again—civil war. I mean, the Jeffries and Austers are bitter enemies, not just competitors, and especially since 1807—"

"Jeffries is a fool!" said Jonathan.

"Hush, sir," said Beatrice, half in jest, but with a warning look.

"Why do you say that, Jonathan?"

"What I mean, Catherine, is that the good Captain Jeffries is still living in the 18th century. We have separated from England—well, some of us are certain that was unwise. But it's time to 'bury the hatchet' and treat England with the respect she deserves. Jeffries talks as if we were at war with her again! He and his crowd refuse to trade with her—our mother country. It's ridiculous!"

"But they say that there are thousands of American seamen forced to serve on British warships. Thousands! And some Americans have been hanged for refusing to fight against the French."

Catherine didn't want to antagonize this couple by displaying too much knowledge of current affairs. But she knew a great deal about the issues affecting the United States and her precarious role as neutral trading presence between warring France and England. Some of her information had come from Amy Jeffries. Federalists hated Napoleon, almost as much they hated Madison's Republican-Democrats.

"We were fighting the French ourselves, until recently," Jonathan reminded her. "And French ships and ports detain as many Americans as we hear are claimed by the British. In any case, Britain has the right to protect herself at sea. She is preeminent there after all. These reports of Americans imprisoned or serving on British ships, if they are Americans and if the reports are accurate, only means that we have to sort things out with England. She struggles for her life, the Empire, mind! This is an international war, remember. Napoleon has duped those idiots Madison and Monroe time and again. As far as England is concerned, we have simply a misunderstanding between two maritime powers—and we had better be careful! Our merchant fleet is a concern to them, and rightly so.

"Personally, I think these reports of impressment and so on are highly exaggerated. But we are in no position to dispute England's sea routes, even if we should wish to do so. She has the largest navy the world has ever seen, over six hundred warships. What do we have? A handful of small vessels. Six frigates. Not even one ship of the line! Our mother country is engaged in a life-or-death fight with France, and we can hardly blame her for becoming impatient with her interfering child."

Catherine looked at him, then shook her head. "That is the way Richard talks—because the Austers and their partners trade a great deal with England! But that is small comfort to those unfortunate individuals whose rights as Americans have been stripped from them! And England has no more right than we to the use of open ocean. We are at peace again with France, and ought to have the right to trade with her as a neutral, as long as we abide by the international conventions applying to neutrality. The Atlantic is not a British lake! I grow weary of the insults we receive at the hands of our 'mother.'"

Catherine realized she had crossed over the line. Beatrice had not spoken for some time; her lips were compressed into a thin line, and her face clearly showed annoyance. Now she attempted to take charge of the situation.

"These are complex issues, Catherine, hardly a woman's concern in any event, and perhaps when you are older you will understand. Though I'm surprised your visits to England and France have not taught you more."

Catherine's face turned red at this rebuke but her breeding forbade her revealing an excess of emotion. She chose to conform to Beatrice's mocking style.

"Naturally I bow to the greater insight and sophistication of my superiors, ma'am. And do not wish to seem ungrateful . . . for your help and the forebearance of—but let us get back to my question, if you please. Is there more to this struggle between the Jeffries and Austers?"

"Why would you think so, my dear," said Beatrice with her condescending sneer, "and what would you hope to gain by that knowledge, if it were available?" She smiled at Jonathan.

But Catherine said nothing and only smiled back at her patroness.

Beatrice, about to speak again, stopped and looked sharply at Catherine. The helpless look on Jonathan' face almost made Catherine laugh. But then he smoothed the waters. "Ahem. Quite. Let us proceed then to a somewhat more demanding question. What shall we do about dessert?"

Indiana Wilderness

Drop by drop flowing down river, shot by a white man in blue, now slipping into the cold, where nothing matters. Barbara Steward. Nathan Jeffries. Why had he lingered with white men—he knew the red arrow, the red stick, broken hatchet, the buck knives, Tenskawata and Tecumseh, his last great hope as he lies by the river, Wapalaneathy—lost eagle, lost fool.

In Peter's last moments of lucidity, stubborn flickers in the night, the burning of his tears, knowing his mother would suffer unavenged, her dreams for her son unfilled, but the embers drift on and on. So the master creator has no more need for this half-breed. And really, why had he lingered with white men who had betrayed him more than any other—his blood brother Nathan—don't focus on that one; consciousness slipping and then the blood drops into the still flowing river. His memories swirl up in the dark like scattered embers, to meet his people and perhaps find forgiveness.

Harrison's soldiers had put a musket ball in his thigh, and Peter had lain on the cold ground for almost two days until a young Shawnee found him.

Now, opening his eyes and feeling warm inside a *wickiup*, Peter assumed he was dead when he saw that lovely face—but the vision was no angel. Her name, he struggled to remember.

"I am *navrika*, cousin of the great Tecumseh. I am Connumoch, Never Cries," she said soothingly. "You were right, of course—they have all run away."

Connumoch, the beautiful young niece of Prophet Tenskwatawa was said to be a witch disguised sometimes as a great black panther, frightening men not easily frightened, not cowards. Because of her power, none would marry her.

"Why—why did you stay?" Peter croaked as his beautiful young nurse wiped his face with cool, moist linen. She then sniffed his leg.

"I stay for you, Walpalaneathy. Now hush and rest, get strength back. I remove the bullet from your calf—so poor a job the soldier did—and your shoulder is hurt only slightly. I see no injury inside and I clean the worst of the wounds and they should heal nicely good—your fever down. You have excellent health. You not lose any fingers or toes—I have make you drink sassafras and gamablyss for pain as body—"

Peter tried to rise and collapsed immediately.

"Your fever returns if you not rest," she scolded.

He nodded, still exhausted, grateful and worried about this Connumoch. He realized that she loved him, the poor girl. And so this went on for—how many days? Weeks? It was now a dry December but Peter knew his luck would not last forever. He must return again to the East, and find his mother's killer, who is surely his father. If his mother Elizabeth had been cared for properly, this pregnancy should not have been a problem.

Peter often forgets where he is and wakes up in a cold sweat, to feel Connumoch's sweet, soothing hand or a cool cloth on his forehead. Once he thought she kissed him gently on the lips. Peter wakes up in pain and panic, but seldom alone, always safe and cared for—or is that the dream? Peter feared that he would never again see his friend Nathan and his parents, Barbara and the Stewards, the people who cared for him without ever formally acknowledging his existence or real parentage. After all, he was a half-breed. The only thing lower than a half-breed was a pure Indian, or pure Negro, most worth less than a good horse. The Stewards had read about the sufferings of the American sailors, taken at gunpoint off their own ships, forced to obey every order, virtually slaves aboard "his majesty's armed ship *Bastard*." Many times this was a life sentence. Were the New England shipowners devastated by the snatching away of these employees? Then Nathan, Tippecanoe, the Prophet, Barbara. Peter drifts on . . .

No! Barbara straddles him in bed, raising a tomahawk over his head. Peter jerked awake. "It is all right," said Connumoch. "There is no one else here. You are safe with me, and we have plenty to eat and drink. Later you hunt for us." And then, as Peter healed, he became in many ways the model patient and they began to make increasingly frenetic love. But he knew there would be tears and anger when he insisted on returning to the East and crossing the Mississippi again. She warned he would die unattended, especially in the winter. When he rode out of the nearly deserted village, she who had nursed him now cursed him and turned her back, her long black hair switching furiously like a horse's tail. That perfect, oval face and large brown eyes; curved, love-hungry lips that would haunt him as he made his way east.

Late afternoon in the middle of December, just above freezing, Peter Hughes was riding east, urging his horse more quickly than would normally have been necessary. The beautiful weather and clear blue sky would not last long. So far, the rolling hills showed only a light dusting of snow, but soon this would be a white and difficult world for travel. His sense of anxiety and urgency about getting home was also heightened by visions of his mother, the Jeffries, Nathan, Barbara, Richard. Peter was dizzy with fatigue and worse; he feared gangrene and was haunted by thoughts of death or the loss of his right leg as he nodded in the saddle.

The wide road through the vast woods was frozen, hard packed and almost dry now; dozens of individuals and families had passed him, mostly in coaches, carriages and wagons, mostly going west. Some men walked, alone or with women and children. It hurt him to see one middle-aged woman in a shawl carrying a small infant, staggering with weariness. She stared at him sullenly as the baby cried.

But now the road was clear; even the small amount of dust picked up by normal travel earlier in the year had settled. Peter had seen no one for over an hour. In a few miles, just this side of the Ohio River, he would reach Steubenville and could rest, feed and water his horse. Then he would cross into Pennsylvania, and in about fifty miles reach the busy town of Pittsburgh. Some fifty miles to the south was Wheeling.

Peter was not wearing his buckskins now, but looked rather civilized in a white shirt, dark soldier's waistcoat, homespun wool overcoat, flannel trousers from Nathan and a felt brim cap. Peter was also worried about his friends among the Shawnee, and could not stop thinking about his last words with Tenskwatawa, now defeated and disgraced.

"In a vision, my brother saw Harrison's face and saw our father die in battle when we were boys. Now Tecumseh will probably kill me, for disobeying him and losing everything—you were right, Wapalaneathy, my brother—yet the Mysterious Creator told me we would destroy Harrison. It seems my visions are ... but I have seen more of your future," he said. The Prophet's voice and eyes were thick with smoke and ruin. "You might well listen, even though it comes from ... me. You will soon be unable stand in the middle of the stream, as you are doing now. You will be forced to ford the stream and fight on one side or the other. I know your loyalties are confused, and they will continue to be, but action will become necessary, whether you wish to act or not."

"How so, Prophet? In what manner will I be forced to act?"

"It won't come from your people, Wapalaneathy—but it will come very soon. Be careful, and use your own sight, your own abilities to see ahead—that can be a curse, but it will also save you. I may end up like Black Hoof, a disgrace to my people, but I will never sell out to the white man."

One of the young warriors nearby, Two Moons, had laughed derisively. "Since he has not the heart or stomach to fight beside his brothers, perhaps his great vision can save him from his own fear."

Peter had walked over and hit him in the face with the back of his hand. Two Moons had looked at him blankly, stunned, with blood trickling out of the side of his mouth. Peter struck him again, this time with his fist, and Two Moons fell down.

"Since you think I lack courage, my brave friend," Peter had told him, "maybe we should put your conviction to the test—just say which weapons you choose and I will be glad to stay and fight you. One of us may enter Mother Earth this day."

In spite of his pain, the Prophet had chuckled, and then shouted at Two Moons.

"You are a fool, and a disgrace to this tribe. Why don't you go hunt bear, and maybe when you return, you will be a man. Leave us!"

Two Moons had galloped off, with a murderous look at Peter. No one had doubted his courage then, but he had not won any friends and had made at least one new enemy. The Prophet had begged him to stay, but mainly to help protect himself from Tecumseh's wrath, when he returned from the south, the land of the Seminoles.

Then Peter's reflections were rudely yanked back to the present.

"Hey, mister! Whoa, boy, hold up a spell!" A thin, bristly-faced, gap-toothed young man was grinning up at Peter. Dressed in tan trousers, and patched jacket, dusty, tired boots and a floppy, wide brimmed hat, he was now holding the reins of Peter's horse. Where had he come from? Peter realized he had been dangerously oblivious to his horse's slowing pace and the surroundings.

"What do you want?" Peter said.

"Well, that ain't very neighborly, is it, Jake?"

"No, sir, it sure ain't, Zeb!" A giant man with long blond hair and a whining, high-pitched voice crashed out of the woods and stood on the edge of the road, pointing a long rifle at Peter. The two men laughed.

Zeb now produced a short, sawed-off musket he had concealed behind him. Peter now realized they had picked this ambush spot with some care; the road had turned abruptly to the right. That and his dangerous daydreaming had enabled the men to surprise him on the open road.

"What do you want? I have little money," he said.

"What do we want, Jake? We'll think of something, won't we," said the man still holding the reins of Peter's horse. The mount shook his head nervously. The big man nodded, smiling, now standing beside his partner.

"Now, my young dark dandy, I think you'd better relieve that horse of your weight," said Zeb. "Careful, now! My brother's got a mighty itchy trigger finger."

Once Peter was dismounted, he was quickly and expertly frisked.

"I'll just take care of these for ya," Zeb chuckled. He was holding Peter's knife and money purse, with its five silver dollars, two gold coins and assorted bits of change. "Now, mister, you walk on ahead—but not too far, ya hear? I'd hate to have to shoot ya down, right, Jake?"

"That's a fact, Zeb." The giant man produced his annoying, tinny laugh again; his voice buzzed irritatingly, the high-pitched, inane scratching of a huge insect. Peter speculated that his intelligence was sharply limited, even compared to his partner's. Except for Jake's size, both men looked like the average dirt farmers or trappers in their nondescript western jackets, leather vests, broadbrimmed floppy hats and dirty bandanas.

"What else do you want?" Peter asked again. "You've got everything of value," said Peter, without turning around.

"Oh, not everything, pretty boy," Zeb growled. "Just keep walking."

Peter now realized that they were after more than money and thought desperately for a plan.

"You part injun or nigger, boy?" asked Jake. "Naw—too pretty for a nigger. But you seem a little dark for a white boy."

Peter said nothing.

"Hey! I'm talking to you, boy." Peter felt the muzzle of the rifle prod his back, hard. He felt a sharp pain, and stumbled forward, almost falling on his face. But he still said nothing and did not look around.

"Now, Jake, is that any way to treat our guest? There's time enough for that later!" Both men laughed.

Peter wondered why the men seemed oblivious to the risks of discovery on the open road. Maybe their concern was allayed by their knowledge of the area, or a story ready to tell anyone who came by. If Peter did shout out or try to run, he would almost certainly be shot.

And part of the answer was revealed a few minutes later.

"Turn up here on the left," Zeb ordered. Peter could see a path that led off the road—a trail not overly conspicuous, but clear enough in the brush and overhanging dead growth. Once they passed through this tunnel of dry branches and vines, they were on an open, yellow walk, with plenty of clearance on either side, shaded by pine, aspen and ash. A beautiful setting, under other circumstances.

Eventually they came to a large open space, surrounded by large, old oaks, still impressive even without leaves. The trail evidently continued off to the right, but the three men stayed to the left. After about a hundred yards, Peter noticed that all the saplings and underbrush had been cleared away. He heard the sound of running water, and saw a small, crude cabin made of raw pine in a patch of afternoon sunlight.

A black dog, chained to a post outside the door, started barking as they approached. "Shut up, Wolf!" Jake snarled. He tied the horse up at the post while Zeb shoved Peter inside the cabin.

There was still ample light streaming in the windows to reveal the rude furnishings in the room. Two canvas cots on either side, a couple of wooden chairs, all rough hewn, a stone fireplace, and a plank table.

Zeb grabbed a jug from a shelf against the back wall and took a swig. Peter could smell the rum. Jake came in and closed the door, eyeing Peter in a lascivious way.

"Now, here's the way it is, boy," said Zeb. "My brother here fancies youngsters like you, and I want him to be happy. If you don't give us no trouble, why, maybe you can be like part of the family. We won't tie ya up, or sell ya, and we won't kill ya—but if ya don't do like you're told, yer dead, or worse."

Peter felt sick to his stomach.

"Here, give me some of that," said Jake, lifting the jug from his brother. He tilted it way back and poured a pint's worth down his throat, spilling some in his short black beard. Peter estimated his age at twenty five. And he smelled as if he had not bathed since birth.

Zeb, still holding the musket, nodded to him. "Enjoy yourself, brother."

Jake slammed the jug down on the table. "OK, boy, just don't fight me."

He ripped off Peter's jacket, twisting his arm half off in the process as

Zeb laughed. Jake yanked Peter's trousers down to his calves and shoved him to the floor, face down. Peter almost passed out from the pain in his thigh, now bleeding again. On his hands and knees, Peter heard Jake pull his own trousers down with a grunt, and felt a hard cock against his backside. His head was forced down by Jake's large hand, the other hand grabbing his buttocks, and he felt the man's foul breath heaving against his ear. Now.

With his left hand, Peter whipped a knife out of his left boot and reached behind him to bury it in Jake's massive side. With a shriek, the man rolled off him to the right and hit the floor beside him with a crash.

Peter rolled quickly to the left as the musket roared. A flash of searing pain in his left shoulder told him the ball had only grazed him, punching into the floor. He was looking up at Zeb's furious face. The man started for him as Peter wriggled away, meanwhile pulling his trousers up.

Peter stood up and ducked as Zeb swung the musket at his head. The stock banged against the wall behind him. Peter shot his right fist into the man's stomach; but as Zeb bent over and yelled in agony, he backed away and Peter's big knife appeared in his right hand.

"All right, boy," he gasped. "I'm gonna stick you now but good."

Peter dashed for the door, grabbing Jake's rifle on his way. He could hear the thrown knife stick in the door as he ran out. He made for the woods and in a few moments was hidden in the brush, reddened by the setting sun. In the waning light, he checked the rifle. Thank God, loaded, primed, ready to fire. Peter cocked it, careful not to dislodge any more powder from the pan. The flint in the lock looked new.

He crouched there, a hundred yards from the cabin as the day darkened. Then he listened quietly for a moment to the sound of mourning doves. An owl hooted nearby. He could hear sounds inside the cabin, and then vaguely saw the shape of Zeb stumbling outside, untying the barking dog.

"Come on, Wolf, let's find us some meat! Boy, I'm gonna skin you!" Zeb shouted, almost shrieking. "You killed my brother, boy, and I's gonna hurt you real good before you die!" Peter saw him leave the cabin and start walking back up the trail, his own big knife and the musket ready for instant use. The dog had already disappeared. That was going to be a problem.

Five

Ohio Territory

Peter Hughes could see through the alder bushes that Zeb was coming right for him through the gloom of dusk. By chance, the man would practically run over him, even though Peter knew he was concealed. Zeb was less than ten feet from him.

Heart pounding, Peter stood up. His adversary halted abruptly, almost dropped his musket in astonishment. The rifle was pointed at his chest.

He saw the big black dog running at him, and he shouted, "Call him off, or you'll be the first to die!"

"Wolf! Here, boy!" The dog growled and barked but stayed beside his master.

"Drop the musket, Zeb," Peter said.

Zeb laughed nervously. "Why, I'd be crazy to do that, wouldn't I, boy? Especially at this range, with the help of ol' Wolf here; we both got loaded pieces, ya know. I'd say we both got an even chance."

"I wouldn't. Drop the gun. Now."

Zeb scowled, then quickly cocked the flintlock and swung it a few degrees. Peter fired a moment before Zeb, but they were so close together that the sound was almost one long explosion. Through the smoke and flame Peter saw Zeb fall with a yelp and groan. Zeb's shot had missed him. Wolf lunged, and Peter swung the rifle as a club, hitting the dog in the head and breaking the stock of the gun.

The smoke cleared, and a full, orange moon was rising. In the clear twilight he saw the still bodies of man and dog that lay before him; the man dead, the dog stunned, dying, now whimpering and struggling to rise. He found his knife in Zeb's waistband and thrust it into Wolf's neck, an action which upset him more than the fate of the two men. Then Peter walked back to the cabin, pulled his knife out of Jake's bloody side and cleaned it off. He also retrieved his money. The jacket was torn but still serviceable. He swallowed a generous portion of rum, and briefly looked around the cabin. He found a more or less clean cotton rag to tie over his still-bleeding upper left arm, where the first musket ball had grazed him. The moonlight shone through the window on the huge body of Jake and the pool of blood. Everything else in the room was now in darkness. Peter raised the jug again to the corpse, with a bow and a vague saluting gesture.

"That's the way you wanted it, boys."

He carefully placed the jug on the table, and made his way outside, where he could clearly see his way back to Zeb. After relieving the dead man of another knife, he picked up the musket and cracked it hard against the side of a big hickory tree several times, until its stock was also broken off. Then he listened to the night; only birds, late locusts, some scurrying of small predator and prey. He fancied he could hear hunters on the prowl—rats, snakes, fox, bear, racoon, opossum, creatures of the night. He imagined tall flames roaring out of the cabin, the bodies and evidence inside, and decided against a burning. The murdered men would not be missed, but even if their murders were investigated. . . eventually perhaps all of us will have paid for our sins, one way or another. If the Creator pleases; if there is a Creator. Peter was no idealist; nor was he yet bereft of all hope. I hope to find my father, he thought. And punish him. Call it revenge. If men could only create as easily as they destroy, he thought, as he packed his belongings, mounted his horse and slowly, carefully made his way back up the trail.

The dinner meeting of the Daughters of the American Commerce had begun normally enough; held in the Steward's east wing on an unusually warm day in January 1812. Most of the snow had melted and from the Mount Clare overlook, they could see other mansions, countless mills, tobacco bins, Otterbein church, the Town Clock in the tower of First German Reformed Church, the Courthouse straddling Calvert Street, even the horse races near the Bay beyond Fells Point basin. This informal gathering of the first ladies of Baltimore and the Daughters of the American Commerce brought out the wealthiest and most powerful in Maryland. The male escorts were smoking up the other room. While Mrs. Randolph had delivered a speech on the need for more generous budget for extending the quay along the South End—a most unladylike subject—the women had been served at the long tables, roast turkey and the last of the season's peas and green beans, cheese and pie with their discrete glasses of sherry. Talk had been animated. The mostly white and blue gowns of the participants contrasted pleasantly with the dark walnut paneling, oak floors and severe classical design of the hall.

Now Barbara was cross-examining Catherine at their table. "So what did she say about your mother and father?"

"Not much, I fear," said Catherine. "My father may have been an officer—as if that helps much. Yank or Loyalist, army, navy, she doesn't know, or rather won't say. What a frightening woman. Well, you know her. After what has occurred, she reminded me of my duty—and you know about the health of Jonathan. At best, you would anticipate the ultimate jeremiad—yet she seems to envision . . . certain communications, meetings . . . with Richard . . . and will not tell me about them. They laugh and then scowl when I pry for secrets."

"You should not press so hard, Catherine, but you are so right—officers from the war are not rare."

Then Barbara shrugged. "No doubt they try to spare you ugly details about your real father—"

"But maybe now I can find out what happened before 1807 . . . if the Jeffries really are trying—I asked them to contact—"

"You had better let it rest, my dear. For years you have searched in vain for your parents' identities. The Charles are your parents, dear. And soon you will be married."

"Yes," said Catherine. "You know, I think Richard does know something about young Nathan Jeffries whereabouts."

"What did you say?" Barbara asked abruptly, staring at her guest.

"I . . . do believe that my fiancé knows more than he is telling me about what happened to Nathan in November. Mrs. Charles—my dear mother? She 'asked' me to refrain from asking anyone further . . . on the same topic."

"Well, then, what did you tell her?" said Barbara sharply.

Catherine looked at her, and arched her dark brows. "Is it that important, Barbara?"

Her inquisitor looked away. "Of course not. What do I care what others think? I was just . . . curious."

"I could turn the question around, my dear. The fact is, you know, all they say is that he and his father have behaved . . . badly through this affair. William Jeffries seemed brave enough—or foolhardy enough—to stand up to Jacob. It's difficult to believe he would cheat and fire early . . . but not according to my fiancé. You know the Jeffries much better than I do, Barbara."

She then looked sharply at her hostess but Barbara had turned her face away.

"I don't know, I . . . never did quite understand their . . . ugly disagreements. Though of course everyone knows that the Austers and the Jeffries are on opposite sides of the British question . . . of every question. Some had rumored of a 'liaison' between the boy and I—nasty gossip, you know."

"That's part of it. But tell me, Barbara." Catherine smiled wryly. "You know I shall probably never find out, but really, besides being *persona non grata*, Nathan Jeffries had visited here often before 1807. What do you think happened to the boy?"

"Why, Catherine, I—"

A loud voice carried clearly across the parlour. It was Rachel Conrad.

"Are we ready to discuss the continued candidacy of Barbara? Catherine? Remember only ladies may be members. Still, what an honor and delight it is for us to have known the two most beautiful and shall we say experienced princesses this side of the Fells Point Wharf!"

Catherine couldn't believe what she was hearing and Barbara looked down at the floor in confusion and embarrassment.

Catherine had ignored the vicious look of her rival, Rachel Conrad, sitting at the nearest table when she arrived. But she could not ignore what Miss Conrad was saying now, ostensibly to the young woman next to her, but loud enough for the benefit of the other tables.

"My friend Betsy, who is in a position to know, assures me that Richard Auster had been seen at all the more fashionable parties, always playing escort to the most charming young ladies of Baltimore, New York and Boston. You would never think that this gentleman was contemplating marriage. Certainly there was something going on we haven't been officially told about. Perhaps there is more to his behavior than we have been told."

"Excuse me," said Catherine, tossing her serviette aside and rising, her face darkened, almost ruddy. Barbara looked at her in alarm, but said nothing.

All eyes were on Catherine as she walked slowly over to Rachel's table. Talk quieted down, and Rachel now looked over her shoulder at Catherine standing behind her.

Miss Conrad delicately put down her glass and stood up, facing Catherine with a tight smile on her thin lips, which opened as her dark eyes grew big and round.

"Why, Catherine, my dear, forgive me if I spoke out of turn. You know I have only your best interests at heart."

Someone giggled, and then there was a moment of silence as Rachel looked into Catherine's calm brown eyes. Her face was impassive, her body too still.

Rachel became uncomfortable. "Really, Catherine, I—"

Out of nowhere Catherine's right hand came across Rachel's face in a slap so loud it could be heard clearly across the room. In a blur, Miss Conrad fell sideways, knocking over the woman next to her. Dishes clattered, food was spilled and two women were sprawled on the floor.

In the stunned silence that followed, Catherine turned to address the hall. "You all know who I am. Does anyone else have any lies to spread about Richard or anything at all to say about my relationship with the Austers? Or anyone else?"

She glared around the room and eyes fell from her burning gaze.

Then she walked back to where Barbara now stood.

"I am very sorry for this, my dear, and I think I had better leave."

Barbara knew her duty, but she could not move or speak. Then she stood and the two women walked out of the hall; Catherine, taller, slim, dark and regal in a light blue demi chemise, looking only ahead, and Barbara, porcelain white, full bodied, in a darker, ruffled gown, looking around furtively at women she felt she could never face again

Aboard *Scourge*

Someone was shaking his shoulder, a gravelly, unfriendly voice forcing itself into his dreams.

"Roust yourself, boy! Hit the deck! Mr. Logan's got some more holystoning for you to do!"

Nathan opened his eyes to the waking nightmare, the bos'n's mate, Joseph Coker, getting ready to flip over his hammock. He was in the fo'c's'le of *Scourge*. This was the end, he thought, as he remembered his impressment. The sun was just clearing the horizon as he struggled to climb out of the hammock, quickly slipped on his deck slops, and clambered up the companionway ladder, jumping at the sting of the starter on his backside, courtesy of the master-at-arms, Eller Clough, before he stepped in the bright deck. The bos'n, Mr. Jack Logan, was aft. Some of the hands on watch were still in the forecastle, a few were working around the deck, more aloft.

The topsail schooner *Scourge*, built in 1800, recently overhauled and fitted out with ten 12-pounder carronades, carried a crew of fifty men, mostly for prizes. She was handy and fast, about 80 feet on the water line, 100 feet on deck. Her two towering masts were sharply raked, and her transom extended far over the rudder. Her knifelike bow sliced through waves, in this fine breeze carrying fifteen sails, all but two fore-and-aft. Her bottom had been scraped and caulked and recoppered. Her crew were mostly English or New England stock, with some "southerners" and a Negro cook's mate. There was no surgeon, no minister and no French or Spanish aboard.

Mr. Jack Logan was cursing a hand for a poor job securing the fore topsail halyard.

"Where did you learn to tie a hitch, Williams? On your momma's knee, no doubt. We'll have to send you back to knot school!" Several crewmen laughed. "Get below, and join your mess."

As usual Logan wore his faded felt brim cap and dark blue wool waistcoat, white linen shirt and white duck trousers. The quartermaster's mate was at the wheel aft, several men worked near the larboard main shrouds and at the windward quarter to starboard stood another man, gazing with imperious authority at all of the goings-on. From the crew on deck Nathan received mostly curious looks, neither hostile nor friendly. The man on the quarterdeck studied him the way one might study a young race horse or farm animal.

"That's Lieutenant Wilkes, the mate, second in command."

"We've met," said Nathan, with a grim smile.

"Remember, you say 'aye aye' when you're following orders, Jeffries," Logan told him in a quieter tone. "Don't hurt any more men."

In spite of the gruff tone, Nathan couldn't help smiling as he saw Logan's weatherbeaten face crack into a grin. Up close, the man looked fifty, with ruddy leather skin that had spent a lifetime working in the sun. His sandy colored hair was almost completely covered by the cap; Nathan could see unruly tufts emerging from beneath it. He had an altogether robust confidence, matter of fact. Able to take care of himself. Here was a man who would tolerate no nonsense, Nathan thought.

"Cap'n wants to see you." The bos'n led Nathan across the heaving, heeling, spray-soaked deck, and prepared to descend the after hatch. Off the stern Nathan saw only azure horizon, no other sail, no land. Then he glanced forward and saw Morgan staring at him. He felt a chill come over him as he followed Logan down the gangway and further aft on the main deck toward the Captain's cabin.

The door was open, and Logan bellowed in the narrow space.

"Bos'n with Jeffries, sir!"

"Enter."

Captain Coxe was sitting at a small writing desk, his long arms and legs enveloping it spider-like, the early sun just starting to slant in the after cabin windows on either side of the ship.

Coxe turned from his writing and looked calmly at the two men. His black hair was curled neatly over that high, smooth, skull-like forehead, and the pale, penetrating blue eyes missed nothing as he gazed for a moment at the two men.

"Sit down," he said, indicating the two chairs on the either side of him amidships. "What was all that noise on deck yesterday?"

"A misunderstanding between young Jeffries here and Mr. Morgan, sir," Jack Logan answered with a glance at Nathan.

"Morgan, eh?" Coxe gave Nathan a shrewd glance. "Well, lad, it looks like you're off to an auspicious beginning. You've made a bad enemy. Seems Morgan likes you no more than I do myself, but you will work. Morgan knows his business—I dare say better than you." He looked meaningfully at Nathan.

"Aye aye . . . sir." Nathan could not keep the bitterness and fear out of his voice.

"Thank you, Mr. Logan, that will be all for now."

The bos'n left with a barely audible grunt and closed the cabin door behind him.

Nathan remained seated, impassive.

"Now, Jeffries. Bos'n'l assign you general duties and we'll see what you're fit for. We crowded, but we can certainly find work for you . . . you've got the build for an able bodied seaman, just not the stomach—"

"I have the day free, if you care to fight me yourself, man to man—"

The long hand came out of nowhere to slap Nathan.

"Remember, you are nothing—if you cause me any more trouble or start to tell any one about your past . . . other than as a volunteer aboard . . . I'll have you flogged. Or keelhauled. Or worse. Now git."

Six

Slave to the Lash

Eight bells in the forenoon watch. Nathan heard them ring out clearly in the south-east wind as he stood near the hatch down to the crew's mess. Jumping over these worn planks, down into darkness, down into Peter's "inner circle"—no, Peter told him the writer was Dante. Only Peter knew the truth. Does that make him more or less of a threat now, his ex-confidante, his ex-friend, now his enemy? He fought back nausea. Jumping overboard, or thrusting a pike through Archibald Coxe or that troll Clough or Morgan . . . before he—what did Peter always say when they were discussing these things? Something from Shakespeare! With his heart pounding, he braced himself for the next roll. And now bitter enemies—it seemed absurd. The steps were slippery, probably diseased from countless bloody bare feet; his own were still curing into the leathery pads of most crew. Nathan felt lost. How could he survive on this vessel? It was obvious that no one would save him from a long Hell or quick oblivion, and send him to meet his maker. Nathan had begun to pray every day, to make his peace with God for all of his errors and weaknesses.

The only good thing about watches of four on and four off was that he seldom saw Morgan from the starboard watch. He automatically hunched over so that he didn't bang his head again on the berth and mess-deck timbers only five feet off the deck. Lack of headroom, however, was the least of his troubles.

"Nate! Get over here!" It was Coker, the bos'n's mate, brusk, square and dark-skinned, who often overlooked his work in the orlop, when Nathan's other odious duties could wait, now signaling him to join the first table.

"My name is Nath—"

"Not no more it ain't!" laughed Coker. "Less you want a worse'n. Sit down!"

Tom Howard, a topman who had come with him from *Bucephalus*, smiled and signaled him to join them at this first table. Neither the Captain nor the mate were anywhere to be seen—or master of arms Clough. Also at the table, a fiesty little red-headed rooster named O'Malley, Kilharn, a gunner, coxn's mate and waister, an older topman named Harris, seemingly too pale and weak for any duty—and the bos'n himself, a powerful blond giant, with a strong impassive features, dead gray eyes and a pigtail, Jack Logan. Several dozen men sat at other crowded tables nearby—most of the crew and prizemasters not on duty topside. They seemed agreeable enough, but Logan's pale gray eyes stared at him unblinkingly, and his expression was impassive as he barely nodded at Nathan, no longer so friendly. The bare wooden plank table was filled with tin plates and cups and wooden or pewter bowls, being served with hardtack, salt pork and pea soup, and grog from the scuttlebutt near the mast. Nathan sat on a cask at the table and heard the rasping voice of Clough coming from the Captain's cabin at the stern. But his tormenter went up on deck.

The fat, sweating cook's mate, Lonnie, was leaning over the table, his round, pockmarked face wound up in a perpetual scowl that belied his good nature. Nathan at first could still barely swallow the food—even his pennywise mother would have thrown it out. But Nathan discovered that, in spite of the generally vile food, the rank bilge and rotten salt sweat of the men, in spite of the enormous rats and his fears and the heeling and rocking of the ship, his appetite had grown.

The corpulent cook's mate began to ladle some pale noxious liquid into their bowls. Suddenly a big hairy hand reached down and grabbed Nathan's leathery "ship's biscuit."

"Ya gotta tap it like this, boy," Morgan said sweetly, his huge ruddy face in a caricature of a smile. "See?"

Nathan watched as half a dozen fat, white maggots, disturbed in their quiet routine, squirmed reluctantly from their tunnels and fell on the table.

"Eat those!" roared Morgan. "I'll eat the hardtack!" The laughter seemed friendly, except for Morgan's.

Nathan looked up.

"Don't drink yer grog too quickly, boy," Morgan now warned. That brought a chuckle from the table. Nathan had drunk his share of rum and beer but now Morgan reached down and took his cup of grog. Nathan looked up at Morgan, with that twisted smile he had already grown to fear and hate, now holding his cup of grog in triumph. Nathan could only stare at him, open-mouthed.

"This boy's too green for strong spirits, Mister Logan," said Morgan, with solemn insolence. "We're tryin' to protect him from evil."

A number of men who heard this guffawed, and Nathan felt his face flush red. He looked at Logan, but the bos'n turned away and shook his head. Nathan knew this was a test; he knew he would fail.

"I don't really want the grog," Nathan said in a shaking voice, averting his eyes from Morgan's triumphant, ugly face. Now no one would look at him in this moment of embarrassment and humiliation. Nathan heard some chuckles and whispers.

"Very well, Morgan, sit yourself back down at your mess," said Logan. Morgan took the damned cup of grog back to his table, his broad back leaning over to his cronies. Muted laughter and snickering lifted up from several tables. Nathan saw in the eyes of his messmates . . . loathing? Contempt? Disappointment? Disgust?

Soon everyone was eating again, with occasional glances and snickers. But Nathan's appetite was gone; he had spinelessly surrendered. As it stood now, his messmates would certainly look on him as a weak boy, even a coward, in spite of his impressive size and robust physique.

"Jeffries," Kilharn suddenly said, prompted by the devil, "is you connected with William Jeffries, from that yankee 'navy,' from aught-one?" This was getting worse and worse.

"Yes, I am," Nathan said after a moment's hesitation, and not knowing whether he caught a sharp look between Logan and Coker.

"The *Argus-Defiant* fight, Quasi-War? Now he's—"

"Yes," Nathan gritted, barely concealing his irritation.

"Well," Morgan, who had overheard this, said in a loud voice for the entire deck, "I guess no one can accuse you of being a chip off the old block." Morgan reached out and kicked the small cask out from under Nathan, and he crashed to the floor—his ridicule complete—amid laughter and whistling and stamping of bare feet. He tried to get up—stumbled over the cask, fell again. Glaring at Morgan, Nathan shot to his feet again and crashed his head into the low beam above. Struggling to keep on his feet, dizzy and weaving, Nathan was finally able to stagger up the ladder, his head bleeding, hearing Morgan's final shout above the hilarity, "See, Mister Logan, I told you he couldn't hold his swag!"

By the time Nathan reached the windward foredeck, he was drenched in cold ocean spray and nearly swept away as the schooner pitched in the heavy seas. He could not quite bring himself to let himself go over the side, to drown in ridicule and shame. He had promised his mother that he would not fight. The last time he had seen someone challenged to fight, a so-called "gentlemen's affair of honor," his father had practically lost his senses, not to mention his reputation. Even if he confronted Morgan—how could he hope to survive? He'd get two dozen lashes, or hang, or worse. Nathan felt paralyzed and cut off, surrounded by enemies, his only escape the surge just below, remorseless, menacing and thorough. He laughed bitterly. Something had replaced his dread of drowning. He now feared death on board, or perhaps both equally. He leaned out over the ship's weather side, letting the stinging salt spray hit his face, to hide the tears welling up in his eyes. All he need do was let go, lean all the way out, kick off the side, or slide over, dropping the mere fathom of *Scourge's* freeboard. What would the water feel like after the initial shock? At the ship's present speed, he would be a thousand yards behind by the time the man overboard alarm was given—if it was ever given. Why not recreate the very accident on his father's ship that had given him that dread of the sea so long ago?

In truth, his other troubles aboard had made his water fear seem more like a drop in the bucket, and he was an excellent swimmer—or used to be. In these seas . . . the thought of dying within the hour wasn't pleasant, but had a certain appeal. He added his meager salt to the ocean.

"Nate! Get over here!" That damned Coker again, yelling from the fore-deck rail above. "Jeffries!"

"Back to your business," he yelled at some curious crew, "I'll giv' ye sum, ye waisters!"

"Jeffries—now!" Hailing him through the freshening winds, no mean achievement, stolid Coker's words probably carried back to the quarterdeck. Nathan recognized Wilkes, the "first lieutenant"—a true martinet, and a master's mate. Fortunately the watch were mostly trimming sail, tarring and splicing a new starboard main brace with stout six-inch hemp. But several sailors still stared, risking Joseph's wrath, and more were now climbing up from mess. The bos'n's mate grabbed Nathan's shoulder and hustled him down to the orlop, saying nothing. Captain Coxe had joined the quartermaster's mate at the wheel, standing by the weather taffrail, almost right astern, glancing forward and obviously ignoring the commotion forward.

Once they were crouched and bent near the chicken coop, Joseph shook Nathan's shoulder and forced him to sit on a sea chest. "Jeffries, what were you doing there?"

"I was—"

"Shut yer gob! And listen good. Or ye'll swim for sure! You must join this crew—ports open, hatches shut, as they say! The officers know they better not meddle too much down here—especially that popinjay Wilkes. D'ya fallah? No one will interfere."

Nathan stared at this brutish, impenetrable face. It seemed more like a force of nature, remorseless.

"I am a man of peace, Coker; I am a gentle man. You just said—"

"I ain't said nothin', you fool!"

"To Hell with all of you and do your worst!"

Coker's stony face actually brightened in pleased surprise, then dimmed again. "Don't make me—listen, you young fool. I never took you for one, but I guess you ain't too swift. I ain't told you nothin' . . . but I don't think you'd want me to do my worst—say t'ain't true, say you'll fight, Squirt."

Nathan said nothing. Why should I, he thought. My life is over. Both men rocked easily as water sloshed in the bilge a few feet below them; the ship rode sweetly over the waves. Nathan had already grown accustomed to shifting his weight from side to the other, perfectly balancing in a smooth motion to compensate for the ceaseless gyrations of the hull, as the horizon rose and dipped and yawed in slow, grand style, or remorselessly pounded the vessel, seeking weakness.

Nathan feared his stutter would return, and the nausea set in, his vision blurred. There was no escape; it had been too long without sleep or nourishment, in spite of the constant fear, and now, degradation, loss of manhood, a living Hell. Why had God deserted him?

"Get some rest, boy. Yer gonna need it."

Neither man said anything about Nathan's humiliation. All the rest of that long dark night, he dreamed he was a Jonah; not a Macbeth or Antony —but instead an ignominious coward, and Logan's flat, impassive features, sea grey eyes haunted his dreams. Nathan felt he was nothing, a bug, a tedious experiment mercifully ending.

Nathan remembered one voyage south, his great "southern cruise" aboard *Bucephalus*. He'd seen a leper colony—from a distance. Now he was the leper; alone, isolated, an outcast.

Scourge sailed on—brief escapes from painful leather stings courtesy of Eller Clough, holystoning the deck, fresh breeze, spray, some horseplay and cold water on bare feet had offered some comfort, companionship, even relief from the blazing sun. Coxe seldom appeared, but Nathan knew they were shipping larboard across those southeast trades not many leagues off Savannah, seeking prey enroute to Europe from the West Indies. Sailors jawed and scrimshawed, repaired ashore rig and read books or letters around the mainmast, but Nathan was a pariah.

So he would select a spot near the foremast, letting the creaking of the rigging and gentle rocking, as they skirted the Gulf Stream—Cape Hatteras now far to the northwest—lull him into a restless doze. As he lay against the mast, Nathan noticed the pathetic twelve-year-old cabin

boy studying him, with shadows of the rigging playing across his frightened, triangular-shaped face, the dramatic thrust of his pale forehead,
that weak, narrow chin. Nathan knew that the Captain enjoyed watching
his relentless torture, and might throw him overboard if he complained.
Morgan, Clough and even Kilharn now, made life a carefully orchestrated
Hell in which exhaustion and panic commingled with murderous despair.
He remembered his father harping on fear and haste—that's when danger
and risk soar. "First time at sea, boy," said his father, William, "Well, yes, I
felt nervous, at first, Nathan, my son, but that is . . . nothing, it will pass."

But it did not pass, and Nathan could not forget his father's duel
with Jacob Auster—paralyzing the lives of Amy, William—along with
Nathan. His own near-drowning in that fight with Richard Auster so
many years ago. He knew the loss of breath, those last few dim seconds,
had little enough to do with his solemn promise to Amy never to leave
coastal waters and never take up any weapon in anger or war, no sword,
knife, tomahawk, hatchet, ax, pike or gun, in short, to be careful and all
times on or off the water. Nathan eventually managed to conduct himself
with some decorum. The last fight between Amy and William—but Amy
never fought, she only dictated terms of his father's surrender.

His father and many of his colleagues and crew seemed simple and
loyal; proudly wearing their best duck trousers and jersey ashore—but
they seldom knew how to conduct themselves among civilized folks.
Nathan felt secretly grateful that Amy had forced him to heel, his terror
of the seas avoided in the countinghouse. Then the duel virtually destroyed
the Jeffries; William and Nathan had disobeyed Amy for the last time. But
more violence?

Now he thought how his life had terrifyingly changed as he and
other "waisters" rubbed the stone against the deck planks, mostly on
hands and knees, around the main hatchway. Nathan's heart grew cold
again, thinking of Morgan and his threat. But he couldn't see Morgan on
deck as he glanced around in the bright sunshine. Most of the rigging
was secure and most sails were set and drawing well, including the two
topsails. Nathan could see that *Scourge* was born to sail. A great deal of
banter and light-hearted insults and shouting greeted his ears as he made

his way farther aft. But even Tom Howard would hardly look at him, and left to man the pumps.

Like most seamen who wanted to survive, he knew that he'd feel the starter or worse if he fell behind. It was bad enough to be considered a coward on a merchant ship—this was not one of those. "Wait 'til we run out the great guns agin' an American frigate—that might give us a sport." But no one shared fighting stories or any other kind with him now.

"Watch it with that block, look at that gaff!" Coxe roared. "You whore's son, How'rd—where'd y'learn seamanship, in good Sarah's shore-locker?"

Laughter and derisive whistles and huzzahs followed this. "Heave, you lot o'scabs!"

Nathan spied Lieutenant Wickes sniffing around after the mainmast, like a nosy terrier—only uglier.

"The crew'll put you through your paces soon enough . . . you better learn your lines, boy. That's the way it has to be—it's always has been that way. You think you have special consid'ration here? Life at sea ain't for malcontents, work with men you're running from ashore. I don't know what you're runnin' from, boy, and I don't care; you'll do yer work, and stay out of trouble, or you'll be very sorry. Jeffries, we don't much care what a man's background is—all we care's what a man does. Ye'll have to make friends with us, or else. Close friends.

"Now go about your duties, boy, and remember: if you do the best you can, you may live for a while."

"You and Reece, set that spanker right or I'll have your hides!" Logan shouted behind the mainmast. His voice pierced the late sky near the other end of the ship; constantly in motion, cajoling, shoving, berating, jumping, threatening. The bos'n could rig and handle the entire ship alone. Nathan saw his empty stare—and Morgan's ugly sneer—everywhere, in his nightmares and on deck. But the bos'n only watched with those blank gray eyes, severe face, that betrayed nothing.

Nathan struggled to learn or re-learn many duties—despite the frequent ridicule by Morgan, and frequent stings from the master-at-arms and his starter.

"You're our new powder monkey girl, Nathan . . . I mean, Natie boy,"

said Morgan. Nathan shuddered; he could barely squeeze into the magazine room when ordered to do so as punishment. Where was the cabin
boy? Only small people were suitable for powder monkeys. Nathan began
to "hand, reef, and steer." He scrubbed decks and shined brass, helped
repair casks, hemp and spars, pumped the excrement from the bilge, the
heads and the stern galleries, learned all the lines, reefed and shook out
topsails. He even won grudging approval at the helm, almost falling from
a yard, assisted the kindly sailing master with navigation and the cook
with mess (much to the amusement of Morgan), and helped the purser,
steward and captain's clerk in writing letters and balancing the books.
Nathan was careful to make light of his learning; this only reinforced
his own sense of isolation. Morgan bullied him on deck as well as at the
mess table, sometimes tripping him, and mocking his efforts whenever
possible. Morgan would put his arm around Nathan's shoulder, in mock
friendliness, and guide him to the seat next to him at the table. Nathan
silently acquiesced.

"You know, Nuthin," he said, looking at his messmates, who would
snicker—especially Kilharn, Morgan's favorite—"some ships carry quite
a few women aboard . . . now, of course, here on *Scourge* we have only one
big one."

As everyone laughed, Nathan jerked away from Morgan's beefy arm
and stood up. Morgan always needed an audience. Often the bos'n was
there, not to mention other petty officers, even Coxe himself. Or Kilharn
and the rest of the foretop gang. Any witnesses would do for this section
of the watch.

"Excuse me," Nathan often said, foregoing dinner, and heading for
the top deck as the laughter flared up again.

"I didn't mean you, boy. You are a big boy, ain't you? Nancy-un." The
laughter burst upon his ears with renewed force, a loudness that would
echo in his memory forever. His face was burning, and tears rose perilously
close to the surface. He was trapped in the Hell of his own fear and shame.
Now Morgan didn't even bother asking Nathan if he wanted his share of
grog; it was understood that Morgan got both portions. Sometimes Morgan helped himself to all of Nathan's food, as well, such as today.

"Yew ain't hungry, are ye, boy?" he would laugh.

Nathan even preferred the brutal work in the orlop, since after long acquaintance with its miseries he felt at home—safe within his abiding terror of drowning. Stow that—see the carpenter's mate—see the captain's clerk; said he wants you to help the clerk and then the sailmaker. Glimpses of the bos'n stare, the Kilharn leer, not to mention Clough pointed like an ugly boxer by a sneer from Coxe himself, because no one else dared interfere —certainly not Lieutenant Wickes or the petty officers. The sailing master was old, tired, never actively hostile. Harris, captain of the maintop, bullied him—that'd b'extra spars and canvas, buckets, number two hoops, iron, not the hickory, damn you, get forward of the water casks and hogsheads of salt beef and pork.

Nathan figured that the carpenter's mate would let him do all the work—but the bos'n's mate was more than willing to help out—at first. "It's warm down here, ain't it?" he had asked. It was dark and stuffy in the hold, and Nathan sweated already. He could hear the pounding of feet on the deck above, and the ship was rocking. Another tack.

Coker chewed thoughtfully, "I once saw'm beat a man's head senseless against the number five starboard carronade. Morgan is bad, Nate; tangling with him, you'd best not."

Nathan preferred working with white-haired, sun-tarred and irascible Eleazar Adams, master's mate, a wizened, wrinkled curmudgeon who hated "off'cers" and crew equally, wore his long hair in the old-fashioned tarred pigtail. Yet perhaps only Mister Jack Logan was less replaceable— or expendable—according to those who knew the welfare of *Scourge* generally. Anywhere from twenty to fifty years old, Eleazer repaired all manner of casks and hogsheads—everything except weapons, flints, slow-match and powder, stored in the magazine room. He could set his hand to anything—marlinspike flashing, bending new iron hoops, new strakes of oak, tarring, caulking, pitch and oakum. "Life blood of this vessel, boy. Once saw my mate cough up a ball of red the size of a 24-pounder—it had everything in it... poor bugger....heard o' schooner *Arnolde*? I believe Captain and most of the crew got sick from bad vittles, foundered off Cape Hatteras back in aught-one, bodies half-et by somthin' on th' inside

out—remember, boy, these high-and-mighty sail trimmers ain't worth a
ha'pence compared t' us keep this good ship workin', and nurse, too!" Nathan digesting these sage observations without comment, if he could.

"Captain's got you on the forenoon watch, breakfast at eight bells."

Nathan followed the stench of rancid, fetid meat, worse than rotten,
ruptured and corrupt cod-steam wafting along the berth deck, thankfully
diffused by the wet breeze pouring down from the open hatchways fore
and aft. The cook and the cook's mate were busy in the galley; the slime-
infested remains of pork or beef of some ancient vintage as well as pea
soup, amid the groaning and humming of timber and hemp throughout the
ship, heeling forty degrees, more noticeably to starboard now, and rocking,
yawing majestically as she met the Atlantic waves on her larboard beam.
He was exhilarated but sick because he could not maintain footing. The
growing number of crew now on the berth deck between the two masts
seemed oblivious to Nathan or the hull's motion, a few men laughed or
stared in disgust, others glanced indifferently. His eyes painfully adjusting
again, Nathan emerged into the insistent wind, now from out of the east.

The sailing master's Bowditch said this early in the year storms this
far south "are as likely as not to blow out quick." Nathan agreed, and
wondered when the southerly trade would reassert itself—he watched
suns settle in the southwestern skies. Anything can happen at sea, and it
will, at the worst moment, said his father. Captain William Jeffries never
surrendered to any man and only one woman, Amy, and then only sometimes. How long would they be out of sight of land? Would he ever see
land again? It must be somewhere to the west, perhaps a hundred miles.
Soon, helm down and bow even farther around, until running free before
the wind, the rollers would lift her stern and help speed the vessel south
to—the Florida islands, the Bahamas, Cuba, Hispaniola, Jamaica, the
Greater Antilles—where?

Unless he was headed across the Atlantic; Nathan did not know; he
heard various versions. Curiously, in spite of his fear, he hiked himself out
on the bowsprit, dipping and rising as the cutwater plunged through the
emerald ocean—or he looked up at the masts and billowing canvas describ-
ing a lazy ellipse in a cloudless sky. Breezes freshening from the east as they

sometimes made two hundred miles a day; mostly southerly, he thought, with the wind over the one beam and the setting sun the other. He was not allowed on the quarterdeck at any time. But he heard bits of conversation and there were enough changes every day to keep most of the top men aloft—"the only real crew, you un'stand, flop-ee?"

The masts dipped and swayed—all sails straining, sheets and tacks and braces groaning and shreaking, *Scourge* had broken out all of her wings, and it was time to reduce canvas.

"Larboard Topmen, aloft! Lend a hand here, lad," yelled Jack Logan. One of the top men, Kilharn, bellowed in false baritone, quickly taken up by waisters, "My love is ashore and I'll see her no more! Haul, haul, haul away boys!" As Nathan and the other waisters on deck walked backward and heaved on the main topgallant and topsail clewlines and braces, the ship rose and then nosed into the rising seas, taking green water over the larboard bow. Nathan looked back to the northwest, where he imagined the Chesapeake Capes or New York or Boston harbor. "Man the braces! Square those yards!" Nathan squinted in the bright sunshine. Every four hours, every eight hours, the transformation from the dark and dank bowels couldn't be more extreme. Ironically these were mostly sunny days.

He thought often of his one-time confidante, Peter; he thought of those who lived on those shores that he would probably never see again, then smiled grimly for the sake of . . . he wasn't really sure . . . his ambition to survive notwithstanding. Logan's opinion of him must be as low as . . . and maybe even the backbreaking labor of pumping the bilge helps would shove him closer to the end, less painfully. "Aye, aye, sir," he would say, even in his hammock. But then he would run afoul of Morgan and the gang and once again show himself to be no Nelson, Paul Jones, Truxtun or his father; voice shaking, his moment of truth interrupted again by Morgan himself. He must not fight! Of course he had already broken that promise.

I promised never to make the mistake my father did! Even if I did, I will suffer a dozen lashes, or worse, he thought hopelessly. And always those flat sea grey eyes calmly watching, from another direction—judgment—perhaps resignation. No doubt Logan had seen many men fall;

why waste time on one more?

"Secure those headsail sheets! Jeffries, topmen, look lively now!" They were beating to windward now, reduced to fore-and-aft sail, plunging along at a good ten knots, and he was ordered aloft—by Harris' connivance. Why? He might easily fail to climb at all. As he looked around and smelled the rising sea on this brilliant day, he felt certain that he didn't care and there was some satisfaction in that. But the panic remained just below the surface.

Then Nathan saw Morgan staring at him from the number one carronade near the windward foremast shrouds. Morgan was a foretopman, furled either of the two yards faster than anyone in his gang. The first foretop watch usually beat the maintop crew. Captain of the foretop, Kilharn, challenged Harris's maintop gang to a match every other dogwatch. Now he climbed, knowing it might easily be for nothing, as other hands on the main ratlines raced ahead of him, all assigned to the main topsail yards.

And his station, saved for him—that baby-sized footrope and gasket, the small spar pointing to weather—grab it with his big toe. "Deck there!" he shouted down. But only Morgan's hateful red eyes looked up, burned into Nathan's and he looked away. Was he finally delirious? Then he saw Morgan talking to Wickes, near the mainmast shrouds below. Morgan looked up his way again and a chill came over Nathan on this warm if blustery day. Under three headsails, fore and main staysails, *Scourge* plowed through the waves, close-hauled on a larboard tack, reaching for the stiffening wind right over her beam, veering now northerly. Why had he been singled out by God, especially by these madmen? Nathan looked forward above the bow one last time. As usual there was nothing ahead but empty horizon, utterly composed and at peace.

Seven

South of Cape Hatteras

His daily torment filled Nathan's dreams with nightmares of a fatal duel between his father roaring around in the dark, "If you seek peace, prepare for war," and his mother firing back, "Live by the sword, die by the sword"—and he is failing both parents, losing his grip on life and thought itself . . . and Amy always right. . . . losing essentially both husband and son, especially her useless, slow son. "Can you blame them for doubting you now?" she would ask her men logically, "You want to be more hurtful to them . . . regardless—"

"But Auster's trying to destroy us!" William's broadsides, relentless.

"And will succeed, thanks to you—you will lose everything, trying to win. Can you blame them for not helping you?" she blasted quietly until he realized that he had failed to help Nathan, only used him to further his own passions—failed to honor his promises to his Quaker wife, failed again.

"Amy," he groaned. "You know I love him as much as you do. Why don't you admit that you never wanted our Nathan to grow up to be—"

"To be . . . what—like you? How many survived that 1801 battle?"

"Damn it, Amy! How could any thing be so clear-cut as the defense of one's—"

"And who do you want him to fight now—the Austers again?" That was in 1807. That usually sounded the last broadside in the battle. Amy defeated William again. And then of course the duel, the day when everything ground to a halt, the ship dismasted, fast on the reef, her belly ripped out. But many of his nightmares ended like this, in drowning or worse.

Fully awake again, Nathan had known since being impressed—even before he met again the master of *Scourge*—that he was not going to survive the daily doses of mental, spiritual and physical abuse, both from within and without. When his need for sleep became obvious and embarrassing through frequent collapse, they pushed him into the surgical cot and woke up the drunk, goggle-necked "Doc" James Adams, who insisted that he was a naval surgeon but was worse than inept and trained only in cutting—or backstabbing—the epitome of his kind. But at least Nathan did get some kind of sleep.

On this day in January 1812, the sun was past noon as this fast ship reached to the southeast, already well south of Cape Hatteras. *Scourge* flew even with topsails furled. Nathan searched for a place forward of the mainmast; the forecastle was far too crowded and confining. Surely this would be the last year of his life. By now the routine was clear: dull pain of exhaustion, muscles, enlivened briefly and unpredictably each day by exquisite pain from Clough, with threats of worse from Clough, Morgan or Archibald Coxe himself.

Suddenly Morgan was there to bar his way.

"Jeffries!" called the boatswain. "Pumps!" Nathan knew better than to delay.

"Where are you off to, boy?" said Morgan with a grin. "It ain't your watch!"

"Gotta get ready for our next race," Nathan yelled, defiant at last, a brief exhilaration that at least he had mastered his fear of racing aloft— one of the oldest topmen, Tom Howard, helped him make it, just when Nathan turned back.

"There will be plenty of time, boy, plenty of time," Morgan growled, with a smile that made Nathan feel sick. The afternoon would glaze in fading slate sky, and dull green swell showed many whitecaps reaching as high as the maintop now as the ship swooped and plunged, her bowsprit disappearing, rising again from the sea.

Virtually every other man aboard ignored Nathan, as if he were not there; or laughed at him, as one laughs at a big fool, a large clown. Maybe he would fall from the topmast yard and save everyone the annoyance.

Nathan knew he could survive the ridicule, but his tormenters beat him where visible injuries did not show and would be explained by any number of accidents aboard. As the days passed in a blur of sleepless fear, he knew he could not survive. He had no allies, although Howard had helped him survive aloft. Morgan, Kilharn and their friends would torment him at every mess, every few hours, the game, "'til Neptune pulls her down,"and there would be more inventive humiliation, even terror. He suddenly remembered one thing his parents had agreed on: if he didn't know what to do or how to do it, learn and learn quickly and well. He had to learn to survive.

"Jeffries! Pumps!"

"I'm surprised the bos'n trusts you with that responsible task, in your present state of ignorance and mischief," yelled Morgan. Several men laughed. "Do you know the difference between a keel and a cofferdam, boy? You know, boy, that *Bucephalus* was a gelding!"

More laughter. But suddenly, finally, Nathan had had enough.

"Yes, I know an ass from amidships," Nathan said. Even as the laughter renewed, the fist came out of nowhere and the next thing he knew he was on his backside on the deck, with a throbbing head and jaw.

"If you report it, you'll be in more trouble than him," said Morgan's friend Kilharn. Logan, who had been watching the proceedings with some interest, was suddenly nowhere on deck; Nathan saw no sign of the Captain or master-at-arms. A crowd had gathered around the deck there, near the main hatch, circling them. Nathan felt the oppressive quiet, only the vessel whistling and croaking to the sea. Fear shook his body. But he realized that this might be his last chance. "I beg your forgiveness, Mother," he prayed, "for all my weaknesses and sins; for I failed, I must fight. I do not have your strength and courage, and I must break my vows to you—again."

Morgan was now smiling again, nodded at his crony.

"Gentlemen," he heard Kilharn saying, as if an outsider to himself, with heavy, mocking sarcasm, "gentlemen, stop hurting this . . . the poor boy!"

Morgan and Kilharn were a smiling, perfect tormenting machine.

There was no intelligence, no compassion; only cruelty, derision, a cruel logic in their dark, wooden faces—standing there, waiting for Nathan to stop his bleeding nose. Nathan looked away and moved as if to leave, then suddenly he hurled himself at Morgan, launching his right fist at the bully's face.

With the luck of the damned, it connected. Pain shot through Nathan's hand as the knuckles smashed into Morgan's cheek. It felt like every bone in his hand shattered. The two men went down and Nathan could feel Morgan's hands and arms ineffectually graze his sides as the two men hit the deck with a thud. Nathan's mangled fists were flying with an amazing precision, crashing into the heavier man's face and body. His left fist finally got in a blow that caught Nathan above the right eye; no quitter, he was fighting back even with Nathan on top of him, desperately pummeling.

Nathan fell off his opponent and both men struggled to their feet, already groggy, but determined. A vibration seemed to charge Nathan to the very marrow. Through his fear, his terror, came an exhilaration. This would be resolved now, the torture would end here. His misery of his life would stop—shouts of encouragement, some for him, some against him. Morgan's face looked encouragingly beaten, bloody lip and nose. He was not smiling now.

Nathan sensed the fist coming long before he launched it. As if he had all the time in the world, Nathan slipped inside, under the right and delivered an uppercut with all his might against that arrogant jaw. Something cracked. Morgan was lifted off the deck and collapsed, falling back on the deck, sprawled, unconscious. Nathan looked down at his foe, felt the power draining from his arms, felt his eye and chin throbbing, and the poundings of congratulation on his back. The crowd had gathered around him, the victor! Then he saw Kilharn, shaking his head, and then smiling at Nathan. Their eyes locked. Nathan amazed himself. He pointed at Kilharn and actually lunged for him. Kilharn ran away. The powerful arms of the bos'n held Nathan back.

"No, lad, you've won your fight. Now let's have a look at that eye, and those hands." And Mr. Logan hustled him down the forecastle ladder.

Later, with a poultice on his left eye, swollen almost shut, and bandages on his aching right hand, Nathan was trying to rest in his hammock as the bos'n returned.

Since there was no real surgeon aboard and "Doc" Adams was drunk, Mr. Logan himself, who had often served as surgeon's mate, decided no bones were broken; at least, nothing he could do anything about. The black eye might take a week or so. Nathan couldn't believe he had broken Morgan's jaw. There had been no fight officially. Official recognition of the fight would have required dreaded punishment. Had that been avoided? It seemed so in this case, even though Tom Howard had warned Nathan that Coxe enjoyed watching the cat-o'-nine-tails cut into a man's back. Thus far Nathan had seen one flogging and he prayed fervently that he might be spared another one.

"Well, it took you long enough."

"Mister Logan, I am tired—"

"Shut yer trap! 'Bout time you showed backbone. I think we may be able to use you to help us. Can you take up the sword and gun? There's some of us want to leave this *Scourge*. Are you with us? Do y'know small boats? Do y'know how we could—"

Then master-at-arms Eller Clough leaned in.

"Captain wants to see you, Jeffries!"

Nathan felt electric shock of nearly uncontrollable terror. Was he prepared to suffer the most unimaginable pain, even death, today? Who would beat him? Perhaps Morgan, or Kilharn, not Clough himself, probably not the bos'n's mate. Permanent injury might result; perhaps they would keel-haul him for good luck. If he were lucky, an early blow would knock him out. Ordinarily the punishment for fighting was at least twelve strokes, in the regular service. Tied to the gratings and lashed with the cat, for any cause the Captain sees fit to charge the poor, stupid soul.

Could he trust the bos'n? What did Logan care about him? But what did it matter, faced with hideous pain and yearning for death? And Nathan had heard rumours about the Captain's private cabin.

Even after he heard it from Coxe, Nathan could hardly believe the words. A dozen lashes over the gratings.

Within a few minutes, he was tied by wrists and stripped to the waist, his back to be lashed, skin split open, blood stinging, nerves dying. Flogging is exquisite pain but so colorful for the crowd—Nathan feared he would disgrace himself, especially after the drum roll began. Even so, he felt energizing guilt over his parents and considered plans, weapons. Nathan began to sink into himself; Peter had taught him the rudiments before his betrayal. But a life or death struggle; this had been his last chance. Even if the outcome had been very different.

He yelped uncontrollably when the cat bit into his flesh, all nine slices of fire across his back, biting back screams and other high-pitched pathos. He was a big strong lad, but he felt he would never survive even half a dozen.

Then the shout that changed all.

"Deck there! Large brig, two points off larboard bow!"

Eight

Double Agent

The early morning horse and carriage clatter and knock on the door could surely not be the "mysterious benefactor" who had provided their friend Mr. Hanson, publisher of the much-reviled *Federal Republican*, with the powder that eased her husband's maniacally disturbed spirit and let him and others sleep.

The escaped negress Gloria looked nervously at Amy.

"Go ahead, Gloria, let her in. I am expecting Miss Catherine Charles."

Gloria opened the door fearfully to find a beautiful young woman wearing a long, green dress of muslin and lace, over which was drawn a cloak of satin. Under her light bonnet, her black hair glistened in the cold midday sun. She laughed gently at the maidservant's silence.

"May I come in, dear?"

"Oh, yes, ma'am, certainly, I'm so sorry, Miss . . . uh—"

"Charles. Catherine Charles." She stepped inside, pushed back her hood, removed and held out her bonnet and scarf which Gloria held as she curtsied; Catherine's smile put her instantly at ease. Catherine's "extreme indulgence" with Negroes embarrassed nearly every one. Then Catherine shook hands with the flustered Gloria and strode grandly into the Jeffries' small parlour, decorated with the medal and sword from William Jeffries' victories in the war of '99; his flag, his ship, crew muster lists, a grand portrait of his father, a friend of Joshua Barney, Barry, Jones, Truxtun, Hull, others who had lived and sometimes died aboard his ship in two wars for freedom of the seas. There was other bric-a-brac and old, threadbare furniture from Virginia and a portrait of Amy's family by Peale. The sofa was draped with Amy's own depiction of her husband's greatest victory, when he was a young captain in '01. Catherine entered like a princess to greet Amy in her dowdy old flannel gown, hand-embroidered but decades out of style. But Catherine, looking around intently, could see the cleanliness, and the quality handicraft and workmanship evinced everywhere, even in the porcelain beauty of Amy's slight smile.

"It's, uh, Miss Charles, ma'am," said Gloria.

"Thank you, Gloria. Please take Catherine's cloak."

Catherine untied the bow and handed it to the girl.

"Thank you, Gloria, please close the door."

Amy stood up from her rocker and knitting, and the two women shook hands.

"Mrs. Jeffries, I am so sorry about all of this; thank you for seeing me."

Amy sat down and Catherine sought the sofa.

"Nonsense—you are blameless, my child—and I expected your note."

"That was my first question, ma'am—"

"I am Amy, dear, please—"

"Thank you, my . . . Amy, very kind of you. After . . . the duel, and those terrible accusations in the newspapers and broadsides over the past few years, your son and his ship missing . . . I . . . I felt someone from the other—I wanted to . . . should have somehow come to your aid, your . . . defense . . . but I was amazed that you did not seem more surprised when I wanted to come here . . . to help my fiancé's enemy—"

"To arrive here at dawn, unofficially and in disguise, without any white person's knowledge," Amy concluded.

"How on earth did you . . ."

Catherine sought Amy's sky-blue eyes in alarm, but then the older woman's crinkled in apparent friendly, gentle laughter.

"Please have no fear of me. I have learned a few things after all these years, and you show commendable caution—as you must. I am very glad you show courage and compassion as well, because you are here, and I thank you."

Catherine seemed distracted. "Some of Richard's associates own slaves, condone the trade, and I have seen the way they discipline their—"

"It would have been foolish not to make these meetings clandestine," said Amy with assurance. "You want to help me find my son. It has been nearly four months now since my Nathan sailed beyond the Capes, and yet . . . I have some fear but . . . I know . . . he is not lost for good."

Amy's apparently calm omniscience shook Catherine.

"Of course not," she said.

"Why are you so concerned about my son, Catherine?"

"No, I—'

"You want to know how our feud with Austers that led to the incident at the ball began? And again, thank you for these documents about the Austers, bills of lading—and a letter from the Governor! Excellent!"

"No, I heard—yes . . . yes, I do—"

"There are things we know about the association between the Austers and the Stewards, and the Charles in Philadelphia, things my husband knows, that would be very embarrassing if read aloud in a duly selected court of law—my husband's present condition assures them, through their agent, Archibald Coxe, for instance—"

"Yes, I have met him—Captain Coxe, British packet *Scourge*."

Amy smiled again, shaking her head.

"Among other occupations," she added.

"What do you mean?"

"Coxe works for your fiancé's shipping business, through the Charles cabal in Philadelphia, as an agent . . . in the slave trade out of Liverpool and Jamaica. We have not yet found this—"

"Mrs. Jeffries! Amy! How can you know—"

"Our dear friend Abraham Steward is their banker."

"Amy, must I remind you that our . . . their . . . shipping interests with the British—"

"Please, are you now defending them?"

Catherine fought back tears.

"The Austers also dismiss impressment as misunderstanding, even off the Chesapeake, worthy of disavowal perhaps in some cases but hardly— and the ugly fate of thousands of American citizens, White or Negroes, some Spanish Indians . . . dismissed as a minor—"

"I am sorry, Catherine, but how can you plan to marry Richard? You already know and disapprove of many of his business interests and we must accept that your putative fiancé insists on complete control of women and men . . . as a slaver, a traitor, a—my dear; we must accept that you trust him at your peril—"

"Amy, I do not wish to interrupt but—"

"You must know the whole truth about the Jeffries and the Austers. Is that not what you wanted to know? And how it affects my son—"

"British warships harass and even fire on American ships from Portsmouth to Savannah, within a few miles of the coast. Now everyone thinks my husband makes sense, now that it is too late. But we must rescue my son. You must continue providing me with evidence."

Catherine nodded, smiling grimly.

"The Austers become angry when I voice my concerns. They almost shout at me, a mere spoiled woman pampered by servants. 'End slavery? This "evil" pays for your tortoise shell vanity!' they tell me. 'Do you really think of Negroes as human? Some light brown faces, I'll grant you'. I sometimes cannot believe what I am hearing. Amy, I know that you Quakers have fought against slavery, in all forms, and I know it has cost you and your husband and I cannot sanction—well, you understand, for that matter the attack on *Chesapeake*. Yours and mine, we agree that certain behavior cannot be tolerated. Lord Wilberforce won a great victory, and . . . I have tried to remain in my place, but . . . these recent events have made me concerned; and Nathan, and Nathan's friend Peter . . . someday the character of a person will not be judged by their outer appearance, as you Jeffries know so well."

"Thank you. You are a perceptive woman . . . you mean the half-breed, Hughes," said Amy.

"Thank you but I am sorry; I do not care for that term."

"I am so glad. Nor do I," said Amy. "In fifteen years I have never called him that, even though Bill has after too much brandy, even in front of Peter's mother, Elizabeth. Embarrassing. But that's my William. Peter's very handsome, don't you think—but tell me, my dear, what do you think of Nathan? Are you really that taken by my son?"

Bewildered, Catherine stared at Amy. "Taken? By your son?"

"Yes, certainly Nathan, my boy—why else would you wish to visit me in person, in secrecy, and at such great risk?"

"I feel, Mrs. Jeffries, that I have fully explained myself—"

Amy laughed. "Of course my dear. Anything you say. . ."

Suddenly Catherine also burst out laughing, delighted by the penetrating but warm wit of this seemingly small and frail woman. Catherine was no match for her.

Catherine flushed and sat back in the chair. "I only really talked with him that once, briefly, as you know, and it was . . . an irritating encounter . . . and he seemed to resent my visiting here at all—"

"Yes, and with you engaged to be married to the brilliant, wealthy, charismatic, powerful . . . and you, feeling, sadly, already *persona non grata*, as you put it. Of course, Catherine, I don't wish to pry. But you must continue to tell me everything you know that could help me find my son."

Amy now seemed distracted and stood up slowly, walking over to the window that looked out on Anne Marie Street. Just below, the Basin glistened in the early sun just rising in the Bay beyond that. Behind them now-bare trees made fine cracks in the pale, determined sky, but the sun washing her face and hair made Amy look even younger. Catherine could see the beauty that once attracted Lt. William Jeffries, shipowner Jacob Auster and others courting her; this steel lady, whose parents had fled without her to Canada, leaving her to be raised by the Quaker Friends.

"Ironic, isn't it?" she asked. "William and I fought mostly over Nathan's future. And now look what I, a professed Quaker, have wrought."

"Not one of us could believe any blame pointing at you, Amy."

"What do you believe, my dear?"

When she turned back to Catherine and sat down, the native intelligence in her eyes glistened.

"I do not share my fiancé's feelings . . . I must investigate, Amy, and perhaps you of all women understand—I must find out what happened to . . . your son . . . and the connection between Nathan—but, Amy, what if . . . what if . . ."

"Exactly, Catherine, investigate me; investigate everyone. That information from friends and enemies is accurate—the Stewards, Austers, Charles; my son, husband and I will be forever in your debt."

"I fear only my own fear and weakness, Mrs. Jeffries . . . that is . . . not from the enemy camp, but—"

"Yes, the camp of foolish men, Catherine. So you like my son that much, do you?"

Catherine tossed her lovely, dark hair up as she stared at Amy.

"Nathan? Excuse me, but what an absurd notion! I am sorry, Amy, but really, that oversteps the bounds!"

"It all begins with Nathan, it seems." Amy stood, this frail creature in the morning light, but her carriage was erect, her spirit indomitable.

"Please forgive my outburst, Amy, but you ought not say . . . ask such things . . . even friends must adhere to some . . . that is, I owe you and the Captain my forbearance, of course, but—that is, the bounds of tolerance—"

Amy sat down again and put her thin hand on Catherine's shoulder. She seemed again to read Catherine's thoughts.

"I know, you feel you owe everything to the very people I condemn, and I am sorry, my dear. You are quite correct. But I must find my son, and you must help me."

There was a brief, light knock at the door, and Gloria entered with silver tray and Chinese porcelain teapot.

"Ah! Excellent! Thank you so much, Gloria. This is perfect."

Gloria smiled, curtsied and quietly closed the door behind her. Amy poured tea for Catherine and herself.

"There is no reason for you to feel responsible, Catherine."

Amy settled back, looking suddenly very tired and older.

"You have done what you feel is right, and we are forever in your debt. Regardless of your ties with our enemies, I hope we can repay your kindness."

Catherine felt speechless. Though less brutal and ruthless than Richard, this obviously intelligent woman had outmaneuvered her. But could she still afford to trust her, or her husband, sleeping upstairs? Or the boy Nathan himself?

Nine

Cormorant – *February 1812*

"Deck there! Large ship two points off the starboard quarter!"

Spry and gray-bearded Capt. Mathew Turner impatiently climbed the main shrouds for a better look. The close-hauled squaresails on the southeastern horizon, almost in line with their immediate pursuer, indicated still another pursuit from a warship. Whether that was good news or bad, he could not say; there was no way to determine the identity or intentions of either ship. If only it had been late afternoon, they might have been able to extend the chase into nightfall, and then make their escape. As it was, there was too much light remaining, and capture this very day seemed inevitable. Well, his old partner Captain William Jeffries had known the risks, of course, and all of his men aboard knew the risks, even though the British and Americans were not officially at war—yet.

"Big frigate," he grumbled. His mate, a small, strange bed bug of a man named "Dee" had been a sudden, unplanned, unfortunate replacement—Turner could not trust any decision or assurance the dark little creature made. There were a dozen sturdy hands aboard, some popgun six pounders. No match for any privateer, let alone a naval vessel.

Turner, master and part owner of the 300-ton American merchant brig *Cormorant,* just two weeks beyond the Capes, had done everything possible to extend the duration of the pursuit. Though no flags were flying, it seemed more and more likely that the large topsail schooner beating towards them was a privateer—since the U.S. was not supposed to be a belligerent—but merely ignoring his own country's various non-intercourse laws that superceded the crippling Embargo.

Clearly a vessel with many men and ready guns, her lines suggested Baltimore topsail schooner; she could be U.S., French, Spanish or British. Of course, why would American chase American with such obvious determination? The United States were at war with themselves as much as any foreign power, but . . . Turner finally ordered the American flag hoisted on the main, in the faint hope that that might help. The pursuer did not waver.

Nothing the Captain tried to achieve a few more inches of speed through the water availed them. Tacking again would give them nothing, not even prolong the inevitable. With all hands on deck, trimming sails, even lining up against the windward bulwarks to even her keel as much as possible, the enemy approached. The light airs had picked up and this probably favored the other ship.

Within two hours the large, square-rigged frigate bore off, clearly relinquishing the race. She was soon disappearing over the south-south-eastern horizon. Their nearby pursuer, unfortunately, showed no deviation. By late afternoon, she was bearing up on their larboard side, only a few hundred yards away, a long row of guns revealed. And a British flag was finally displayed. She was a beautiful craft, heavily sparred. Turner watched a puff of white smoke burst from a forward gun, and a moment later heard the explosion. A geyser of water shot up near the bow, close enough to spray the head, the traditional warning to heave to. The sleek, rakish schooner continued on the same course, now pulling ahead of the brig. Turner had not even bothered to clear the deck guns, the half dozen slide carronades.

He sighed, then yelled out, "Clew up the courses and royals! Brail in that spanker! Back the main topsail! All hands remain at your stations. Lower the flag, Dee. We're going to have visitors. Her name is. . .'pear's to be *Scourge*."

The British ship also hove-to, now almost directly to windward of her quarry. A launch with ten oars was already in the water headed toward them. Turner saw what looked like naval uniforms and the shakoes of British marines. Within fifteen minutes, they were alongside. *Cormorant* had about the same freeboard as the schooner: less than ten feet; and within a moment of the boat tying up, a cocked hat appeared at the entry port. Turner was waiting on the quarterdeck.

The cocked hat belonged to a slim young man of average height in the uniform of a British navy lieutenant. One gold epaulette on the left shoulder gleamed in the mid-afternoon sun. His uniform was impeccable and his footing seemed sure enough as the ship heaved in the waves that were only now developing whitecaps. This sharp-nosed, arrogant youth looked around quickly, spoke briefly to the men behind him and headed toward the quarterdeck; he could see immediately that no one in command was waiting for him anywhere else. Behind the lieutenant the rest of his men took station near the entry port, a midshipman and six marines with muskets. There would be no resistance.

Aboard *Scourge*, Nathan fought against spasms and screeching from his tormented back as they cut him down, and while bleeding on the deck he had watched the British boarding party assemble nearby—along with a prize crew which would be sent over directly—amid considerable laughter.

"I want you to observe all of this," Coxe said to Nathan, writhing and fully conscious at his feet. "And only observe. You, Jeffries, are known to squeal. And if you say or do anything to arouse suspicion, you'll be food for the sharks." Hustled behind *Scourge's* scant bulwarks, Nathan could now see all through the scuppers with a knife in his back reminding him of the penalty for any sound or movement.

Across the scant 50 yards of choppy seas, the lieutenant saluted Turner, who gave a slight, surly nod.

"Sir, I am Lieutenant Wickes of His Majesty's armed packet *Scourge*, Commander Archibald Coxe. I am ordered to—"

"I can guess about your damned orders," snorted Turner. "We are on a lawful commercial voyage to the West Indies as private businessmen and should be of no concern to either the British or the French government."

"Sir, you must know that American ships may not trade with the British colonies, unless they are duly licensed by—"

"You and your damned Orders in Council! You do not own the ocean, sir. You have no right to interfere with a neutral country's free enterprise at sea, not to mention—"

"Would you care to discuss this matter in your cabin? Meantime I have orders to search this vessel." Turning to the midshipman, "Carry on, Mr. Bowman." The search began.

"I guess I have little choice," growled Turner, leading the way below. He knew that he would reach some understanding, and after confiscating any weapons aboard, the lieutenant would hail his vessel and the boat would return with the lieutenant. The prize crew would sail *Cormorant* to England, or possibly Bermuda.

Sweating under his sou'wester despite the stiffening breeze, Turner wondered if the British would find the guns below. Their Captain felt no need to confirm the value of the prize before assigning a prize crew to it. The lieutenant would want *Cormorant's* cargo manifest, crew list, weapons and destination.

Turner would tell the lieutenant everything he asked, and cooperate in every way because resistance was useless and because he wanted to allay any British worries or suspicions that *Cormorant* wasn't exactly what she appeared to be: a harmless merchant brig concerned only with innocent trade in the islands. Her puny half-dozen 9-pounder carronades had not even been loaded. The brief visit in the Captain's cabin followed precisely as Turner expected; his manifest showed 400 barrels of cider, 600 hogsheads of salted cod, 200 casks of molasses, 13 butts of rum, 1,000 hectars oats, barley and wheat, 150 bushels cured tobacco, other assorted items. Would they find the firearms? Would they bother to spike the popguns on deck? One of the marines reported to the lieutenant, confirming that *Cormorant* indeed seemed to carry this cargo and little else of interest. The two men soon returned to the quarterdeck, the lieutenant still talking; then Turner faced forward and called to all hands.

"Men! We are to be taken under a prize crew with a British midshipman as prize master. I regret that we are powerless to resist this action, but obey the orders of the British aboard as you would obey mine."

A sailor nearby started to smile, and then quickly covered it up. Nothing could be attempted while those guns faced them from 50 to 100 yards away; one or two broadsides and *Cormorant* would be a sinking wreck. The appearance of helpless acquiescence was essential—for now.

The weapons supply which Turner had told the lieutenant about, located in a storage compartment near the Captain's cabin aft—a dozen muskets and pistols, with powder, flints, wads and lead balls—had been removed already. They could hear the clumsy clumping of the marines' boots as they covered every inch of every deck, banging against bulkheads, even rattling pans in the galley, overturning cots, tables, in general ripping things apart. No doubt they would raid the pantry too.

The lieutenant gave brief final orders to his midshipman, Mr. Bowman, and two of the marines disappeared below deck again for final private confiscations for the officer.

The rest of the marines returned to the side of the ship, where Turner and Wickes waited. From the original boatload, only the midshipman and the two marines, all fully armed, would remain aboard *Cormorant*. The lieutenant returned to their boat and shoved off. The launch would return with the six prize crew from *Scourge*. That was judged sufficient. Most of Turner's men would be locked up for the duration of the voyage.

As Coxe had ordered, Nathan, nearly passing out from blood loss and shock, had watched what was going on. He had seen his crewmates run out the number four gun and fire on the American brig; then heard their laughter as she hove-to in rage and helplessness. With a smirk, Morgan, still bloody himself, joined the British prize crew. "We'll finish this some day, boy," he said to Nathan.

The plan had obviously succeeded; the lieutenant was already being rowed back in the shadow of *Scourge*. By now, the sun was half-scuttled on the horizon and the dim twilight approaching. He was no nearer freedom than before . . . soon it would be dark.

"Has t'be now, Natie—Nathan," said Logan, waking him to con-

sciousness, forcing him to stand by the main chains. He became aware
that Logan had rigged him to the stays in a swing chair so he could
watch the goings-on in relatively little pain. The two men stared at
Cormorant. The launch was already returning to *Scourge* in the late light,
having delivered Morgan and the prize crew—a half dozen men—to the
helpless brig. Before dusk, both vessels would be under way.

"There's no moon this evening. There she is . . . our best chance, but
no time to prepare, and you—in this condition."

"Two strong swimmers could reach that ship undetected," said Nathan
in a very quiet, offhand voice. "If they possessed a pair of pistols and
knives—and some guts—they might even help those poor devils over
there retake the ship. If they also possessed enough spirit—and luck. Of
course, if we're caught . . ."

The two men locked eyes. "Nathan, my lad, I admire your style.
You've beaten Morgan and showed your mettle—but in your condition,
this is a crazy idea. Coxe'll flog ye—two dozen . . . or ye'll drown."

Nathan said matter-of-factly, "I'll never survive *Scourge* anyway,
Logan. We both know that." Nathan desperately feared drowning, but
at least it would be quicker and less physically crippling than the daily
torture he already suffered, even without Morgan. He felt the power of
his father, and ex-friend Peter. If only words came to him with the facility
they did to Peter, that brilliant bastard, and Barbara, and that mesmerizing, annoying Catherine Charles. But worse than failing to avenge
himself against Auster or Coxe, he feared failing his mother and father,
perhaps unto his death.

Logan made up his mind.

"You stay here," said Logan, "where Coxe and his bully-boys can
see you."

Cormorant's sails were silhouetted now in the fading light—dark
patches blotting the pale, darkening sky. *Scourge's* launch was being hoisted aboard, amid shouts and slapping lines and screeching tackle blocks.

Suddenly his mind was working furiously. It was the dog watch, and
he had no duties for two hours. The water was warm enough, the seas not
too high; this was his chance to get away and hang the threats Coxe had

made. But could he swim 100 yards to the other ship, while they were both hove-to in the gathering dusk, and somehow climb aboard, undetected? Even if they should succeed, his troubles would have only just begun; after all, the ship was in the hands of his enemy. It was madness; and yet . . .

Logan joined him a few minutes later by the foremast. The wind was freshening but the seas remained modest. He opened his jacket to show Nathan a bundle wrapped in burlap and oilskins. "A half-dozen pistols, cutlasses. You'll carry half," he said.

"Why are you . . . why are you doing this?" Nathan whispered.

"I am an American too. I have watched too many men broken by that bastard—and this crew. I just don't care to tolerate that bastard Coxe no more!" He looked around, and grabbed Nathan's shoulder. "I know why yer here, lad, most of it, and it smells worse'n rotted fish. I think yer the man to escape with me—are ye? Have you the stomach for it? After you finally gave Morgan the what-for. It'll mean more killin'—maybe killin' the prize crew. I can't do it alone. And 'tis now or never, m'boy."

The prize crew aboard *Cormorant*, half a dozen sturdy seamen, sober as yet, the midshipman and two marines, were armed with pistols, muskets, short swords, knives. Turner and the midshipman were still talking as the six new stalwarts—capable seaman of long duty—rounded up the ten men in Turner's crew, in the waist forward of the mainmast. Morgan could be identified as the largest and most brutal, but most of the crew looked little different—some Spanish, French, mostly English or American—pigtails on some, some bare-chested, some in the wide-sleeved tunics, tattoos on brown arms, white breeches and bare feet. The looks darting among the hands were ugly and menacing. But there was no arguing with a dozen loaded guns.

The midshipman Bowman was a fluent snob, a bland-looking man, hung over with faded, bulging, bloodshot eyes; a pale, rat-faced creature of average build, whose nose actually twitched like a rat's. He had wispy hair, a forced laugh and an annoying habit of arching his eyebrows and raising his chin in a supercilious manner. His obvious petty tyrant tendencies marked him as the kind of officer who would go far in the British Navy. But not if he could help it, Turner thought calmly.

With an impatient gesture and a few biting words, Bowman signaled one of his crew to go below and find the overdue marine and report back to him on the quarterdeck. Three of the prize crew on deck, still carrying pistols and cutlasses, were getting *Cormorant* ready to sail again, and forcing Turner's crew to the braces; soon they would haul the main topsail to starboard again. But for a few more minutes she would remain hove-to, until the British ship squared away to the south. *Cormorant's* rightful crew would soon, no doubt, be ordered below under guard, probably kept in the forecastle in lieu of a proper brig.

No one had seen Nathan leave the foredeck. He had ducked down near the bow, climbed out over the cathead when no one was looking, carefully hung over the beakhead, praying that there would be no one visiting the head for a few minutes. Then he silently shimmied down the bobstay until he could lower himself into the roiling water by *Scourge's* cutwater. He almost passed out from the shock of the water against his open back. He barely avoided bashing his head against the bow in the surging waves. As he slipped away toward the brig, he heard a commotion, similar to what he heard when the boat returned, and he feared that he or Logan were already missed. Was that Coxe's harsh talk with the lieutenant, now returned from *Cormorant*? *Scourge* was getting underway. To succeed, he must be sharp or die. The pain would save him. If he still had the strength.

He could only hope Logan had dropped off the starboard quarter as planned. And he could only hope Logan wasn't tricking him! They had perhaps fifteen minutes at the most before *Cormorant* braced her yards and stood away in the fresh breeze. If they failed to reach her in that time, they would die—or worse, get picked up by *Scourge*. Her sails were great squares silhouetted in the fading light; her hull barely distinguishable from the dark water. Nathan certainly feared drowning; but his greatest fear remained the possibility of detection. However, Logan and he had planned well, and each man had gone his separate way with a bundle containing three loaded and primed pistols, knives and cutlasses, and extra incendiaries.

That well-tarred and oiled pack tied to his back barely hindered his quiet but powerful stroke as he swam toward the goal. The water was dark but not cold, probably Gulf Stream. His determination helped dampen the terror of the dangers. He tried to avoid thinking about the white panic when he fell over the side of his father's ship years ago, the horror that engulfed and unmanned him. But he survived—remember that! He survived. His "stripes" from the cat burned his back like fire and helped him concentrate on the task instead of the terror. Now could he get aboard without being seen? Could he avoid being caught, found out and hanged? As he neared the stern of the brig, the inevitable action he dreaded began to take place; the yards were braced to starboard and the mainsails began to fill. Heart racing, avoiding the surge around the stern that tried to throw him against the hull, he climbed the vertical rudder pintles and managed to grab the wale near the stern, then haul himself up to the larboard transom. He steadied himself, feet on the wale, hands grasping the taffrail, as the ship healed slightly toward him—he could hear the shouts of "Haul yer starboard braces! Ease yer helm!" *Cormorant* began to slip through the water on larboard tack. A few more minutes in the water, and he would have watched her glide away, leaving him to die in the manner of his worst nightmares.

Standing just above the groaning rudder, dripping and panting, just as a wake began to appear at the brig's stern, he looked carefully into the dimly lit stern cabin, but could see no one. He crawled slowly around to the starboard main back stays, still abaft the shrouds and poked his head slightly over the quarterdeck bulwarks, the wind now on the quarter, the water only a few feet below him, the slight curve of the ship's hull making this a little easier for him. Just forward, his back to Nathan, the helmsman concentrated on the wheel and lit binnacle. He recognized midshipman Bowman beyond that, near the weather rail, and Nathan ducked down, carefully opening his bundle, stuffing the two pistols and knives into his belt, making sure they were both secure and handy—and dry. The rest of his meager supplies found room in his sodden pockets.

He peered over the side again. Across from him at the aft end of the quarterdeck, an older, stouter man in a worn sou'wester gazed upward at the great spanker boom and gaff. Although he could not see his face in the lantern-splashed twilight, Nathan instinctively felt that this was the rightful commander of the brig. Just forward, his face half turned away, Bowman stood easily on the swooping deck, now slapping a belaying pin in his left palm. Nathan recognized the rascal laughing from forward, Morgan from *Scourge*. Then the prize master turned to address the older man by the taffrail.

"After the topgallants are set, Captain, your men will go below—for the duration," Bowman said.

"You might still find the services of my mate useful," growled Captain Turner.

"You are the only one we need now, Captain—perhaps not even you."

Around the mainmast, Nathan saw dark forms hauling the topsail yard and making fast the topgallant clews and sheets. He could vaguely make out other crew moving near the foremast. The stars were out, partially blotted out by the big squares of the topsails. Would any hands aloft see him there? The hull dipped in the swell with the ship now underway with a creaking of spars, hemp and blocks, the slap of canvas and the hiss of water under the counter. The wind brought him the smell of salt, tar and vaguely foul corruption.

Where was Logan? He was supposed to climb up the bobstay at the bow, slip over the cathead and round up the crew before the mast. Some of the prize crew were already below deck. Those would probably be armed and might continue to resist, or even attempt to cut the rudder cables or otherwise slow or sabotage the ship before she got too far away from *Scourge*. How far would the sound of gunfire carry over the water? But if they could retake the main deck and arm the rightful crew and allies topside, Nathan and Logan had thought there was a fair chance of success.

Their plan, such as it was, would soon reach its conclusion with terrifying simplicity. He saw only a few vague shapes of men on deck now.

Did they have pistols ready? How much longer should he wait? Soon perhaps one of the prize crew would report aft for final instructions regarding the prisoners. He could work his way aft again along the hull, climb over the taffrail and . . .

Suddenly the gray-bearded man Nathan had confirmed was the Captain turned and looked directly at him. His mouth opened and a look of shock on his leathery face quickly turned to understanding. It was time! Nathan pointed to the helmsman, then to the Captain, and then to Bowman and himself, raising a knife and pistol.

The Captain nodded and walked over to Bowman, making sure the latter had his back to Nathan.

"Sir, is it really necessary to lock up my men? They—"

"Don't be ridiculous!" the midshipman snapped. "You should be thankful we don't simply—"

Nathan had managed to climb over the side and creep up to Bowman. The helmsman glanced around and tried to yell. But it was too late. As Turner decked the helmsman with one blow, Nathan handed him a pistol and hooked his left arm around Bowman's neck, and with the knife in his right, stuck the point into the man's back.

Two of the prize crew rushed towards them, cutlasses and flintlocks raised. But by now Nathan had stunned Bowman with a vicious blow to the head with a pistol butt, and the man made an excellent shield. Still holding a knife to Bowman's neck, Nathan trained his second pistol at the men forward.

"Drop your weapons—now!" he shouted. There was commotion farther forward, no shots, but perhaps the clump of a body falling. He did not know the fate of Logan, but if he failed to take these men all was lost. They surrendered. Where was Morgan?

"Drop that!" called a voice forward, by the forward ladder. They heard another sound, like the clatter of a musket on the deck below, near the main hatch. To his relief, Nathan saw Logan.

"You two, sit there by the binnacle lamp, facing forward," said Nathan. "Relieve him of his sword, too, Captain" said Nathan, indicating Bowman. Turner had already grabbed the helmsman's pistol and aimed it at the prize crew; now he pointed the midshipman's sword at the helmsman, groggily getting to his feet.

"Keep your mouth shut and get back to that wheel," said Turner, "and stay on this course, damn you."

"Silence! Don't move, any of you!" said Nathan. "Or someone dies!" They were almost certainly invisible to *Scourge* by now, and too far for human voices to carry; but a gunshot or a violent alteration in course could still change everything. Logan had managed to free Turner's men from the forecastle, but they had no weapons yet.

"Jenkins! Take your men and man the braces! We'll wear ship!" Turner looked at Nathan, who smiled and nodded. "Get those British out of the tops and on deck—make sure there's only *Cormorants* aloft!" Turner yelled. Hails came from forward.

"Get those weapons and arm yourselves. Search these bastards for any more guns or knives—get back here, you men . . . and make sure to look out for any British near you!"

"They're no more British than us, Captain," said Nathan. "*Scourge* is American—at least, her Captain is. Her name may change from time to time."

"Damn—where is that useless mate of mine?"

"Dee is dead, Captain," shouted Jenkins. "They were about to lock us in the fo'c'sle—then—"

"One of those bastards shot your mate, Captain," said Logan, "and disappeared!"

"Morgan!" Nathan shouted. "I'll find him!"

"Do you think that pirate saw or heard anything, mister?" Turner asked Nathan, pointing at *Scourge*, still hove-to.

"Nathan Jeffries, Captain, at your service. I wish I knew." He wondered if two minutes or two hours had elapsed since he reached *Cormorant*. And he still might not live through the night.

"Mathew Turner, and the privilege is mine, sir. We'll need your men to help us tie up these boys—we can't leave 'em here unguarded."

"Do you really think you can retake this ship?" snarled Bowman, sitting up and leaning against the binnacle.

"You won't live to see otherwise," spat Nathan, digging his toe into the man's back. "Now keep your mouth shut!"

Bowman squealed in agony. Just then more human forms came aft out of the gloom; Nathan was heartened to see four unarmed and crestfallen prize crew, shoved by Jenkins and Logan, who were grinning broadly. Jenkins approached and knuckled a mock salute to Turner, and nodded to Nathan.

"Tie and gag these bastards at the mainmast!" Nathan ordered. "With your permission, Captain—"

"I am in your debt, sir," said Turner.

Nathan and Logan shook hands.

"I see you held up your end, Jeffries!" Mister Jack Logan said. "But I guess Tom Howard—kind enough to point his gun against the prize crew once he saw me aboard—is the only one of 'em we can trust. And I fear *Cormorant's* mate—"

"Dee. We heard," said Turner.

"Yes, sir. He was the one who relieved one man of his musket and his balance—you may have heard the commotion. We got 'em all now, tied up—and Tom Howard and one of your crew's searchin' for the last two men. Maybe now we can spare some more hands to search."

"There's more weapons below," said Turner. "We were waiting for our chance. You gave it to us."

"Where is *Scourge?*" The fresh southwesterly wind blew across the heeling *Cormorant's* starboard beam, tacks straining but secure.

Turner shouted up the main mast.

"Willis! Any sign of her?"

"I can't see her!" they heard from aloft.

It seemed incredible to Nathan, as *Cormorant* slipped with gentle pitch through the dark night, all plain sail, that they had succeeded; that he would survive. But there was still Morgan.

"There's only my men aloft," said Turner. "Jeffries, you—"

Suddenly they heard a shot forward on the lower deck, and a scream of agony.

"Give me that pistol," Nathan said. "Logan, you take the forward hatch. Jenkins, you come with me—with your permission, Captain. The rest of you, stay and guard these men, and look for *Scourge*." Bare feet padding on the deck, he plunged down the aft companionway, determined to settle the issue.

Side by side, Nathan and Jenkins almost ran into Morgan who suddenly emerged from the darkness near the foot of the ladder; the big man smiled grimly and fired his pistol. The loud bang and flash startled Nathan, who saw Jenkins's head jerk back and spray blood as the man fell back to the deck by the stairs. In the acrid smoke, Morgan swung the butt at Nathan's head.

As Nathan raised his right arm to fire his pistol, the wood and brass cracked against it. Its paralyzing sting and the force of his arm smacking against his own head, rocked Nathan back against the corner of the narrow passage by the mate's quarters. But he did not fall. As his knees started to buckle, Nathan saw the glint of another pistol in Morgan's hand.

"You ain't gonna be in any condition to report back aft," Morgan growled. "And this ship ain't gonna swim much longer, neither."

Nathan smelled iron and blood, struggled against oblivion and nausea as he remained standing, swayed on his feet. He heard the man cock the lock, and Nathan tried to call out. His croaking brought a snicker from Morgan.

Ten

In Dreams, Hanover – *February 1812*

Peter's dream always unfolded the same way: in it, the year is 1805 and his mother Elizabeth still possesses much of her legendary beauty, long, smooth hair still black, her oval face, sharp features, high cheekbones, widely curved lips, large brown eyes, delicately arched brows, thin, slightly arched nose—a remarkable beauty. This had been a source of annoyance for Peter, who knew he possessed that same irresistible quality, yet was still rejected by both Shawnee and white man. Her parents had been Shawnee, but after they were killed she was taken in by the Charles family in Philadelphia and given the name Elizabeth Hughes. Every one knew that Peter's father was a naval man, but that's all anyone knew—or would reveal.

"The quality of linen and ware we receive from New York is much better than Baltimore," she is saying. Peter's patience is at an end. Discussing fashion in a home that was a small cabin hidden in a small cul de sac of discreet rock and pine, a "glen of sin," as he had said to Nathan in that last good year.

"Then I suggest you have your 'provider' ship our supplies direct from London, or better yet—"

"Peter, please stop this constant—"

"Mother! Stop trying to protect him . . . or me. I want to know who my father is, and his association with the Austers, Charles and Stewards."

Elizabeth bows her head as if in shame, abandoned, that helpless look, in disgrace. She stares at her son, and her eyes grow moist.

"Please, Mother! I love you, but I weary of all these fables, and why . . ."

Elizabeth shakes her head petulantly, reminding her son of a young girl caught in a lie, not unlike Barbara Steward. Then she looks at her son, crying softly.

"Peter my darling, I have tried to . . . please don't say such things, and let us part in better spirits."

Peter hugs his mother, feeling in many ways, he was the parent, and she the daughter. But he loves her. She and Nathan, the Jeffries, are his only family, with a few Shawnee from his distant past and Dr. Beatty, the remarkable Dartmouth professor, his mentor.

"I must be cruel only to be kind, Mother. I'm sorry."

"You have triumphed in this white man's world, Walanapeathy—"

Peter laughs derisively. "Triumphed? Please, Mother! My only true friends among the whites—I had been accepted by Nathan and his folks . . . and now . . . Nathan was the only one who truly saw me as brother, a blood friend. I would have fought every day, if I did not have . . . and have to swallow . . ."

In the dream he could see how upset he was making her, and so he stopped. In a sense, he was responsible for fostering her childlike delusions. In order to spare her the pain of reality, he usually kept the dosage as small as possible.

She smiles sadly. Elizabeth's other life remained a secret to her son; a wealthy man would send for her, presumably as his mistress. Peter could only visit her at that roughhewn, plain cabin on the edge of the thickest woods. Peter hated this man, probably his father, with his servile squaw of convenience. He barely hugs his mother goodbye, to swallow that bitter green bile.

His dream travels on to June 1807, when Elizabeth dies mysteriously before he can see her again, disappears in thin air like the treasured "magic smoke" of the Caribs and Lucayans, the same plant family as the hemp planted all over the year for making rope.

Peter laughs, trapped in that same nightmare; Auster, Abraham Steward, whose beneficence had not warmed him, nor the enticing Barbara Steward. Nothing had warmed him as much as the friendship of

Amy, Nathan and William Jeffries, and now in his dream that friendship of Nathan's grows into a raging face in the mist, the rasping voice.

Then Peter runs through the woods, chased by white men waving and throwing spears—pikes! Any three or four men he could have dealt with, but there are hundreds, with muskets and pistols, long knives, tomahawks. He can hear their labored panting, crashing through the undergrowth. He has never felt so strong, or so glorious, fierce anger and despair power his legs as he jumps nimbly over dead branches and dodges dry trunks—light flashes down from their crowns. Then he sees a man standing up ahead, in the clearing, a big man with a long rifle. It looks like Nathan.

"No!" he shouts. "No! This must stop!"

And as usual, the miserable dream stopped, and he drifted up.

He opened his eyes. The bright sun was a candelabra held by his Dartmouth correspondent Professor Beatty; his kind, inquisitive, wrinkled face looked at Peter with an almost comical concern. Now he nodded, seeing that Peter was awake and staring at him. Beatty knew what Peter's first question would be.

"You are at my house here in Hanover on the night of February 24th, 1812. You have been very ill for about a week, tossing and turning, feverish, but your wound is good, it looks and smells much better now. I was about to wake you."

Peter nodded. "It was bad. How long have I been here?"

"About a week," Beatty repeated. "It is still early morning, almost dawn. My niece and I worked on your wounds and gave you some laudanum to help you sleep."

Peter tried to sit up in the bed, but a horrible light-headedness overcame him at once.

"You've lost considerable blood, my friend. Get some more rest, then we'll talk." Beatty placed his hand on Peter's chest. Peter knew the old man was filled with questions and grinned in spite of himself, admiring his forbearance. Then he slipped into unconsciousness.

When he opened his eyes again, he saw three men and a woman looking down at him. The professor knelt and felt his pulse.

"It's good and strong. Try to sit up and drink this beef broth." Beatty handed him a cup.

This time he was able to sit up in bed and thirstily drink the bouillon. There was a look of apology in Beatty's eyes.

"Peter, you remember my niece Serelea, and these men are Army officers who have been ordered by President Madison to explore portions of the lower Missouri first studied by Lewis and Clark in '05. This is Major Harris who actually participated in that expedition as a sergeant, and Lieutenant Gould here. Serelea was recommended by Sacajawea herself in Washington City. And Peter, what an opportunity to continue your study of temperate zone plants and animals."

"A pleasure, sir," said Harris, stocky and self-assured, shaking Peter's hand. The woman, lithe and pretty, dressed in handsome deer hide, her shining black hair braided, flashed her intelligent dark eyes at Peter, leaned over to take a closer look at him.

Peter nodded. "Now that Jefferson has doubled the size of the United States, and before we . . . before any renewal of formal hostilities between us and the British, our government needs to learn more about what is out there," he said. His voice sounded like a croak to his own ears. "And you can learn a great deal before departing from the professor and his associates."

"Yes, sir," said Harris. "His knowledge and understanding of the situation is impressive, as perhaps is yours. This spring we take boats up the Missouri River from St. Louis and then up the western Ohio."

Harris paused and looked at Gould.

"We would like to . . . hire you as scout and guide."

Peter laughed weakly.

"I am sorry. I appreciate your offer, but—"

"Mr. Hughes, I have been authorized to pay you one thousand dollars for your help."

"I am sorry, Major. I cannot help you for any price."

"Listen, boy—" Harris began.

"My name is Hughes, sir. Peter Hughes."

Harris cleared his throat. "Mister . . . ah . . . Hughes, there is something else—we understand you were injured—"

"Where did you get that wound, Mister Hughes? Was it a musket ball?" interjected Gould.

Peter said nothing. He felt the throbbing pain in his leg begin to build up from its previous numbness, and the burning eyes of his inquisitors.

"Fact is, Professor, there was some killing near the Ohio border; two settlers, not long after the fight at Tippecanoe and we noticed that Indian pony outside," said Major Harris. "And, this man is part Indian, Delaware tribe—is that not so, Mr. Hughes?"

"My mother is Shawnee, my father . . .white."

"Well, that being the case . . . we—"

"I must rest, gentlemen," said Peter.

"Let us then return to the parlor and let my patient rest," said the professor, noticeably relieved.

As she left, Serelea held out her hand to Peter; it felt warm and strong in his. Her dark eyes burned into him.

Peter heard bits of the conversation in the other room as he drifted off to sleep.

". . . heard that from a man who was an army officer . . ."

"Maybe. But this one is a half-breed, you know, half Shawnee . . ."

"Gentlemen, I must insist that . . ."

"And I have a report that Fitch and Fulton have developed his ideas for torpedoes and steam-powered and even submarine vessels . . ."

"Major, please . . ."

As he faded in and out, Peter wondered if he could even trust the professor and Serelea. Later that day he woke up alone, got out of bed, threw a cloak over the nightgown he was wearing and carefully walked around the room before sitting in a chair near the window. Some dizziness and fatigue, but much better. Then Beatty came in, smiling.

"Excellent! Your arm is causing you no pain? Or your leg?"

"Only a twinge now and then. I owe you my life, Professor—or in this context, I should say, Doctor."

"Nonsense! I did only what any compassionate man would do."

Peter shook his head. "No. You are naive, sir. But you saved my life, Professor, and some day I hope to repay that debt. In the meantime, I owe you at least—"

"The truth. You owe me nothing, sir, but I would be more than happy to listen to the story you don't want the officers to hear. Do you feel up to joining me for some supper downstairs? It would be just the two of us."

"Then your army visitors—they gave in so easily . . ."

"Harris and Gould are staying at the inn for a few days. They may return, but for some reason the government values my good graces, and they do not wish to embarrass me. And nothing you say to me will be repeated to anyone."

As they ate roast pheasant and sweet potatoes, Peter told his host about Tippecanoe and then the ambush. Beatty nodded as Peter described the grisly details.

"I had never killed anyone, Professor, and this weighs heavily on me."

"Did you have any choice?"

"No, I—"

"So you really think I am naïve, Peter? You are only half Shawnee, and I believe you are the most extraordinary man."

"I am not a white man, Professor."

"And you will suffer this for the rest of your split life—for God's sake, young man, you are gifted . . ."

"And blessed, I know, I know . . ."

"You are cursed, like the rest of us. Serelea was able to survive her parents, her life as a slave, practically; revealed at last as a brilliant—"

"Excuse me, Professor, but I am a murderer!"

Peter looked at Beatty in astonishment as the old man smiled.

"Professor, I have lost my only friends, the Jeffries; my mother has disappeared, probably dead. I have no home, not even with the Shawnee."

"I'm sorry, young man. You are right, you are the survivor, and that's why you must stay with Serelea and me. We will take care of you; we are your friends and we believe in you. We will not betray you, and here you can explore some of your other interests; this natural world, not man's violence, like your new species of Lycaenopsis. Even your work with Fitch and Fulton."

"Yes," said Peter bitterly. "Torpedoes and paddle wheels and steam engine submarines."

"You are caught between two worlds, Peter: the white man's and the Indian's. But we can offer you—"

"—reprieve for my people killed and pushed farther west of Indiana Territory? You are white ... you do not ... are not—"

"Not to be trusted? Are we not friends, Peter? And the Jeffries in Baltimore, I do not know why you think they hate you now."

"I betrayed Nathan with Barbara," said Peter calmly. "And my helping the British betrays everything his parents believe in. There can be no peace."

The next day Peter was even more improved. As much as he respected his professor, Peter was anxious now to return to his mother's house, even as the dead of winter approached—by now it had become urgent. He walked the streets of Hanover, filled now with frozen mud and snow, and bought some goods. Peter looked around carefully, seeing a few Indians shuffling and slouching, eyes averted from boisterous, bearded white men in buckskin. But no one took any particular notice of him.

After supper that evening, Peter insisted that his exhausted host retire, and reluctantly the professor agreed, knowing this was the last time he would see this man, probably forever.

"Very well. I will see you off then, my young friend, with the rising sun. I will miss our conversations."

They shook hands, and Peter felt tears welling up. He grasped the old man's narrow shoulders.

"Thank you for everything, Doctor Beatty ... I'll never forget this ... your kindness ... our talks."

"Please. Well, good night then."

The candle Beatty held splashed its light off the walls as the professor ambled down the hall and upstairs to his bedchamber. Peter stared at the candle on the table, then decided to take a walk outside in the night. There was plenty of moonlight and it was clear.

An hour later, he was back at Beatty's door and quietly let himself in. He was tired now and wanted to leave at dawn. The house was dark, but his eyes, accustomed to the night, could make do with the moonlight leaking in through the hall and stairwell windows. He slipped upstairs to the guest chamber.

Something was wrong. Even though he could hear muffled sounds from down the hall, the good Beatty snoring, he knew it wasn't that. Someone had made a fresh fire in the guest chamber. But it was more than that. Someone was in there now. Had they found out about his fight with the white men? It was a bad moment. But surely Beatty would not betray him, and then sleep! Perhaps it was someone only pretending to snore. And in his chamber—nothing except the flickering light, the fire crackling in the fireplace. It was quiet, warm and yet he knew. He carried no gun but he slipped out his knife and was as ready as he would ever be. He braced himself for another fight or for the blinding flash and explosion of a gun.

He slowly entered the room. He saw the body on the bed and heard the low, quiet voice at the same moment.

"Are you well enough for company? I do not think the knife will be necessary."

Serelea! His heart was drumming in his chest as he approached the bed. There she lay, shimmering in the blue moonlight; her lithe, brown body seeming to glow, naked above the covers, nipples erect, lips smiling, eyes brown pools, brows like dark crescents, hair black against the pillow.

"It is too warm for cloth, do you not agree?" She smiled as he stared at her, dumbfounded, then slowly slipped his knife back in its sheath, still speechless.

"Yes. I do not think we will need that weapon."

"How did you—"

"Do you believe you are the only one who can sneak in and out of white man's lairs? Come join me. I know you feel as I do."

"Why did you tell them—"

"They knew—or suspected. I wanted to make sure your story was defensible; some people can see that you have Indian blood, and I had already been asked if you have another name."

"It is—"

"No, not now," she said, reaching up to him.

Thoughts of weariness and sleep flew from Peter's mind as he quickly stripped and lay in bed next to her; caressing Serelea's warm nude form, he abandoned himself to her shape, feel and smell, her aggressive passion, her tactile delights. For the rest of the night, there was little talk, or sleep; only muffled cries and groans of satisfaction.

Eleven

Seduction

"Your father is at the bank." Richard was sipping the Steward's poor excuse for Amontillado, wondering what had happened to the sherry he had sent over. Or even the Madeira, a bit earlier. He sat near Barbara on the settee in the Steward's east hall. The afternoon sun struggled through the damask curtains Barbara had drawn to protect the paintings and upholstery from its damaging rays, even in February 1812. A thin coating of snow remained on the ground. The sky was chalky as the temperature settled in the low thirties, and little wind.

Barbara looked down. "Yes. He was very short with me this morning. I have no idea why his temper is so frayed."

"Don't you?" Richard squeezed her shoulder gently, admiring the golden shine of her hair, with hints of strawberry, now loose and flowing, the snowy white curve of her breasts, the promising hips under the red gown and the generous pouting of her lips.

She turned to him. "No. Should I? Is that what you wanted to talk to me about? After last night—"

"Well, yes. Frankly, I thought for your own sake I should share what I know—it is a shame that your father has not seen fit to discuss the matter with you."

"What is it? I believe I've heard enough about the Jeffries, or the Charles—or even my brother."

Richard laughed gently. "Your brother."

"Yes." She looked at him sharply but his small smile disarmed her.

Even though Richard seemed more and more the bearer of bad news, Barbara found herself not wishing to execute the messenger. Quite the contrary. He was sympathetic and clearly cared for her, and must have her welfare in mind even when he revealed the worst news. Ever since he had announced that his marriage to Catherine would be postponed and Peter left and Nathan Jeffries disappeared, Richard had told her things about himself, about her family, and she had now felt jittery and nervous. His warm hand on her bare shoulder was soothing.

Now the topic was Abraham.

"My dear, your father . . . some unfortunate information about some of your father's activities in the past has surfaced. And we are helping to keep the past buried."

"What information?"

"It seems there was a potential scandal involving a friend of Abraham's . . . a Miss Martingale, a very young girl—"

"No! You're lying! This is ridiculous!" Yet her heart sickened and writhed in acid; she knew it was true.

She stood up, shaking. Richard stood and held her shoulders firmly, facing her.

"I'm sorry, Barbara, but you must have had some sense, an inkling—your sainted stepmother, Mary, practically living in Philadelphia. I know how hard all of this has been for you . . ."

"He was accused of . . . having relations with this young girl?"

"Yes. But of course your father would not want to upset you."

She pulled herself away, and facing the window, spoke bitterly. "No, my father has not seen fit to mention this. He speaks little of . . . those matters."

"Of course all vicious lies," said Richard soothingly. He stood behind her, caressing, gently massaging her bare shoulders and arms.

"Please remember that the Jeffries may have fabricated the entire story from whole cloth. It is they who betrayed you, not I. We wish only the best for you . . . you know that."

He could not possibly know what had happened, she thought. But he seemed to know and understand everything.

"Richard, you must stop that. The Jeffries?" Barbara turned around and looked in his handsome, calm face. "What do you mean? Are they capable of this kind of insidiousness, subterfuge? Catherine speaks highly of Amy Jeffries, you know, and I in particular—and now, Nathan; nobody knows where he is . . ."

Richard laughed harshly now, and walked over to the other window, looking out at the garden.

"Can we not simply count our blessings? Come now, lovely Barbara! Womenfolk like Miss Amy are another matter! The menfolk are—I supposed you understood my feelings toward William and son."

"Oh, of course, Richard, as far as William—"

"Ah, beautiful, naive Barbara." He stroked her hair and she instinctively lay her head in his palm, before realizing what she was doing. She sat down again, shaking her head.

"I know I've asked you already, Richard, but please tell me again that you know nothing about Nathan's disappearance."

Richard sighed, and sat down again next to her, as he quoted:

"Thy shores are empires, changed in all save thee
Thy waters washed them power while they were free
And many a tyrant since, their shores obey
The stranger, slave, or savage; their decay
Unchangeable save to thy wild waves' play,
Time writes no wrinkle on thine azure brow—
Such as Creation's dawn beheld, thou rollest now . . ."

Barbara closed her eyes. "Richard," she said, relentless. "So you know nothing of Nathan's . . . or *Bucephalus*?"

"Isn't that lovely? A few lines from a satire soon to be published, 'Childe Harold's Pilgrimage.' My friend Lord Byron has great talent. I expect great things from our young George Gordon. Marked by destiny, he is."

"Richard—"

"Yes, of course, again . . . I know nothing of poor Jeffries or his vessel. Sad how so many are taken by the sea—that last relentless mystery, the sea. They say it has no memory—"

"Don't say that, please!"

"I am sorry, my dearest Barbara, but perhaps I should quote Shakespeare as our young ornament, half-breed pride of Dartmouth, Peter Hughes, is so fond of doing:

> On such a full sea are we now afloat,
>
> And we must take the current when it serves,
>
> Or lose our ventures.

"But of course I am no Brutus, and hardly a philosopher or classics scholar. I can only remind you that the lad is a proven coward. You surely do not want me to—"

"You men are such fools!"

"Of course we are, we are all madly in love with you . . . if we are men—"

"Stop it. And here you are engaged to beautiful Catherine—"

"Barbara my love, let us be honest with each other, at least here and now. I love you, you know that, but I also feel you and Peter . . . well, we can put that chapter behind us. "

"What are you talking about? First my father . . . now my brother, I want—"

"What do you want, pretty Barbara? I can understand your feelings for the boy, since you are discrete. You know, the rubes and huckleberries on this side of the Atlantic notwithstanding, I see no need to treat the pagans any worse than other servants—or even respectful and honest, hardworking trade neighbors—especially if the uneducated ones remain beyond the Mississippi. Peter is well-behaved, well-trained, respectful. He is intelligent and knows his place . . . except with you—unlike some of these uppity stable slaves, right? But I understand how you must feel after . . . those you trusted pawed and mistreated you."

Barbara stood up again, pale and trembling, followed immediately by her inquisitor, the Harvard attorney and hardened shipmaster; sinister, detestable, irresistible.

"I feel it is time for you to leave, Richard."

"Certainly my dear, certainly, if you wish it. But remember Solomon's proverb, 'He that troubleth his own house shall inherit the wind, and the fool shall be servant to the wise of heart.'"

Barbara felt her knees collapse beneath her as Richard held her by her shoulders.

She allowed him to guide her to the sofa.

"Why did you say that?"

"Oh, gentle Barbara, I do not enjoy intruding on your fantasies, but please remember that your esteemed father has contracted . . . certain obligations and expenses since the unfortunate misunderstandings and certain gambling notes—not to mention those ugly accusations."

Barbara squirmed and trembled under his magical touch and breath.

"Please stop, Richard, please . . . please, no; oh, that feels so . . ."

She could hardly concentrate on what he was saying, his hands and lips causing her mild spasms of ecstasy. "You don't love Nathan, for God's sake, you love me. You must love me. I love you madly, you know that I do—it is only you I've wanted since, that time at the shore, when we walked—"

"Richard! Please stop!" But when he did, her eyes pleaded and she pressed his hands onto her warm, buoyant breasts.

"You don't love him," Richard whispered, "and you know the Jeffries are not to be trusted. I won't share you with anyone, I cannot. In any case, how could Nathan love you? Where is he to protect you from your father's enemies, as I am doing? You cannot even trust your own father, let alone Nathan; they do not worry enough about your welfare. You know that I am the only one you can trust, and you must let me guide you—you know I am only with Catherine as a contractual . . . obligation. I do not love her; you are the only one, Barbara, and I am the only man for you."

"You are the only one . . ."

Barbara sobbed quietly and sucked avidly on his lips and tongue as his hands played her neck and breasts and belly and thighs, and his enormous hardness pressed into the crushed fabric of her collapsed gown. She groaned and her buttocks ground into the sofa as she lost control, floodgates opened.

Barbara, her father Abraham and Catherine rocked and swayed down cobblestones by four-in-hand coach on their way south on Bond Street to Shakespeare near Market Square for a New Year's ball at Right Honorable Samuel Chase's forty-room "cottage." In the late sun to the west, they could see the silhouetted spires of St. Patrick's Church, the Courthouse "on stilts" at Calvert on the hill, St. Paul's, the Town Clock in the towering German Reformed Church and the First Presbyterian Church. The cold gusts from the northwest blew a thin, powdery snow across the road. The deepened basin and Patapsco river glittered beyond, only frozen near the banks, inshore and barely brine. The shipyards were nearly deserted, but a forest of masts still swayed at the wharf and moored in the harbor, some decked out with lanterns and moat lights. The women especially wanted to see Elizabeth "Betsy" Patterson, who had returned to Baltimore after her short-lived marriage to Jerome Bonaparte. All the wealthiest and most famous shipping interests were invited, even the rich Salem ship owner William Gray, New England through and through and yet notoriously loyal to Madison, not the Federalists. The Jeffries, who lived a few blocks away, were not.

"We will be at war within a few months, Abraham; is that not so? The President's latest edict via Congress, while they try to call up volunteers from—"

"Catherine, I am with the two most beautiful women in Maryland— how can I discuss such sordid matters?"

"Bah! Come, Abraham! Please indulge me. Richard will not discuss any of these matters in my presence, and I do not see how neutrality can be maintained after all these coercive economic policies have failed, after the *Chesapeake-Leopard* and *President-Little Belt* attacks—"

"What can we do against the British navy, my dear? And the northern states do not want the war. 'Twill only cost more money, with the original northern commonwealths like Massachusetts footing the bill. The British are friends now, not the French. But remember Copenhagen? I am sure that Congress does the best it can—the ninety-day Embargo . . .

well, first Macon's bill—"

"What about the American crew men pressed off those American ships to serve the British navy? That is not good enough, Abraham. You sound like a Federalist."

Abraham laughed with false bonhomie, turning pink with embarrassment.

Barbara leaned forward and impatiently pointed her finger at her world-weary friend.

"Catherine, please, you know my father cannot afford political allegiance—he must be neutral."

"As Richard is neutral?"

"What do you mean?"

"Here we are, ladies!" said Abraham with evident relief. He leaned forward and rapped the ceiling, and when the coach came to a snow-rattling stop, horses snorting, he squeezed carefully out.

He escorted the ladies into the hall, waddling comfortably, his boots knocking loudly on the oak floor. In his new beaver hat and light blue silk suit that fit well over his rotund frame, he looked like what he was: a prosperous banker. But today these two lovely women turned heads in this affluent society; faces turned to gaze, even the Commonwealth Club stood up to bow and nod appreciatively at them. The brilliant ball with its naval presence, all bullion and polished silver; the gamine beauties, bare necks and shoulders, twirling diaphanous gowns; and dark blue uniforms and gold fittings bending and graceful, forming stately squadrons, fleet actions on the floor.

Barbara's heart pounded when she saw Richard looking magnificent as he sailed into the Chase's reception hall, wearing a snowy white shirt with ruffled cuffs and cravat, and a formal dark blue silk suit cut for a British country gentleman. The servant took his newfangled top hat—its beaver skin the same as the Negro's deep mahogany so cherished in English furniture and racehorses. The man's alert, clear eyes darted to gauge his targets, his prey; but always calm, in control. Richard's masterful aplomb reassured and helped others govern their fear of his paralyzing gaze, known to be terrible to behold.

Before he could even enter the ballroom, Barbara came quickly to the vast foyer, followed by her father and Catherine.

Both Barbara and Catherine felt the inevitable thrill of the victim, watching the Devil approach—with dread and eager delight; depths of depravity suddenly appearing in real life. They knew they belonged to Doctor Faustus now, and there was no hope, only everlasting torment. Barbara begged God to get it over with, skip the torture. But she knew little of that sordid world of male pride and revenge, a great cataract that would never end, never purge. She had been taken by a pirate, and become that pirate's woman. No better than the soiled "wives" who come aboard ... worse, even ... curse me, bless me.

Barbara forgot about Catherine or Abraham or anyone else—only Richard. She loved this man who threatened morbid mischief against everything she thought she held dear ... her father ... her secrets. Abraham's gambling and other pleasures had become even more expensive with finances from Austers to "help clear up this ugly matter of his indebtedness."

Now in debt only to the Austers (and for a staggering sum—worse than she might have supposed—that brutal, ugly term, half of one million dollars would definitely settle it, Richard said sadly) and about the old men pawing young girls, Barbara remembered her father kissing her when she was young with hard candy on his tongue, that sickeningly sweet taste. She had fallen into the arms of Peter Hughes not long after.

But her fondness and delight with her "brother" Peter paled in comparison to this addiction to the mastery of Richard, like some kind of wizard, or magician; detestable, yet irresistible. Abraham no longer pressured her to marry Nathan or anyone else. Richard could destroy Barbara and her father any time. She knew his hatred for the Jeffries was more than even Barbara had imagined and would destroy them all. But Richard had of course singled out the coward and traitor Nathan Jeffries for special sacrifice. Barbara cringed and said, You are mad! Yes, he said. Richard had her almost believing that his marriage to Catherine was not—in any case his heart belonged totally to Barbara—of course. Now here he was again, haunting even in the wakefulness of day.

"We had not expected you," she breathed up at him, hand fluttering over her chest.

"Ah! So fortunate I could leave Boston early and see you, and even if only briefly."

"Only briefly . . . you mean . . . you—"

"I called on you, my love, and Abraham out of courtesy to dear friends, but I shan't stay long. So many duties to perform."

"Duties?"

Barbara Steward's smile noticeably faded. She was dressed in green emeralds, matching her mesmerizing green eyes. Now she felt those vaulting arches of desire surrender her to most unholy and unrighteous acts, a slave to carnal pleasures she could not resist.

At first, Richard had eyes only for his fiancée.

"You look lovely, my dear," said Richard, bowing to his lady Catherine, then taking her two outstretched hands. He smiled at Barbara, and she blushed even more beautifully, her lips curving into an involuntary smile. Abraham looked down and cleared his throat. Richard smiled at Catherine's seemingly arrogant and haughty stare, hiding profound fears; that lonely seeker of a true soul-mate, her dark eyes and gold flecks reaching into the abyss. And yet, he believed that she loved him. They had been joined early in life, as kissing cousins, except that all knew Catherine had been adopted. But you overlook problems with her pedigree when you look at such a fine filly. However annoyed, she would say or do nothing in a public arena such as this; she would feel it only appropriate in private. He hated her, but he could not imagine life without her. Even now that he had fully tasted her enticing lips.

Richard had to admire the strength and fiery brilliance of his fiancée, as intolerable as those qualities were—repulsive in any young woman of beauty and breeding, any woman, really. Even the joy at the terminus of the hunt paled with Catherine, because she showed no sign of yielding to his control—quite the contrary. Her courage, her daring, no quarter asked—but he reminded himself that the patient predator can achieve more than the impulsive one. In time Catherine would pay bitterly for every act of defiant will or challenge. Disobedience is the mortal sin. In the meantime the least he could do was ruin Barbara—and all in a good cause—their sacrifice would help him turn the Jeffries against each other.

At length he would be avenged; no doubt, in fact, the process had already started, even though neither Barbara and Catherine, nor even poor old Abraham, suspected anything. They do not think beyond their seemingly innocent "neutral" visit to a rich Fells Point favorite, Chase and his daughter Rachael, not quite as beautiful but immensely popular, on whose bare shoulders a necklace of lustrous pearls lay entwined.

"And how are you, sir?" Richard inquired politely of Abraham.

"Unfortunately, not well enough to remain with you young people," said Abraham. His voice rasped and rumbled hoarsely.

"I am sorry you cannot continue to grace us your presence, sir, but I know you will recover quickly."

Abraham bowed again. "Thank you, sir. Now please enjoy yourselves."

"Get some rest, Father," said Barbara.

She watched bitterly as Abraham waddled off to the portico and Richard carried off Catherine in the other direction and the two lovers danced the newfangled waltz. Richard, with his betrothed Catherine—but he said he loved only the golden fleece, that I was his—that he wanted only me—but Catherine had all the power.

Then Catherine was gone and here was Richard, looking at her with concern. So kind. No, no physician, please, only Richard.

Now she could see that the entire episode had been choreographed by her new master, Richard Auster. Did Catherine or her father know about her new, secret status as a kept mistress? But Richard felt so comforting, he could not possibly be lying to her about everything; how he felt, even after all those ugly rumors, no doubt spread by the Jeffries and their kind, as Richard says. And if only half of what he says is true, I dare not anger him; and what shall I say to my own father, after all these years of denial, the horror . . . bedding his own daughter. Now just say nothing, nothing. Barbara could not hold back the tears, in spite of all her training.

Barbara looked out the window, playing her part. "I . . . I can't believe it. I've known them for years, and Catherine vouching for the Jeffries . . . and I—where is she?"

"Of course my love. I understand, and I will do all I can."

She was choking back sobs, and the trail of a tear glistened as it traveled down the side of her rosy, round cheek.

Richard kissed her wet cheek, held her more tightly.

"I want to help, my lovely Barbara," he whispered. "Please be assured that I will always be here when you need me . . . when I need you." She needed him now; trembling, her hands and arms resting against him, feeling the firm warmth of his torso. Some eyes darted their way inquisitively, but many guests had already departed—but what difference did that make now, she asked herself. Richard loved her—not Catherine.

"Stop it, Richard," said Barbara. "Did you ask Catherine about the new Empire gown? Those horrid French hairstyles? She wants me to read this novel *Sense and Sensibility*, that new British author Jane Austen— please desist, sir—"

But she leaned against him, nodded her head on his strong shoulder, and held on to him, trembling slightly. Her hands and arms were resting against him, feeling the heat of his muscles. Were they dancing? There must be music, if music be the food of love, play on. And then, suddenly, there at the dwindling ball, he was fondling her, in front of everyone; only they couldn't see, because they were at the far end of the room and he was between her and everyone else. His hands were so clever and insistent. She kissed his lips and licked his neck and felt too giddy. If he would only carry her away from her sheltered world . . . he was caressing first her back, then her buttocks, and suddenly she was on fire! She knew it was so wrong, but she was his; she let her fingers graze his fingers and hands, as his tongue and lips played with hers. Those madly addictive hands, that voice, reassuring, seductive. Hateful and omniscient. All-powerful.

"Richard, not in front of all these people; please you must not! You . . . must . . . stop . . ."

"You will look even more luscious out of your lovely dressings, my dear Barbara."

Barbara was terrified; she wanted him, hated him for making her need him so desperately. She was not crazy, she never wanted him to stop, she wanted those maddening hands all over her, inside her, and release . . .

"How do you know—" she gasped. "Stop, please, Richard."

And suddenly, he did.

Richard gently led her out onto the nearest Flemish Balcony above Stodderts Wharf and Yard. He released her arm, but said nothing. He looked at her, then shifted his position slightly, as if reluctant to continue.

"Oh God, please! Do not stop now, please, my love!"

He sighed and backed away.

"Go on, Richard; please do not stop now, I beg you. Please, more, Richard! My . . . darling . . ."

"I am sorry, my dear, if I have . . . upset you in any way."

"No, Richard, I only wished to—oh, please my love, let us continue . . ." She groaned, pleading with the Devil.

And then he was gone.

Twelve

Retaken

"Say your prayers, boy!" Morgan raised his pistol slightly higher, pointing it at Nathan's chest. The explosion of the weapon seemed simultaneous with Nathan's forward lurch and the blinding pain in his left side. "Aahh!" cried Morgan, with the hilt of Nathan's dirk protruding from his belly. He had just thrust the point viciously into the man, meant to pull it out again, but could not. Morgan half turned and almost collapsed on the deck between them, but then recovered. His pistol clattered across the deck near Nathan. He swept his arm around as if to shoot another weapon at Nathan's chest.

"Jeffries, I'm still gonna get out of here," he croaked with a crooked smile. "And you ain't."

But as Nathan fell backward to the deck, Morgan crumpled also. Nathan saw the look of horror and puzzlement on Morgan's face as he slumped to his knees in agony on the deck, his chest covered with blood; he jerked forward and then lay still, his face barely visible, a frozen ugly mask of pain and fear.

More feet were pounding down the companionway now. Several men crowded into the passageway; was that Logan? Poor Mr. Jenkins; his blood pooled on the pine deck near Nathan's bare foot. It seemed like hours since Nathan had clambered down the steps himself, and he laughed sleepily at the thought of it. The dark form of Morgan's body was now concealed by moving forms, and voices buzzed around his ears.

"Look below," Nathan sighed to indistinct faces. "Find the slow match and keg of powder. He's probably lit the fuse. Hurry!" He felt someone gently shifting him onto his other side, more scurrying, shouts and voices, and then nothing.

The light warmed his face and he warily opened his eyes into the blinding glare. Bright sun streamed in through a window two feet from his head. The rippling glass was square, with a cross of lead separating it into four smaller squares. He could only be lying in the berth of the ship's master. He felt very thirsty, and with the gentle roll of the hull, tried to sit up.

"Don't think of trying it, boy," said a stern voice. But the gray-bearded face that went with it made Nathan relax. "We sail free, thanks to you and your men. You know Richard Auster?"

Turner was leaning in the door from the main cabin, under the low ceiling, with a smile that told Nathan the ship was safe.

"I take it she didn't blow up, and your prisoners are secure," said Nathan. His voice sounded like an old woman's. And then it registered.

"Aye, thanks to you, lad. We found a keg with a fuse, just like you thought we would, far aft on the orlop deck. Got her out just in time."

"Did you say Richard Auster?"

"That I did."

"Might I trouble you for a drink, Captain?" asked Nathan.

His croak seemed to echo like the creaking of oak timbers reverberating through the wooden bulkheads, the groaning and moaning that told Nathan the ship was alive and sailing—that he was alive. But the nemesis of his life already returned.

When the Captain handed him a glass of brandy, Nathan managed to smile and toast to Turner's health before quickly downing the liquid.

"It was either fight . . . or die . . . Captain," Nathan said self-deprecatingly. "And I am not brave like my mother."

"Your mother is a Quaker, God bless her soul. Thank God you will recover, Jeffries!" said Turner, his face, like dark wood, briefly brightening with emotion.

"Morgan almost killed you, but his aim was poor. The ball removed only a small strip of your right side, son, and did not stay with you. There was a goodly amount of blood, but seems to be no infection according to your Jack Logan, who knows as much physic as anyone aboard. And a lot more than any bosun I seen."

"Wh . . . why did you ask me about Richard Auster?"

"Because he is the reason why we are here and I was wondering . . . if you had any business with him."

Nathan almost laughed in spite of himself. "Where should I begin—and how many watches do we have?"

As he spoke, Nathan grimaced with the pain. His right side below the ribs felt pierced by a splinter of wood, and agonizingly stiff. Eight bells, he heard on the deck above. It must be early morning. Then he heard two splashes, following by the pad of many feet on the pine planking. He looked at Turner, whose face was impassive again.

"Let me tell you a few things then," said the grizzled old Captain. "My shipping business had just about gone belly-up as they say, when Auster offered me . . . a special voyage. A very profitable voyage."

"Africa," said Nathan.

"Yes," growled the old man. "May God forgive me."

A nerve in Nathan's side suddenly snapped him into electrifying pain. He groaned, "I am the son of William Jeffries."

"Jeffries! Of course. How could I forget the dishonorable duel in 1807? I am sorry, that was one story. Can I get you something for the pain? We have no more laudanum I am afraid—"

"No . . . thank you but—what about the other wounded and . . . the dead? Morgan?"

"Morgan," the man said. "He got no service, nor the marine."

So the bodies had been summarily tossed overboard.

"Don't try to talk any more now," said Turner. "You look as pale as lace. Our prisoners told me a little about *Scourge* and about you, with some persuasion. They know you were 'pressed, but they don't know why, or what Coxe's game is with the Americans. That damned Archibald Coxe, I heard of him, sure. Should have recognized that fast boat of his. Couldn't have escaped anyway, though. And at least you got away from the bastard."

Nathan raised himself up again to drink.

"Lie down, man! Henry, fetch a fresh sheet here!"

But Nathan leaned against the bulkhead in the tiny compartment. "The marine was killed? Who else?" he asked, his head buzzing again as he fought nausea.

"Tom Howard found him, lighting the fuse! They nearly killed each other in a knife fight, my boy. The marine died only a few hours ago. Howard is recoverin'. We had some laudanum, which eased his pain. I'm sorry—Jack Logan said Howard was a friend of yours from *Scourge* and we can trust 'em. Can use him aboard. It was Morgan shot my mate with a pistol ball. That son of a whore's one step behind the Devil. Four bodies, two committed to their Maker with all the decent words and prayers we could muster. Four bodies, food for sharks. Wilkens is alive, if you please, but God in heaven, I know not how, with a musket ball in his head. He sleeps next to death, has not spoken. Bad business. I need a new first mate. No other serious wounds, at least; the prisoners are locked in the cable tier. We got the boy leader Bowman tied to the taffrail. He ain't said much . . . but he will."

Turner's face set in a grim and frightening mask—and the focus softened as Nathan's head began to yaw and his eyelids droop.

"Here, you, get some more rest. Henry! Where is that clean sheet!"

Nathan realized he had started to fall sleep sitting up. When he started to think about the horrors of the past few hours, he was sure he would never be able to sleep—and now he drifted off promptly again, fears and worries and busy thoughts notwithstanding. He had lost a lot of blood, was tired, so his body's needs took over. Images of his parents floated through his mind, and Peter, and Barbara, and Catherine—and Auster.

When *Cormorant* crossed the Gulf Stream, a sail appeared ominously similar to *Scourge*. But there was no sign of her the next day. By late afternoon, after sleeping through two watches, Nathan awoke to find a waister standing outside the captain's door When the sailor saw Nathan's eyes open, he nodded at Nathan and passed through the day room into the Captain's small after-cabin. Nathan's eyes continued to follow him aft to the stern windows, where Turner was looking over a chart on his table. Late afternoon sun still offered plenty of light, slanting in now through the windows. Nathan struggled out of bed, shrugged on a nightshirt, shook of the dizziness and staggered out of the compartment. Turner and the sailor looked up when Nathan approached, still weak but standing. He frowned.

"Belay that nonsense, Jeffries," Turner growled, then smiled and lowered his voice.

"All right, Henry, carry on. Send Howard in here."

"Aye, aye, sir." The slight but competent man nodded again to Nathan, and left.

Turner signaled Nathan to sit down, nodding to one of the small straight-backed chairs, and stood over him.

"I'm glad to see you are better," he said. "We're making for—"

"Antigua."

Turner stared at him with his mouth open. Nathan almost chuckled over the man's wrinkled face and bewhiskered chin. "We're due for a talk," he added, indicating the chart.

"And it's certainly time I slept somewhere else," Nathan said. "So that you can have your own quarters back."

"Nonsense," Turner said. The small but resilient Tom Howard, now steward and acting surgeon by his own insistence, appeared at the door.

"Tom, would you fetch Jeffries' clothes, and bring us some of that cold beef and beer. Now, lad, suppose you tell me the rest about you and that wind witch Coxe, and Auster?"

Nathan heard six bells in the evening watch before he finished the story; Turner was a good listener, only occasionally interrupting for clarification. With only a slight tremor in his voice, Nathan told him everything.

The Captain nodded at the end, and stroked his chin hair knowingly.

"First dogwatch. You've been lucky, my boy—and resourceful. We need to talk about getting you home. And my cargo sold. The cargo you saved—and my ship."

"Yes, Captain, I must get home. Thank you."

"Only thing is, we're almost south of the Tropic of Cancer now—within two days of Antigua, if this fine trade holds."

"Yes," said Nathan blandly. "*Cormorant* likes to reach a beamy wind. The headsails—all the fore-and-aft—are drawing well for a brig. Main's luffing too often. And we are not rid of *Scourge* yet. Coxe won't dare return to his master without me, rest assured."

Turner stared in amazement at this laconic new warrior. "Uh, yes. We're roughly 19 degrees latitude. Leeward Islands are south-southeast 160 miles. You remind me of your father," he said.

"I am taller," said Nathan. Both men laughed.

"But my father did teach me how to read a chart," Nathan added, "and a sextant with the help of Bowditch and Bunt."

"I did not know your father well, but I could not believe that he would fire early or behave in any way not a gentleman and honorable hero—"

"Yes, I know," said Nathan. "I have heard all of the accounts. That duel ruined our family, thanks to the 'honorable Richard'—but I will set things right, I . . ."

He shook his head silently, decided not to tell Turner about breaking all of his promises to his revered mother, Amy. And his father's buffoonery since the duel.

This young, quiet giant continues to astonish, Turner thought. In his long years at sea, he had never heard of a man seemingly transforming overnight (according to Nathan) from a craven coward false Quaker to a bloodthirsty, *bona fide* hero who saved his ship and his men. If I had a son, Turner thought sadly.

"What did you say, Nathan?"

"I said I understand why my return to the United States will be delayed," said Nathan.

"No longer than absolutely necessary, I promise. It is possible we could get word to—"

"Yes. That is always possible. We had better start preparing for our friend Coxe."

This young man has learned how to sink his fears like a man, he thought, a natural warrior discovered—what a wasted skill in a counting-house or ropewalk. And yet he remained a puzzle.

"Yes. We are not rid of him by any means."

"You have a plan, Nathan? Are you sure you are . . . well enough?"

"Captain, if I have any more time to rest and think about my night-mares I will go mad. Helping us to survive will keep me occupied for a while."

"Of course, my boy. Look, I can have you sign aboard *Cormorant* as my mate. If we speak another ship, you can join them and try for a faster return, some time in March."

Jack Logan's sun-darkened face lit up when Nathan joined his mess for supper shortly thereafter. He grabbed Nathan's shoulders, then, em-barrassed and concerned for his health, gestured to a chair.

"I knew you fared better," he said, "but didn't wanta 'sturb you before you were up and about."

"I am much better," said Nathan. "And grateful more than I can say that you—" He looked down. "I heard about the four men. What news since then?"

Logan looked away. "Aye, poor bastards; dogwatch services, sunset, if you would—"

"Of course, my friend."

"But I forgit my manners. This here's Reynolds. He supped with . . . Jenkins, and Tom Howard here, I guess you know; he's been taking care of you real good."

The crew treated him with the simulated deference reserved for strangers. He nodded to Reynolds.

"I am honored to serve with you men, along with my friends Mister Jack Logan and Tom Howard, best topman in Maryland."

Tom Howard laughed in embarrassment.

"In the world, if you please, Mr. Nathan," he growled. "I wish this brig of ours was a frigate," he added harshly.

"Why?"

"Why, so we coulda blowed that *Scourge* out of the water, o'course!"

"But we're merchant seamen, Tom, we're . . ."

"That won't stop us from ending up in a wrong ship again, or the prison, with stripes on our backs, if we can't fight," said Reynolds.

"You are right. And we are going to fight, men, and soon," said Nathan. The others smiled.

Late the following day, after helping to trim the sails in the afternoon, Nathan escaped to the bow, sat himself alone near the port cathead, and let the wind and warm spray from a stiff northeasterly breeze buffet him. The bow rose and fell in stately fashion, the white bow wave ceaselessly churning below. Topsails and topgallants were drawing well, and the jibs strained above him as the forestay hummed. Worried about the last of the Sargasso doldrums, the horse latitudes, Turner was working the little vessel for all she was worth.

Behind him the sun had already set, but the empty horizon was still pale mother of pearl. Over the mainmast Nathan could see the first stars appearing. For a blessed, magical time, Nathan knew no language, no past or future, and was at peace, at one with this ship and this sea.

He had succeeded; he had killed one enemy. But even racing to the south-south-east, *Cormorant* was flying toward his future. What would happen at his next landfall? Nathan's nostrils were assailed by the sea breeze, the last of the smell of the Gulf Stream, the Sargasso, the tang that seemed so alive and insistent. He felt a sudden spike of sorrow and anger as the ship flew south, directly away from his loved ones and enemies. His feeling of humiliation, his lust for revenge was awash with his guilt for the suffering he had caused. They were mixed in together, like the roiling waters in the wake of this ship. His mother had warned him, pleaded with him, ordered him never to fight, never to duel! Tears came to his eyes. He had come so close to death, and he did not want to leave this world! He had failed his mother, but he wondered what his friends and family would have thought of his death. They might think he was dead now. No doubt a few would mourn, but Nathan shook himself, wishing he had spirits. Turner favored beer and whiskey. If he survived to return to Baltimore, what would he do about Auster? There was no way he could ever claim a victory. His father had . . . and his best friend Peter . . . and Barbara.

He went below, as seven bells sounded in the evening watch. He backed down the forecastle companionway, ready to sling his hammock. Aft at the bos'n's table, he saw his friends playing cards. A lantern flickered fitfully over their faces as they waved him over. But his was the midnight watch; it was time for sleep. He shook his head, and joined the bodies cocooned and gently swaying in their hammocks forward, returning some written pages and scraps of paper to the snoring body in one; it was another letter from or to a wife or lover. The main deck and forecastle were crowded with hammocks, supplies, guns, equipment and cargo everywhere, and one ailing pirate in the cockpit. The rest of the prisoners were even more densely packed below in the cable tier. An alert man with two pistols and a musket, who happened to be the cook during this watch, kept a wary eye and ear on them, just below some of *Cormorant's* crew. The guard duty was relieved every watch. Nathan wondered if Bowman was with them, but soon drifted off.

After standing the uneventful midnight watch aloft, he was anxious to return and join those in the land of dreams, and crawled eagerly back into his hammock to sleep until breakfast.

Hours later, though it seemed like minutes, someone was shaking him.

"Nathan! Cap'n wants you on the quarterdeck," Tom Howard said urgently. "It's six bells in the morning watch—and there's a ship following us!"

A ship! He was instantly awake. It could mean nothing, but . . . Nathan knew better than to delay in any case. He quickly slipped on his roundabout jacket and hurried aft. There were still four snoring forms in their hammocks, swinging gently to the motion of the ship—Howard would soon destroy their peace, too.

The early morning breeze, just starting to freshen, was delightful— still cool, but promising a warm day. The sun was just breaking the horizon off the larboard quarter, the wind from the southeast. The darkness was still dissipating to the west. Nathan saw no clouds and no land. As he made his way to the quarterdeck, he saw Turner and Reynolds staring abeam, off the larboard quarter, where the loom of sails of a two-masted ship, hull down, was becoming clearly visible, on the same tack as *Cormorant.*

"Bowman!" Turner shouted to the *Scourge* midshipman, after a nod to Nathan. The Captain seemed calm, smoking his pipe and leaning against the binnacle. But the number of men gathered near the helm was anything but usual. Bowman, whom Nathan had hardly seen or spoken to since the recapture, now approached Turner. Nathan knew that Turner had wanted to "persuade" him to help *Cormorant*, in exchange for better treatment during and after this voyage.

Two of the crew held pistols trained at nothing in particular, but Nathan could see several weapons near the wheel.

"All hands to their stations, Mister Reynolds," said the Captain quietly, and the new mate strode forward shouting orders.

"Nathan, I will have some of the same questions for you that I have for Bowman, so kindly keep your berth here for the time being. Later we may need you aloft, as well. Hanson, ease your helm. Ease the braces!" The sails of *Cormorant* filled again as she hauled off to the west; not her desired course, but calculated to once again prolong a chase. The other vessel instantly came around, and now was almost directly astern, bows on. Their worst fears were realized.

Turner squinted at the pursuer, perhaps three leagues distant now, less than ten miles. A dozen pairs of eyes followed his. The Captain rapped his pipe on the taffrail and looked hard at Nathan and Bowman. There would be many questions, but the first one Nathan knew.

"Well, is that *Scourge?*"

Nathan nodded, certain that the long night with little sleep would now be followed by an equally grim day, with every man needed for duty.

Bowman remained motionless.

"It is *Scourge*, is it not, sir? You know the orders," said Nathan.

"It is all right, Nathan," said Turner.

"Now!" Nathan suddenly demanded of Bowman.

"Nathan, let me . . ." Turner began.

Nathan saw Bowman's insolent stare and something snapped. He grabbed a pistol, cocked it—loaded or not—and shoved the muzzle hard in the man's belly. Bowman gasped and went down, doubled over. Nathan jerked him upright and bore his face into those startled, pain-filled eyes.

"You answer me now, or by God I will send you to Hell this minute!"

"Yes, yes," croaked Bowman, hate and fear flickering across his face as he turned away. Nathan marveled at his own effectiveness while at the same time felt sickened that he had fallen so low. He was a man of peace who had vowed never to resort to violence; now he readily threatened to kill—and had killed.

The ship's routine went on almost as before; except that wherever more than a few men were gathered, talk reverted to their chances. They had heard of a surprise that Nathan Jeffries was working on. Their little popguns were loaded but not run out. Try to keep their powder dry. The sails were constantly trimmed, never made to Turner's satisfaction. Midday mess was subdued; no jovial skirmish over the grog took place this time, as was usual. Howard and his new cronies were quiet. The next hours were the longest Nathan could remember.

Thirteen

Northwest of Catonville – *February 1812*

Peter Hughes gazed up at the northern night sky, broken by empty poplars and gangly pines—he probably should have stayed in relative safety with Professor Bailey and his delightful niece. Her sounds of pleasure were echoed maddeningly in the northwesterly breeze among the bare branches. Nathan Jeffries would have compared their sighing to the surf—did his one-time friend feel this breeze, wherever he was? Peter sighed. Nathan was still alive somewhere. When they were boys, they came often to this forest, several miles from his mother's cabin, to listen to the night and the spirits of Peter's ancestors. But tonight he was meeting someone still part of *this* world.

They approached noiselessly from the west, one older man and one younger, of the Shawnee tribe now living west of the Ohio Territory. Under the moonlight they signed to Peter, and the older man approached. His long, black hair was covered by a faded tricorn hat adorned with two eagle feathers. He was dressed in deerskin leggings and a coat decorated with bears' teeth and red painted trimmings. His large, brown face was wrinkled, but the black eyes were bright, and his prominent nose dipped majestically. The older man spoke in English.

"Tecumseh told me to find the young brave Wasabogoa, or Wapalaneathy. But I see only a boy wearing the clothes of the white man. Have you seen no Shawnee?"

"Yes, Grey Wolf, I have . . . I am Wasabogoa, Dark Sun, or Peter Hughes," said Peter, accepting the insult with no apparent emotion.

"Your people moved from North Carolina to Tennessee and now live west of the Poconos and the Ohio; there is nothing for you in this land stained by the white man."

"My people?" said Peter, looking at the young man, who had said nothing. "My people made my mother a pariah, an outcast. My people have abandoned us; they are no better than the lying Yankee. Don't talk to me about the Shawnee who left me and my mother to die."

The young man, who had remained silent up until now, stepped closer. His small, lithe form was covered in a simple tunic and loin-cloth, beaded headband and moccasins. He carried a knife in a scabbard strapped on his left side, and a musket slung over his right shoulder. Now he said a few angry words in Shawnee.

"Yes," said Peter. "I live among the lying Yankee. Speak in English, little one, if you can. I understand your words but choose English as my tongue for now."

"For now?" said the young man haughtily. "I'm surprised you remember any of the ways of your ancestors. You, the great inventor for the white invaders—and they stole all of your inventions anyway!"

"*Poosetha*? Who is this tagalong?" said Peter, sounding bored.

"I am Banded Snake," hissed the wiry youth, rearing up and then crouching, hand reaching for his knife. "And you would do well to remember that. We are cousins, I have been told; though I find it hard to believe."

"Silence! We did not come here to bicker," said Grey Wolf, feathers twitching as he shook his head and raised his hand imperiously.

"Why did you come here?" Peter asked. "Just to—"

"Just to deliver a message, Peterhughes. Tecumseh asks that you meet with a new British contact. Actually an American who poses as a—"

"Who is it?"

"The white man is here in Baltimore; he is the rich shipping man, Richard Auster. He can supply almost everything we need, even guns and powder, but—"

"Richard Auster!"

Now his nightmares made sense—he should have foreseen this!

But Grey Wolf was right. He was only half-Shawnee, and his sight was not clear. Of all the individuals on earth to work with against the Americans! Even if Nathan could forgive him for Barbara . . . how could he betray his friend again?

"What did you say?"

"You are asked to meet with him as soon as possible, in Annapolis. His local contact there is the harbormaster, Eli Newirth, or his son."

"Annapolis? Why there?"

"That is a good place to hide secrets," said Grey Wolf. "That is what we were told."

"And then you may be asked to help deliver the weapons across the great lake—unless you fear traveling that far to the northwest, the Canadian border." The two young men glared at each other.

"You know, after all this time with your friends, the white Americans," Banded Snake continued, "we wondered if you would ever honor your ancestors and fight the settlers who lie and take our land, spreading death and disease across the great river."

"Are we talking about the British, or the American traitor, Auster? You trust the British priorities?"

"They do not seek our lands, only our friendship and freedom," said Grey Wolf. "Look at the Winnebago and the Keokuk, the Minnesota. They are still free and hunt with our brothers in Canada. Tecumseh has gathered many tribes together to fight the white men. It is our last chance. We join as one, or we die one by one, disappear like saplings in a fire."

"It is true," said Peter, "that the British soldiers do not like the Yankees, and promise you guns, protection, supplies. They sometimes fight alongside our warriors to burn the Yankee forts and settlements and take back what is ours. But other times—"

"It is not too late for you to rejoin the old ways. They are good ways. After you finish with the Yankees—"

"Are they? I am no more accepted there than I am here. I will be considered an oddity wherever I am. Even if I was willing to forget the fact that my mother's family left us here."

"What is your answer then?"

"My answer is, I will help you, but I must also uncover the mystery of my mother and father . . . and a few people here . . . remain important to me. Someday, if I stay in the west, if I survive, I may be accepted. I am honored that you came here, and I regret that I cannot at this time offer you the hospitality of—"

"We did not seek it, Wasabogoa," said the old man sadly.

"Nor do we want it," said Banded Snake. "The smell of this white man is making me ill."

"It appears the boy you brought along is in need of your medicine, wise one," said Peter, "or perhaps more of mother's milk."

"You die for that!" hissed the young man, who pulled out his knife— and in a flash was pinned on his back, Peter's knife at his throat.

"If anyone is to die tonight, foolish boy, it will be you," said Peter calmly. The young man had stopped struggling, realizing the futility of his efforts.

"A brave but inexperienced warrior," sighed the old man. "I brought him along as a favor to his mother, my sister. She asked me to . . . well, your mother's cousin wishes that you would rejoin your people now and bury the tomahawk. I feel the sadness about your mother—"

"Yes," said Peter grimly, letting Banded Snake struggle to his feet, and handing him his own knife. He thought better of inflicting further humiliation on his would be antagonist. "Thank you for honoring me with this mission. And tell my mother's people that . . . tell them whatever you think is right."

"So be it, and know that the Prophet and Tecumseh will winter again near the western bank of the Erie. Farewell," said the old man, signing. Peter stood nodding, his eyes large, dark pools, watching the two men disappear silently into the brown and snow-covered underbrush.

February 20, 1812, was the first conference with Catherine and Amy that had William in attendance. Captain Jeffries was not always rational and coherent, but at least he was temporarily sober. Amy had salvaged the best of the man to help find Nathan and deflect some of the attacks in the newspapers. Both now believed that Catherine was indeed intent on ruining Richard Auster's reputation.

"But there seems little to show for it, my dear Catherine."

"We must be patient, sir, I . . ."

William and Amy smiled at each other.

"Patience," said William.

"I am sorry, I have no right to—"

"Not at all, Catherine, you are one of our only supporters now, and we are eternally grateful for your help and efforts on our behalf."

Tears welled up in Catherine's brown eyes.

The banging on the front door startled all of them.

In the crowded front room, Catherine herself answered the door; the wind from outside forcing sparks to spray out of the hearth.

"It's a parcel," she said, sneaking the messenger a shilling twopence and handing the package to Amy who steadied her rocker and put down her knitting to open it.

"It is from the harbormaster in Newburyport," she said, reading the note and then standing ramrod straight.

"It . . . it is . . . Nathan's glove . . . I knitted for him, with his initials NJ."

"Amy!" William took the note.

"From wreckage believed to be that of *Bucephalus*—oh no!"

"Oh, William!"

Catherine and William tried to catch Amy as she collapsed on the rug near the fire.

Off Antigua

When he was thirteen, in 1805, during the Essex Junto, Nathan fought with a young Richard Auster aboard his father's ship—the fight ended in the water, where the larger Nathan panicked and almost drowning, gave up the fight. Nathan might be a coward, some said now, but others said he is a very honest and modest man, pleasant but not exciting, but has he no courage? Most close friends said he was an exemplary friend and loyal—and too large to antagonize. Except for Richard Auster,

of course. Nathan's mother Amy had pushed him in another direction—
some reported that with laughter—a sea lawyer of the worst kind, a man
afraid to defend his family honor. Then more humiliation when his father
was accused of firing early in the duel in 1807. Bless his mother's soul,
she would not allow him to fight, after the Quasi-War. But your father
broke his promise, and look what has happened. Do not argue with me,
son, not about this. Do not break your solemn promise to your mother . . .
and to God . . . you must be true to Quaker vows . . . our faith. This is for
your sake and mine, son, and you know it is wrong to resort to violence.
Remember that, and please save yourself for higher pursuits. Don't break
my heart, Nathan.

Only Peter had seemed to fully appreciate Nathan's dilemma. Peter
had saved Nathan, then turned around and betrayed him. But Nathan
knew that Peter was the most brilliant man or woman he knew, of any
skin color, who lived a dual life that was forced upon him by the frustration of competing loyalties. He knew little about his father, but his
mother was the beautiful Elizabeth Hughes who was all Shawnee squaw.
Peter had warned him that the disaster of 1807 would not be the last major fiasco; ugly events seem to shadow him. How unfortunate that Peter
had not warned him about Barbara, Nathan thought bitterly. Now, at the
lofty age of 21, Nathan was second in command of this fast-sailing, 300-
ton brig, copper-bottomed, with bags and bales and casks of grain and cod
and homespun and perhaps a few illicit muskets wrapped in dry goods.
Rifle muskets. Wads and powder. Just the cargo for his Captain Mathew
Turner's plantation slave-owning friends on Antigua—if *Cormorant* managed to escape capture again, or some other disaster.

When Nathan returned to the quarterdeck near sunset, it was crowded. Turner, his new number two and Bowman all seemed to be shouting
at each other all at once—an amusing scenario, but no one was laughing.
The two men at the wheel, Jack Logan, now the acting bos'n and quartermaster, and the new master's mate, the feisty little Corker, O'Reilley,
were grim-faced, standing the watch. Turner and Bowman were near the

starboard taffrail, gesticulating and shouting, until Turner finally pushed Bowman away, while a few other hands near the main fife rail were trying to listen to the words while trying to look busy with their duties.

All hands were ready, and every man would be needed above deck. The six-pounders, port and starboard combined, were loaded, cartridges and shot in the racks, not yet run out; but it seemed like a futile gesture. Six little popguns, six-pounders, and not even enough hands to man them. They dare not let loose the prisoners to serve aloft or as gun crews. Meanwhile *Scourge* boasted 6 eighteen-pounder carronades in a broadside, twelve guns, possibly a swivel, and at least four times as many men.

Every golden sail was set; the late ruddy light seemed to burnish faces and wood as it slanted across the deck. Light westerly airs washed over the starboard quarter, easing the ship along in an orderly fashion, her stern rising and falling sedately in the light, long, even swell. Pitch increased and she sometimes buried her bow into the steep waves.

The captive Bowman shook his head impatiently, and then O'Reilley spoke in an most agitated manner, ignoring Nathan at first and then staring at him.

"Captain! You know the men agree with me—and Bowman knows that damn *Scourge* and her captain! For your sake and the sake of this crew, we insist a change in our course of action, since—"

"Some men agree with you, maybe," snapped Nathan.

"We will resist, sir," said Turner calmly. "Anyone who feels ready to submit now will go below . . . or overboard." A heated discussion requires two to rise to the bait, and Turner refused to do so again.

"But this is madness! Soon Jumby Bay will be southwest—"

"Silence, sir—"

"How can we possibly resist—"

"Shut your hole, O'Reilley," said Nathan, "or by heaven you and Bowman can jaw in the cable tier for the duration. Helm, steer two points starboard! Haul your larboard tacks and braces there! O'Reilley, give them a hand there, if you please."

One look at Nathan, with his eyes slitted, now slapping a belaying pin in his big palm, silenced both men.

After a long watchful day, sleep was unavoidable. Nathan headed down the companionway ladder to sling his hammock, half asleep already. No one disturbed him during the dogwatches. But at first wakening, he shot up the ladder to learn his fate.

On the quarterdeck, Turner nodded at Nathan while Logan stood at the leeward rail gazing at the brilliant moonlit night sky, the invisible but nearby lethal coast.

"We'll be able to make our offing."

They both laughed.

"Bowman ain't gonna join us, Nate," said Jack, now back at the wheel, with his usual taciturn manner.

"Oh?"

"He scuffed it up with one of his own Brits—a couple of heads were knocked, sir—he did not give good as he got, so . . . but ol' Bowman he's laid up for several weeks, they tell me." This was an elaborate speech for the laconic Jack Logan.

Turner hid a smile in his beard.

"Very good. Send the hands aloft, every other gun, if you please. Topsails and headsails."

"Aye, sir."

The ebb happened to coincide with the bright moon that peeked beneath a few distant velvet clouds as *Cormorant* worked her way along the Atlantic coast of the Nonsuch Island, dangerously close to shoal water, not far enough east to calm any responsible navigator, master or pilot. The sails were now dying blue steel in the moonlight. And there was O'Reilley in oil-skin weather coat again coming up the quarterdeck from forward.

"Wind's fresh out of the nor'nor'east, Captain, and veering," said O'Reilly, shoulders hunched under the slick hood, small face drenched with salt spray. "No bottom . . . yet . . . but soundings—"

"If it doesn't veer more than a point, we can do it. It will be a long beat to the sea. Thank God for the ebb."

"Too much leeway, Captain! We must not follow this . . . lucky novice's course! We's near abreast of Indian Town Point, and with no other sail in the offing. Willoughby Bay is—we'll be on the rocks before ye can spit . . . we must wear—"

"Prepare for another tack, Mister O'Reilley—that will take your personal attention on the fo'c's'le!"

"Sir—"

"Now, damn your eyes, O'Reilley!"

"Aye, sir!"

"It appears we have beat the odds again, Mister Jeffries," said the angry Irishman, with all the passion but none of the generosity of his type, brushing by the big man on his way forward again. Nathan could only feel sorry.

"It does indeed, Mister—"

"Sail ho!" rang from the maintop.

"Where away?"

"Two points on the larboard beam! Looks like a topsail schooner, sir! Fast rake!"

"Belay that order, O'Reilley! Bear up, sir!

"Back the mainsail! Back your helm!"

"Heave you lubbers!"

"Clew up topsails!

Echoes shouted with precision all the way to the head.

"Heave to!"

"Aye, sir."

"Very well, Mr. O'Reilley. Well done."

"Thank you, Captain. Gun crews ready, sir." The man was efficient.

Nathan and Turner looked at each other. In the next half hour, the grim truth was plain to all. Groans could be heard as the race seemed already lost.

"*Scourge*, blast him!" said Turner. "This was planned all along!" *Scourge*, beating into the wind, close-hauled on the starboard tack, clawing toward them less than a league off the starboard quarter, would overhaul her victim before the midnight watch. It was time for *Cormorant* to bear up again and steer southwest, to prolong the chase and avoid the reef around the island. But it would make little difference. The wind would inevitably cause a collision by eight bells; boarded, sunk or captured by *Scourge*, or her guts ripped up, strewn on the teeth of those beautiful, deadly coral reefs, sometimes less than a fathom below the surface. Nathan nodded to Turner, noting Reynold's sour looks, the clear skies and full moon rising. Visibility was at least a league; they were in extreme danger for hours. Would they see the sun again?

"Captain," said Reynolds, "Tell Mister . . . Nate here that we do not want to do anything to that boat yonder—at this distance any move on our part, without another signal of surrender—and we don' want that. Even if *Scourge* don't blow us to bits, I know we'll git severe punishment for all aboard, for doing his best to keep this ship away from that one. As it is, many of us—"

"Do not speak to me!" shouted Turner. "Go bother Jeffries."

"We will sail as the Captain wishes," said Nathan confidently, "and I have no doubt he will make the right decision." His look discouraged further speech from Reynolds.

God is overdoing this torture, Nathan thought to himself, briefly awash in self-pity. Captured again—by that same miserable tool of Richard Auster's—or on the reef . . . and whatever happened to his father's *Bucephalus* that he lost? Could one man be so unlucky, so dogged with catastrophic failure, at the moment of salvation?

Nate was no deep thinker, but as usual he could figure out that his mother had been right about everything—again. But hard to think about anything but the pain on the reef or torture from Coxe—perhaps both! The Quakers do not believe in fate. But they have faith. To sleep, perchance to dream . . . that is correct, sir, focus yourself on the sea bottom or in some equally useful fashion.

There were only the two vessels in sight—almost as if it was planned.

"Our escape was too easy," Nathan said. "They came down the Straights long before us, to prepare this little *tête-à-tête*. We just need to find the rest of the trap. The rocks to leeward there are no doubt part of it. The reef circles the entire island, but there is a channel to the naval dockyard and Falmouth Harbor."

"How in the name o' Jezebel do ye' know that?"

Nathan smiled, "I've been here before. A long time ago, but I remember."

"We will only get one chance. If we fail, they will probably slaughter us all. In which case, submission would have been the sensible course."

"I know, Captain," Nathan said. He concealed his impatience and refrained from reminding Turner that this long chase with no better alternative except abject and disastrous surrender had frayed the nerves of every man.

"Baltimore-built, do you fancy!" O'Reilley complained, watching their fate bear down on them. "One of our own craft against us! My word, she is fast! Yessir, she's got her teeth showing! *Scourge*, I reckon, will be the last of us," the man said with an eager tone.

"I know," said Turner and Nate in unison, and both laughed. But, unlike most Irish, O'Reilley never laughed. Yet he called himself a good Anglican, not Papist, nor a severe Calvinist. More importantly, they needed him to help Tom Howard and the rest of the able-bodied crew.

Scourge was already clewing up her topgallant, full of men and with carronade muzzles protruding from either side. Six on a broadside, more than enough to sink *Cormorant* with the sun—or bright full moon.

All hands were on deck; every man aboard knew his assignment. As *Cormorant* lowered her flag in token of surrender, observers on the swift schooner saw little activity on deck of their prey. Quartermaster at the wheel, the Captain and a few hands staring aft. Coxe, master and commander of the British privateer and naval cutter, knew that this large but otherwise typical Yankee merchant brig had no more than a dozen crew in any case, and was not surprised that he could see no guns . . . or prisoners. *Cormorant* probably had no teeth, only empty popguns, empty words. Thank the Lord for their passive, greedy foolishness! Another easy capture. This time they'd keep that bastard Nate Jeffries. They were even spared the need for a shot across her bows, though the guns were ready to fire, double shotted and slow matches lit.

"A little closer," said Turner to the helm, as Nathan nodded. "That's it, lad. Now, would be a good time to let the wind take her."

Cormorant lay hove-to with jib and stay sail on the port tack and the foretopsail aback. All the other square sails were loosely furled. The stu'n'sail was luffing. *Scourge*, now with only topsail and mainsail showing, wore neatly and heaved to just a hundred yards directly to windward of them, as if pinning her quarry to the distant beach, her starboard quarter facing *Cormorant's* port bow, ready with a touch of the helm to deliver a broadside. This was the usual maneuver. The prey apparently helpless, obviously supine, poorly handled, too close to *Scourge* to escape now even if she had thought to—and so of course she had surrendered. The launch filled with armed men and a dozen oars lowered away to fight the steep waves, like a giant water bug struggling over the watery rims of a scalloped horizon, spume blasting from gun'l. The distance between two vessels narrowed, the launch rising and falling in the moon's cold, angry glare.

The men on *Cormorant* were tense, waiting for the order, watching the approaching boat, slipping up the troughs and skipping crests. The enemy was now less than pistol shot range—fifty yards to windward; a dozen men at the oars, another dozen ready to climb the sides of the brig with a rush of death, and Nathan could clearly see cutlass blades gleaming.

"Do you think it is time, Mr. Jeffries, to greet them?" asked Turner, smiling through that gray, wet mop of a face.

Fourteen

Broadsides

This was the moment! Heart pounding, Nathan shouted forward.

"Haul on the fore braces, men! All hands aloft! Prepare to shake out all sail! Starboard three points!"

Nathan looked at Turner again. The old Captain nodded.

"Fire as your target bears, Mr. O'Reilley!"

O'Reilley went to each larboard gun, and each banged at the hapless longboat. As ten of the best topmen hurled themselves into the top hamper, the rest pulled for their lives on the braces to heave over the foretopsail against the wind as *Cormorant* fell off. Nathan felt pangs of guilt as he saw the last shot hit the longboat. He watched the crew near him clew up the big stu'n'sail temporarily, with O'Reilley back to his station forward. She was pulling away! Shots were even fired from the boat's survivors, now at their stern, nearly awash and breaking up. Nathan heard a lucky musket ball thud into the mainchains.

"Good shooting, Mister O!" Nathan shouted. "Extra beer for number four gun!"

"Thank you, Jeffries!"

"Aye, she's taken the bait," growled Turner, studying the black schooner. "But we'll only get this one chance."

How many more times will he say that, thought Nathan. Starboard guns would now get their chance—the same crews had simply moved to the unengaged side.

They had gambled that the predator would tack, once she saw the prey wear as if to fly off the wind. The escape attempt made sense; running to the south again, into Willoughby Bay maybe, *Cormorant* would be no worse off than before, and at least safe from the coral and rocks. With the sky still dark she might elude her pursuer, especially if the latter delayed to pick up her boat's crew in the water—but the chase would end quickly, and this time there would be no mercy.

The schooner's stern, with *Scourge* emblazoned on it, had swung around neatly and she was now showing her port side, sails still luffing. Nathan looked to Turner, who nodded.

"All hands! Loosen all sail! Helm, hard a larboard!"

Would *Cormorant* come about? The two men at the wheel fought to bring her over through the wind as the big sails dropped on both masts. The stu'n'sail, full again, would help her tack.

"Heave over the headsails! She's tacking!"

For a moment it looked like they would be in irons, hung up in stays. But she came over, and the deck sloped sharply as the quartermaster fought against her tendency to fly up again.

"Ease off! Two more points off the wind! Steady on that course!"

Scourge, caught off guard by the surprising change, had decided to take advantage of the opportunity presented for an easy broadside and remained on the starboard tack. It wouldn't be long now.

"O'Reilley, are your men ready?"

"Aye, sir!"

In a Herculean effort, most of the hands had quickly completed sheeting off and run down to O'Reilley's station on the starboard, and now windward, foredeck.

"Two more points to port."

Cormorant surged bravely along, with the wind now more than a point abaft the beam, in a race with the schooner—except the two vessels were on an oblique collision course. The moment of truth was only moments away.

"Will she hold?" asked Turner. "Ah!"

The black sides of the other vessel suddenly erupted in flame and smoke, and Nathan heard the terrifying roar of the six guns, even in this brisk wind. At that range, they couldn't miss.

There was a howling rush of wind and a scream forward as he heard three or four balls crash into *Cormorant*. No time for that now. He felt a writhing, tingling in his chest. Even Turner's voice sounded strange.

"I'm going forward, Mr. Jeffries. That's . . . where it is going to happen. I need you here, to get us out and away, if . . . all goes well."

"Aye, sir," Nathan croaked.

"Nathan, that is—you are bleeding . . . that is your blood!"

"It is nothing but a scratch, Captain . . . I am not—look out!"

The schooner was terrifyingly large now, all her sails set, as the two ships charged toward a meeting point less than a pistol shot ahead. In a moment, it would be too late to avoid a collision, even if one of the captains did lose his nerve. There was not even enough time for another broadside from the schooner, though Nathan heard the higher pitched sounds of small arms banging their way.

God! He could see men waving, gesticulating angrily from the other vessel. They would not give way, and the long bowsprit of the schooner started to fall away towards the wind at the last, still disappearing behind the brig's forward rigging. Coxe apparently deciding too late to avoid the collision.

"Hold your course," said Nathan grimly, bareheaded, his hair like wet straw, tortured in the wind, flat eyes squinting in the direction of their pursuer, shivering in his roundabout in the warm spray.

Two events occurred in rapid succession: there was a roar from the starboard side of *Cormorant* as the three guns went off together, right into the bow of *Scourge*. During the last run, the canvas concealing them had been quickly removed and the matches lit. All of the other weapons had also been directed at the bow. The crash of the guns was followed almost in one sound by the crash of the schooner's bow into the side of the brig, at an acute angle, just behind the starboard cathead. With a shuddering jar, both ships settled in the water. Nathan was thrown against the leeward taffrail, and several men lost their footing. He pulled himself over the splintered, bloody bulwark to see one man fall from the schooner into the sea.

The jib boom of the schooner snapped off, and Nathan heard a crack and loud thud as the schooner's foretopmast wobbled on its cap. The topgallant spar slapped down against the foreshrouds and then cracked and toppled onto her deck. The rest of *Scourge's* bowsprit was swinging overhead, roughly amidships, as her stem slid and shrieked against brig's sides, grinding and breaking her female figurehead with its hair of snakes as her bow swung along with the wind. Her hull, more delicate than *Cormorant's*, even with bulwarks and decks reinforced for the twelve pounders, was less suitable for this rough treatment. The two ships were roughly the same length, but *Cormorant* was more stout, with higher freeboard, and more rounded construction; better suited for this abuse, a maddening blend of guts and sweat and despair in the warm, driving nor'easterly.

But now the wind, still veering, was swinging *Scourge's* starboard side towards *Cormorant*, and some of her guns could almost be brought to bear. Men who weren't firing their pistols and muskets or brandishing their cutlasses were frantically heaving the cannon around towards their opponents aboard *Cormorant*. The two hulls were almost bow to stern now. It was time for him to play his part. Nathan heard men forward shouting "Reload, reload! Run-out!" In the powdery smoke he couldn't tell if it was from *Cormorant*, or *Scourge*, or both. His own men were firing chain shot, broken barrel staves, some old cannister and grape, bar shot and a few round shot, whatever was handy. Other crewmen would take shots with a handy musket or even pistol. There was a large crowd of attackers on the cathead and ruined bowsprit of *Scourge* waiting for a chance to cross over onto the mainchains of the brig. But Nathan knew he would find his target on the quarterdeck of the schooner. From the foremast shrouds he could see down to the stern of the enemy. There he was, Coxe; snarling, jumping around the deck like a giant spider, yelling and gesticulating, clubbing the helmsman and then Clough with his cat, barely glancing at *Cormorant*. In a moment Nathan was aiming his cocked musket at that creature, not 50 yards away.

Just as Nathan pulled the trigger, Clough lost his footing on the rocking deck and then was hit by the musket ball meant for Coxe. Through the crack and smoky roar of the musket, Nathan saw Clough fall into Coxe. Both men went down. Nathan heard a ball snap the ratline near his head, and half fell to the deck without breaking anything. Blood smeared his chest, and a sharp pain came with every breath. He pulled out his loaded pistol and checked flint and touch-hole. No sign of the giant spider now. Why could he not see or hear clearly?

Cormorant was in trouble; if she didn't get away quickly, she would be destroyed or captured. Time to return to the helm and get away—if they could. Several men seemed to be walking toward him now; Turner was one of them. The gunfire was continuous. None of *Scourge's* larboard-men were needed on that side and their overwhelming numbers would bring about a speedy capture of the Baltimore brig if enough should make it over. Then three of her starboard guns banged out as her leaders barked orders, shouting against the wind. The three guns of *Cormorant* fired at almost the same time. Their explosions and the acrid smoke filled the air again, and was not so quickly blown away. A geyser of splinters ballooned up the air as iron crashed into wood, and he heard screams and saw men fall on both vessels. Several things happened at once. Nathan saw sharp-shooters in the maintop of *Scourge* aim at the quarterdeck—at him—and at the Captain approaching him. He forced himself to stand where he was; a lead musket ball hammered the rail near him; he saw the wood shake with the impact. Then the man at the wheel groaned and fell to the deck. Mr. Logan took over the helm again with a nod to Nathan. But when he looked again, Jack was gone.

Then he looked over at the schooner, and saw a man throw a grappling iron aboard the brig to insure that they would stay together; the waves had lessened slightly and *Cormorant's* fate seemed settled. Where was Turner? He saw O'Reilley busy with the guns. Red stained the planks, guts strewn among muskets and pistols. Fighting nausea, Nathan aimed his pistol at the scowling man heaving on the grappling hook; they were almost at eye level, the enemy in white duck trousers and dark blue coat. He pulled the trigger, and the gun kicked as the powder exploded. Through the smoke he saw the man bend over and disappear. His latest killing—murder, really—of the new year, he thought bitterly. Nathan swallowed his bile as he saw another horrible sight; another longboat from

Scourge was now approaching their weather side, where there was no one to resist them. They were doomed.

"Cut that line!" he roared, almost screaming. The grappling iron was caught in the mainshrouds, fortunately within easy reach, and the line was cut by another hand, wielding an ax, burying the ax in the gunwhale with the fury of his blow. The two vessels were both hove-to with *Scourge* to windward, but gradually her starboard stern was making its way aft along *Cormorant's* starboard side. The wind was almost easterly now; only a few of the big guns could now be trained at any target. Shots were still being fired from the longboat; they were now less than fifty yards off, fighting wind, current and small-arms fire from *Cormorant*. They could not approach without the risk of collision with their opponent. Thank God for Tom Howard! He and several men were making life Hell for that longboat.

Jack Logan watched him, knowing instinctively what Nathan was planning. "Ease the helm to starboard," he said. *Scourge's* maintop windage was pulling them around in that direction. It was still dark, and flashes of gunfire had become more scattered—lovely, ruddy, loud sparks in the night, topsails were luffing.

"We're going to come about on the larboard tack. Now!"

This was their last chance; their defeat otherwise assured. He knew that Coxe was preparing for another boarding attempt. The enemy's fire, and especially their aim, had slackened; hits were only sporadic. Nathan could dimly see men clambering on her rigging to repair her injuries aloft. How many holes between wind and water? Was *Cormorant* sinking? Where was that damned carpenter?

"Braces! Haul for your lives!"

The yards slowly came around, and wind bellied the sails. She was pulling away! The deck heeled over to larboard as she now caught the northerly wind square on her beam.

He heard groans from one of the less stoic wounded near the mainmast. Rigging hummed and creaked as *Cormorant* plowed to the west, with the yards hard over. The breeze over the starboard side was dying, however. It was getting darker, and except for the wake and a murmur from the men, it was quiet.

But he knew they had not escaped.

"Sir, he means to run us into Half Moon Bay," said Jack Logan.

Scourge, still faster and more weatherly, would race towards *Cormorant's* starboard quarter. She could gradually force the brig ashore, or into action again, cutting off any chance of escape to the sea. If they didn't choose the correct course now, they might still be sunk—or prisoners—before the morning. It might already be too late.

"We'll wear, Mister Logan," Nathan said.

Reynolds was also bleeding and black from cuts and powder.

"He will not yield, Nate—" he began.

"Keep your mouth shut!" roared Nathan. "Starboard a point, helm!"

It truly looked as if Coxe would hold his course and the two ships crash into each other, with considerable damage if not the loss of both. But Nathan knew this was their only chance.

After wearing, *Cormorant* had run down to within a cable's length of the enemy's stern. Seeing that maneuver, *Scourge* tacked and beat southeastward, then wore in turn to confront her stubborn prey head on. This was the last dance, the final card.

"He's heading down, sir, he's bearing away!"

"Aye, sir. Course east by sou'east."

"Nigh on six and a half knots!" shouted the man with the chip log.

"By the deep five! Coral sand!"

Six knots, even with their damage and enough water for now. Five fathoms, nine feet under their keel. The waves were still ominously peaking into enormous green and silver caps in the lurid moonlight.

"Archibald Bloody Coxe," said Nathan to no one in particular. Balancing on the rocking deck, he heard O'Reilley order his gun crews to their guns, to be ready again for action, loaded with dismantling shot.

"So much for ambush," said Nathan, in spite of his pain and fear.

"So you have said," yelled Reynolds in his ear. "Guns already run out!" He was nearly dancing with anxiety.

The crew looked to him. They seemed calm.

"Prepare for another volley, O'Reilley," Nathan said.

"Are you mad! You aint' the captain, Nate Jeffries!"

"Maybe you would surrender."

"Well, at least we need more time! Wear ship, man! We need sea room, or we'll be trapped against the Green Island Shoal or Nonsuch Bay."

The two vessels were on convergent courses, *Scourge* running before the wind less than three cable-lengths distant; *Cormorant* close hauled to leeward.

"Port your helm," said Nathan, quietly, to the Captain. "With your permission, sir. We can fight her."

Turner nodded, saying nothing.

"Steady. Steady. Meet her."

The crew stood transfixed as the bows of the two ships, though still distant, crept ever closer—again.

Nathan shook off the mesmerizing slow motion of the impending collision.

"You are deliberately—"

"Gun crews, are you ready?" The men cheered.

"We may have a little surprise for him," said Nathan. "Ease your helm, man!"

"Aye, sir!"

Every stitch of canvas, all plain sail, was drawing.

After one of the longest days, it promised to be one of the longest nights Nathan could remember. The deck near the mate's cabin below was still stained with blood. That moon simmering near the southwest horizon could be his last. Nathan prayed that he would live to see the dawn, his position now nearly to windward.

Nathan gulped. Soon they must bear off again! They could hear the surf onshore thundering, pounding on the rocks.

"Mister Jeffries," said Turner, "I wish—"

"Captain, I suggest we stop running and haul our wind, tack and beat towards *Scourge* again."

"What, man, are you daft?" asked O'Reilley.

"Nathan, we skirt shoal water now," said Captain Turner.

"Deck there!" It was a shout from the foretop. "Sail two points off the larboard bow!"

This electrifying news brought a dozen men to the windward bulwarks. Turner stared at Nathan in shock.

"What is it?" Turner shouted up, after a long look at Nathan.

"Looks large, like a full-rigged man-o'-war, Captain—she could be a frigate, sir. Sailing off the wind, near enough."

The vessel might not be hull up for hours, might even stand away to the east. In any case, had *Scourge* seen her?

Nathan turned to Turner. "It is time, Captain! This is our chance! And the moon won't set 'til near dawn!"

"By God, yes!" shouted Turner. "Might as well be shot for a fortune as a farthing," he said to Nathan, who returned from hauling braces. "Aloft there! Alert us of any change of course—that vessel may be—"

"Deck there! Large sail ain't American! I can see her ensign! She's British! And overhauling us fast!"

"I think I know her, sir," said Jack, relieving at the helm. "She looks like our British Frenchie *Guerriere*, 38-guns. And she'll be wanting to add some of us to her crew, I'm thinking."

Turner groaned, "Any flag, sir, but *Guerriere*! Mister O'Reilley, send the men to the braces, and prepare to come about!"

"But, Captain—"

"Now, sir!"

In a few minutes, the critical maneuver began. If they hung in stays, the jig was up.

"Ease your helm up," growled Turner to the two men at the wheel. Did she have enough way on? Or would they end up in irons?

"Cap'n, she's hauling her wind!"

"Clew up courses! Sheets in! Tacks aboard! Braces there! Back the main! Ready about! Hard over!" Turner shouted. Foresails luffing, *Cormorant's* bow began to swing through the eye of the wind, forced around by the main topsail pressed back against the mast. *Scourge* also bore up, instantly close-hauled and now almost directly abeam, still on the same tack, but not for long.

"Starboard braces, haul! Foresails! Starboard tacks aboard! Ease your main sheets!" Turner shouted with a practiced eye and confident timing.

"Switch over your headsails! Ease your main topsail braces! Fore t'gallant men, haul!" Though still too distant to see clearly, the men aboard *Scourge* must be staring in astonishment, Nathan thought, as her prey came around to put her starboard bow toward the enemy, and kept turning.

"Braces there! Haul your fore yards around hard to starboard! Haul main braces! Set your starboard tacks! Trim main yards full and by!" The foretopgallant and head sails volleyed as *Cormorant* came around, then the main topsail; a sudden silence fell as the sails filled and she paid off. "Loose and set the topgallants and courses!" Turner shouted.

The wind still dangerously forward of the beam as she kept turning, close-hauled, *Cormorant* soon had the rising wind, now a fresh breeze still out of the west, forward of her beam. Now the brig was beating on a larboard tack, directly toward *Scourg*e, almost head on; on the opposite tack, with all plain sail drawing well, surging toward her fate.

"She's making six knots, sir," said Tom Howard, approaching the two men leaning over the windward quarter. Turner's beard cringed up in what Nathan charitably called a smile. "Send 'About to engage.' We'll soon know," he muttered, nodding at *Scourge*. Their little popguns were loaded and run out again, but could do little more against *Scourge's* carronades. The two ships were less than a cable's length apart, slowly converging; Nathan thought he could see men in the top hamper. The moon was setting; it would soon be darker, and then lit from the sun. The air was clear and the fresh breeze would carry the ships together and into shoal water in a few minutes.

"She's tacking, sir, she's tacking!" shouted one of the crew forward. But they could see for themselves. The bow ahead turned to starboard; yards came around, and they could see the great main boom and foresail swing over from larboard side to starboard. The evolution was neatly done, but now Coxe would have to make up for the lost yardage. He knew as well as Nathan the lack of searoom to leeward, as they approached the wide outer teeth of Mamora Bay and English Harbor at the south end of the island.

"Captain!" shouted O'Reilley, gesturing from the southwest to the towering vessel now racing beside them to windward. "We skirt the reef . . . we must heave to, again, before it is really is too late." He made as if to personally surrender to those black gunports and yellow strip along the hull. "We been spared the true wrath of *Scourge*, and Nate—certainly the young man . . . should be—but we'll not be lucky a second time—"

"Deck there!" came another hail from the maintop. "They's firin' guns! There it is!"

They heard the shouting and saw a flurry of activity from *Scourge's* gun crew, as the forward carronade bore, then a puff of smoke followed by the bang from the starboard bowchaser, both smoke and sound quickly dissipating in the breeze. Nathan fancied he could hear the high-pitched *whurr* of the iron ball, and did see the small geyser of water just off their own starboard bow; but then he could hear no further sound. Soon there would be an order to heave to—and more gunfire.

"This is madness, Captain!" pleaded the second mate. "They mean to—"

"Mr. O'Reilley! Send the men to braces!"

Turner knew that if anyone had the coolness, skill and experience to implement Nathan's own suggestion, Nathan himself was the man; the Captain had already seen what he could achieve.

"Back the fore topsail! Not the main! Clew up the courses! Helm, when she pays off, ease up to southwest and keep her steady."

"Due so'w'st sir, aye," said the quartermaster, with a cool gaze at the schooner, now racing close-hauled to come up on their larboard quarter.

"Sir, we'll soon have Juggy 't leeward," O'Reilley pleaded. "Wind's still veering!"

"Hard up now! Clew up the spanker, Mister O! We'll wait for 'em."

"Aye, aye, sir!" The odd-looking man shouted angrily, shaking his head.

"Prepare to heave to but not yet." They would wait, rocking in the waves, but relatively motionless for Coxe crashing down ahead of them. Those towering muscles of canvas were now beginning to merge as the schooner came up into the wind, less than a hundred yards distant. Even without her foretop, that Baltimore-built craft was a miracle of strength and handiness. But so was *Cormorant*.

The big privateer was just past them now, and preparing for slaughter; the two ships would be side by side again, converging like a recurring nightmare. Men on the larboard side started to cringe away instinctively from the horror to come.

"Steady boys! Stay cool!"

Nobody moved. Not one man let fear get the best of him. Nathan silently prayed that he was not grandstanding and leading these good men to Hell.

Scourge had overhauled them—again; now to windward, heaved to. Nathan thought he saw faces and uniforms now, at the entry port and the quarterdeck; the moon had set but there was enough light to see the launch being lowered. He stared at the boarding party, a dawn attack by small boat, too. *Cormorant* fell off drifting slowly inshore toward the reef, shore off the starboard bow, fore and main topsails acting as brakes on one another.

"It is time. Helm amidships! Weather braces haul!"

"Shift over your head sheets! Foretopsail braces, haul away! Loosen courses! Shake out that stays'l reef! Haul yer guts, my ladies, haul! Open her spanker! Helm, hard over—heave!"

The next few minutes would probably decide the outcome.

The bow of *Cormorant* swung to larboard, and Nathan could almost see the shocked faces of the British crew as their helpless victim suddenly bore off and headed right for them. Then *Cormorant's* bow swung further away, and he glimpsed *Scourge's* stern as she was also coming around on the starboard tack, imitating *Cormorant's* maneuver. There it was! Small-arms fire and the boom of sternchasers. But after two cannons fired with no hits, there was silence again. Nathan could read the faint *Scourge* under the undamaged stern gallery windows as the ship swung to starboard and showed her larboard quarter, then that menacing line of larboard eighteen-pounders.

This was the ultimate gamble. One good broadside at less than two cables' lengths would probably sink *Cormorant*. At best, she would be crippled alow and aloft; crashing iron balls of death or knife-like splinters of smashed wood would create wounds worse than death, horrible injury aboard. Every yard of open water *Cormorant* had put between herself and *Scourge* had made capture less likely; yet during the night, the dogged pursuer had reacquired her quarry. The next few minutes would be critical.

No one spoke. Now with *Scourge* once again to leeward they were less than pistol shot distance, beam to beam, when both ships erupted once again in flame and smoke. Round shot crashed into *Cormorant*, and several lines parted. Nathan heard another scream, but then there was a mighty cheer as the men saw at the last possible moment *Scourge* haul her larboard braces and steer toward the south. Her sails shivered and her broadside showed plainly; then the square sail sagged and dropped forward in a tangle of cordage and canvas.

"By the deep four!"

"We've caught her on her quarter!" one man shouted.

"She's hauling her wind!"

"Aground, you fool! Silence, you men! Steer south!"

That one exchange of broadsides had not brought down the jury-rigged fore topmast of *Scourge*. Her luck had run out with the ebb tide. Struggling to heave to, she was helplessly driven further onto the reef. *Cormorant* watched in amazement as *Scourge* lay heeled over, nearly on her beam ends, the hull already slowly sinking below the northeastern horizon. The remains of the lofty masts and deadly hull of the graceful schooner that had raced them hundreds of leagues lay almost dead astern now, already half a league away. Except for the faint loom of her remaining top hamper, the hapless vessel nearly disappeared in the moon set, and then soon became lit by the sun's rising fire.

In the gloom of near dark, smiles of relief broke out everywhere. Her canvas seemed to burst into fire as the first sun shone on her big ragged main sail and topsail spars. A spectacular, menacing sight. She would be hull down, bulwarks below the horizon, before sun was fully up. As they left the British ship astern, with Union Jack now flying upside down, Turner stroked his beard and nodded again to Nathan. The blinding sun pulled itself from the sea, glaring and searing in all its harsh glory. No one spoke.

But then another hail from the foretop finally broke the spell.

"Deck there! No sign of the big ship! Nothin's 'n sight—except the Dockyard and Falmouth—and the wreck we left behind!"

The crew cheered wildly.

"Three cheers for the Cap'n and his mate," roared Mister Logan.

The crew burst into cheers, and invaded the quarterdeck, laughing and pounding Nathan.

"Silence, all of you, get forward!" Nathan yelled angrily, trying to wave them away and retreat.

"Captain—" he began, face beet-red.

But Turner and Jack grabbed him and pounded him on the back. Others raised belaying pins, pikes, cutlasses and guns, and all aboard basked in an unavoidable sense of magic, spiritual grace, even, the Lord's genius exactly where they wanted it to be. Turner now looked on Nathan with amazement and Logan smiled knowingly; Nathan was so embarrassed, he made to leave the deck.

Turner blocked his way. "Easy, there, Nathan. Madeira for you, at our ease." And to the crew, "A tot all around, men! Well done, boys. Secure the guns."

When the cheering died down again, he pulled Nathan aside.

"How did you know that they would tack? How did you know they would run aground, and somehow we would not? The crew thinks you are a wizard, a sorcerer."

"I did not know, Captain. I just hoped. We were just lucky, really, Cap'n Turner—Mathew—I am sorry, but I won't be a captive again . . . I gambled with your lives, and that was wrong; another solemn vow broken. I hope you will forgive me, but now—I must get those bastards—and get home."

Turner was silently shaking his head in disbelief, his beard wagging behind.

"How many did we lose, Captain?"

"You are a good man, Nathan. A mighty good man," said Turner. "We lost a few . . . wounded are well cared for by that damned . . . that bos'n of yours . . . also reigning surgeon—I just checked, everything's bein' done by Mr. Logan and his boys. May you never feel the need to gamble like this again, Nathan, if that is the case, but you saved us. Almost all of us. Quite amazing. You are . . . you and your boys . . . are powerful good. I am certain that it must be . . . a blessing from God, and your father and mother, if you will pardon, will be proud of you—"

Nathan looked up to see *Cormorant's* flag whipping stiffly in the breeze, forcing back tears. Am I good enough, oh God, to even see my mother and father again?

"No bottom!" shouted Tom Howard in the forechains. "No bottom with this line!"

Fifteen

Mistress

It had all been so easy, almost too easy. Richard Auster smiled to himself as the early sun slanted in through the bedchamber window of his suite overlooking Baltimore's Inner Harbor. Cold, bright, devious. The light crept into the room across the Persian rug and brought out the ruddy floral patterns weaving through the fabric. Looked like a pleasant but unreliable southwesterly breeze, backed last night, a barely freezing day near the end of March 1812. It would veer soon to the north again.

Catherine already was or soon would be in a position where she must comply with all of Richard's demands, perhaps not quite as vulnerable as Barbara but certainly in no position to make his life difficult.

Young oaf Nathan Jeffries was suffering his Hell at sea, if he still lived. Richard looked forward to enjoying further torture of both father William and son Nathan before finishing them both off.

But the articles did annoy him . . . the news stories about his slavers . . . and other private matters. Richard's people had assured him that the source of those stories would be found soon and brought to him alive.

So he decided to indulge in a few days at his rooms at the Lord Baltimore tavern, close enough for business next week, but feeling a respite from his other duties to focus on Barbara.

When he escorted her into the carriage at the Steward mansion, Richard took Barbara in his arms and kissed her warmly. She did not resist; their lips parted and their tongues melted together. He crushed her breasts to his chest, and she could feel his hardness pressing against the loose folds of her gown. He could feel those stiff magnificent nipples, and ripped open her gown to get at them.

Barbara had slapped him when he had first kissed her breasts; he remembered smiling. As she grew to depend on him more and more, he started kissing and licking wherever he pleased whenever they met—innocently at first, at the Steward mansion, and then with increasing violence. Richard asked nothing of her, except all of her; took care of her and—he was compelling.

"I want only what is good for you, Barbara, you know that," he whispered. "I don't want you to concern yourself with anything. You know how I feel about you." She nodded and sighed—in her mind, the warning flags of a storm brewing were ignored. She did not want to think about Nathan, Catherine or anyone else. Anything that interfered with these moments was too confusing and unpleasant to deal with. She wanted to keep her father and the bank alive, with its rich comforts and extreme vanity—but she was intelligent enough to realize that she was now controlled by Richard. And he had known all along about Peter!

When Richard took charge of her life she resented it at first, but the trade-off was too appealing. Memories of her father in her bed had led to the long infatuation and then virtual obsession she had with Peter; more as a object, a plaything, rather than a thinking human being. Her need is to keep the truth from escaping, and keep her reputation as a good Lutheran girl. She laughed when she thought about the church, "Thank you Lord for all these, thy blessings," and knew that the proverbs had been written for the Austers and her father, never to protect her. Could she remember a time before her life had been soiled by these craven men, her own father? She could imagine some, like Catherine, who apparently believed in a higher side of humanity, even among men. The fool.

Barbara, always the little princess, Daddy's little darling and profoundly mistrustful of women, preferred the company of men; as did Catherine, but for different reasons. And she dared not talk to Catherine about . . .

How had it come to this? she thought wearily. Thinking appeared irrelevant and hopeless in the event. For Barbara, life was a constant sunset, glorious in her transitory pinks and blues; the end of the day.

She had not the nerve to ask her father about the story of the young girl that Richard had told her. And Abraham must know about her liaisons with Richard. He must know.

When they reached the tavern, Richard lead her inside his rooms and kissed her voraciously. As their kissing became more heated, he lifted her effortlessly and carried her to the bedchamber. His lips were on her neck and breasts as he released buttons and began to disrobe her; she half fought, half helped him, and began to fumble with his own scarf.

The rest of a bottle of port remained at the bedside. When Barbara looked up at Richard's face, it was so kind, so beautiful, so intent. He knows everything, how to excite, how to control everyone; those bewitchingly mild brown eyes, gold-flecked beacons, slightly hooked nose, imperious but exuding charm and tact. He was a delight to the eye, always pleasingly impeccable, handsome, dashing, trim but not tough; a soft face really, not ostentatious, but smart, proud and confident. She knew he was arrogant, compassionate—dangerous. But to look at him, so brilliant, compelling, frightening; she was giddy with passion.

Suddenly Richard broke away. She thought he had been about to take her, but he smiled and paused, holding her lightly.

"By the way, you'll never guess who I saw late this morning on his way from the bank—our friend, William Jeffries, no doubt asking for another loan; and the boy Nathan Jeffries still missing! What an unfortunate affair that was at the Stewards. The boy a coward, and now, his father, much as I tried—"

"Oh, Richard! Damn you!" She felt a white heat of anger coursing through her body, now covered with a film of perspiration beneath the light green chemise and straight flowing gown. She tried to push away, but he held her tightly again, hands slipping under her dress, fondling her thighs. She squirmed, only faintly struggling, feeling his body against her.

He bit her softly on the shoulder and laughed. "I'm sorry, my dear, that was tactless of me."

She knew how deliberate his timing could be, and how cruel. This man frightened her and excited uncontrollable passion in her. He squeezed her body against him again and she wriggled delightedly in spite of herself, hugging his face to her neck, then her lips against his as his expert hands played with her skin. Hours of bliss sailed on.

Richard had allowed himself the luxury of spending the night with Barbara, still sleeping next to him in the large canopied bed. This reckless activity, this risk of exposure, was to torture her and please himself. She was being rewarded for her loving loyalty, a delightfully perverse service. Any pretense of a decency between them had long since dropped; and she knew by now he would continue this for years and never let her free, never marry her. And she dared not protest their arrangement—the last thing she wanted was any wider knowledge of their affair, ruining her reputation and her father's, but certainly not Richard's.

What gave him a special pleasure, beyond her sensual bodily charms and willingness to experiment, was the fact that she would have done what he said even without the threat of publicity. He had unleashed within her a passionate, insane need for him, a habitual ache of longing, a primitive obsession, madness. With him she had performed acts of love and hate which would have been unthinkable, unimaginable in 1810, even with Peter. His seduction and control of her were complete.

It had amused him to have her write a letter to Captain William Jeffries in the guise of a friendly advisement, warning him that he had dishonored his trade and the naval profession on the dueling field as well as with *Bucephalus*, mysteriously lost, along with *Cormorant* engaged in smuggling with the British, and offering a few other observations to goad the old man and further spit on his reputation.

Richard would continue to wreak his revenge on that Jeffries boy, if the wretch still lived; but the father still enjoyed some powerful backing and was still beyond his reach legally—at least at the present time. It had been quite a shock when Richard learned that someone was reporting on his business activities, some of which was damaging, all of which was true. Surprisingly, he laughed out loud. Let the games continue!

Barbara groaned and shifted her position beside him.

He had trained her to violate all decorum and sleep naked, and now he pulled back the covers and slapped her firm round buttocks. She cried out and rolled over, now awake.

"Richard! Please do not do that—let me sleep . . ."

He rolled over on top of her, covering her generous lips with his, and began to roughly explore her perfect curves, squeezing her large breasts and biting her neck. His urgent hand and then rigid manhood quickly found their way between her muscular white legs.

She twisted her head away for a moment, gasping—the pain and pleasurable tingling were equally mixed now.

"My love! Not now . . ."

He grabbed her face with one hand and squeezed her lips together into a vertical caricature.

"Yes, now! And whenever it pleases me!"

Still recovering from the soreness of several hours of amorous play a few hours earlier, Barbara would have screamed—would have, except that her mouth was mostly covered by his and because he would inflict more pain if she had complained any further. More and more, he enjoyed watching her suffer before giving her any pleasure or respite. Sometimes there was only his brutal greed. She cried out in spite of herself; the pain was gradually replaced by a raw desire. He was a silent, powerful machine, oblivious to her.

"No, Richard," she moaned. "This is wrong." She closed her eyes.

"But I love you, Barbara, that is all that matters!"

Suddenly he pulled away and she heard the door open—he was slipping out. The door quietly closed again. Barbara sat up in bed, bewildered, tingling over every inch of her skin, her insides screaming with need. She got up and started to reach for the door knob. No! Would he return? He must return! Barbara's hand swept across her exposed breasts and then she reached for her shawl, her heart pounding. The heat from the fire seemed oppressive. He must come back! He must be careful! What was she thinking? She could hear the crackling in the fireplace, the hush of the dead eaves trembling in the March wind.

Enjoying her protests and the risks, Richard would often visit her bedchamber at home, but not always—she felt bitter jealousy, even towards Catherine. Especially Catherine. She envied that fool. Richard would sometimes slip out before dawn to return to the Auster mansion, or someone else's home. Abraham would come up to see how she was before leaving, and it was easy to feign illness.

Now, in Richard's rooms, she looked at her bleary expression in the gilt, oval Louis VI mirror of the dresser. Barbara looked and felt like an overused strumpet, a working girl used to sleeping all day and lying with many men. She was repulsed and excited by the image.

Her thoughts drifted back to vague memories of her mother, who had died when she was six. Mary Steward had been a seductive beauty herself, and loved flirting with men. Barbara remembered seeing her father in tears once, over some impropriety Mary had committed at a social affair. She had hated to see her father suffer, in spite of his own perversities, and had gone to great lengths to present to him an image of the ideal daughter, a pure and innocent creature of the day, the perfect hostess, who would marry the right man and maintain the Steward's honorable and upright role in the community. Part of her enjoyed this image, and she knew that men of power appealed to her, men of prestige, or bright, handsome and gifted young man, poets. She enjoyed the prestige of her father's reputation. Even if it was all a sham.

By all accounts, Nathan was never to become a pillar of the community. If he did return . . . but it seemed hopeless now in any case. The Jeffries had become a joke among the many Auster associates—and the Stewards were counted among those, at least in business. She knew Nathan had loved her, but now Nathan would never share her bed; assuming he was still alive.

Oh God, Richard must come back, he must return, please. Do not leave me!

She was a slave to his whim; she must have him. Then she heard the door open.

"Come in," she whispered. It sounded like dry leaves, the hush of those dead leaves trembling in the icy wind.

Now dressed in a maroon, brocaded evening robe, Richard closed the door of the suite and walked across the dark mahogany and oak floor of the outer vestibule and parlour room into the bedchamber. Almost all of the furnishings—his robe, even—were imported from England. But I must have them replace those sickening portraits of Washington, Hancock and Adams in the hall, he thought to himself. One was a valuable Gilbert Stuart painting, which was the pride of these rooms, but he had no doubt that the owners would accede to his wishes, rather than risk losing such a generous patron. In most respects, these rooms were imminently satisfactory for the purposes of a discrete rendezvous. And he was hardly worried about anyone seeing Barbara. But it would be unfortunate at the present time if the general public became aware that she was not visiting her cousin—an actual cousin—who had been persuaded to provide reliable testimony of Barbara having stayed with her if her legitimate whereabouts should be seriously called into question.

"Maybe you should be left alone, my dear," he said.

"No! No, please, Richard, please stay. I am sorry that I angered you!" She felt every warm pulse coursing through her body.

"*Amor et melle et felle est fecundissimus*," he said, smiling. "Love is rich with both honey and venom."

"But Richard, I feel guilty about Nathan . . . I fear, you know . . ."

He sighed and told her more fictitious stories about Jeffries' misdeeds and escapades, fictitious, some of which included Peter, including indiscreet liaisons in New York, sufficiently colored to paint a very bleak picture. Her eyes glistened, and a tear slipped down her rosy cheek as she listened to Richard discredit William and Nathan and the relationship between the Stewards and the Jeffries.

"As I said, he is a fool, Barbara, to have abandoned you this way—while you were becoming a young lady! Any man would give his right arm to have you! But he doesn't want to marry you now—or ever—because he doesn't really love you. Can't you see that? Where do you think he has gone, anyway?"

"But his youth! His father's . . . financial plight."

"Enough!" Richard quickly masked over a frightening scowl, shook his head, smiling sadly, gently wiping her tears with a handkerchief.

"Nathan is gone, my dear! And I'm sorry to have to tell you this, but he does not love you—the Jeffries are untrustworthy in any case! Oh, you surely know he has not saved himself—he has not been faithful to you or anyone, my dear! I know you two were childhood friends, but it is time to grow up, Barbara!"

Then Barbara did look at him. His face seemed misty, mythological in the cheerful, dramatic glow of all the candlelight.

"But what about you and Catherine?" she ventured. "Everyone knows you and Catherine . . ."

Richard grimaced again briefly.

"I thought we understood each other regarding . . . I thought we loved . . . but I was sadly mistaken—please do not bring up that subject again."

He bowed and turned.

"No! Please do not go now, please do . . . stay with me." She sobbed.

The moment was right. He held her closer and kissed her, and her arms snaked around his neck. She held him and returned his kiss passionately, and he knew she would always be his. His tongue filled her mouth, and her legs quivered then relaxed as his erection pressed home. She was on fire, she wanted him, she hated him for making her crazy, she never wanted him to stop, she needed release.

Suddenly there was a loud knock on the outer door. Richard paused and pulled away with a curse as she trembled beneath him. He threw on his robe and left the bed. At the outer door he heard a rasping voice.

"Captain Auster! Captain Auster! Please! I must speak with you!"

"Enter!" Richard roared from the outer room.

The short, wiry man came in smiling nervously, wearing a faded blue roundabout and nervously dropped his beaver hat as he handed a newspaper to his angry employer.

"Clough!" Richard growled. "What in the name of Christ are you doing here?"

"Cap'n Richard, uh, Archie sent me to report—"

"Where is Coxe? Where is *Scourge*?"

"Sir, Cap'n Coxe is in Fells Point with the surgeon and the wounded."

"Wounded? What has happened?"

Barbara could hear an ominous scuffling of boots in the outer room of the suite.

Auster's menacing face frightened Clough.

"Out with it, man!"

"*Scourge* has been lost, sir, we—"

"Lost? Lost!" Auster growled.

Clough pulled out a letter.

"It's all here, Mister Richard. *Scourge* was ... we was chasing an American brig *Cormorant*, off Antigua, sir, the Devil—shoals and reefs in those waters—she ... *Scourge* ran aground, sir! A total loss—we salvaged some of the ordnance and supplies—the Governor's assistance—liberty was ... expensive. The crew we lost—we was lucky—"

Auster snatched the letter from trembling hands.

"Between the salvagers and a French privateer—and *Guerriere* was sighted, sir, but she made off—"

"Fifteen thousand pounds lost! Fifteen—and that puffing Jeffries boy? He's with Coxe?"

"That is the other part, sir," said Clough, shaking now. "We'd run down *Cormorant* and we was in the process of securing her with—"

"Where is Jeffries?" yelled Auster.

"Uh, the boy and the bos'n, Logan, some others, managed to escape to the brig, and—it seems ...uh ... recaptured her."

"What! The devil you say!"

Auster's face was as red as Clough's was white.

"And you failed to retake this brig?"

"I don't how they did it, sir—escaped—the boy's ga' more gumption than we—"

"Jeffries ... where is he?"

"He's aboard *Cormorant*, Cap'n. We lost thirteen men, sir, all together. After that last week in the Leewards, you know, Cap'n Coxe decided to—"

"You lost *Scourge* ... and the boy ..."

"*Cormorant* has already sailed north, sir," said Clough, now clearly terrified.

He cringed as Auster walked toward him, their eyes on the same level. Auster's face was already more red and working. Clough watched Richard struggle to control his rage. The latter looked at the newspaper and read aloud with disbelief.

"Auster's *Merlin* and Liverpool slaver partners! Damned son of a whore!"

Barbara heard the sickening crack of Richard's cane on Clough's head. Clough started screaming and Barbara threw on her nightgown to run to the door. She felt nauseous as she watched Richard swing the cane again and again at the writhing, bloody body on the rug; her lover's dark hair and bright blue eyes wild and horrible, thin lips twisted ferociously as he beat the man.

"Richard! Please! You will kill him!"

He turned toward her. For a terrifying moment she thought he would attack her. Then he stopped. All was silent and still.

Sixteen

Divided Loyalties

From the southwest shore of Lake Erie, Peter Hughes admired the islands five miles away, solidifying through the early morning haze. How had it come to this? "Partners" with the despicable Richard Auster and his boys. Peter heard the clumsy approach of the white man long before he appeared at water's edge, and turned to see an ugly, battered creature, slightly taller than him, with two pistols and a cat-o'-nine-tails in his belt and a sneer on his face. Peter did not recognize him.

"You the half-breed?" the man challenged. "Friend of those Injun-lovin' Jeffries?"

"I am Peter Hughes—and you are?"

"The name's Clough, boy, Eller Clough. I work for Captain Auster . . . same as you!" he added with a bitter laugh.

He gazed out at the islands in the mist, beyond which lay the Canadian shore.

"So—supplies arrive tonight—your Injun friends are still west o' here?"

"Where is Auster?"

"Captain Auster sent me with the shipment—and that is all you need to know, boy."

"I want to inspect the guns and powder now—last time half of them were useless."

"You want to . . . who do you think you are, boy, prancin' around here like the noble savage? The Captain put me in charge of this—and now I tell you what to do."

Peter sighed. "Your master must be desperate to send you, especially after you have evidently earned his wrath by failing at some other task. He beat you quite badly, didn't he? Let me clarify matters, Mr. Clough. I do not work for him, and I certainly do not take orders from the likes of you!"

Clough spat on Peter's moccasin. Dark spittle dripped down his chin like burned blood.

"Shawnee Boy, you are asking for hurt."

"The British say they want to help in the conflict—but Tecumseh trusts them no more than I. In a few months, war will ignite the frontier and they have betrayed us before. Most Americans simply want to destroy us, but have no use for the British. You, however, care only for gold and silver—no loyalty, no side to call friend or enemy, no human soul, only a sick spirit to whom it is useless to try to explain morality."

"What . . . morality? What s-s-spirit? What're you yammering about?"

"You are a whore," said Peter calmly. "You and your master. Loyalty, truth, honor, compassion for the deserving, even those who seem undeserving—these things mean nothing to you; you are a blight on this earth, black spit on the great windswept waters."

"Why you m-m-mouthy bastard . . . ungrateful uppity redskin—I'll whip you!"

His long arm snaked down to his "cat," and in the blink of an eye Clough screamed and lay writhing on the sand, groaning, with no apparent bruise, no discoloration or blood.

Peter gently raised Clough's head by his hair, as the latter's face contorted in rage, pain and fear.

"I recommend that you never speak that way again to any Shawnee or 'half-breed' unless you are prepared to die—and tell your master that we have concluded our association as of now—is that clear? I will no longer lower myself to this level—even for the sake of my people."

Peter let Clough's head fall to the sand.

"Is that clear?" he repeated quietly.

The man sobbed while nodding his head. Moments later, when Clough opened his eyes, Peter had disappeared.

The servants had been dismissed and the two remaining people sat at a long and exquisitely carved French mahogany table in the western dining room of the Auster mansion in Baltimore. At one end Richard Auster fiddled with slices of Roast Pheasant *á la Galatine*; across from him, Catherine tried to enjoy the rest of her scrod. She sipped her wine and glanced uneasily at Richard, whose eyes glittered as he half-heartedly sampled his dinner.

"I must remember to compliment Francois on this pheasant. Excellent," he said, with a noticeably false pomposity.

"Yes, excellent," said Catherine, absentmindedly.

"So, my dear, welcome back once again. I missed you, even though Philadelphia seems to agree with you."

"Thank you, Richard, but don't they say, 'Philadelphia is a birthright, not a city.'"

Richard's laughter sounded forced.

Catherine watched her fiancé's fingers drum across the table.

"So, my love, how did this new business come about?" Catherine could not resist probing Richard regarding his mysterious "trading voyages" and other business; with a kind of sick fascination she persisted in learning all the details of Richard's engagements—especially the ones that she dare not probe too closely.

"Why, it is nothing to trouble your lovely head about, Catherine. That fool deliberately provoked me. There was nothing for it but to give him his chance and call him out. They still insist that I was somehow responsible for—"

"The way I heard it, you struck him, Richard."

Richard neatly patted his lips with his napkin, and his blue eyes looked into Catherine's brown ones. The look was disturbingly vacant, almost wistful. She couldn't return his stare, and gazed at her wine while he spoke.

"My dear, the silly man insulted me in front of half the ship's crew. I couldn't very well ignore that, could I?" Richard smiled, but his eyes were cold. With his imperious head back, tall stock and impeccable dark blue jacket with gold trim and ruffled white linen shirt, he seemed remote, almost godlike. Catherine inwardly trembled before his self confidence and virile presence. But she felt she had to resist.

"But you went there—"

"Come, Catherine, there is no need for you to get involved in such unfortunate matters," he said, waving his finger in mock reproof as if in league with the devil. "There is nothing sordid about the business of shipping the Negroes. I visited the Captain with an honest proposition, as a gentleman, and answered his . . . objections . . . as a gentleman." Catherine, looking down, did not catch the warning look Richard gave her.

"Richard!" Catherine said loudly, looking up again at his bright, piercing blue eyes. "There must be a better way for people to resolve their differences!"

Both smiled broadly now, as if in innocent affection.

"Of course, Catherine," said Richard. "I agree with you completely, and really the only unforgivable action is treachery, is that not so? We can't very well ignore the traitors among us, can we?"

"Why do you mention betrayal?"

He waved the recent *Federal Republican,* then read, "Hanson says, 'the great Baltimore ship owner Richard Auster and his Cabal . . . the commonwealth to order examinations of *Medusa, Minotaur, Montauk,*' . . . God in Hell! . . . 'the Black Angel. . . Auster to appear before . . . the city aldermen.' Governor Thompkins in Annapolis . . ." Richard turned to her, "We found out who has provided our friend Alexander Hanson with so many lies about our shipping ventures."

Catherine shivered. "Who has—"

"Should I order dessert, Catherine?" said Richard.

"Who has betrayed you?" Catherine demanded.

"His Honor Mayor Johnson has not treated this rascal Hanson quite the way I indicated. Nor has he proven reliable with regard to William Jeffries. So I have asked the good citizens of Fells Point to lend a hand."

"I thought Edward was your friend—"

"It is time to tie up those loose ends, as they say," Richard said. "The Jeffries and their friends."

Catherine could only stare into those bright blue eyes, petrified.

"We 'leaked' misinformation . . . my dear. At first I could not believe it. Thank goodness for our favorite vole Abraham Steward, eh? But you know what wounds me, my love," he said, "is that you of all people know the special place I hold in my heart for the Jeffries."

Catherine stood up and walked toward the door but Richard blocked her way.

"And, my dear Catherine, you know how much I dislike being treated like a fool. Are you sure you wouldn't care for some dessert?"

"No, thank you, I . . . I must catch up on my correspondence tonight." She barely trembled.

Catherine tried to go around Richard, but he grabbed her bare shoulders, pulled her up to him and kissed her brutally. As his arms went around her, she stopped struggling and felt excitement and fear. Then he let her go.

"Richard! I—"

His right hand, horny and calloused as any tar, hit her left cheek with a blinding crack and she crashed to the floor.

"How stupid do you think we are?" she heard, through the shrieking, electric pain.

Nathan smiled as he stood on the quarterdeck, his well-salted, wind-beaten face, now covered in a downy beard, cracking with the effort. The Antigua adventure had brought him many benefits; one in particular was the loss of his virginity with the help of Maria, a dark and exotic creature of indeterminate years, an erotic *señora*; a Spanish Gertrude or Moorish Desdemona, Peter would have called her. A widow lady of Spain whose intimacy with officials and admirers made her queen of this British island. Maria had taught Nathan many delights, and he was loathe to leave her lithe copper body. Her exotic features reminded him of Catherine's allure. Too intelligent for her own good, sailing circles around Nathan, Maria had understood and met his needs.

Thanks to her, Nathan and the *Cormorant* crew had outwitted their rapacious enemies on Antigua, especially the British frigate *Guerriere,* and managed to net a profitable cargo of British musket rifles, powder, rum and other items, not necessarily for the interests of the United States in general, but mostly for the profit of the southern Jeffersonians and the powerful young settlers from the west. They neither knew nor wanted to know the buyer, and suspected it would help either the Indians or the British, or even the settlers, the War Hawks, at least officially. The crew feared but were loyal to Nathan because he had delivered *Cormorant* several times. His relentless fight to save them never wavered.

Turner joined Nathan at the top of the quarterdeck.

Nathan grinned again at the laughter from Jack Logan and other friends who dared make jokes at his expense. They already had a song, another version of "Spanish Ladies," dedicated to him—the greatest honor imaginable. Nathan fought to contain his excitement. At least he was returning in triumph to his mother and father. Under the circumstances, how angry could she still be at her wayward son? Decaying his excitement about returning to Baltimore and seeing his parents was the dreary memory of Peter and Barbara. He also thought about those dark hypnotic eyes of Catherine Charles "Auster"—his bitterness towards the Austers dying of surfeit.

"Brisk wind out of the east, Captain. Not much of spring in it. Cape Henry in sight!"

"You're setting the topgallants?"

"Yes—we have done it, Cap'n."

"Don't say that . . . yet!"

But the old gray goat smiled and nearly laughed.

"Think of the stories we'll tell."

"Yeah . . . I uh . . . I like the story of a boy who feared the sea and then thanks to a great captain Matt Turner took to it like a dolphin . . . or whale . . . or maybe a flying fish!"

"Not me—took it like a man; a credit to your own father . . . and mother."

Turner put his hand on the taller man's shoulder.

"Yew have a brilliant mind, Nathan—don't let nobody tell ye different. And ye'ar a brave man, our kinda' mascot, and no mistake!"

Nathan fought back tears.

"Deck there! Topsails just off—now dead astern!"

Turner and Nathan spun around.

"Let me see that glass. God'struth—looks like a big ship—frigate maybe. You don't s'pose—"

The lookout suddenly shouted again, "Deck there! Large sail ain't American! I can see her ensign! She's British! And overhauling us fast!"

"I think I know her, sir," shouted Logan, relieved at the helm. "She looks like *Guerriere*, all right, that same damned 38-gun frigate from Antigua. French built with eighteen-pounders. Underhanded and she'll be wanting to add some of us to her crew, I'm thinkin'."

"Damn your eyes! Son of a scorpion fish whore slave—" Turner clamped down on his pipe, struggling with his emotions, seemed about ready to explode with anger and frustration.

"Aye, aye, sir," said the bos'n with a practiced straight face, no wink.

"Sir," said Nathan quietly, "we only need stay off till dark. If I may make another suggestion—"

Nathan and Turner began going in and out of the Captain's cabin. O'Reilley was not invited to join them and grew increasingly agitated. When Nathan returned to the quarterdeck near sunset, it was crowded. Turner and O'Reilley were shouting at each other again—an amusing scenario for the two stolid men at the wheel, Jackson, now the acting bos'n and master's mate, and another feisty Corker named Dobbs, a friend of O'Reilley's, not so grim faced but silent and tense. Most of the crew was at hand, studying the progress of the race. Turner and O'Reilley, near the starboard taffrail, gesticulated while other hands near the main fife rail pretended not to listen to their words while looking busy with duties.

Reacquired practically within sight of home! Could be another pursuer —but every yard of open water *Cormorant* put between herself and their pursuer, possibly the frigate *Guerriere*, made capture less likely. During the night, it would be difficult for the pursuer to again reacquire her quarry. The next few hours would be critical.

Fells Point

Gloria was away and William sleeping, so Amy was alone when there were four rapid knocks on the door. Do not be afraid, she thought.

"Come in," she said from the Queen Anne wing chair, facing the door.

The man who quietly stepped into the still sunlit entranceway was of above average height and trim, ruggedly built under his elegant blue suit. As he paused in the short hall, Amy could see that he had changed little in the four years since their last meeting. He was handsome, still used to getting his way, with lean features, steel-gray eyes and blazing white shirt, stock and neckcloth. But Amy's face registered only a faint repugnance, and said nothing.

His gaze swept the small Federal parlour, with its round looking glass topped by ormolu and brass Girandole eagles, the mahogany sideboard with inlaid maple, the pair of gilt sconces, the patinated bronze spout lamp, the Danforth pewter and Chinese punch bowl on the John Vanderlyn tea table. He nodded with vague approval and bowed in front of Amy, studying her. Yes, he thought, the son has the same wide nose, broad cheeks and hazel eyes, small lips, brown hair. But his overall face and head is more square, flat, like his father's.

"At your service, ma'am. You are as beautiful as ever, and this chamber is even more beautiful than when I last visited. A number of recent additions?"

"We are quite alone," she said evenly. "My husband will sleep for several hours."

"Yes, that is certainly a wise precaution. May I sit—"

"Let us get to the point, Michael—or whatever name you are currently using."

The man smiled slightly. "Most of the local citizens know me as Michael Fredericks, rather than—but whichever you prefer."

"How amusing. Now, suppose you begin with an explanation of what happened to my son."

The man's raptor stare could easily attract women and frighten men. But now Fredericks himself seemed strangely intimidated; the glare of those bright eyes seemed dimmed, muted. He sat back.

"As far as I could determine, there has been no contact between . . . your son and Richard Auster."

"Don't take me for a fool! I know Nathan was taken aboard *Scourge* by Auster's man. Where is he now?"

"I don't know, Amy. I admit the impressment and this financial . . . arrangement with *Scourge* came as a surprise to me. Still, your son seems none the worse for his sea time. From what I hear, Nathan acquitted himself very well indeed, and I do not believe you can divert his course without divulging facts which you do not wish him to know."

"You had better keep my son alive, Mister . . . Fredericks—oh yes, you had better!"

"Madam, I have been unable to track down the few remaining individuals responsible for taking him to *Scourge*. I still find it difficult to believe Auster would dare make the attempt. Yet, it is possible."

"There is another matter," said Amy. "Last year we received a letter and bank draft from my cousin in Baltimore stating that additional funds had been discovered, even though earlier he had reported my father's estate completely exhausted." She stared coldly at Fredericks.

"I trust some of these new furnishings are a result and thanks to that pleasant surprise."

"Did you provide them with that money?"

Fredericks looked out the window. "Yes."

"Damn you, sir, I told you never to attempt any such maneuver. We do not want any contact with your sordid, ill-gotten gains!"

"I assure you, Amy, it will not occur again! It happened that I discovered your incomes were dry, and, knowing that much of your husband's limited resources are squandered on other causes, I merely filled in the gap."

His sneer concealed the fact that only significant sums of money diverted from other sources were saving his own hard-hit properties in

Baltimore, staving off even greater financial disaster if he liquidated. He had warned the Austers to stay out of slavery before the Embargo, when England had outlawed transport of slaves. But they had been more worried about keeping their ships active, and now sufficient pressure, exerted on the right people in Baltimore and Boston, could make them reveal the identity of the individuals and vessels which flouted the law. It could ruin the Company, and possibly drag down Fredericks.

His sneer also concealed his undying love for this diminutive, aging woman. The two people gazed at each other, a few feet apart and at the same time peering across a gulf, from an infinite distance. Two different lifetimes of handicaps and suffering, some agonizing part of it shared; two people struggling with severe flaws, stronger for their flaws, a pair of walking wounded filled with sinister secrets. Except that Amy's instinctive response to that throughout her life had been to reach out, to use her strength to take care of her own and help others overcome their difficulties and handicaps, and to find some joy in that effort. Ever since he was a young man on his own, Fredericks had reacted coldbloodedly to oppression by operating in an even more ruthless manner himself, oblivious to law or morality; efficient, calculating, deadly. He did not ask again about the Captain; Amy did not expect him to. He owed loyalty to no one except himself.

"Do not ever come here again," said Amy. She spoke with quiet conviction. Fredericks said nothing, but stood up, while she remained seated. "We can communicate, if we must, through Abraham—I trust that is still suitable?"

He sighed. "As you wish, Amy. Quite—"

"Another thing. Stand by your promise. No one else can control Auster; you know that as well as I. Tell him—or rather, remind him . . . to stay away from my son. And my husband. I do not want to hear about any more surprises on the quay or anywhere else."

"I shall continue my most vigorous efforts. But, Amy, after all, he really is difficult to control, without—"

"Find a way. You had better do your utmost. If I find out otherwise . . . don't forget, I know who you really are." Her narrow hazel eyes were blatantly threatening and dismissing.

"Of course." He bowed. "Take good care of yourself, Amy."

She looked away. The sun would set in less than an hour. Fredericks was the most frightening, dangerous man she had ever met, utterly beyond the conscience of the world. And yet, and yet . . . his English leather boots snickered quietly on oak floor; the door opened, and he left.

On a wet, bitter, early Fells Point spring night, the loud pounding on the Jeffries door on Thames Street startled Amy. But the visitor shocked her even more. She immediately shouted for Gloria as she helped Catherine, the toast of Europe, the great beauty of Baltimore, now blue and shivering, battered with face disfigured, dripping blood on her once-white linen gown; a pale and dying waif out of the glistening streets and sizzling lights. Carefully inspecting and drying her beaten face and black avalanche of sodden hair, Amy tried to restrain Catherine as she weakly thrashed and moaned.

The servant Gloria had not arrived, and the good Captain William Jeffries was no doubt still engaged at his sodden throne at Saucy Sal's tavern. Amy could only think how this poor creature, obviously out of her mind, confirmed Richard Auster's worsening mental condition. He had clearly thrown off all restraints and now burned pure evil. Her beloved husband was undoubtedly next. William was all she had left. This bold young woman had done so much to save the Jeffries and hurt Richard. And now she had paid for her treachery.

Seventeen

The Tide Turns

In a meeting with his "attorney" Michael Fredericks, his father's old partner, Richard delivered the mostly bad news. With most of his American ships, crews and shipments mired in customs house detention and otherwise requiring his presence in Washington City, then New York, now in Boston; the once-distinguished name of Auster was on the run. Too many charges from those relentless articles in the *Federal Republican*; charges of slave-trading, running arms to the British and the Indians, trading with the enemy, treason, despite the nominally neutral status of the United States. But of course the last act of the Jeffries revenge tragedy was yet to be played, as he haltingly explained to Captain Fredericks. But Richard hesitated again.

"Who could have thought that my fiancée . . ." he started, then paused. "The relationship between Catherine and the Jeffries is unexpected, and in the face of the old man's drunken status and son's firm position as a lost and presumably dead coward, I am now betrayed by my—"

"Yes . . . but it was an obvious possibility you should have investigated; that was the failure of a careless fool."

"What did you call me—" Richard Auster growled, then closed his mouth when he saw the look in Fredericks' eyes.

"Now listen and keep your mouth shut, and maybe we'll let you live," said Fredericks with some heat. "The boy Nathan lives in all likelihood, and this time I will take care of him myself personally, understood? You are acting the part of a bully, not a gentleman. How could you let that boy outwit and escape you? And who gave you permission to beat your fiancée?"

"Who gave . . . who says I could—"

"Shut your fool mouth for the last time, Auster. I could have done so to your father and I could still do . . . solve all of your problems, *n'est pas*?"

Auster said nothing.

"Now, that will work out eventually, no thanks to you. Amy, whose wrath we have skirted, knows me as Captain Fredericks, but she taught Catherine well. Somehow unbeknownst to you and your men and to me, she spent many hours learning how to cut with precision into your precious cabal, hurt the Austers . . . and the Charles in Philadelphia . . . and at the same time help the Jeffries. Why? Meanwhile you waste your time with Barbara and Abraham Steward and the other parasites, yes. Overall, things are going quite well, aren't they? As the lovely young woman sinks your sorry ass!"

After dropping his eyes from Fredericks' awful stare, Richard croaked. "I . . . I . . ."

"And you . . . you do nothing! You are to go home and do absolutely nothing! Do you understand? After I take care of old William and his boy, I will decide what to do with Catherine . . . and you."

Richard's mind ratcheted back and forth. When he got away from this lunatic, he would get his final revenge on all of them, including Fredericks, the Jeffries and his would-be wife, herself a lunatic, all still running amok. He would repay the debt. It would not be pretty. He could already fondly savor that last scene with Catherine; how the slap had cracked loudly and opened the cut again on her cheek. She had stopped smiling. The defiant traitor was now silent and *persona non grata* throughout the civilized world. Richard smiled and licked his lips hungrily. Then he remembered that cockroach Nathan Jeffries—the boy's defiant, bug-like resilience had surprised Richard. You think he's been squashed but he pops up somewhere else, seemingly impossible to kill. But all the plans had been laid. The game was over. The old man, the boy, Catherine . . . none had quite been humiliated, ridiculed, debased or tortured enough.

Slightly more to it than I originally thought, that is all, just a slight delay, almost erotic, Richard said to himself. "The boy will never return

home—what is left of it! And of him!"

Peter disliked Boston but knew that he must go there. Without know-ing clearly why, he had ventured south again, avoiding settlers and occa-sional hunters. Men of all colors who did see him stared at him suspiciously until he stared back. His own people. Who were they? But he must find his father, or what was left of him, and decided to begin with Abraham Steward.

A fearful man, Steward knew he was in trouble but seldom stayed sober long enough to focus on it. It did not take long for Peter to squeeze from him that Richard Auster currently resided at the Huntington in Boston, meeting with a Captain Michael Fredericks, Esq. With Abra-ham's daughter, Barbara, the unrivaled "Belle of Baltimore," accompany-ing him, seemingly immune to the rumors flying rampant like malaria; soon it will be obvious to all, they say. They say she is lying or he is lying about being deceived. You'll never get to the bottom of this, Mr. Steward.

"Never could I have imagined," sobbed aged, balding Abraham, in his silk undershirt and slippers, at noon, "that my beautiful daughter, and . . . Captain Auster . . ."

"Enough, Abraham," Peter impatiently interrupted the man he once thought of as father. "And she saw Catherine—"

"Yes! Yes, I told you. Barbara returned from Auster House in tears because Catherine had been beaten up badly by highwaymen, according to Richard, who also calmly tells us the engagement with Catherine is off. Catherine is no longer a member of the Auster-Charles Cabal, or even a lady, after her disgraceful behavior, and Barbara later told him . . ."

"Told him what, Abraham?"

"Barbara told him that she was . . . two months—"

"What did Richard say, damn it?"

"I . . . I am afraid of that man, Peter, my—"

"What is to happen to your daughter, you old fool?"

Peter shook the man, who nearly fell over, with tears on his cheeks.

"Barbara told me she wanted to leave, but it was too late now, and we both know that if Richard beat Catherine senseless, what he would do if Barbara tried to get away from . . . his influence. She said that when she sees him, he is able to make her do anything he wants. But when she explained to him that she is in a panic about being a pariah and that he must marry her, Richard laughed and said that he would soon be done with her, so she knew what would happen to her if she disobeyed."

Peter had listened to his heart and felt driven to confront his white demons starting with Baltimore, and instead now must journey north again to Boston to save a crushed and distraught Barbara Steward. She was apparently in the north end of Boston which he could monitor discreetly from the remains of his secret cabin outside Newton, just a few miles away. One of the same cabins his mother had "shared" with the mysterious white, rich lover, his presumptive daddy, his perverse quest. Not that the man, living or dead, would be of much use. Peter sought help from some source he knew did not exist.

Catherine, with Amy's care and the services of her remarkable "doctor," the freed black Andrew, recovered her senses in a few days. As she calmly studied her scarred and lumpy blue face in the mirror, she quickly disobeyed Andrew's order not to talk by completing her report to Amy, both orally and in writing, on the Austers and the Charles, up to the moment Richard beat her into unconsciousness. Amy wrote it all down in her journal.

"When I left Auster House it was empty, I am fairly sure," she concluded.

"Oh, Catherine, I am so sorry—"

"Do not say that, Amy," said Catherine. "You are my rock and I knew the risks. I accepted them." Catherine held Amy's blue eyes with her one open brown one. "I still accept them."

"Please do not speak any more and rest, my brave girl!"

"As I think of more details . . . he . . . destroyed many . . . too powerful, too many allies frightened off . . . he reached around the world to capture or destroy any great shipping family . . . any other 'Cabal'. . . and

Canada."

"I know, my dear, you must rest now. You have hurt them so badly—"

"But not . . . destroyed . . . not yet."

Washington City - *June 1, 1812*

President Madison, the small, brilliant, quiet man, gazed out the new, pearl-colored President's Mansion at the dark, watery sky. Cloudy stars and moon failed to dispel the gray gloom that matched Madison's agitated sense of doom. Bitter fighting raged far to the south, west and southeast, from Tennessee to New Orleans and throughout the northern Floridas. It was past midnight, now June 1st, and Dolley had gone up to bed. As the tall beeswax candles burned low, Madison, in his spotless wig, linen shirt and dark homespun waistcoat, looked around the oval office with dismay. He wondered once again if the Republic would survive, in either Federalist or Democratic form; already sour with the bitterness of the older Adams opponents and President Jefferson's catastrophic 1807 Embargo, non-importation laws, Non-Intercourse Act, Macon's Bill Number Two and farcical French promise to repeal the Berlin and Milan Decrees. Whoever lifted their neutral trade restrictions and depredations would receive the same cooperation in kind from the United States, so Napoleon Bonaparte's French foreign minister, the Duc de Cadore, had hoodwinked the Americans with a letter rescinding their decrees and hostile actions—in a letter that was not worth the paper it was written on. "Little Jemmy" Madison had chosen to believe Napoleon.

The piratical British were more honest and open about their robbing and hostility, and so the end result was an official continuation of the non-importation policy against the British and her colonies, while the French continued to prey on American ships. But the British sea lion was the big problem. American foreign policy had come full circle, from non-importation to non-exportation and now back to non-importation again. American capital, not goods, accumulated in England. Many, if not most, shipowners were disgusted with Washington City and of course chose to ignore the letter and intent of the law. Privateering was on the upswing again. Spanish, British, French, Indians and Americans fought under madmen such as Andrew Jackson. All along the coast fires burned ashore and at sea. Jefferson's economic sanctions had failed, yet the new policy was also hurting England's people. With poor crops that year, the country was threatened with mass starvation.

In the bloody battle late in 1811, the heavy United States frigate *President* had pummeled the British corvette *Little Belt*: an ugly night on the high seas, especially for the much smaller, weaker sloop of war. When the guns stopped firing, nine of the British were killed, 23 wounded. When the identities of the two vessels were finally established, the British refused assistance and limped away. Both sides accused the other of firing first. To most Americans, it was just retribution for the *Chesapeake* affair. To the outraged British, it was unprovoked brutality.

"The blood of our murdered countrymen must be revenged," said the *London Courier*. Most Americans were proud, but the episode did not enhance U.S. naval prestige abroad. The outspoken Captain Richard Dacres, commanding H.M.S. *Guerriere*, a frigate on the North American station, displayed a topsail and flag bearing the words, "Not the Little Belt," and harrassed American shipping and seamen even more. Impressment increased. While thousands of American sailors suffered on British ships or languished in British prisons, the British Foreign Secretary, Castlereagh, dug in his heels. Madison sighed again, reading more papers and documents on his desk.

"We do not want to destroy the trade of the Continent, but only to force the Continent to trade with us," Prime Minister Spencer Perceval had said before he was assassinated. King George himself had become even more obviously insane. In New England, the Republicans tried to drown out the leading Federalist voices such as Boston's wealthy Harrison James Gray Otis, New York Governor George de Witt Clinton, Daniel Webster and the "Essex Junto."

From the south and west, Republicans who knew nothing of the sea champed at their bits and rattled their swords. Ministers presented decrees, fought with words. Ships were captured and condemned, hundreds of them. Less fortunate shipowners lost their businesses; crews lost their freedom or their lives. Carrying most goods from France to America, for instance, was perfectly legal now, but unsafe except in a warship. Many American vessels supplied food to Wellington's army, fighting Napoleon on the Spanish Peninsula. And now at last the 90-day Embargo, which everyone knew was supposed to be a prelude to war, had sent hundreds of vessels scurrying to sea for at least one last chance at profits. Madison shook his head; the candlelight shining against the large dormer windows on his intelligent, irresolute face. Was the United States really going to declare war? Who could believe it? They were spectacularly unprepared. The War Hawks didn't want to wait, but they knew as well as he did that the country remained totally unprepared for war. They wanted to fight, but with what, where and how?

"Remember, sir," said Monroe, "that according to Jefferson, it is merely a matter of marching into Canada."

"Yes." Madison absent-mindedly reviewed the papers and documents on his desk.

"We can call for 50,000 volunteers and 10,000 army. Gallatin is asking for a 50 percent increase in tariffs to give us 13 million dollars from customs duties and other revenues . . . to outfit all vessels of war, arm merchant vessels and destroy British fisheries and commerce . . . at St. Lawrence, York and Queenstown. Barlow says France is poised to invade Russian with 600,000 men. Pinkney's left England . . . for protection and patriotism. Tippecanoe war fever is at an extreme pitch out west in Indiana and Ohio . . . Henry Clay and Calhoun . . . the John Henry affair. Randolph condemns the War Hawks! And Congress will never vote for enough taxes to pay for an actual war."

Monroe sniffed. "Any true Federalist already hates Clay. Carrying the flag to Canada, Mobile and Key West—the western flock seem to forget we purchased west Florida and Louisiana from Spain and France—"

"But the fighting continues, after all, legal or otherwise . . . General Jackson . . ." Madison paused.

"I know, Mr. President, but those army appropriations bills will pass through the House, and I believe the Senate as well. And next year is an election year for—"

"I know, I know. But look at this, another petition from Josiah Quincy, J. Q. Adams, Rufus King, the Clintonians—"

"They don't control the Congress, sir. Langdon Cheves, Felix Grundy, Giles and Lowndes—they're the committee, Mr. President. You must side with your own party or . . ."

"Or be branded a Federalist. These young southern and western Republicans know nothing about foreign relations—they know nothing about war! But they want to invade Canada."

"And the French still claim they have repealed the Berlin and Milan decrees," Monroe said, "and the British will not repeal the Orders in Council denying us free trade with anyone else—"

"Napoleon has played me like a fool."

"Well, sir, it is too late to concern ourselves with that now. And we lose many more ships and men to the British than the French."

"That's true. And we cannot declare war on both—we cannot!"

The more fortunate Federalists, many of them New England merchants and shipowners, made fortunes in trade and fought the notion of war at every turn.

The late spring night breeze wafted through the mansion's tall windows in this great half-completed smelly swamp and marsh of a city, extending from both banks of the Potomac. Not to mention yellow fever and other sickness brought on by the gasses or, according to one odd theory, the remorseless attack of mosquitoes and other minute pests. The nation's capital, just ten years old, consisted mostly of the worst roads of yellow clay, huge muddy holes, streetlamps with no oil, loose hogs, and boardinghouses like Captain Coyle's, Mrs. Cottringer's and Miss Shield's, where most members of Congress lived.

Clay and Calhoun presided over the "war mess." Two of the loudest opponents were Federalist Daniel Webster and Alexander Hanson with his damned *Federal Republican* libel out of Baltimore. The *Lawrence* and the *Hornet* had finally returned from England in May with no good news, no budging on the odious Orders in Council or impressment. Now after midnight on this first of June, seeing the grim face of his Secretary of State, Monroe, facing humiliation after humiliation. The United States were debased, defamed and maligned in the eyes of the world.

Taking Canada would be merely a matter of marching, Jefferson had said. It took nearly a week to travel to Philadelphia; how long to the Canadian border? Here, Madison felt that he was mired in a wilderness. But at least it was a Republican wilderness. The much-threatened, now-realized War Congress consumed Washington City. Madison turned again to his Secretary of State, James Monroe.

"Any more word yet from that naval committee?"

"No, sir. But Porter, Rogers, Bainbridge, Decatur, all say that the committee agrees that some sort of . . . accommodation . . . might still be possible. But since there is nothing in writing yet, and no new commitment from the Representatives that we can live with—of course, most of our naval professionals recommend an offensive use of our . . . naval assets."

Madison waited for Monroe to continue; when he saw that nothing was forthcoming, he nodded and said, musingly, "I wish we could get some reliable counseling on what to do about our navy and coastal defenses."

Monroe, dressed impeccably in a dark blue silk suit and paisley waistcoat, loosened his cravat and settled back down in the leather Louis XV straightbacked chair, stretching out his new long trousers and tall leather boots, in contrast to the older president, still wearing the old-fashioned breeches and stockings.

"No one wants to pay for a standing army or navy, sir; only a standing promise of regulars and militias numbering 12,000 men. Remember when President Jefferson told Congressman Walden to 'hold on like a good and faithful seaman, till our brother sailors can rouse from their intoxication and right the vessel.' That was during Preble's command against the Barbary Pirates. Tripoli."

"Yes. I believe you mentioned him earlier. Excellent record. Flinty character. We need another Preble now. Not just 'Preble's Boys.'" Madison paused again and looked over the letters the secretary had handed him, some new, some old.

He read from one, "'I must warn you, sir, of the folly, begging your pardon, of sending soft emissaries and money to the British, any more than we did to Barbary corsairs. London, like the Bashaw of Tripoli, only understands force of arms. It is my understanding that one fifth of the annual budget, over two millions, was paid to the pirates of Morocco, the Bey of Tunis, Algiers and Tripoli. In addition to the need to protect our citizens in their lawful pursuit of neutral trade, it will be more economical to teach a sharp lesson to all pirates in their kingdoms, and at the same time, to provide training for our future naval officers, instead of dismantling our most potent weapon to discourage outrage and loss of trade freedom at sea.'"

"Is that the letter from Jeffries, sir?"

"Yes," said Madison. Then he continued, "'There is no price you can pay for a fighting force of the caliber of men which the likes of Secretary Hamilton would squeeze dry of life and substance. Many of us have chosen a merchant career—to fight for profit rather than patriotism—there being so few public ships. Certainly I myself "took up the quill and lay down the cannon" because there was no Navy to speak of at the time I resigned from the service. As Paul Jones and Truxtan have urged, we must have a training school for officers, and a large fleet at least of small vessels. No other nation will treat us with respect if we lack even the most minimal naval force. I remain ready to command any fighting vessel, except one of those damned rotting, useless gunboats. We cannot prevent blockade, but we can still quickly build many more sea raiders like the *Argus, Wasp, Hornet, Enterprize,* and we must, to force the British to end impressment and other interference with our free trade! I remain, Honored Sir, your most humble and obedient servant—'"

Madison looked up again, shaking his head irritably.

"'William B. Jeffries, Captain, United States Navy.' Listen to that!" Madison exclaimed. "The man is incorrigible. After that duel with poor Jacob Auster and the disagreeable details of the disappearance of his son Nathan, and his lively career as a drunk, he wants us to give him a navy ship to fight. I was told that he was now virtually an invalid."

"Yes, sir, but apparently, sir, Richard Auster is now the one under investigation, and the Jeffries have been more or less exonerated. And Joshua Barney and William Jones, whom Jefferson had offered the job of Naval Secretary, have vouched for William, and have also badgered your

naval secretary, Hamilton, for dozens of small warships, corvettes, schooners, brigs, 12 to 22 guns, unleashed against British trade—"

"All of this advice, except for how to pay for these vessels. Why do
these captains ignore our privateers? Surely they would be enough to
tame the British lion as far as *guerre de course*? Shipowners are paying
their crews up to 50 dollars per month! And how on earth can we fight
the largest navy the world has ever seen? Our navy consists of a few
dozen vessels—and not one ship of the line!"

"Yes, sir . . . but these gentlemen insist that we must and can augment
the private vessels with small public vessels to bring British merchant
fleet to heel. Baltimore, for instance—"

"Speaking of Baltimore, look at this article from that devil Federalist Hanson in Baltimore, that damned *Federal Republican*, rousing others
among that infested den of surviving Federalists."

"Sir, the *Baltimore Whig*, the *National Intelligencer* and Niles' *Weekly
Register* remain faithful to you."

"Yes. I must ignore that demented editorial excess, just as Jefferson
did. Would you please read my letter to Congress again?"

"Certainly, Mr. President."

Monroe began to read aloud:

"British cruisers have been in the continued practice of violating the
American flag on the great highway of nations, and of seizing and carrying off persons sailing under it . . . thousands of American citizens, under
the safeguard of public law and of their national flag, have been torn
from their country and from everything dear to them; have been dragged
onboard ships of war of a foreign nation and exposed, under the severities
of their discipline, to be exiled to the most distant and deadly climes, to
risk their lives in the battles of their oppressors, and to be the melancholy
instruments of taking away those of their own brethren . . . Not content
with . . . laying waste our neutral trade, the cabinet of Britain resorted at
length to the sweeping system of blockades, under the name of orders in
council . . . as might best suit its political views, its commercial jealousies
or the avidity of British cruisers . . . And as an additional insult . . . the
commerce of the United States is to be sacrificed . . . as interfering with

the monopoly she covets for her own commerce and navigation . . . She
carries on a war against the lawful commerce of a friend that she may the
better carry on a commerce with an enemy—a commerce polluted by the
forgeries and perjuries which are for the most part the only passports by
which it can succeed . . . We behold our seafaring citizens, still the daily
victims of lawless violence, committed on the great common and highway
of nations, even within sight of the country that owes them protection.
We behold our vessels, freighted with the products of our soil and industry, or returning with the honest proceeds the revocation of her decrees,
as they violated the neutral rights of the United States, her Government
has authorized illegal captures by its privateers and public ships, and that
other outrages have been practised on our vessels and our citizens . . . We
behold, in fine, on the side of Great Britain a state of war against the
United States, and on the side of the United States a state of peace toward Great Britain.'"

Monroe paused and looked up at Madison, who nodded.

"Not for much longer, Mr. Monroe."

"Unless the Federalists have enough votes in the House or Senate to . . ."

"We will soon know, Mr. President."

Eighteen

The Last Prize

Nathan, Captain Turner and O'Reilley were all on the quarterdeck at dawn. The sun pulled itself out of the sea in a glorious morning. Even in Antigua there had been talk about the United States actually, finally declaring war on Great Britain, but no one believed it. The early June sun burst gloriously above the clear horizon off the starboard quarter—then the shout came from the maintop.

"Sail in sight . . . fine on the starboard bow!"

"She's overhauled us, sir, but how?" asked O'Reilley.

Nathan said nothing.

"We don't know how," said Turner impatiently, "but that is a frigate. Nathan will figure out a way for us to dodge the bastards again."

But the northerly breeze said otherwise. Nathan went below without a word and stared at the chart again. The frigate, close-hauled now on starboard tack, had somehow beaten them to the Capes and now held the weather gauge. This time, practically within sight of home, they might not prevail. Nathan and *Cormorant* were returning in triumph after defeating *Scourge*. Turner had virtually turned over the ship to Nathan, after all the bold risks and financial success of their adventures on Antigua. The ominous sail—almost certainly a British frigate; the chase was on . . . again.

His thoughts churned—come about and abandon the Bay altogether? Deliberately run her aground? Sink her? It was a bad moment for the strapping young man, one of the worst, as he stood alone in the Captain's cabin. Then he mastered himself again.

Still, Nathan felt sick; their luck could only last so long. But maybe the wind would back and weaken, favoring the smaller vessel. An unmarked shoal might hold the frigate in its grasp. Maybe some miracle ... would save them. All hands were ready, and every man would be needed above deck. The guns were heaved overboard to marginally increase *Cormorant's* speed. Precious cargo and supplies were shifted, some tossed into the calming sea, bilge water was pumped ... all futile gestures.

Every sail set; the early ruddy light seemed to burnish faces and wood as it slanted across the deck, and lightening airs washed over the starboard quarter, easing the ship along in an orderly fashion, her stern rising and falling sedately in the light, long, even swell. The frigate, also beating into the wind, clawing toward them less than a league to the northeast now, and off to larboard, Cape Henry, as if mocking them. The warship would overhaul her victim by noon. They could perhaps prolong the chase by giving up on Chesapeake Bay, wear away and steer *Cormorant* southeast. But it would make little difference. The courses of prey and predator, barring damage, accident or dramatic change in wind, would inevitably intersect within a few hours. Time to return to the quarterdeck. The men abruptly stopped talking and stared at Nathan as he approached.

"Sir!" Nathan greeted Turner, who nodded, and then Nathan looked at O'Reilley.

"Tell the master here," the latter said impatiently, "that we do not want that ship to close the distance any more than he has, without a signal of surrender on our part. Even if she doesn't blow us to bits, that captain will treat with severe punishment anyone aboard who he thinks most responsible for the long chase, this recapture and for doing his best to keep this ship away from that one. As it is, many of us—"

"Shut your mouth," Captain Turner said. "Nathan?"

"He is right, Captain," said Nathan. "I have failed. You must say nothing, and at least allow me to accept full blame in front of these bastards—"

"Nonsense—we are all in this together. None of this is your failing."

Now, maddeningly, in spite of the determined efforts of the crew to get every inch of speed out of *Cormorant*, they were about to be captured again. The large ship, towering above the northern sky, sails still glowing from the early sun, a molten ball simmering near the horizon. Nathan barely glanced at Logan and his other mates, who silently shook their heads.

"You have not failed, my boy," said Turner. "You have performed . . . splendidly. Heave to, lads," he added sadly.

"Mr. Reynolds! Send the men to braces!"

"Back the fore topsail! Clew up the courses! Helm, when she pays off, ease up to east and keep her steady." *Cormorant* fell off to the larboard now, fore and main topsails acting as brakes on one another.

"It is time. Helm amidships! Helm hard over!"

"Shift over your head sheets! Fore topsail braces, haul away! Brail the courses! Ease the spanker! Helm, hard over!"

The frigate, now hull up dead to windward, bore down on them. Those towering pyramids of canvas now beginning to merge as the frigate came up into the wind, less than three hundred yards distant, the big ship now preparing prepared to heave to. The two ships would soon be side by side, less than a cable's length apart.

In less than an hour, the 38-gunner, ensigns on the fore and mizzen, Union Jack flying at the maintop, was less than 100 yards to the northeast, main deck guns and carronades run out.

"Not takin' no chances, is he?" said Logan, with a dismissive snort.

Nathan could see faces and uniforms now, at the entry port and the quarterdeck. The sun rose and warmed the clear air, and they could only wait, rocking in the waves but relatively motionless as the British 10-oar launch was quickly lowered.

"Boarding party and prize crew, sir," said Jack Logan, with a cool gaze at their persecutor coming up on their larboard quarter.

"Mister Logan, Reynolds! Not a word."

"Aye, aye, sir!" Reynolds shouted angrily.

"Nathan, you know where the strong box is."

But then Nathan froze as he recognized the face of a spidery-armed lieutenant in the boat.

"Oars!" shouted the British cox'n as the boat came along side, secured by the British crew.

"Holy Christ, it ain't—"

Cormorant's men stared at the boarding party, had then started groaning with curse and roar as they too saw what Nathan and Turner did.

"Silence!" Turner shouted, turned to Nathan. "Good Lord, my boy, this can't be true!"

It was none other than Archibald Coxe who strutted across the gangway toward them, smiling and licking his ugly lips. Those black eyes now crinkled at Nathan in delighted amusement. Should he have tried to hide? If he had known . . . would it have made any difference? Surely this was an act of God—or the Devil. The men could only fume silently.

Coxe turned to his midshipman. "Mr. Halley, take four men and search the ship."

Nathan looked at his Captain, whom he loved almost as a father. And at his mates: Duffy, the cook and surgeon's mate; Murphy; Tom Howard; Jonas Green; Old Halley Sobery, who had sailed as cabin boy and powder monkey with his father on *Medusa*; Sam Tripe, steward, clerk and acting pursar; Sobery; Roger Lovitt, best liked man aboard and one of the best singers, hornpipers, topmen, indispensable everywhere, including the quarterdeck where he had nearly bled to death. The wonders they had seen: Fort Nelson in Barbados, St. John's, Antigua, Maria, the living coral seas. Nathan's stomach turned and he glanced at the bright sun, his mind was in turmoil, knowing this could be his last day on earth. Would he see the sun rise again?

"Search them—not too gently. Is this your entire crew?" Coxe asked the Captain.

"All except our prisoners," said Turner, as the marines and sailors searched, beat and pushed his men into a line amidships.

"We will not resist, sir," said Turner coldly.

"I should think not," said Coxe.

"If you will accompany me below—"

"That won't be necessary—strong box in your cabin? Papers—"

"Proving our bonafides, sir."

"Shut your mouth, old man! Spare me your protests of righteous indignation. You and your shipmates will be tried in London. No doubt your contraband Baker rifles, muskets and pistols . . . for the Indians and the

British? Or Colonial rebels? Hidden, I gather, behind a false bulkhead. You there," he said, turning to O'Reilley. "Go with Mr. Halley and show them."

The men of *Cormorant* fumed silently.

"Certainly some of these seamen are British deserters," Coxe said.

Now Coxe's pockmarked face came up to Nathan's and sneered. "Did you really think you was going to escape, Jeffries?"

"Well, it took you two ships and 4,000 miles to capture us again—that won't please your master, will it? Who rescued you? At whose bidding are you now?"

Coxe raised his fist as if to club the taller man, but then smiled.

"Captain Dacres and *Guerriere* were kind enough to offer me this temporary berth aboard; he and Captain Auster are old friends. You will live long enough to see my employer again—even though you will pray for death when you do. Who knows, maybe I will entertain you aboard my next ship!"

"I doubt you'll get another ship or crew soon, Archie—the way you lose them! Fourth lieutenant, I'd guess—"

Coxe stopped smiling, nodded to a man behind Nathan, and a pistol butt suddenly slammed into the back of his head. In blinding pain, he crashed to the deck and saw his own blood staining the deck it. Before he passed out, Nathan prayed for his parents and their pardon, prayed that he would not disgrace himself.

Baltimore

"I wish you had explained the realities of a sea war to Madison himself," said Alexander Hanson with a profound sigh. "Or even to a few congressmen."

"Would that I could have," said Captain William Jeffries. "We tried, remember? Sam Dana did his best. Even Monroe favored a limited maritime war. Now Captain Barney is at sea on *Rossie*, and Jones is back in Philadelphia."

"These Republican fools! Well, they have their unlimited war—right here in Baltimore!"

The two men sat apart from the others, two dozen in all, sleeping in some cases, in the county jail lit fitfully by candles in the thick darkness. They were all known Federalists and had been rounded up and escorted from Hanson's battered South Charles Street "fort" early that day by General Stricker's militia, with some injuries sustained. And now, without weapons, they could hear the growing mob outside calling for blood.

"This was a mistake, Alex—you cannot trust Mayor Johnson any more than Stricker—and now we have no guns or swords."

"I know. I am so sorry I dragged you into this."

"You did not—nor did that lawyer friend of yours, Francis Scott Key or General Lee. I disagree with your politics as much of your politics as ever—but any enemy of the Austers is a friend of mine, and madmen and mobs . . . cowards . . . deserve all they get."

"Well, thank you for that. Yes, Richard is certainly an enemy now, thanks to all the information Catherine Charles and your wife provided. Auster is ruined in Baltimore, maybe up north too; he is on the run from charges of slave-trading, running arms to the British and the Indians, trading against all federal—"

"Tar and feather the traitors!" someone yelled just outside. "Treason means death!"

"The distinguished Auster put the mayor up to this," said Hanson, "and instigated this riot, this gang of cowards."

"With the help of the *Whig*, the *Sun*, the *National Intelligencer*, the *Weekly Register*—not to mention the *Federal Republican*!"

Hanson smiled. "You are right. How is Amy?"

"She still talks about Nathan—"

"Yes, I am so sorry."

"She forbade me from coming to your aid, in Georgetown or here. And yet, here I am again. I . . . don't know what the President of the United States is thinking, invading Canada—"

"The fool thinks we can just march in, as Jefferson said. He thinks that Napoleon will defeat Russia and we will conquer Canada and then Great Britain must end impressments; maybe after some sea raiders and armed merchantmen cause enough damage, no navy is needed."

"Castlereagh has scuttled those damned Orders in Council, but they will never willingly end impressment. How do you feel, Harry?"

General "Light Horse Harry" Lee had suddenly sat up, resting against the wall, shaking his head and groaning.

"I badly misjudged this situation," he said. "I only hope I live to see my son Robert again."

"If I have anything to say about it, you will," said Jeffries.

"Thanks, Captain. You have been a good friend."

Suddenly they heard the outer jail door open and a roaring crowd charging inside.

"Get the lights!" William shouted. "Harry, you and Hanson stay with me!"

The bloodthirsty crowd broke down the cell door and swarmed on top of the men inside. "Kill the Tories!" shouted a man William recognized as George Wooleslager from Fells Point and the butcher John Mumma. They heard thuds, hacking and screams as William secretly slipped Lee and Hanson past the rioters, yelling for blood himself, squeezing through the crowd.

They gained the street, but then Hanson was recognized as well as Lee. Suddenly a dozen drunken fanatics were beating them with rusty swords, and knives and clubs, and William lost contact with the other two. He punched and flailed as the mob descended on him. One of the other victims from the jail was tarred and feathered and lit on fire. He saw children ram a stick down the throat of one prostate body, and pour molten wax in his eyes.

"He is still alive! Cut his heart out!"

Captain William Jeffries, though now on the fringe of the horror, was fading fast and could still feel his tortured body and face being hit as he fell to his knees. He thought once again how he and his son had disobeyed Amy, and now she would be alone, her foolish men gone. Then he thought he recognized Dr. Andrews and a flashing, whirling figure, Peter Hughes, leveling everyone around him.

"Let's go home, Captain."

The rest was darkness.

Nineteen

War At Last - *June 29, 1812*

Before Lieutenant Coxe left for *Cormorant*, Captain Dacres had ordered him to leave Capt. Turner alone. Despite that direct order, Coxe had his men ransack Turner's cabin with particularly destructive thoroughness, then forced the Captain to sign over his papers with ship and cargo for delivery to Dacres, minus a few personal gifts for Coxe. *Guerriere* had fewer than 300 men as crew, so Dacres had no men to spare to leave a prize crew aboard the ship. In fact, Coxe was ordered to impress the best men from *Cormorant* and bring them aboard *Guerriere*. He gleefully chose Nathan, Jack Logan, O'Reilley and Tom Howard.

Nathan silently fumed at this turn of events. He had succeeded in getting good profit for *Cormorant*, avoiding capture and death on the island of Antigua, then within sight of Cape Henry had been impressed again, probably for the last time. After he was lifted roughly from the deck, Nathan broke away from the two British marines and looked Turner in the eyes.

"You . . . you and every member of this crew will . . . survive, or I . . . I will die trying to . . . to save you."

But now, since his arrival aboard *Guerriere*, Coxe had isolated Nathan from his *Cormorant* crew and managed to punish him every day, in any way he could; freely laying on the cat-o'-nine-tails and using his fists, only in the most undignified and awkward places, but he eased up when that did start to show. A recently captured American, Captain Orne of *Betsey*, in gratitude for Nathan's saving his life one day aloft, somehow procured laudanum for Nathan's daily agony—but no one else would openly defy Coxe's injunction against helping Nathan Jeffries. This seemed to include Coxe's superiors; Lieutenants Kent and Ready must have closed their eyes to this blatant violation of orders. Coxe persevered in Nathan's torture, and soon Nathan would be permanently crippled, in both his mind and his body.

Most of the crew laughed when they read or heard about American and British newspapers announcing the war; the U.S. Congress had barely squeezed the declaration of war in front of the American people, and many protested; in any case their land forces were a joke, and the U.S. Navy? The London *Times* described it as "a few fir-built frigates manned by a handful of bastards and outlaws."

Nathan yearned for the release of death, even though he was trained to despise surrender and self-pity. But this last bizarre event, his recapture by Coxe, made all seem hopeless. Five years ago Nathan's world had shattered when he secretly witnessed his father killing Captain Jacob Auster with a pistol at Bladensburg, and since then Jacob's son Richard had waged a perpetual campaign against the Jeffries, always stopping short of personal challenge. Now Nathan found himself slave to the lash, again, his ship taken, his back side opened, captured twice—by the same little troll, Archibald Coxe, supposedly a British privateer, now trumped-up royal naval lieutenant, whose real master was Richard Auster. And after all that Nathan had endured, Auster and his man Coxe would win the game anyway. All for nothing, and now both of Amy's foolish men, son and father, broken by men they should never have challenged in the first place.

July 16, 1812

Dacres had finally found the patrolling British squadron. The commander, Commodore Broke, aboard the 38-gun frigate *Shannon*, had already heard from the packet the latest news of war from the British side. The squadron included a captured brig, the former *USS Nautilus,* the old 64-gun ship of the line *Africa*, and the smaller frigates *Aeolus* and *Belvidera*, the last having learned of the war in the most dire way, barely escaping an American squadron weeks earlier, believed to be Commodore Rodgers', consisting of at least one large frigate, possibly *President* with 44 guns. That afternoon, in the haze and baffling breezes four leagues off Little Egg Harbor, New Jersey, they began playing nip-and-tuck with a big ship to leeward, possibly a heavy American frigate. It had taken hours to sort out the identity of the ships of the British inshore squadron to the north and west. At sunset, with meaningless, futile signal lights hung, the ship to the southwest was slowly closing with *Guerriere*. Later that night, with shifting breezes, the other ship bore off again to the southeast.

July 17, 1812

At dawn the next day, Nathan witnessed something startling: amid rockets and guns, the entire British squadron was chasing the unidentified but clearly American vessel, perhaps a league to the south, now just to windward of what little wind remained. Ahead the fitful airs died altogether, and the chase was becalmed. The hapless ship looked familiar to Nathan. Could she be *Constitution*, and his friends George Earleigh and Captain Hull? Up until now, except for *Belvedira*, the British had faced only small, inconsequential vessels at sea. Captain Dacres was obviously excited at the opportunity to engage a worthy opponent. Eventual capture of the American seemed certain; there were four British frigates, and one old ship of the line. The U.S. ship would be overwhelmed, surrounded by superior force, and there was almost no wind. It was a spectacular sight; every ship had every stitch of canvas spread, clouds of sail, from courses to royals, skysails, stun'sails, staysails.

But even while the occasional breeze usually favored the British, and one or more ships remained in extreme range of the prey, the capture eluded them. For the next two days, the frustrated British hounds bayed fruitlessly at the heels of the American fox. Ships were towed, kedged, tried to take advantage of every breath of wind that occasional arose. Long shots were occasionally fired; none hit the target. The quarry teetered on the edge of being in fatal range. Sometimes five ships were hull up; but the fox somehow kept away from *Guerriere* and the other attackers.

Nathan was stunned. The feat was almost unbelievable. And yet when he gave it more thought, who more likely than Hull and his crack crew to escape the British net? Hull and his boys were easily the best sailors Nathan had ever known, totally dedicated to their craft and their men—the consummate technicians and managers when it came to seamanship.

A squall had finally come up, a strong northwesterly. The American ship was to windward, several miles south. When the British officers on the quarterdeck looked through the rain and saw to their surprise her flying with all sails set, they cursed in a most ungentlemanly fashion; the United States frigate had slipped out of their grasp.

August 9, 1812

When *Guerriere* overhauled a small merchant brig and sent over a boat for its register, it was Lt. Coxe who reported to Dacres when the boat returned.

"It is *John Adams*, sir, Liverpool to New York," he said, handing the register to the Captain. Coxe stood and waited patiently, and was surprised to see Dacres smile.

"Shall we burn her, Captain?"

"A moment, Mister Coxe," said Dacres, who began writing in the register.

"Return this to the brig, sir, and let her go on her way," said Dacres, waving dismissal.

"Aye, aye, Captain."

A Welshman named Wells had befriended Nathan onboard *Guerriere*, and given him assurances of his sympathy and promised discretion. When Nathan found out that the brig was American, he wrote a note of his own, determined to get it somehow to the brig. This was his chance. Wells, told off for the cutter's crew, had returned aboard with Coxe. Now the latter read out loud what Dacres had written in the brig's register while he and Nathan listened.

"'Captain Dacres,'" read Coxe, "'commander of His Britannic Majesty's frigate *Guerriere* of 44 guns, presents his compliments to Commodore Rodgers of the United States frigate *President,* and will be very happy to meet him, or any other American frigate of equal force to the *President*, off Sandy Hook for the purpose of having a few minutes of *tête-à-tête.*'"

Those within earshot laughed as Nathan slipped Wells his note to be returned to the brig—just in time, as Coxe triumphantly and contemptuously looked in his direction.

"Wells, let's go," said Coxe.

Dacres was eager for a showdown, and Nathan wanted to help. "Urge you to get word to American frigates. Frigate *Guerriere* headed alone for Halifax for repairs," he had written. "Believe H.M. frigate is overmatched in crew, weight of metal and size by the large American frigates. I am an American citizen impressed aboard her. Nathan Jeffries, master of neutral United States merchant brig *Cormorant*, Boston, legitimate neutral trade."

We'll see about that, he thought.

Now his hands started to shake as the boat rowed back to the brig. If Wells revealed the note or was forced to tell all, Nathan would be flogged again, or worse. Ironic, indeed, that everyone wanted to fight. There was no secret there. But Nathan knew, or at least more fully appreciated, the advantages the big American frigates would have against the British, singly fought. And in *Guerriere's* present condition, and severely undermanned—it was the best chance the Americans had. Timing was all. His hands still shook; Coxe was watching him suspiciously.

Why did he take this chance? He admitted to himself it was hate of Auster, and even Barbara and Peter, that drove him, not love of country; neither his father's nor his mother's way. That spurred him on. He didn't care who was right or wrong—only cared about the U.S. frigates as a way to release him from this bondage and pain, and perhaps to enable him to exact his own revenge.

From the quarterdeck, Captain Dacres caught sight of Nathan midships larboard and thought, that big silent American, Jeffries, seems to have become the leader for all the Americans, his quiet demeanor notwithstanding. Evidently claimed to be Quaker. Dacres saw the tall young man approaching the quarterdeck ladder, now limping, with new and old scars, and favoring his left side as if partly paralyzed; clearly hardened and used severely through many hard months at sea. But there was something else about the man, an apparent humility, not given to idle talk. He seemed to get in trouble with Coxe often but never witnessed by Dacres; suffering the after effects of it, seemingly random and sometimes severe—contusions, broken ribs, crushed foot. His back suggested recent flogging, no doubt from his last captain. In the vast panorama of extra hands, caught and dragged aboard by the voracious British sea net, this man interested him more than most.

Dacres turned to Lt. Kent. "It seems to me that Jeffries is a very able seaman and a leader among the Americans. Do you believe any part of his story about being an innocent Quaker and legal master of *Cormorant*?"

"Sir, Coxe swears to me that the story is not true—Jeffries is just a sea-lawyer and notorious pirate, his mother's family from that damned nest of thieves—speaking of which, did you read, sir, of that riot in the town in June? Mutilations of loyal Federalists—"

"Dammit, Mr. Kent, do you believe Coxe or not?"

"Sorry, sir. Yes—that is, I believe Number Four. I do not care for Coxe personally, but—forgive me, I mean—that I do believe Coxe as a naval professional over the American ruffian. Everyone can see Jeffries is a common rogue, a robber jonathan, yes sir."

"Well, I guess our Mr. Coxe is no martinet."

"Sir?"

"Yes, thank you, Number One. Dismissed. Carry on."

August 19, 1812

Log of U.S. Frigate *Constitution*: "Lat. 41, 42 N. 1on. 55,33 W. Thursday, fresh breeze from NW and cloudy; at 2 pm discovered a vessel to the southward, made all sail in chase; at 3, perceived the chase to be a ship on the starboard tack, close hauled to the wind; hauled SSW; at half past 3, made out the chase to be a frigate; at 4, coming up with chase very fast."

Guerriere was sailing west, close hauled under reefed topsails, heading alone toward Halifax, ordered in for some much-needed repair and perhaps to pick up a few hands. Nathan also suspected that he would be imprisoned or hanged there, but Dacres had not come out and said so. In any case, Auster and Coxe would never let him live. Nathan wondered if *Constitution* had returned to Boston or New York; if she or other heavy American frigates would ever find them, would see his note.

And even if they did—what chance did the United States Navy have against the enormous size and experience of the British Lion? In fleet or single-ship actions, for centuries, the limeys had won a victory virtually every time, fighting French, Spanish, Dutch. They were certain of an American defeat at sea now. The midshipman had just rung four bells in the afternoon watch, 2 PM. The previous day had been foggy and rainy, but the wind was slowly rising again out of the northwest and the seas were starting to pick up. Flying cumulus clouds gathered to the southeast, promising heavy overcast later. Ideal sun and fresh breeze right now, though, as Nathan made his way aft.

But this wasn't to be just another day of no sail in sight. The foremast lookout had seen something to windward and Nathan heard the call to shorten sail. As crew poured out of the hatchway for the change, he saw on the quarterdeck his colleague and fellow prisoner, Captain Orne, talking to Captain Dacres; the first lieutenant, Kent, was with them, pointing.

Nathan walked boldly over to the group, narrowly missing a collision with the quartermaster's mate at the helm; that wheel was going to become very busy soon. The bos'n's mate made ready to rudely remove Nathan from the august presence. "Permission to join you briefly, sir, on the quarterdeck?" Nathan said to Dacres.

"Granted, sir," said Dacres politely. "Captain Orne here suggests that sail to the north may be American."

Lt. Coxe appeared and saluted his Captain; he glared at Nathan but said nothing.

"What is our position, Mr. Coxe?" asked Dacres.

"It is 41 degrees 42 minutes north, 55 degrees 48 minutes west, sir."

"Very good. So, it is a Yankee, you think, Captain?"

"Tremendous sails . . . a great vessel. 'Tis no Frenchie, in my opinion, sir," said Orne, looking through the spyglass again before handing it back to Lt. Kent.

There was a hail from the foretop. "Deck, there! I think she's a United States frigate!"

The men looked at each other. Kent rubbed his hands together but said nothing. He was kind enough to offer his glass to Nathan.

"What do you think, Jeffries?" asked Dacres, peering through his own glass.

"I think Orne and your lookout are correct. But she's a small American frigate—*Essex* or *Congress*, likely enough." Nathan spoke calmly, but his heart was racing. He knew it must be one of the big frigates—*United States, President* or *Constitution*, nominally 44 guns. This might be his last chance.

Dacres sniffed. "She's running free before the wind—coming down too boldly for an American—pardon me, gentlemen." Dacres bowed and smiled. "Well, that is all to the better for our glory if he behaves well . . . look how that ship tries to slip inshore! After taking her I shall be made for life! An admiral, like my father."

Captain Orne shook his head and went below.

As Nathan watched the vast pyramid of sails rise above the horizon and the distance slowly lessen to a few leagues, he felt like he was staring at his own destiny. In the late afternoon, as the two ships approached like wary duelists, and in spite of his own lack of experience on the field of honor, he shivered with a kind of terror. But it passed. Then he felt a surge in his heart that was almost painful; he was confused because he should not be having feelings like these, an awful resurgence of—a kind of patriotism. Of course, how would he feel after the American frigate was captured?

Futile attempts to communicate by signal flags confirmed that this was clearly the enemy. The sails were obviously from a large vessel, a frigate. And though no flag could easily be seen, Nathan felt certain in his bones, almost as a feeling of predestiny, that this ship, bearing down on them from windward and then from the northwest, was *the* ship, Isaac Hull's ship with his friend George Earliegh, son of poor old Enoch, aboard. And he also somehow felt that in a few hours, by sunset at least, he would be a free man again—or he would be dead. The fresh breeze suddenly took on a chill, though it was August.

Orne returned to the quarterdeck before 3 PM, Nathan looked around the ship—most of the crew were already on deck, of course, studying the other ship. Dacres followed his gaze, then shouted, "Beat to quarters, Mr. Kent! Fighting sail."

Amid the drum roll, shouting and pounding of feet as the gun crews were called to stations, Dacres studied the other ship carefully, and decided to back the main topsail and wait on the enemy. The rising wind would bring them together soon enough. He looked at his two "guests" and smiled slightly. Just then Lieutenant Coxe came up and saluted him before herding—actually shoving—Nathan toward the companionway.

"Main deck ready for action, sir." But with a glance at Orne and Nathan, he said, "I don't know where we will place so many new prisoners. Forward with you, Jeffries."

Soon the large frigate was not merely hull up, but within a league, perhaps only two miles distant. "What make you, sir, of that ship?" Dacres asked Orne. "Will she fire her guns when we get into long cannon shot range? Does she know how? Is she one of your largest? Perhaps *Constitution?*"

Something took hold of Orne, and he answered in a manner somewhat foolhardy. "Not only is she that, Captain, but she is your defeat bearing down on us!" Orne nodded, looking apprehensively at Dacres.

But Dacres only laughed. It was obvious that he was eager for a fight, for an acceptance of his invitation of a "few minutes of *tête-à-tête*" with an American ship, and hoping desperately that he could now become the first British captain in the war to humble the upstart Yankee in a free, fair and open ship-to-ship duel between two sizable naval vessels. Two frigates, nominally an even match.

Half past 4 PM

By now every tick and rat aboard the converging frigates, lofty clouds of topsails, topgallants furled and courses brailed, knew that shortly they would slug and pound and throw iron, lead, wooden spars and splinters like harpoons, pikes and cutlasses, tomahawks and muskets in the tops and fire and smoke and wet blood and acrid death—probably wet and salty, very unhealthy, no doubt mostly aboard the insufferable Yank, but no names, no nationality remaining, only bloody red body parts washed overboard, as the broken enemy vessel lurched in the steep seas.

Grinning happily at this prospect, James Richard Dacres studied his American opponent, thinking of how this fabulous prize, if not too badly damaged, would be worth at least 10,000 pounds sterling for the victorious captain's share. It would also accelerate his rise to Admiral, possibly a political career, if he could curb his acerbic wit; not to mention how it would please his new wife, Arabella. He shouted for another report from the mizzen lookout, voice already hoarse. He gripped the weather taffrail tightly with both hands, inhaled the crisp, freshening nor'westerly; this was his moment. A confrontation with the U.S. frigate *President* or other American, and he would be the first British captain to beat the upstart Yankee in a fair fight, a gentlemen's duel in "Madison's war," and no dodging, no more excuses or delays, matched evenly enough after that long afternoon of maneuvering. Probably—he hoped—John Rodgers himself would be on *President*, so he could see the words "Not The Little Belt" on *Guerriere's* foretopsail.

Dacres knew perfectly well these American ships were hardly what the *Chronicle* called "fir-built frigates" of "pine and striped bunting." On the contrary, they impressed naval professionals as outstanding and powerful frigates with heavy crews. But could these rebels fight? Barbary pirates and the French are all well and good, but these mere colonials could never defeat the British sea lion. Touch wood.

Dacres waved the American Capt. Orne to him.

"Captain?"

"Well, Orne, what do you think—a bit timid, eh? For such as imposing vessel, new white sails and all. But we still have two hours of light."

"You'll never take that ship," said Orne.

"Is that Jeffries' opinion, as well?

"Sir, we only ask that Americans remain below during the battle."

"That again? I have discussed the matter with my officers and assure you that no American will be forced to fight against other Americans; now, if you will excuse me—"

Dacres turned away.

"Yes, sir. But Captain, you need to tell Lt. Coxe . . . again—even now Americans are being forced to serve the guns, all—"

"Are you deaf?" asked the corporal, shoving Orne toward the ladder with his musket. "Get back down to your friends—"

Below on the gun deck, walking away from the number eight 18-pounder "Long Tom," Nathan met Orne at the quarterdeck ladder to receive the last of his laudanum. Nathan knew that after these blessed hours of physical numbness, the pain would increase again exponentially.

There would be no escape for Nathan this time; Coxe would see to that. He would almost certainly be dead, one grisly way or another, by the end of the dogwatch. If Coxe didn't get him, British or American shot would; and he could expect no less from the inventive Richard Auster, somehow always several moves ahead, unreachable.

And now, after breaking all of his promises to his mother, conquering his lifelong fears and commanding a ship of steady men, sea warriors, he certainly would not live long enough to see his parents again, let alone confront Richard Auster—by now married to the seductive Catherine Charles and on his way to becoming one of the most powerful and dangerous young men between Boston and Baltimore, well known and respected in New York and Philadelphia.

Standing on the gun deck with Logan, O'Reilley and Tom Howard, Nathan had stalled near the break to the quarterdeck to hear Dacres, but now Coxe returned, furious.

"You men, what are you lollygagging for? I want one of you each at number five, six and seven gun, here—"

"Sir," said Nathan, glancing at the nervous Americans, but otherwise unmoving, towering over Coxe, "may I remind you Captain Dacres ordered that you cannot order American civilians, non-combat citizens to—"

He didn't see the belaying pin in Coxe's fist until it smacked into his side. He threw up his arm to guard against another swipe aimed at his head. That pain was nothing compared to the agony when Coxe's pin landed square on his back.

Nathan felt paralyzed, and his legs buckled as Coxe tried for a fourth hit. Nathan forced himself not to cry out again, with tears in his eyes and his spine throbbing, pounding, on fire. Now Coxe slashed at him with his cutlass. He slipped under the blade and swept the deck with his good right arm as Coxe, carried forward by the momentum of his swing fell over and clattered to the deck near "Dear Sally" on the larboard side, much to the amusement of the crew; collapsing like a hammock, cutlass sliding, his legs swinging into the pinrail as his head banged against a carriage truck.

From the deck, Nathan looked up to see Coxe swinging up his cutlass, his head bleeding badly from a cut, running toward him, raising his bright blade with both hands to hack at Nathan, his bloody face a mask of hate.

"You . . . will not survive this battle—" he gasped, or rather squeaked.

"Mister Coxe!" roared Dacres from the quarterdeck. "Belay that! See to your duty and leave that man alone—and don't ever threaten any unarmed man with your own weapon!"

"Sir, do I—"

"Do I make myself clear? He's a prisoner of war, and only I can order punishment! The Americans—we'll not force 'em. They stay in the cable tier until the . . . action is decided."

Coxe locked eyes with Nathan as the sun glared from a purple, bruised horizon. Nathan knew this was his last chance—very soon the situation would be out of his control. But with hatred brimming in his eyes, Coxe's own instinct for survival mastered his fury.

He raised his for'n'aft to Dacres. "Aye, aye, sir."

"Carry on, then! I told you Americans to go below, now! See to it, Coxe—quickly! Then report to Mr. Irvine or his mate, clean up and return to duty. I want no more of this!" The ship writhed massively, twisting and pitching in the angry steep swell, forcing everyone to hold on with both hands. Other gun crews paused.

"Aye, Captain," said Kent. "See to it, Mister Coxe. Will the American ship even fight, Captain? He seems to be wearing."

"Really?" said Dacres, with a glass to his eye, staring intently at the rapidly growing mountain of canvas. "Well, the wind's still rising. We will see."

Within the space of a few minutes, both ships had taken in most of their sails; only fighting canvas remained—reefed topsails, jib and spanker. This was the moment!

"A large frigate, sure enough!" Dacres shouted. "Excellent quarry! Good sport! I do believe it is one of their best we will bag today!" Soon she would be within long range of the maindeck 18's. Dacres rubbed his hands with savage anticipation.

"Come about on the starboard tack," he roared to the quartermaster at the helm. "Man the braces!" The big ship slipped over through the wind as the yards were dragged around.

"Up ports! Run out!" *Guerriere* bravely shouldered the steep waves as the mesmerizing din of banging wood, creaking tackle and the squeaking wheels of the carriages filled the wind, then ceased abruptly as the cannon were run out and the strain and ecstasy ended. *Guerriere* showed her teeth; the guns had been hauled outboard, their muzzles protruding several feet beyond the side of the ship.

"Back the main topsail! Starboard battery, prepare to fire all guns! Lieutenant Ready, keep an eye on the foreward spar deck guns!"

"All guns ready to fire, sir," saluted the first lieutenant, then the second lieutenant and the gunner, Williamson. They waited as the large vessel bore down.

"Very good, Number One. Wait for my signal," Dacres said, calmly. He had the look of a man anticipating a good meal.

"You heard the Captain!" Coxe shouted, and chaos resumed. Nathan was dragged out and carried below by the corporal and two privates. "Give them a taste of our broadside, Number One!" Dacres finally ordered in the brief, groaning silence.

"Fire!" Lieutenant Kent shouted and the deafening roar of the guns erupted, the deck momentarily blanketed in acrid smoke.

Nathan saw through the larboard entryway the other vessel yaw and neatly avoid the metal wrath just unleashed at less than 500 yards, a group of useless splashes suggesting that the target had dodged the broadside by anticipating the precise moment Dacres would fire.

And like a giant parasitic insect from a nightmare, there was Coxe again, face clean and calm. "Just remember, Jeffries, one way or the other, you ain't surviving this—but . . . I surely did enjoy beating you—you made an excellent slave!"

Nathan spit in his face with what little saliva he had.

Coxe backhanded him so hard that the Marine corporal lost his grip and Nathan fell to his knees.

He could not focus and hear, but then that whine: "Always got to get right back up and fight—never give up, is that it, Jeffries? I'll give you this. You got more salt and vinegar than I gave you credit for. You—a big pale sea lawyer! A man of peace! Hiding behind that Quaker cloak! Never thought you'd last, you're a bloody sprig turned Baltimore pirate—you're a born pirate, boy—that's what you—"

"Privateer," Nathan rasped, coughing blood. "You on the other hand are common rat shit—"

Coxe raised his fist again, then looked for Lt. Kent, who was back on the quarter deck. He smiled.

"I promise you one thing, Jeffries, that it will be a very long night for you, and your last. Dacres nor anybody will hear from you no more. And when I finish with you, Captain Auster will be well pleased with me, but maybe not so much your goddamn papa—maybe give that pretty wife of his something to remember, too! Your mother will need comforting!"

Nathan lurched toward Coxe but ended up crashing back on the deck.

Coxe laughed. "Goodbye, Yankee Dumpling."

Nathan barely felt the loud slap of the cat against his back, although that pain would soon return and register. He doubted he could survive the agony to come, even if his tormenters left him to die in some dark corner of the brig, or the bilge itself.

"Get below!" cried the young corporal, brandishing the cat he borrowed from Coxe. Nathan somehow managed to stagger and stumble down the ladder.

Or would the sea take him? Wonderful how the mind can conjure up worse fates. Even now, after weeks of daily creative punishment by Lt. Coxe, the other crew lay low and bet on Nathan's life span in hours. Peter Hughes had taught him loyalty and then betrayal, both in Shakespeare

and in his personal life with Barbara. And yet he was right about everything else. Damn the man. Nathan collapsed again. Then the corporal's
sharp boot probed his liver as he rolled over, coughing blood, shivering,
and felt the crests of agony surging higher and higher.

"This isn't the cable tier," he croaked. "It's the brig. Are you lost,
corporal?"

The little pockmarked man laughed. "Just following orders, Mr. Jeffries,
and now . . . bend over that handsome blonde arse . . . Lt. Coxe sends his—"

Because it seemed he had little to lose, Nathan backhanded the twit,
and the muzzle came up as he backed away. But suddenly the man collapsed forward, adding his own blood to his red uniform. Orne appeared
behind him; smiled and firmly handed over the bloody silver butt-end of a
pistol.

Nathan gripped Orne's other hand in silent thanks. "Is it primed?"
Nathan asked. "Dry? Can we get more? Help me to get to the foc's'le
ladder," he croaked. "We'll have to go through the main deck to get back
down to the cable tier—"

"Are you mad, Nathan? What if Coxe or Dacres or the sergeant see
you? If they don't kill you, American shot will. We . . . we are fairly safe
here—our fellow Americans are safe, too, I'm sure—"

"Help me!" Nathan ordered. He tried not to think of his battered left
shoulder and the signs of bleeding below the surface in his ribcage. For a
moment he felt bitter, but at least his father and mother would approve
of this effort to save life, although his own seemed to be lost.

"I'm going up, Captain!"

Orne, bleeding from a diagonal cut above his left eye, shook his head
at first, but then helped the big man up the ladder. Their gray and brown
civilian clothes, now torn, wet and bloody, seemed to blend in with the
swirling dust and thick smoke. Once they were standing, still crouched,
Nathan and Orne were barely noticed in the organized bedlam of the
gun deck. They made their way forward, until Nathan looked out the
first larboard ports and saw the American frigate clearing the smoke and
bristling with heavy guns run out.

Twenty

Long Guns and Carronades - *5 PM*

As he limped his way forward, Nathan could see and hear most of the action. The two ships were within long gun shot range; their guns were loaded with round shot. Eighteen-pounders on the main deck, 24-pound carronades on the foc's'le deck, two decks above Nathan, and aft, on the quarterdeck. In moments, 25 cannon would explode and hurl 350 pounds of iron at that beautiful, towering ship. Nathan and Orne heard three cheers and shouting.

"Let's try a ranging shot! And hoist the ensigns!"

Then something very strange happened. Even as the lieutenant shouted "Fire!" and the deafening roar of the guns erupted, the deck momentarily blanketed in acrid smoke, Nathan looked out and saw the other vessel yaw and neatly avoid the metal wrath just unleashed at extreme long range. The useless splashes all around her, though admittedly early testing shots, to find the range, clearly showed that the target had dodged the broadside, almost as if the other captain had again anticipated the precise moment Dacres would give the order to rake.

Just when this happened, Nathan gulped as he saw her colors break out, fifteen stars and stripes bursting open from atop her masts, as if in mockery and defiance. He could hear faint cheers. And still the other vessel came on, obliquely, on the other tack, but not firing, even though her range was probably comparable, or perhaps even superior, to *Guerriere's*. Nathan knew that the big American frigates carried long 24's on the main gundeck.

"A worthy target. Let the main topsail fill!" Dacres shouted, judging the appropriate angle for another attempt at the enemy. It seemed to Nathan that the look on Dacres' lean face was an intriguing mixture of determination and—wonder? Confusion? Anxiety? Was this arrogant man struggling with a frightening thought? Could this enemy be superior? The American Captain obviously knew what he was about, in the very least. The big guns bristled from her sides now; she was somewhat larger than *Guerriere* in all dimensions they could see, and she carried a big crew, swarming in her yards and along her decks.

"Fire as your guns bear!" Dacres yelled at the port side as *Guerriere* began to wear again. A ragged broadside again filled the air with smoke and the crash of cannon fire. Again, though, the American frigate wore at just the right moment. One hole appeared in her fore topsail, the only evidence of the effect of the shot, of *Guerriere's* best efforts at the rapidly closing range. The American was now close, and time seemed to speed up, or slow down, Nathan couldn't tell which. He could only wonder why the other ship had hardly fired. But now, he knew return fire was moments away.

The other frigate was less than 1,000 yards to windward and gaining on the British ship, almost abeam, running down on to her, parallel to them, in the most painstaking and exacting manner, an almost fastidiously careful approach. Both ships could fire at will now. But the American was still virtually silent. Dacres' men kept up a steady barrage, and some shot were beginning to tell, but—what was that? Nathan looked closely again, unable to believe his own eyes. A splash quite near the American hull; British shot had apparently bounced off the side of the American ship—at less than 500 yards.

Half past 5 PM

Dacres bore off and both ships now ran free. Looking to larboard, Nathan could clearly see figures swarming the decks and rigging of the American ship as she began to overhaul *Guerriere*. Soon they would be side by side, broadside to broadside, at about half pistol-shot, less than 50 yards. A lethal range for every gun aboard. The Americans set their colors at every mast.

6 PM

"For God's sake," someone said, "is this *Chesapeake* again—why does he not fire?"

Then it happened. Nathan saw a round figure on the entry port, the Captain, jumping up and down, and he heard a familiar voice faintly carry over the water, "Now boys, pour it into them!" It was Isaac Hull. He heard the American crew cheer, and the frigate's starboard side became engulfed in smoke and flame, and a terrifying roar split the air. The wrath of the other ship's broadside was suddenly upon them.

"Oh God," Nathan said.

"What is it?" asked Orne. "I—by God!"

"Quiet! Drop to the deck! Now!"

There was an ominous whine that drowned the hum of the rigging, a rush of objects through the air. They heard a loud crashing tattoo pounding the entire ship; *Guerriere* shaking amid screams, lines snapping, wood cracking, groaning and the bloody face of the corporal sprayed with spinters—a 24-pound ball hitting and punching through the ship's timber, not twenty feet from them. Gaping holes in the bulwarks raggedly framed blue sea and sky beyond. One 32-pound shot cut a groove into the deck not a yard from Nathan's feet. He could hear below shot hitting 'tween wind and water; the entire ship shuddered violently with the impact of the double-shotted broadside, over 700 pounds of iron, 27 solid iron balls, 24- and 32-pound smashers, and various round grape shot, and even lead musket balls against the wooden hull. A powder monkey, a 10-year-old running to the other end of the deck, suddenly became blood spray. Another seaman went down at the eighteen-pounder behind him.

"I'm going up!" Nathan shouted at Orne, pointing with his thumb; *Guerriere* throbbed with her guns running out as well as occasional crushing hits, 24-pounders, 32-pounders from the carronades on the heavy U.S. frigate. They were on the windy banks of Hell, ghosts in the smoky, dimlit air of the cockpit, ship pitching violently, the tortured iron and wood screeching below the deafening explosions of gunfire and crash of solid iron balls against the wooden hull.

Orne tried to cradle Nathan's left shoulder as they staggered up to the main companionway hatch through the fear-naught. Several powder monkeys dashed by them. But the men at the guns, even Lt. Symms in command, ignored them. The visibility was so poor here, they might not even have noticed the onlookers; everyone held on desperately as the ship wore to the starboard tack.

"Are you insane?" shouted Orne. "You will die up there!"

"And I will die here, sir, I will—"

Nathan waved his hand dismissively and limped forward.

"No, Mr. Jeffries. I'll go with you," he heard behind him. In a few moments he was walking up the forward companionway. A red-coated marine gave him a questioning look, but then turned away to work his way up the larboard ratlines. Most of the guns were still firing deafeningly as he looked over the larboard cathead at the vast masts and top hamper now gliding slightly ahead. The wind was dead astern; the American ship, apparently uninjured, still less than half pistol shot range. Orne was at his side.

"Oh God," Nathan moaned quietly, terrified; he was afraid to stay, and afraid to run below again, to escape this Hell laid out before him. Perhaps it was more merciful to be frantically busy as the crew. *Guerriere* bore down on her fate. A seaman went down behind him. He looked up at Dacres and the other officers on the quarterdeck who remained standing, uninjured. But Dacres immediately turned and called to him with a lopsided, forced smile.

"'Tis time for you to go below, sir," Dacres said to him, not realizing Nathan had been below. "This is not your fight—yet."

Nathan knew it was useless to argue, and in any case Dacres was right: he was on the wrong ship to be showing bravery. Nathan didn't feel heroic either; in fact, he was scared to death. Thoughts of one of those idiot iron or lead objects hitting him were unmanning him. It could decapitate him, or remove an arm or a leg, or split him at the middle. He wanted to live! And not as a piece of a man. But how could he leave the action now, even as a spectator? As he stumbled back to the main hatch and hesitated, constantly jostled by the running powder monkeys and the wounded, who went below; the din redoubled again as the American frigate unleashed another volley. And then—was this the fourth broadside?

Standing near the foremast on the main gundeck, he stopped in his tracks as an awful crash, even louder than the cannon, came from farther aft, almost right astern. It could only be the mizzen mast, fallen by the board. Nathan and Orne looked at each other, and ran aft again. They could feel the ship falling off and slowing down with the drag of the useless mast in the water. He could imagine the devastation above, the desperate attempts to cut loose the unwanted sea anchor. Another broadside from the American, this time forward, almost in a raking position, seemed to shake every inch of *Guerriere*. More screams and crashes. One of the guns suddenly lurched off its carriage and the desperate gun crew dodged the angry breech and flying bore. The guns were still being fired rapidly, those still in operation with sufficient crews. The two ships must be very close now. But Nathan knew now that *Guerriere* was doomed.

Looking above the smoke off the larboard side, he could just see the tops of the other ship, now pulling ahead and across their bow to rake.

The next broadside was low, and Nathan could feel the tortured deck shudder as round shot crashed through timbers. Would she sink from under them? Another broadside swept by him in a terrifying black and gray hail. He heard the rush of a 24-pounder less than a yard from his left ear. Two men fell by the forward carronade; their blood splashed against the bulwarks in a macabre pattern. Nathan stepped on an arm, saw that it was unattached and almost vomited. One ball crashed into the foremast, near the deck; splinters showered everyone, a deadly storm that erupted as high as the fore course yard.

Then there was silence, as momentarily no guns would bear—then several banged in unison.

Nathan dodged and squeezed his way along the larboard guns, averting his gaze from most of the men, especially those serving the eighteen pounders. The carnage was already dreadful; white bone shone through red, mangled flesh; pieces of human bodies lay scattered across the deck. Was that a loose iron cannonball or a decapitated head rolling on the deck? But most guns were still in operation.

"We have only a few moments, sir," said Orne as Nathan clambered up the companionway to the foredeck. "Just stay low, please." Nathan looked aft to see Lieutenant Ready busy with a group of men, chopping away the rest of the mizzen rigging to free the ship of the broken mast. The British cheered early when they saw the ensign on the American's foremast fall, thinking they had surrendered. But the flag was quickly knotted in place again. Now the grim faces told Nathan everything.

But the American now hovered, pitching sharply, stalled with her topsails aback, apparently in irons. Nathan could see that her braces were mostly shot away, making maneuvers difficult.

"We can rake her stern, sir!" shouted Lieutenant Kent to the quarterdeck.

Dacres nodded. "Steady your helm, men!" he shouted. The two men at the wheel struggled to keep her bow pointed off the American stern in the heavy seas.

"Now we have him!" someone screamed. "Now let him get a real taste of it!" A few guns were firing now, mostly forward. But then the bow of the American ship began slowly to swing to larboard, and they saw that the two ships would collide.

"Oh, God . . ."

This was it! The bowsprit of *Guerriere* swooped down in the trough of the wave, seemingly joined to the mizzen rigging of her opponent, and then rose in the swell, now entangled thoroughly as the British starboard bow crashed into the larboard quarter of the American frigate.

A few men fell down, and the two remaining masts whipped violently as the jib boom and bowsprit of *Guerriere* snagged and pulled on the shrouds and boat davit of the towering U.S. frigate. Timber groaned and spars splintered. In all the yelling, a peculiar pattering sound became even louder than it had been. Splinters flew everywhere as musket balls hit the planks like deadly, gray sleet.

Coxe was on the deck near Nathan now, furious enough to strike this American down.

"What are you doing here? Get below!"

"Fire your starboard bow chaser, Mr. Coxe!" they heard from the quarterdeck. It was Dacres. "Is that Jeffries? Send him back below!"

"Aye, sir!" Nathan and Coxe locked eyes briefly; he saw the lieutenant's hand flutter toward his sword, as if tempted to kill Nathan on the spot; but then he turned to his men.

"Aahh!" cried Dacres. He leaned heavily against the binnacle.

"You've been hit, sir!" said Lt. Kent. "Let me—"

"Get back to your post!" roared the Captain. "Call for boarders! This is our chance!"

Most of the surviving midshipmen, led by Kent, ran toward the bow along the gangways of *Guerriere* to board the enemy. Small-arms fire was constant now, and Nathan fought to control his fear. Men were falling, screaming in pain. In spite of the stiff wind and violent rocking of the ship in the heavy seas, there seemed to be a red mist over his eyes. His clothes were torn, but he seemed uninjured.

Where was Dacres? Belatedly, as if moving in tar, Nathan started to follow the men running forward as boarders. He saw similar activity near the stern of the American now. A musket ball whizzed overhead, and he ducked. Another one cracked into the rail nearby. Lieutenant Ready went down, and several others. He saw a blue-coated man on the American ship fall, probably a lieutenant—he had been trying to lash the ships together. A lieutenant of Marines also went down; Nathan could see his head explode in red.

But the fire from the tops of the American ship was twice as heavy against *Guerriere*. Her decks were showered with lead; great guns still fired, but few could be aimed effectively at a target. Men were falling all around him; the deck was slippery with blood. The cabin of the American had been fired upon by the bow gun of *Guerriere* and was now in flames. Just before he ducked behind the foremast, he saw Hull, with burst white breeches, calling for boarders, pulled down from the "horse head" arms locker on the other vessel by a sailor who pointed at his epaulets, evidently throwing discipline aside in his concern for his Captain's safety.

Hull called again from the deck, and brave men forced the American's sails away from the wind. As they filled, she drew ahead in the plunging sea. As if reluctant to let her go, the bowsprit of *Guerriere* pulled and snapped her spanker boom and tore away the stern boat; it dangled, fell and disappeared into the huge, heaving waves. But the American was pulling free, and suddenly the bowsprit of *Guerriere* snapped up, released from the tension as the two ships completely separated.

Then the terror really began. As the forestay sagged, he heard an ominous cracking groan from *Guerriere's* mast; it shivered, the base weakened by several 24-pound balls of iron in its heart. Nathan panicked as he looked up and saw the yards sway much more than seemed possible. Musket balls and rifle fire still peppered the deck, but he dashed aft toward the entry port as the foremast toppled with a mighty crash, taking the mainmast over with it. Like two great trees, the foremast fell over the starboard side, the main to larboard, mostly on deck. Nathan narrowly escaped the carnage of spar and canvas and hemp piled suddenly all around him and in the sea along side. There were more screams; he saw one body severed cleanly in two, and looked away, fighting down bile.

And just as suddenly, there was silence, except for the cries of the wounded and dying. He could see the American's name now: *Constitution*, looking virtually untouched except for mizzen damage, severed lines and holes in her sails. She sailed away, now several hundred yards to leeward. Stunned and speechless, he watched her heave to with the wind abeam at perhaps a quarter mile. *Guerriere* yawed, rocked and pitched violently, her gunports rolling into the green-and-white water, muzzles dripping as they drooped and dropped and raised pointed high again. A sickly movement; the ship had no masts or sails to steady her. Men were moving again now, and Nathan shook of his stupor and walked aft through the awful carnage.

Half past 6 PM

With less than two hours of light remaining, Nathan could hear Dacres shouting orders again from the quarterdeck now, along with first lieutenant Kent. Both men were badly wounded, the Captain in the back, Kent bleeding from a splinter wound. There was only gray clouds and darkening sky above as they tried desperately to get *Guerriere* in order. Wind and seas were rising ominously.

"Clear away the mainmast! Get those fore shrouds cut and over the side! Secure that gun! Hurry!" Men with cutlasses, axes and knives struggled against injuries, weariness and the rolling of the ship, knowing it was futile. But orders were orders.

Then Coxe walked past Nathan as if he wasn't there to oversee the men at the bow, working on setting the spritsail. Nathan could feel many eyes follow him as he walked over to the main companionway ladder. How many of these men were eager to kill him? He glanced around, his eyes resting momentarily on Dacres; the man could barely stand. Orne had vanished. No Americans to be seen, none of Nathan's men on deck.

The horror that had been on deck was now repeated below, only it was worse. In spite of the freshening wind, the air was both wet and smoky; heated and reeking of vomit and blood, excrement and death. Shot holes were everywhere, wreckage festooning the frames and knees, slapping in the violent rolling of the hull. He could hear the wounded screaming and moaning in a constant chorus, mostly forward and below in 'tween decks in the Hell of the cockpit; but pieces of human bodies were still scattered everywhere, some imbedded in the timbers themselves. He lost his footing and almost stepped on a hand, attached to no arm, just the portion neatly beginning at the wrist, fingers still gripping the tompion it had been wielding. Nathan knelt and fought the urge to vomit again.

There! In the hazy nightmare he saw Orne, accompanied by Tom Howard and Logan. There was some comfort in seeing their anxious faces, filthy, clothes torn and dirty, but otherwise apparently uninjured.

"Captain!" Nathan shook hands with all of them.

"Would you come with us to the cockpit, sir?" Logan asked. "O'Reilley has been . . ."

"I'll come." They walked forward, dodging the litter on deck and the hurrying surgeon's mate, who carried a bloody saw, splints and dressings, some clean, some not.

"Over here, sir," said Mr. Logan.

"He . . . he volunteered to bring down a wounded American, sir, one who had served a gun, damn him, decided to throw in his lot with the British, and . . . the gun was hit and backed off. He was behind it. The breech caught him, sir, crushed his ribs."

In the crowded sickbay, Nathan saw men missing an arm or a leg, swathed in red cotton, pale, near death. One man sat up, patiently waiting for a ten inch splinter to be removed from his cheek. Then Nathan recognized O'Reilley, with Surgeon Irvine leaning over him.

Now the doctor looked up, saw Nathan, and shook his head.

"There is nothing more I can do for this man, sir. I am sorry, I must return to these others. Three more men will lose a limb . . . at least. Many of these men will be fortunate to survive the night."

The gleam of recognition seemed to light O'Reilley's eyes as he saw Nathan, and the four Americans leaned over their erstwhile comrade.

Breathing was difficult for him, and Nathan gently pressed his shoulders down as he started to rise, swathed in blood soaked bandages, obviously feverish. He started to speak. But it was not to Nathan.

"Emma? I know I am late, Emma . . ."

"O'Reilley, rest yourself," Nathan's lips trembled, as O'Reilley's did.

"I have missed you, my dear, have you been lonely? Ah, my love, I shall not leave you ag—aah! Aah!"

"Help me hold him down!" Nathan shouted. O'Reilley writhed in pain.

But he quickly quieted down again and spoke conversationally.

"When is dinner, Emma?" He coughed and choked, and gulped blood. Nathan's hand shook as he pressed it against the delirious man's shoulder.

Captain Orne stood up. "Poor devil. Gentlemen, I—"

"How are you today . . ." O'Reilley began to speak rapidly, a gibberish no one could understand. He smiled. Orne remained standing.

"It is time . . . aah . . ." he finally said, clearly and calmly, almost confidently, his eyes wide open as if peering into the dark. His mouth stayed open, filled with blood, such a dark red against his white face and staring eyes.

Amidst the suffering and anguish of the other wounded, the men all stood and bowed their heads in silent prayer.

"He is now at peace, at least," said Nathan, his voice shaking.

"Captain, he helped a man what helped the limeys, it is truth, but would you take this, sir?" Howard spoke quietly, almost whispering in his ear. "It should go to his fiancée, he asked me to entrust it to you before . . . when he was still of right mind, sir."

"What?" Nathan found it difficult to avoid sobbing.

"This, sir; this belongs to his fiancée now." Howard handed him a chain and locket, with a portrait inside of a beautiful young woman. Tears streamed down Nathan's face and he was not ashamed. The eyes of the other men glistened, too. He took the locket silently and slipped it into his pocket, nodding.

Then an even stranger thing happened. Here, among their fallen enemy, the injured in their agony, the Americans, including Logan and Howard, with hardly a glance among them began to help Bates, the surgeon's mate, in his odious duties to the hurt, the dead and dying. It was an instant, unspoken understanding that here, for the moment, was where they belonged. Nathan even assisted in removing the splinter from the stoic seaman's cheek. It was all he could do to stay on his feet as he handed the surgeon's mate some additional rags to cover the bleeding face.

"We will try to sew it up later, Miller," Bates said matter of factly, as if talking about a sail that needed mending. Miller nodded, almost cheerful. Nathan thought the pain must be excruciating. But Miller had enjoyed a healthy draft of grog and seemed content. Soon most of the crew would be drunk on the "switchel" they had prepared for their Yankee prisoners.

"Thank you, Mister Jeffries, Captain Orne, men," said Bates as the surgeon returned from cutting with the other assistant. "I do not know how else to express my appreciation—"

Just then a midshipman, once neat and spruce, now his uniform in bloody shreds and tatters, approached Nathan and saluted. Nathan could see the boy struggling to appear cool, stern and manly as he forced his emotions down. Now they heard loud shouting and cursing erupt on the deck above them.

"Captain's respects, sir, and would you please return to the quarter-deck—you and Captain Orne."

"Very good, Mister—"

"Harding, sir, James Harding."

"Thank you, Mister Harding . . . Captain Orne, after you."

The meaningless formalities accorded gentlemen and officers helped all of them to get through this, to move on.

7 PM

The sun had just touched the highest waves. The ship's rolling was even more pronounced now as Nathan and Orne struggled up the companionway to join Dacres.

"Ah, gentlemen, thank you for reporting so promptly," said Dacres. His voice sounded hollow, empty of emotion. The man was still stunned, in a state of shock and in great pain from his wound. He was like a dead man walking, with no nerves at all. Nathan remembered the wounded seaman who had snarled him away when he had tried to help. But he also remembered again how Dacres had prevented Coxe from running him through. Here, surrounded by defeat, sick, injured and dying, the man still maintained a semblance of civility.

"Captain Dacres, you must have Dr. Irvine look at that wound immediately," Nathan said.

"There is no time for a physician now, sir—look there! *Constitution* is standing down for us."

It was not exactly a rebuff. Orne and Nathan followed where Dacres now pointed and felt exhilaration. The frigate appeared fresh and ready for action, a great ship about to cross their bows. Nathan noticed no spritsail on *Guerriere*—the effort had finally proved futile to keep even one square of canvas before the strong wind; in fact, several had been carried away.

"Fire that gun! Jumping Jack!" Dacres yelled.

"Aye, sir," came a sad reply. One of the 24-pound carronades on the leeward side barked loudly, a signal of surrender.

"As you can see gentlemen, we have no flag to strike," Dacres said. Now a trace of bitterness had crept into his voice.

Constitution backed her main topsail and lowered a boat that began rowing over to *Guerriere*.

"No one could have fought better, or more bravely," said Nathan. He was not sure why.

Eyes glistening on the verge of tears, Dacres fought against emotion, held himself in check, seemed ready to break, but did not. "Thank you, sir." He turned to Orne. "It seems now, sir, our situations are reversed. Now you are free, and I am a prisoner."

"Captain, I will not say that my colleague and I are not proud and relieved at this turn of events, but—"

"*Guerriere*, ahoy! Have I your permission to come aboard?" It was a young man's voice hailing from the *Constitution's* boat, now right alongside, bobbing in the heavy seas.

There was no need to ask for identification. Dacres nodded at the bo's'n, who roared down, "Permission granted!"

This was it. Nathan was at long last released from the hell ration of Coxe and life aboard this accursed ship. And yet, in spite of himself, he felt sorry for Dacres. Maybe he was just growing faint, finally losing his mind.

The American lieutenant left his escort, half a dozen armed Marines and sailors, at the entry port. As the former approached them on the quarterdeck and saluted, the drama of the moment was inescapable, and Nathan gulped. He saw Captain Orne was strained too. After a stunning thirty minutes of heavy action, the British had lost to the upstart Yankees. The sky darkened as the sun set on the tempestuous sea, on England's conceit of invincibility, and on Nathan's life in captivity. In a few minutes, he would be a free man, and the next day would usher in a new reality.

Something gnawed at the back of his mind, and he struggled to grasp it. He had survived, he was free, he would soon, God willing, see his friends, then what else troubled him?

"Captain?" asked the lieutenant, looking at the right man, in his now battered half moon, fore-and-aft cocked hat and best uniform coat.

"Dacres, yes, I fear so," said Nathan's ex-captor.

Nathan could imagine the glee shared by almost every American on the two ships—this was the once-arrogant man who had humiliated and harassed and mocked the United States along the northern coast for years. But none of this was apparent; the scene was an almost rehearsed tableau of exquisite tact, as if at a social gathering, surrounded by the hopelessness and agony of this battered vessel.

"Sir, I am Reed, Third Lieutenant of the United States frigate *Constitution*, and it is my duty to officially inquire of you and confirm as to whether your ship has struck."

Dacres produced a slight smile. "Well, sir, our mizzenmast is gone, our foremast is gone and our main is over the side—I suppose, on the whole, you might say we have struck."

Reed did not even crack a grin. "Then, Captain, it is my duty and honor to offer you our boat, with Mr. Gilliam in command, to return with you to *Constitution*. I shall remain aboard here in command of the prize crew."

Dacres nodded.

"I have also been ordered to ask if you are in need of surgeon or surgeon's mates or other medical assistance."

"Thank you, but I would think you have need enough aboard your ship for all available medical staff . . ."

Reed visibly relaxed from his stiff posture. "Oh no, sir, we have only seven wounded, and their injuries were dressed half an hour ago."

Dacres paused to digest this. "We have suffered 100 casualties, sir, one third of my crew; we could use any assistance you would be kind enough to offer," he finally said, then turned to Orne.

"Lieutenant, allow me to introduce Captain Orne and Nathan Jeffries."

Twenty-One

Old Ironsides

Later, at 8 PM, as Dacres was being rowed back to *Constitution* in the gathering dusk by midshipman Henry Gilliam, the battered ship was becoming crowded with new, fresh faces—Yankee faces. Other boats had begun arriving from the American frigate to remove prisoners, wounded first. Sailing master Aylwin brought a hawser to attempt to get the prize under tow. A surgeon's mate arrived to assist the British surgeon, Irvine. No one would sleep for some time. Lt. Reed had promised Nathan that he could almost certainly sleep aboard *Constitution* if he chose, rather than the shattered *Guerriere*.

Where was Coxe! No one had seen the bastard since the battle began. Nathan would have to conduct his own search, if necessary; a disguised fugitive? Had he been lost overboard, killed outright? Nathan knew he wasn't with the wounded in the cockpit.

At one point Nathan was alone near a handful of skylarking hands on the foredeck; needing fresh air, he had briefly escaped from the frantic activity below, where his men and Orne still helped.

One seaman, a short, thin man with a overly large, pitted, bluff prow of a face, spread his hands several feet apart.

"That round shot weren't more'n this far from my ears, Ned—not more'n this!"

"That 'twern't nothin' lad," said a taller man; he made a dismissive gesture. "When Old Ironsides was laid alongside, a ball, 18-pounder, mind you, sailed right through our gunport, it rang off metal like a song, boy, and missed my nose by an inch!"

The man pointed to his nose: a sharp, long, curved specimen, shaped like a beaked figurehead.

"Uh, pardon me, sir," said Nathan. "You said 'Old...what?' I do not understand—"

The sailors laughed. "Bless you, sir," said the taller man. "Old Ironsides—you see, *Constitution*; she were named that when round shot bounced off her stout oak neat as you please. Moses Smith shouted 'Huzza, her sides are made of iron!' This poor ol' tub here could hardly touch her; ain't that so, mates?"

"Aye, you should see her iron sides shrug off them poor British peas," said the one called Ned. And he nodded his head judiciously, before an angry shout from the master's mate and the bosun's mate sent them all to work again.

Guerriere had suffered fifteen dead outright, 62 wounded and 24 missing—some lost overboard with the masts. She mounted 49 guns, though rated a 38: the main deck carried 30 eighteen-pounders, spar deck 16 thirty-two-pound carronades, as well as 2 long twelves and a twelve-pounder howitzer. *Constitution*, officially a 44 gun frigate, carried 56: 30 twenty-four-pounder long guns on the main deck, 24 thirty-two-pounder carronades on the spar, and 2 long eighteens at the bow. By weight of metal, hull strength and crew (440 to 302) she outgunned and outmanned her opponent by a factor of three to two. So it was hardly a disgrace for the British to lose, though the execution and damage done was all out of proportion even to the relative strengths of the two ships.

By 10 PM, surgeons Evans and Irvine and their mates, now aboard the victor with most of the growing crowd of wounded men, had amputated and dressed and splinted as best they could. The efforts to tow *Guerriere* had failed, and boats constantly crossed between the two ships. Work continued feverishly on *Constitution*; but on the battered British hull, the struggle was to keep her afloat. In a weary haze, daydreaming, Nathan helped for hours wherever he could.

Many of the British crew were already drunk. Fighting down his nausea, Nathan had helped remove bodies and pieces of skull, brain,

tissue from the deck, and comforted the wounded, all the while search-
ing for Coxe, dead or alive. He had not been removed from the defeated,
battered hull; he was still aboard, that much was certain.

A group of British tars near the bow raised glasses to him in the dim
light of the foremast lantern, as if in celebration rather than defeat. They
knew he had shown compassion towards their comrades, and now they
could throw caution to the winds.

"Here's to you, Jonathan," one said, "an' a better Yank I'll not speak in
this cruise—Mister Yankee, we greet you as friend."

They laughed.

"Or this lifetime, mate—"

"Hear him! Hear him!"

"The best of good fortune to you, sirs, and my name is Nathan—"

"Say that again, Jonathan!" They laughed and waved as he moved on.

Some of the Americans had already transferred to *Constitution*,
including Logan and Howard. Others had been left aboard thus far,
especially those few who had fought against their fellow citizens, along
with some of the unwounded British tars. It was rather dark, with less
than half a moon and a few stars struggling through the cloud cover. Two
figures approached him at the taffrail, one holding a ship's lantern. It was
Lieutenant Reed and Captain Orne.

"A boat is waiting for you and Captain Orne, sir," said Reed. "And
my thanks for the help you two gentlemen have given us here."

"We were glad to do it," said Nathan. "But I shall remain aboard,
with your permission—at least for this night."

"As you wish, sir." Nathan seemed to detect a mischievous glint in
Reed's eyes. They shook hands. A few men had come aboard *Guerriere*; he
saw an officer cross over the entry port, a young midshipman and a few
others. In a few minutes Orne's belongings, in a sea chest donated to him,
were lowered and Orne and others were rowed to "Old Ironsides," along
with more British prisoners.

The black, mastless hull he stood on still rolled wildly, and ahead lay
Constitution, neatly hove-to, her tall spars and clean white canvas reaching for the heavens.

Then he saw an exhausted, filthy lieutenant approaching, his black-ened face breaking into a grin.

"George!" Nathan shouted. "It is you!"

"The very same," laughed George Earliegh, giddy with fatigue himself. They shook hands and then hugged warmly.

"How are you, Nathan? When Captain Hull told me you were aboard *Guerriere*, I could not believe it! We thought you were—"

"I know."

As they stood near the mainmast, swaying with fatigue, Nathan gave a brief summary of the events that had led him there.

"How are your brother and sister, George—how is . . . my family?"

George looked down. "After my father was . . . lost, like you were, Jason and my sister lived with my aunt and uncle. And my brother and I feel like you about the Austers, and Barbara, you know—"

"Lieutenant! Signal from the Captain!"

Over the next few hours, though constantly interrupted with the need to give or execute orders, George and Nathan caught up on events, eating cold beef and warm rum in the remains of a cramped little cabin on the starboard side aft. There were bodies and noise everywhere: some sleeping through the din, others repairing, pumping, eating, talking, laughing; some even sleeping on cots or hammocks; and underlying all of that, the constant moaning and screeching of the wounded hull.

George marveled at Nathan's tales of adventure and hardship, and told him about how cool and calm Hull had been as Lieutenant Morris asked again and again for permission to fire as they approached, and how, finally, at less than a cable's length, the Captain had shouted, "Now, boys, pour it into them!" He had jumped up and down in rare excitement when he ordered that first broadside, and split his white breeches from belt to knee. It was one of the many stories that would become immortal, in Hull's moment of greatness.

"We went into battle with the Captain in bursted breeches!" George laughed. "And you know, all you could see were a few smiles! The men love him, we all do. We respected him before and now we're even more proud. Daniel Hogan, Richard Dunn, Moses Smith—he attends to them all personally, all of the wounded. He treats each man as if he were a brother, a son! Even the niggers, he told me how impressed he was with their courage, stripped to the waist, fighting like devils. I think he is more loved now even than his boys on *Argus*. He cares about the suffering of the men; the mutilation was dreadful, Nathan."

"I know. I saw him. George, Coxe is aboard this ship."

"Auster's man? Why did you not—"

"Let me bring you up to date." Nathan finished recounting the last three weeks, his torment and torture from Coxe and the latter's disappearance just before the battle.

"Are you sure he is aboard? Perhaps he is now on *Constitution*, or was lost over the side earlier on—"

"No! No, my friend, he is here, somewhere, I just know it! And I must find him!"

Nathan stood up and felt a moment of panic as he began to fall, but George grabbed him and saved him from a hard meeting with the floor. Nathan looked up at his friend, fighting consciousness as his fatigue and pain overcame him.

"George! I must find that bastard, I . . ."

George nodded. "We will find him, Nathan—I will round up one or two Marines to help."

Nathan cracked a smile. "Mister Logan and Tom Howard have already searched for me, but I must be sure."

It was only a few hours after dawn the next day when Nathan, finding himself alone in a cot off the wardroom, struggled wearily through a chunk of hardtack and heard Lieutenant Reed hail from the deck above.

"Leaks still gaining, Captain!"

"How much water in the hold?" Hull bellowed from the other ship.

"Five feet!" Dimly Nathan remembered men slinging hammocks, walking in their sleep with fatigue. Progress had continued through the night, transferring prisoners, treating minor wounds, trying to shore up the prize and pumping clear green water out of her bilge to keep her afloat. The enemy's hull below the waterline had been holed and damaged from end to end on the larboard side, with long gaps in the planking; impossible to fother a sail and slow in pouring water. Most of the remaining British prisoners aboard were drunk and refused to man the pumps.

"Prepare to abandon her, Mr. Reed!" yelled Hull. His prize would not reach port. Nathan had run up the companionway to borrow a glass, and could see Hull across a third of a cable's length, squinting in the glare off the water between the two vessels. The face revealed none of the disappointment he must have felt; no doubt, in the intervening hours since his victory, he had hardened himself to the possibility—indeed, likelihood—that the prize could not be saved. The enemy had been smashed too badly even to survive another day, but the hull might remain barely afloat indefinitely. She must therefore be destroyed.

During the morning, the rest of the prisoners and their belongings were removed to *Constitution*, the gentle commander taking great pains that every single man had his bag. A special trip was made to retrieve Dacres' Bible, a gift from his mother. However, some cloth taken from American prizes was confiscated and distributed among the American crew. Nathan searched and searched for Coxe, even daring to explore the stinking darkness of the flooded orlop, where one misstep might be his last.

At 1 PM, the last boat, but for Lt. Reed's, had been secured aboard the U.S. ship. The American crew still aboard began to lay a powder train to the ship's magazine. Nathan determined to make one last look below. The gray sunlight filtered down through the dust and filth of the gun deck, then down to the berth deck and down again to the orlop. Here the water had risen above the planks; even in this flooding Hell, Nathan felt all too familiar with the ruin of a vessel. In the semi-darkness of the chain locker, the cockpit, the cable tier, he stumbled, bent almost double, hurting his back in numbing, reeking twilight. He could hear the men returning to the boat, mission complete. He must quit this fruitless effort; almost falling into the coal hole as he twisted his ankle near the magazine, sealed

from water but still containing tons of powder that could ignite. Time to give up and get to the boat.

He thought then that he heard Peter's voice. What was he saying? He turned and saw the pale sheen of the knife in the grayness, slashing at him. The blade caught his arm and he gasped at the pain, falling to the wet deck and sending sharp agony to his spine.

That face again, now red-eyed, the insane, bony spider-devil's face of Coxe with a death's-head grin, now in his moment of triumph, loomed before him. He held a pike at Nathan's chest.

"All your searchin' and I was here the whole time, breathin' coal dust, waitin' for the right moment—you fool! And then movin' from time to time when you got too close! Once I was up there in the captain's realm, you know it?"

"They are waiting for me," Nathan gasped and twisted violently to his left, rolling desperately away from the pike. He heard the blade bite into the deck. The water was rising.

"And they'll wait in vain!" Coxe flipped over the long pole of the pike and slammed it into Nathan's side. This time he screamed in pain and fought against blacking out, fought against the terror he felt, the madness; a sinking ship, trapped near tons of gunpowder with a man determined to kill him—and succeeding.

How will this nightmare end? he thought insanely, as if he were calmly watching all of this through his pain and fear. But instinct and reflexes had taken over. Just as Coxe was about to finish him off with the pike, Nathan suddenly rolled the other way, knocking the man off his feet, and they both splashed and struggled on the deck, banging into casks and cable.

He was too weak to react quickly enough when he felt his hair grabbed, his face pressed into the foul water.

"You are one resilient son of a—I give you that!" he heard. "If I can't kill you one way, another will serve!" shouted Coxe.

Out of breath, Nathan desperately pushed off the deck with his hands and twisted free enough to swipe with one fist. It connected on Coxe's jaw and he fell off Nathan.

"God damn you!" Coxe searched wildly for his knife in the dark ooze, until Nathan kicked him and struggled to stand, ignoring the throbbing anguish. Coxe also rose, and the two men circled warily; then, with surprising speed, Coxe dashed for the companionway. Nathan, too slow in his present condition, hesitated in following him. By the time he reached the bottom of the ladder and started up, he could see that Coxe had managed to find a grating and was sliding it over the hatch.

"You'll die down there, Jeffries, one way or the other!"

Couldn't Reed's men hear all of this? Nathan yelled for help as the water rose to his waist. Then he did hear shouts from the gundeck and above. But down here, there was no escape now from the orlop except through this hatch, and Coxe had tied it securely. He could raise it slightly, but ex-hausted, slipped back down into the grimy water.

Shivering, fighting panic, he dived down into the murk and felt along the deck for Coxe's knife. Again and again he dived. The water level climbed the stairs; soon he would drown, even though the ship herself was far from sinking.

There it was! He felt the knife, clutched the handle and flopped up the stairs, now mostly underwater, to the grating. Reaching his hand through, he carefully felt for the knots the held the grating down. Forcing himself to saw effectively, he loosed strand after strand. How much longer? One side was free! He focused on the other and cut the last line, slamming himself against the grating. It slid over, and he rolled out of the water and onto the still surprisingly dry berth deck. His back was bleeding.

Smoke! Good God, the ship was on fire! He almost sobbed in anger and frustration. The after hatch to the gun deck was surrounded by flames now and he was still trapped. Within a few minutes, she would blow up. His strength all but gone, he managed to limp forward to the main companionway, remembering that the gaping holes in the gundeck should allow him access. As he pulled himself up and rolled again to avoid the fire racing forward, he heard and felt footsteps running toward him.

"I'll get off this damned frigate, but not you!" shouted Coxe. He carried a pistol now.

Its touchhole ignited by the flames, one of the great guns suddenly roared nearby and lurched backward toward him. As Coxe dodged the recoil, he stumbled and dropped the pistol. Nathan charged him and both went down in the smoke. Nathan smashed Coxe's face with his fist and plunged the man's own knife into his belly, ramming it up toward his chest as he screamed. They were both covered in blood.

In the thickening smoke, Nathan could see the life leaving his enemy's eyes. He had to get out of the ship. He shook Coxe's head savagely.

"You'll see Auster down there too, damn you to Hell!" Coxe was dead.

More guns exploding; *Guerriere* was on fire from end to end, flames flashing along her gundeck and licking her gunports; cannons fired as if in action. Explosions rocked her upper deck; the magazine would go up any moment. Coughing and feeling light-headed, Nathan stumbled and limped over to a gun not yet surrounded by flames, climbed up and pulled himself up to the wale using a loose line, then threw himself over the bulwarks into the water.

Swimming weakly for a few yards, his skin on fire, he looked back toward the ship's stern; the entire hull shuddered as the magazine ignited. The quarterdeck and after end rose like a wounded beast and she disintegrated in a shower of charred wood and smoke, spewing fireworks hundreds of yards into the air. Some burning wood fragments fell sizzling in the water around him, but he declined to duck his head underwater. Amid bright, glowing cinders surrounded by black clouds, the remains of the hull slipped below the waves with a frothy hiss and groan.

From his left, he heard a young voice. "Mister Reed—look, over there!"

Reed's boat had evidently pulled away, but now returned from Nathan's left to pull him out of the water. Nathan found that he could not use his arms or legs effectively, and swallowed a gallon of salt water before he was safely in the long boat.

"Thank you, sir," Nathan gasped, choking and coughing, "but why did you remain so close after firing the ship? How did you find me?"

"We did not fire the ship, sir, but had pulled away." said Reed, pointing to the debris and the slick area. The dissipation seemed to be farther away than *Constitution* herself—at least 500 yards. How could he have traveled that far?

"My men had laid the powder train to blow her up, but we waited and waited for the last crew. I sent two to find you when, suddenly, the fires were started. We could not stay aboard and I ordered them off. What the Hell were you doing—"

"Thank you, sir," gasped Nathan. "I am sorry. I owe you and these men my life." So Coxe had begun the blaze himself.

"What happened to you, Jeffries?"

"I was repaying an old debt to a—I'll explain later, Lieutenant, if I may."

Halfway between the two ships, Nathan looked back again; all that remained of the proud *Guerriere* was some floating debris, bits of wreckage, a slick, dark oval patch and the last wisps of gray smoke trailing in the afternoon breeze. Nathan shivered and fought back the panic, the urge to scream or vomit.

Twenty-Two

Homecoming

During a peaceful second dogwatch, Nathan found himself at the lee taffrail, the pitch not unreasonable, a gentle roll, the sun setting through the mainsail ahead, the constant hiss of water alongside as the southwestern swell joined *Constitution's* wake under her counter and trailed away as wounded white waves to the east northeast. He felt soothed, lulled yet weary, and contemplated an attempt at sleep. George had saved him a bit of pork from the officers' mess. Now Captain Dacres approached him and offered him a cigar.

"I am sorry, again," said Dacres, "that I did not discuss with you the situation with poor Matt Turner, *Cormorant*, and about my—"

"Free ships make free goods," Nathan said to Captain Dacres, "and we need to end this m-mockery . . . of . . . of justice, impressment, orders in council, extorting—"

"Nathan, please—"

". . . extorting promises of cash and cargo you aren't legally entitled to—no Brit can tell us when a voyage is broke."

Nathan had learned that much from his father's rantings.

"Of course, Mr. Jeffries, but it is not quite that simple. I was following official orders."

"We'll see."

"You know you cannot win at sea, or on land; it is ludicrous, surely—"

"We could win if we had built enough . . . raiders, like you, only smaller than a frigate, sloops of war, corvettes, fast brigs and schooners—"

"Your father is a great man," said Dacres.

"Yes, I know that—what did you . . . how do you?"

"I saw him in action, off Barbados, in 1800. And I did acknowledge your right not to fight your own countrymen, did I not? I even had that bet you heard about with Isaac, Captain Hull. Many good hands aboard my ship are American, just as many are British on *Constitution*."

"You and your . . . friend Richard Auster have greatly wronged us, Captain—"

"Yes, yes, but it has not all been the United States as the victim—"

"Surely, sir, you try to slide—"

"May I call you Captain Jeffries then, and may I tell you about your father now, facts you may not know?"

They sighted Cape Cod and took on a pilot early Sunday morning, August 29, beating up against the southwest wind, and then they sighted Boston Lighthouse.

"Clew up courses and headsails," said Hull. "Reef topsails."

"All hands! All hands to take in sail!" the bos'n bellowed, and bodies tumbled aloft or sweated down the halyards as Nathan let their movement mingle in his mind with the frenzied activity. Thirty minutes later they dropped the bow anchor near Little Brewster Island. Nathan could see Fort Warren on Georges Island, Lovell, then Gallops Island and Deer Island beyond. Long Wharf was still almost ten miles away. Nathan was in a daze, with no official duties to perform aboard *Constitution*, watching the crew clean and prepare for the next day as the launch took wounded prisoners to the hospital on Rainsford Island. Already, boatloads of visitors were crowding around from the Roads, having heard the news, yelling and banging on their craft, throwing hats in the air.

Panic struck early the next morning as *Constitution* lay anchored in Nantasket Roads, when a number of large ships suddenly entered the harbor at dawn with a northeast breeze. Hull calmly ordered the cables cut, and prepared to face the British fleet, fighting to the last man. But it was U.S. Commodore Rodgers' squadron, and so *Constitution*, flying

Guerriere's flag upside down, led a grand reception farther into the harbor. There were six ships in all. The others were Rodger's frigate *President*, Decatur's *United States*, James Lawrence's sloop of war *Hornet*, the brig *Argus* and *Congress*. All consumed with envy that their long cruise was nothing compared with Hull's brief sojourn into history.

As they passed Spectacle Island and Castle Island, Nathan heard shots, distant thunder of gunfire, and squinted into the late sun, scanning the Boston city front still several miles away. The copper dome of the new State House caught the sun's rays, and the familiar high spires of Christ Church—the old North Church—and the Old South Meeting House pierced the burnt orange skyline. He could barely make out Cobb's Hill burial ground, the grasshopper weathervane atop Faneuil Hall, the Salem Street markets, the north battery and even the Park Street Church, where the Granary used to be, bordered by the Common and Tremont Street. The Granary had been torn down in 1809, but his father had told him that *Constitution's* flaxen sails had been sown in that loft in 1797, and that several Jeffries were buried in the granary cemetery across the street. What were their names? He could not remember. He did remember that Samuel Adams was buried there. A few days earlier, a master's mate had told him that gunpowder was now stored in the church crypt, and it had already acquired the name "Brimstone Corner."

Despite the relief and joy of returning at last to his own land from his voyages, Nathan fought down another strange sense of panic and despair. As certain now as anything was, he would actually survive to see his parents once again. He must cling to that, he must head south, by sea or land.

The approach to the harbor was calm, barely any surge or swell. The cheers of Boston's thousands echoed around the harbor; quays were covered by the throngs, yards were manned. Careful years of studying current patterns on the surface told him the tide was ebbing—fortunately the remains of a stout sea breeze still carried them in, not more than two miles now from Long Wharf. Certainly one of the great harbors in the world, surpassed now of course by Baltimore and New York, it was still a sight. The schooners and coastal craft, the fishing boats, pilots, barges and

gigs, bumboats, bladders of rum spirited aboard, the music, the screeching gulls, and porpoises and seals, the eddies and unique flow, purposeful
movement and shelter that was Boston Harbor. In a few days he would
be home at last in Fells Point, upper Thames Street, Baltimore. How many
different sights had he seen? How many more would he? He knew his
mother would forgive him, eventually. The driver behind and above him
luffed with a sudden backing of the breeze; the dead fish and seaweed
smell so pervasive in the harbor wafting him to childhood. They moored
at Long Wharf, where he met a procession of captains and lieutenants,
losing track of young gentle midshipman George Earliegh, Mr. Logan
and Tom Howard, but renewing his acquaintance with Lawrence and
Perry; drinking, and falling, and drinking again, and then convincing him
to wait until Monday to travel south to Baltimore.

Four days later, when Nathan finally reached Fells Point at night,
he nearly forgot which door was his. Ah, Forty-four Thames! Lanterns
burned on either side. His heart pounding, he left his trunk outside and
charged on in. Just inside the door, in flickering tallow lamps, he saw not
his mother's face but Catherine's approach him. Her flawless face now
appeared slightly misshapen, cut and bruised, with purple swelling and
gauze on her left cheek.

"My God!" Nathan exclaimed. "What happened—why are you here?"

"Nathan, there is so much—"

"Where is my mother?"

Then he saw behind her William Jeffries sitting at the table, staring
at him, his old, battered and hairy face barely recognizable.

"Where is my mother?" Nathan asked again, and ran upstairs without waiting for an answer; she was not there, and he charged back down.

"Where is she!" he roared, startling the two silent figures. Nathan lost
all control and began to ransack the house but suddenly an arm snaked
around his neck and he felt all his strength and air choked off. Peter
released his hold to prevent him from collapsing full length on the rug.
Nathan glared at Peter and Catherine, fighting back tears.

"When?"

"Yesterday, Nathan. She is with Dr. Andrews now, to prepare for—"

"No! No! This can't be happening! My mother can't be dead. Peter, what are you doing here?"

Was he screaming inside his head?

"Nathan," said Peter, "your father and you know she always loved you, and had . . . come to terms with your . . . disappearance, she was . . . at peace, I think. We did all we could—your father was badly beaten in that July disgrace on Calvert Street by some of Richard's scum—and Catherine by Richard himself."

"Nathan," said Catherine, "Peter knows more than most doctors—he saved your father's life, and he tried everything he could to save Amy's as well. We worked with Dr. Andrews and Dr. Michaels—the best care possible. He has saved the Jeffries—"

"No . . . no, Catherine is the savior. Nathan, Catherine worked night and day with Amy for months to discredit the Austers—a brilliant campaign. Catherine has lost everything, and became your mother's joy, almost like a daughter, and her injuries—"

"So," said Nathan, "I am so glad about Catherine's new place in the Jeffries' household and about the other side of that most sinister savage Peter Hughes, more dangerous than ever, but also savior of the white man along with Auster's—"

Nathan saw Catherine wilt under his pitiless rant. Am I an ingrate? He thought to himself.

"I am sorry, Nathan; but you must listen now," said Peter. "I know you see me as a traitor, but I am your father's nurse—or one of them. I also want to continue as one of his protectors. Both Catherine and I have been . . . hired to protect him against the Austers—there have been threats against his life . . . and Catherine's."

"Hired? Hired by whom?" Nathan rasped, but Peter said nothing, even smiled slightly.

"What threats? All right, all right, but you are just one man," said Nathan, struggling for some sense to this maelstrom.

"The Austers have already lost most of their support in Baltimore, but Richard Auster is 'at large,' as they say. Probably far from here."

"Probably? Then let's assume he is near . . . here and find the ba-bas-
tard! Why don't I go visit old Richard and say how de ye do—"

Peter grabbed his arm like a vise. "You are in grave danger, Nathan;
make no mistake. There is little I can do for you out on the streets. Richard is also a changed man, even more powerful, vindictive, implacable. I
know that he has put all of his remorseless energy into ruining you and
your father. That is until—"

"Until we started hunting him."

"But he is also a survivor, intelligent and patient," said Peter.

Nathan's broad, flat face, with its wide, small nose, small and honest
mouth, paled and became still, almost prissy, but Peter missed Nathan's
smile, all gone now. Peter saw in those steel-blue eyes only a fighter, a
survivor, with sharp instinct dormant for years, now blazing. Peter feared
and sympathized with the new Nathan.

"I don't know what to do," Nathan said simply.

"Yes, you do. I know you cannot possibly see me as a friend, but if you
persist, on- or off-shore, there is a very good chance you will soon be arrested or killed. Stay here with us, Nathan, regardless of what you think of
me. Your father will be safer with you here, and Catherine—not far away—
for now."

"Just as my mother was?" Nathan asked. "And what about—"

"Barbara and Richard?" Peter smiled. "You must talk to her—but
as Catherine said, you must avoid Richard at all costs, for now. Be very
careful."

Nathan looked sharply at the other man.

"You know I can't promise patience regarding Richard—"

"I know."

But Peter clearly meant no disrespect or mockery. A remarkable
man, Nathan thought. My lifetime once-friend, now enemy. And his
dreams after that were consumed by that half-breed and that raven-
haired witch. That way he didn't grieve and regret as much having failed
his mother in every respect—in essence killing her himself.

Then came the *tête-à-tête* with this entrancing, damaged woman.

"Damn it, Catherine, you understand why I must find Richard before I sail! And I sail with *Merlin* at the end of September. Don't pretend you don't understand!"

Nathan was shouting now, and there was palpable menace that repelled and fascinated her. She was facing a stranger, a frightening man; his thick eyebrows a solid squall line on his angry forehead. She could not look at him any more and turned away, walking towards the sofa. But she would not back down.

"No, Nathan, I do not understand, and we will not agree on this. But I would hope that you and I would have no secrets—and my duty to your family will never include servile and unquestioning obedience to every whim and maneuver that you decide upon. It is for your father's sake, and your own, that I urge you to stay with us. Is that clear? I am not anybody's 'woman,' as they say. I belong to no one."

"No!" he shouted. She jumped as she felt his powerful hands squeezing her shoulders, and she knew that, in spite of her anger and his, she was ready for him. He kissed her neck, and she trembled. His hands slipped down her sides and felt for her, and found her, agile and knowing, as his powerful erection sought her through the fabric of his clothes and her own. He so carefully avoided touching her wounded face, hurting her injuries; she was losing control of her own body's movements, her small, round buttocks and upper thighs beginning to sway and rub against him, gyrating and dropping slightly as her knees weakened. His maddening lips were all over her neck and bare shoulders as he turned her around. She sagged into his arms, open lips seeking his. After a fierce kiss, they held each other tightly.

"Oh, Nathan, damn you," she moaned, every inch of her skin on fire. "Do not leave me, I cannot—I need you, Nathan."

"Do you think I want to leave you? But I was lucky to find a ship, a command, so quickly, and have already signed the papers. And *Merlin* sails—with or without me."

"My Philadelphia 'mother' has of course banished me," said Catherine, filled with insinuation, "and no one has returned from England. No one is here, Nathan, and I don't know when I will see you again!" She stifled another sob, half erotic, half sad. But when he leaned over again to kiss her, she looked away. No comment on Peter, William or Amy. Nathan said nothing further that day, and only glanced at his mother's headstone on the hill behind the house, from time to time wiping his eyes angrily.

The next day he found a hackney and raced southwest toward the Stewards Federal home, bouncing over the cobblestones, dodging horses and pedestrians. The brick buildings and copper roofs blurred. Thames to Hanover Street to Prince, North, Union, Congress, State to Washington and School Street, past the Old State House, the Old City Hall, Granary Burial Ground and King's Chapel, Federal Hill. Finally Beacon Street, along the Common, past the New State House with its shining golden dome, finally Beacon Hill, past Gay Street, then Walnut. To the east, there was still enough light to make out the forest of masts in the harbor.

Barbara had written to him, begging his forgiveness, and . . . the post-chaise carriage took less than 15 minutes to reach the Steward Mansion. Abraham Steward banking away downtown, Richard Auster at large, in London, probably, or across the northern border, or even at sea, on the run—but Barbara! He remembered the way she had looked at the ball, before she betrayed him with Peter and Richard. Thoughts of Catherine notwithstanding, he ran out of the carriage and up to the house. Barbara opened the front door herself; her voluptuous mackerel and blue gown, and sumptuous, radiant smile briefly dispelled the gloom that had threatened to take over Nathan like a tidal wave. She was the victim, Peter and Richard the betrayers. Richard Auster meant nothing to her. They held hands, and she hugged him and pulled at his coat.

"Nathan! I was so sorry to hear about Amy, but, you're . . . here! And you forgive me! And . . . look how handsome . . . you look, my dear!"

"Thank you—yes I am here. In the . . . in person." Nathan stammered again at the stunning pleasure of this golden-haired beauty, outshining the September sun itself.

"Come in, come in! How you have changed. Tell me everything!" She pulled him inside. Once he was in the vestibule, she hugged him again, and this time their embrace was long and close. She reached up, her lips sought his and they kissed deliriously. She led him to the sofa.

"Nathan! Tell me everything," she said, inviting the horrors of the recent months, *Cormorant*, his capture and torture. Barbara's shining lips moved suggestively, her large green eyes caressing him. Her long lashes, her sleepy, seductive look, her mouth large, round and intense, sweeping, expansive yet vulnerable; Nathan was enchanted. Her light, flowing hair shone with angelic luster. She stroked his hands and they leaned back, feeling a heat that went beyond the late sun.

"And what of your father?" she finally asked him.

"I must find Richard Auster!" Nathan blurted.

Barbara looked annoyed, staring at Nathan, then away, but said nothing. Nathan felt a sudden chill in the air.

"I—damn it, Nathan! Why can we not put all of that behind us?"

Barbara stamped her lovely foot, pouting like a child.

"You know I can . . . cannot do that."

"You must stay ashore now and work for my father, or study for a career in law, or even—any landsman's occupations. You promised your sainted mother—end this fight with Richard, forget the Austers. Your war is not with them . . . it . . . must not continue."

"Yes, certainly, I know I disappointed my m-mother—"

"Leave it be, Nathan! Haven't you and your family suffered enough?"

She frowned and shook her head, looking utterly bewitching. He felt a longing overpower him, his arm over the soft shoulder of her pale blue taffeta, her large breasts half exposed by the daring *decolletage*. She seemed so helpless and so alluring, as her wide mouth worked in its effort not to cry. He leaned over and kissed those sensuous lips, smothering her wet face with kisses, and she put her arms around his neck and drew him to her, pressing eagerly against his body. Nathan knew now that this was what she wanted. Words were superfluous. But after a few more minutes of passionate exploration, she whispered hoarsely.

"You have changed, my darling Nathan; do you still love me, then?"

"Yes . . . yes, Barbara, of course I do." He wondered if she knew how much he had changed.

Nathan knew he was being taken advantage of by the young woman who never really loved him. Barbara knew it was the touch of another man driving her to seduce this man. Richard had talked to Abraham, and on leaving, he had smiled and held Barbara briefly in his arms; sophisticated, dangerous, worldly, wealthy. Barbara felt the heat and strength in Richard's sun-brown hands, the desire. She had looked into his eyes, filled with dark promises; his eyes were the color of greed, or jealousy, deep and rich, life-giving. She had given herself to him, many times now, and she would never marry, unless, somehow, Nathan could be maneuvered.

She was startled by her own voice.

"Marry me, Nathan. I know we can be happy . . ." Nathan was gazing into her distracted eyes. How long had she been thinking of Richard.

"If I swallow the anchor."

"Oh, Nathan! You know how much I—we can't talk of marriage if you insist on this life at sea—not knowing when and where you'll be . . . and this vendetta—"

"What about Richard? Where is he? He probably would object to me with you here."

"You know I cannot . . . tell you that, my love."

Seeing a frightening scowl form on his face, Barbara was staring into his eyes, fear and worry wrinkling her forehead as her hands fluttered to his cheeks and shoulders, finally resting on his chest.

"That . . . that damned Auster—" The one phrase had become wearisome, even to him.

"Nathan, please! Catherine Charles has effectively ruined Richard; isn't that enough? And you escaped his wrath!"

"What about *Cormorant* and that devil fish Coxe? And my parents . . . Mother—"

"I know, dear, I know. But please, remember your promise to your mother, to me. You have returned, this is a magical day! Aren't you . . . happy to be with me?"

He hugged her. "Of course, my love. I am sorry."

Barbara felt her control of the situation slip, and the face she showed this young, strapping man was the same calm facade she always displayed when threatened. Nathan wasn't fooled. "Still you refuse to accept the reality of the situation, continuing the education of Nathan Jeffries."

This alarmed Barbara. In the salon, he poured two brandies from the Wedgwood crystal decanter into rare exquisite snifters and offered one to her. She broke the silence again.

"So will you promise me to avoid Richard?" Her voice was louder this time.

"I tell you, forget about the Austers!"

His face became a frightening scowl and he walked up to her, his hands working at his sides. He was taller. Faces inches apart, he did not touch her. She was afraid, but stood her ground.

"You're right, of course," she heard him saying calmly, as if they were not consumed with passion. "The truth is, we will put all this behind us for this evening . . . at Blackstone or Saucy Sal's . . . my love!"

This bitter, lying, hopeless Nathan was more like Richard! As his lean, hard body pressed against hers and he molded her breasts, lower back and legs, she shivered; he thought it was only the sexual excitement. But she knew he was lying, that he had won. He was in charge, and she let him carry both of them along. He was lying! And she wanted him, now! Shaking, she abandoned herself to his expert stroking, his fingers, his tongue, and she reached for him. Soon there was a path of clothes leading to the day bed, and they were coupling madly, bare skin delicious, flesh feverishly working, quivering, forcing its way. The climax came in black gulps; they died together, floating on an alien sea.

Now he had shared both women with Richard. When would they meet again? Nathan cursed himself for his lack of judgment the moment he left the Steward house—could he return to a time before the betrayal, before Peter and Richard? Before he had betrayed his mother? Could he forsake Catherine so easily?

Walking back toward Fells Point near dusk, Nathan ached from still raging desire, wondering if he had now completely lost his mind, walking down Beacon to Broadway along the Common, now mostly illuminated by rising moonlight and the new whale-oil street lamps the runner had just finished lighting on this section of the street, near the Court House. The rising gibbous moon would ensure some additional light. Candles and fireplaces were already blazing in the wealthier homes.

These women acted so loving, as if the loss of so many—he could not possibly be that kind of man, like Richard Auster, alternating between a god and a devil to the women, moods so quickly mixed together in his mind. He made his wayward way down hill in this churning sea of his guilt, hardly realizing when he passed the Granary Burial Ground and found himself heading south on Somerset toward Hay Market and the Middle Patuxent River. A block later, at Charles and Cambridge Street, the road to the left would take him North Point, and to the West End. He took the road bearing right which turned into New Sudbury and would eventually lead him to Blackstone and Ann Street, then Hanover, and down Thames on Fells Point, a half mile or so east and south.

He remembered his father, drunk on Ann Street years earlier, when he first realized the "nymphs" cajoling sailors were women of the town, who lived in the rows of shacks that lined the street. He once saw two drunken tars beat each half to death on Richmond Street, with fists and belaying pins. The taverns and gaming rooms of Fleet and Battery had been just another source of argument between Amy and William; Nathan had felt both disgusted and drawn to "Murder Square," where at least nine men had died violently. "Not all that brick was red when laid," they said.

But tonight was quiet enough in the Neck. He heard one bottle smash against a gable and something that sounded like the squealing of a hog. The few shouts creaks, and smells from the river faded, the piles of corrupting sea weed renewed, the dirty brick buildings on either side, sometimes oppressive during the day, seemed comforting, sheltering, in the fading twilight. The North Point Woods, an occasional hack or carriage clattered by, or couples headed toward or returning from festivities. A half dozen sailors, surprisingly civilized, eyed him curiously from across the street. He recognized one of them as loyal mate Tom Howard, who nodded.

Twenty-Three

New Command

By the time Nathan finally left Tom Howard and his colleagues at Saucy Sal's, it was quite late. Suddenly the silence on the street was broken by a familiar voice.

"Whoa, Moses!"

At the Square he heard a shout from a carriage, a chaise drawn by two shiny black horses, which stopped in front of him; the portly, impeccable black driver impassive in the high seat. That dark face sprouted out of the window.

"Well! If it isn't the wandering boy!"

Even before looking in the dim light of the carriage interior, Nathan knew it was Richard Auster. But beside him, Barbara! Before he could think of anything to say, his tormenter started in again, leaning his smirking, arrogant face out of the carriage window into the faint light of the moon and lamps.

"On the way home to Mother, are we?" he sneered. "Oh, I forgot, she died waiting for your return; you managed to destroy Amy even without my help, the prodigal boy fool. And your father is . . . a blithering idiot? Why are you still in this town, oaf? Do you crave ridicule that earnestly? Scratch the surface of a Jeffries, I say, and find an ignorant waister, not even legitimate deckhand, fit for scrimshaw and tarring, taking up jail space in various hellholes. Ever heard of Beethoven, boy? You probably prefer 'Hail, Columbia,' to the 'Emperor Concerto!'"

Thankful no one could see his red face, Nathan shouted in return,

"This boy made a fool out of you, Auster—and my—"

"As Mr. Wordsworth said, 'the child is father of the man,'" said Richard, "and no doubt you miss the acrid stench of bare bodies, hardtack, rats and sweat. Does the close proximity of 250 men excite you, like it did your father—I must admit I am amazed you have lived this long."

"At least I'm man enough to do my own dirty work, rather than hiring someone else for it!"

"Must we explain yet again the way the real world works to this boy, Barbara—"

"You might fool some of your dupes afloat, Auster, but you and I know what your company does, what *Scourge* was, and what you have done to me and mine! Does Barbara really know what Catherine—"

"As usual, you are slow—well," he said amiably. "Barbara's taste, really, but I should congratulate you for surviving this long—no more hiding behind William and Amy, eh? I must say you were smart to return to this pretty wench—to align yourself with adults, briefly. Come, my dear, and let us join the adults up the hill."

Before Nathan could respond, Auster looked up at Moses, his driver.

"Hadn't you better leave town before you're arrested?" Nathan shouted. Auster smiled and turned to Barbara.

"The fugitive fears the Jeffries," said Nathan in desperation. "Once a coward, always a coward! A rotten chip of the old, rotten block!"

The carriage door burst open and Nathan jumped back, startled. A few passersby paused, then walked on. Richard's face was suddenly right in front of his, still smiling, filled with hate, and Nathan tried to weigh his options.

"Excuse me a moment, Mister Jeffries." Richard turned back and spoke to Barbara.

"Please get back in the carriage," she said.

"No, my dear, please don't concern yourself. I shall return shortly. Stay put, Moses," he said to the driver.

"No, Richard, I—"

"Silence! Remain here, and be quiet!" Richard ordered brutally, cruelly. "This boy and I are merely going to discuss his mis-impressions, so do cooperate, will you?"

Nathan saw her face staring out, framed under a dark bonnet and golden hair. He could see her lovely, oval face, whose large eyes, also dark above those high cheekbones, bore into his; her sensuous mouth now a thin straight line. She opened and closed those exciting lips, but no words came out. Then she sank back into the gloom of the carriage. Behind her, above the nearest buildings, he could see the pale white steeple and spire of the City Hall tower against the moonlit sky, the golden grasshopper weathervane shining faintly in the night.

"Shall we saunter down behind Union here to discuss this privately?" Richard seemed happy and carefree, as if he were inviting Nathan on a picnic.

"Certainly, Mister Auster." Did his voice sound shaky?

"Don't you want us take care o' him?" asked a voice in the dimness on the other side of the carriage. A knot of Richard's men suddenly appeared behind him.

"Not so fast there, my boys," came the answer out of the gloom, from the surviving members of Captain Turner's crew, who had suffered with Nathan aboard *Guerriere*, Tom Howard and Jack Logan, and four hands from *Constitution*. Nathan saw Richard and his men dart a worried look around them. More satisfying to Nathan, he could see, for the first time, even in the dim light, a look of concern in Auster's face. This was something Richard had not counted on. He was briefly surprised, even shocked, that this boy had anticipated him.

"I think we have both been encouraged not to fight a duel, boy," he laughed, with some degree of confidence. "So, why not settle our differences in a more common way, not as public gentlemen, but as private brawlers? Hand to hand, just the two of us, any rules you wish, here in the half light? I promise to keep it as fair as possible." Richard laughed.

The wide alley wasn't completely dark; its gray shadows revealed brick facades and pine clapboards, stout doors of oak, bolted casements, lonely roofs of slate and tin, feeble candlelight from a few windows. Blackstone's was a hundred yards away on the other side of the alley, and not farther, Saucy Sal's. It seemed lifelessly quiet, except for the crunch of their boots on the grey stone. As if by common, unspoken assent, the other men hung back. Nathan felt anchored to a balloon in the near-darkness. The air seemed crawling and alive. Auster suddenly stopped and turned to Nathan, who could barely make out the sneer on his lips. Under his cloak, he was resplendent in a black silk suit, snowy white neckcloth, flawless stock and beaver hat. He seemed to wear the same sardonic, patronizing smile he had displayed at the Stewards.

"You know you cannot win, my boy; any fight, though, can help a man clear his thinking. But we can talk about this all night, and my fiancée is waiting. Unless you haven't the stomach for this? I will be happy to tell Barbara . . . or Catherine and William."

"You bastard!" Nathan raised his fists, and was just starting to back away and remove his open coat when he saw Auster's right hand flash under his heavy wool cloak. Too late he saw the heavy blackjack gleaming dully in the dim light; it flashed out as Auster shot forward, and a blinding pain paralyzed Nathan's right arm, another broke his nose. Auster slashed at him, then the end of the blackjack shot forward into his stomach as Auster came on again.

"Aagh!" Nathan felt the bile rising in his throat and he could feel the second swipe seem to pass through his belly. He couldn't breathe, and crumpled onto his knees, then lay curled on his side, crying and gasping for breath. He could barely hear Auster between his nausea and the ringing in his ears. Richard knelt almost gently at Nathan's side, his hand on Nathan's ribs as he heaved, fighting for breath. He spoke quietly in Nathan's ear.

"I guess it's true what they say; when you want something done right, do it yourself. Of course, Archie had his turn at you, and you didn't learn the lesson properly. Maybe now you will behave yourself, eh, boy? I hate teaching manners to inferiors—you should feel honored, Jeffries, that I am handling this personally. But you were lucky this time. Don't make me get involved again. You tell your friends and family that you have learned the error of your ways and will cease and desist, if not cooperate, from now on with the Auster Company. I must say you and your old fool of a father have been a small enough nuisance—compared to Catherine or Amy; but if you don't mind your betters . . . understand?"

Richard didn't really expect an answer, of course; Nathan could feel him pat his side as he panted and fought between the need to breathe and the urge to vomit.

"Give my best to your father." He heard laughter, vaguely saw the man's cloak swirl overhead and heard footsteps crunching into the distance. There was almost a relief in his head as the gleaming streaks behind his eyes fluttered and fell, and the loud pain in his gut subsided and settled into a dull roar. It was cold; the shivering was now more unpleasant than the ache in his arm and stomach and receding nausea. As the specific pain dwindled, the sense of humiliation and freezing air forced him to move. First he squeezed into a tight ball, still curled on his side, then slowly began to release his cramped muscles and rise.

"Oh God!" Nathan groaned and struggled to stand up, quickly gave it up as the dizziness overcame him. He knelt with his head forward, almost touching the hard ground. He could faintly hear the sound of a carriage passing on the street as the driver cracked his whip and the wheels and hooves clattered over stone. There was a light breeze. He shivered again, gritted his teeth and slowly stood up, head still bent down. The nausea was under control now.

Shaking his head gently from side to side to clear the cobwebs, he saw his hat nearby where it had fallen off. He dusted it off and gingerly put it on, feeling like he must be eighty years old—and a sick eighty, at that.

His right arm worked well enough, though stiff and sore. He gently rubbed his stomach and grinned insanely.

"Thank you for the valuable lesson, Mr. Auster," he muttered. He staggered, shuffled and stumbled out of the alley and squinted under the painful light of a *flambeau*. He leaned wearily against a carriage wheel, tasting his own blood.

He saw a dark figure about to enter a carriage at the end of the alley. Somehow he shook off the nausea and staggered toward his opponent.

"Excuse me, Richard!" he croaked. The arrogant, assured face that turned to him was amused, surprised, then shocked.

With all his strength he swung at that face. His fist miraculously connected. Auster went down, and Nathan fell on top of him.

"I am going to kill you!" he heard a voice shout, and his fists were a wonder of precision and force. He could hear and feel the impact of his knuckles crashing into that face, splashing, and he could vaguely feel the blood and pain of bone on bone as he battered that head and face with this fists. An ecstasy of horror ensued, machine-like, as he proceeded to pound his enemy without thought, without mercy.

"Nathan, stop! You have won! Please!" He seemed to hear the voice of Barbara, and then he was panting, out of breath, exhausted, as he was pulled by his right arm. He suddenly felt Peter's presence and he twisted his arm, hooked it under Peter's and easily swept him away, head over heels. Both Nathan and his enemy felt shrill buzzing, as Nathan pounded Richard's nose and jaw, blood spraying from both faces.

But rude hands were now pulling at him on both sides and a powerful arm around his throat forced him up and away from this drill. It was Jack Logan. From both sides he was lifted to his feet and the fog cleared. The face of a friend forced its way into his conscience.

"You don't want to do this, Nathan," said Mr. Logan. "You don't want to kill him. We have better ways."

As they slowly staggered away, a battered Richard groaned and rolled over, curled in pain, then slowly lifted himself to his knees. Miraculously, he found the strength to reach inside his coat for a pistol.

"Richard!" Barbara screamed.

"Get back!" he croaked, shuddering back the blinding pain as he felt the gun, hard and solid in his hands.

Half-carried by Peter and Jack on each side, Nathan turned as they heard a cackling roar from behind them, and then a hammer cock. The mangled, bloody face of Richard Auster twisted in a gargoyle's grin as he raised the pistol and aimed it at Nathan. A loud crack! An explosion of light and thunderous smoke behind Auster shook his torso like a rag doll and he dropped his gun with a shocked and horrified look on his face, half turned, then toppled. The beautiful woman behind him slowly lowered her matching pistol, still trailing wisps of gunsmoke.

"Barbara!"

In the blue, pungent haze, she cried to Richard, to Nathan, to the darkening sky, 'Good night, sweet prince, and flights of angels sing thee to thy rest.' Her sobbing almost sounded like laughter.

Dawn, last day of September, as he stood right aft on his new command, privateer schooner *Merlin* paying off and standing out from the Fells Point basin, that hysterical laughter reverberated in Nathan's mind. "*Mundus vult decipi, ergo decipiatur,*" said Peter. The world wants to be deceived, so let it be deceived! Time to fly, time to fly, those blue piercing eyes in Nathan's broad, flat face no longer pale and naive, but a scarred fighter, a survivor, whose warrior instinct, dormant for years, had fully emerged to fly, wayward, rampant, insidious, alert to the aromas of deceit, tolerating Peter's great learning and intelligent, fiery life, although they might fight for opposite sides. But for now, he could seek maritime prey.

Barbara and her father had sailed to England, and Catherine and Peter would remain with William Jeffries—for now.

"You and I may no longer speak to each other as friends," Peter had said, "but I have never given up on hope, however flawed our dreams and executions—they are OUR dreams, to be given up, OUR executions! Nothing . . . it is all for nothing."

"So why do we kill? Why do you fight the white man?"

"Because . . . what else is honorable Injun supposed to do, my one-time brother? *Quis custodiet ipsos custodes?* Who will watch the watchers themselves? Besides, William, Catherine and I have begged you not to leave here. Not to mention your promise to Amy."

"Bah!" Nathan looked away.

And on his last night ashore, Catherine sounded like Barbara.

"Nathan! Richard is dead now, the Austers finished—"

"Are they? I can't forgive, Catherine, I cannot—I hope my mother . . . can forgive me."

"I know."

But they kissed each other for a long time. Later she watched from Cobbs Hill as *Merlin* warped out of the Patapsco River into the

Chesapeake Bay, overlooking the river and the harbor, where a cemetery contained his mother's remains. Catherine promised to take care of his father. Now in command of a swift privateer with 10 nine-pounders, Nathan was at sea again. But now hardened, bitter, seeing a beautiful, lonely girl like Catherine in the distance, looking out beyond the Bay at a distant ship standing out, top's'ls filling, sheeted home.

"Everything squared away, Captain," said Mister Logan, standing near the helmsman.

"Very good," said Nathan. "Stead south by east," he said. A bit too northerly, this early autumn breeze. Ignore the scuttlebutt and raise the ground. "No more shoals, Mr. Jack."

Logan smiled. "Sou' by east, aye."

This was no trading voyage. Would they find prey? Would they become prey?

Nathan stared at the sun bursting above the horizon; red skies. Hope is a dangerous thing. Jack Logan would make sure guns were secure and see personally to powder kegs safe below in the magazine. Would he ever see Matt Turner and the *Cormorants* again? Would the spirit of his mother ever forgive him? Twisted emotions tumbled through his head. His father. Catherine. Barbara. Peter. The Austers. The young lad at the wheel also stared to the east. Captain Enoch Earleigh's promising son, Jason. The least he could do.

"*Deus gubernat navem*," as Peter used to say. God steers the ship.

"Mind your helm, Jason," Nathan said.

Made in the USA
Charleston, SC
25 February 2014